All Our Tomorrows

Benita Brown

First published in 2001
by HEADLINE BOOK PUBLISHING

First published in paperback in 2002
by HEADLINE BOOK PUBLISHING

10 9 8 7 6 5

ISBN 0 7472 6619 0

Typeset by Avon Dataset Ltd, Bidford-on-Avon, Warks

Printed and bound in Great Britain by
Mackays of Chatham plc, Chatham, Kent

HEADLINE BOOK PUBLISHING
A division of Hodder Headline
338 Euston Road
London NW1 3BH

www.headline.co.uk
www.hodderheadline.com

To Norman with love, as always

Chapter One

Newcastle, December 1905

Thea sat next to her friend on the bench seat of the open four-wheeler and stared at the Christmas displays in the shop windows on Grainger Street without pleasure. She was too ill at ease to enjoy them. Her father would be horrified if he knew what she was going to do tonight. In fact he would forbid it.

But then her father was opposed to anything she wanted to do. She was still inwardly raging over his refusal to allow her to go to university. Instead of being proud that she was intelligent enough to have secured a place at Cambridge, he had condemned her to a life of boredom at home with nothing interesting to fill her days.

Perhaps that was what had prompted her to agree to something that was so against her nature – it was an act of rebellion.

'Thea, I'm so cold!' Ellie's breath frosted visibly in the chill air. She leaned closer. 'Your aunt must be made of bell metal – just look at her!'

Thea did so. Miss Marjorie Gibb's homely face, topped by a flat tweed pancake hat, was all that was visible above the piled-up boxes of clothes and Christmas gifts that filled the well of the coach. She was clearly in the best of spirits and not at all discomforted by the chill of a dismally dark winter's afternoon.

Suddenly the coach lurched over a junction in the new tramlines on the corner of Westgate Road and the girls nearly slithered from their seats.

'Oh, no!' Ellie wailed.

Thea looked at her in alarm. 'What is it? Are you hurt?'

'No, I'm fine, but my nose is dripping. Is it red? I'm sure it must be red. What a disaster!'

'Disaster?'

'Of course . . . *tonight* . . . you know,' Ellie whispered, glancing surreptitiously at Miss Gibb, but Thea's aunt had turned to give directions to the coachman and she had not heard any of their conversation.

Thea understood her friend's concern. 'Sit back a little so that I can see you,' she said quietly.

Ellie edged away, turned full towards her, and sat as still as though she were posing for a portrait. Her nose was not at all red, but it was about to drip. Thea reached into her coat pocket for a clean handkerchief and handed it over. Her friend was obviously suffering. Her usually pale complexion had lost the delicate pink flush that made it so appealing; in fact her face was as blanched as the tiny snowflakes that were drifting down and melting in the air before they could land on the glistening cobbles.

Some of the snowflakes settled on Ellie's silver fox fur hat and in the curling tendrils of her blonde hair; they sparkled in the light of the streetlamps for a moment before blinking out and disappearing. Her blue eyes were wide and anxious and her long dark lashes trembled as though she were on the verge of tears.

'Don't worry, you look beautiful,' Thea reassured her. 'A little pale, perhaps, but that only adds to your romantic appeal.'

'Don't tease!' Ellie's cheeks flushed and Thea smiled.

'There – you look better already. But what about me?' She pulled off her gloves and adjusted the pin in her grey homburg – her old school hat pressed into shape and trimmed with feathers – before tentatively feeling her own dark hair. 'This damp air is making my hair curl like a wild woman's!'

'Or an Amazon!' Ellie exclaimed. 'That's it – you will look like an Amazon, so tall and dark and striking. Oh, Thea, a blonde and a brunette – won't we look marvellous together?'

'Yes, we will.' Thea tried to sound enthusiastic but, in fact, she had regretted agreeing to her friend's plan almost from the start.

'Thea! You haven't changed your mind, have you?' Ellie was looking at her worriedly. 'I mean, you promised to come with me – I couldn't go without you – there would be no point to it. It just has to be both of us. You can't let me down!'

Thea summoned up a smile. 'Of course I won't let you down. I never would. I'm your friend, aren't I?'

Ellie smiled, reassured. 'Oh, Thea, it will be such fun!'

'Hush!' Thea saw that her aunt was smiling at them. 'Yes,' she raised her voice a little, 'helping Aunt Marjorie at the Charity School Christmas party will be tremendous fun. Aren't you glad that you agreed to come along?'

Ellie frowned and then her eyes widened and she smiled. 'Oh, yes,' she placed the spread fingers of one silk-gloved hand across the fur tippet on her breast and looked skywards, 'I'm so-oo pleased to be able to help in such a worthy cause!'

Behind the cover of the piled-up packages Thea delivered a swift kick in the direction of Ellie's ankles.

'Ouch!' her friend exclaimed. 'What was that for?'

'Don't overdo it,' Thea muttered. She knew she had flushed

3

and it was because she hated deceiving her good-hearted aunt. Her mother's sister had never criticized her parents but she had made it obvious in so many ways that she knew what Thea's life was like and she had never been anything but kind to her.

'Sorr-ee,' Ellie mouthed. She began to giggle, but stopped when the cab left the main thoroughfare and turned into the archway that led under the railway lines to the gloomy ill-lit alleys and the cramped, squalid housing that lay behind the Central Station and spilled down the river bank to the Tyne.

Both girls were silent as they peered ahead. The white glazed tiles of the roof and walls of the tunnel were cracked and dirty, and the flaring overhead gas jets barely lit the gloom. The sound of the horse's hoofs clip-clopping from one pool of yellow light to the next echoed eerily around them.

'Isn't it strange?' Ellie asked softly. 'It's as though we'd left the normal, everyday world behind us.'

'I know what you mean,' Thea replied, 'and you're right. But not in any supernatural sense. It is another world at the other side of the railway tracks, and it's not a world that either of us should like to live in.'

The next moment a terrifyingly loud noise rumbled and thundered above them. Ellie flung herself into Thea's arms. 'What's that?' she gasped.

'Only a train!' Thea spluttered through a mouthful of fur, and then she began to laugh. 'Oh, Ellie, you're such a child sometimes.'

Ellie moved back and pretended to be offended. 'Let me remind you that I am already nineteen years old, and a full month older than you are. But you're right,' she squeezed one of Thea's hands in its damp woollen glove with her own silk-gloved hand, 'you are much more grown up and clever than I am. That's why I'm so glad that we are friends.'

4

Once they had emerged from the tunnel the day seemed even darker than it had before, though it was still only mid-afternoon. It was lucky that the coachman seemed to know the way, Thea thought. It would be so easy to get lost in this maze of ramshackle overhanging tenements and foul-smelling streets with their open drains. She noticed that Ellie was now holding the handkerchief over her lower face.

As her eyes became accustomed to the gloom she saw that their progress was observed. Thin curtains twitched at grimy windows, and occasionally she made out a dim figure and a pale face in an alleyway. She knew that her aunt often came to these dwellings quite alone so Thea supposed they were safe. But, nevertheless, she was pleased when, at last, they came to a halt outside the tall, grim building that housed the Charity School.

'Quick – here comes the ladies!' A tousled head peered round one of the red-brick pillars that supported the iron gates. 'Get yersels in and get weshed!'

An excited group of children ran away across the yard and up the short flight of steps to the school entrance.

'Poor bairns,' the cab driver remarked. He was unloading the boxes on to the pavement. 'The only bit soap they ever set eyes on is at school – and most of them divven't know what a square meal is.'

'At least these children have homes to go to,' Aunt Marjorie said. 'There are many more children in this great and prosperous city of ours that simply live on the streets. And some die there.'

'Aye, it's grand work you do, you and the other folks like you.' The driver reached up to help Aunt Marjorie down. 'The free breakfasts and the holidays and the sanatorium an' all.'

5

'But it isn't nearly enough, and there aren't enough of us – folks like me, as you put it. Nothing will change until every citizen—'

'Now, divven't start on me, missus!' The cab driver held up a large gloved hand as if to ward off the lecture he sensed was coming. 'You know very well I've got five bairns of me own to provide for – and as a matter of fact, wor lass is expecting, so that'll be another mouth to feed.'

'Tom McGrath, how could you?' Aunt Marjorie shook her head. 'Poor Kathleen must rue the day she met you.'

The big man pretended to be offended. 'Nowt of the sort,' he said. 'I work hard and I'm a good provider. You know that fine well.'

'But, nevertheless, that will be six children in as many years. The day I first stepped into your cab, Kathleen and you were not long wed and expecting your first.'

He laughed good-naturedly. 'Well, now, if the lecture's over, I'll think about helping you into the school with this lot – after I've handed these bonny young lasses down.'

Thea was pleased to see that her aunt took the rebuff in good part and soon they were all carrying the boxes of brightly wrapped gifts, and washed and mended second-hand clothes across the yard and up the steps to place them in the entrance hall of the school. After each trip Thea noticed that the boxes they had just deposited had vanished; someone, staff or pupil, was carrying them off into the echoing depths of the building.

'Thank you, Tom,' Aunt Marjorie said, when at last they were finished. 'I have come to rely on your good nature and I'm grateful. Wait – before you go . . .' Thea's aunt opened the door of the carriage and brought out a box that she had tucked away under the seat. 'Here are some presents for your little ones. They're wrapped in green paper for the girls and red for the boys. As for the new baby, I'll see you get something when the time comes.'

'That's real kind of you, Miss Gibb. Kathleen'll bless you for that.'

Thea and Ellie stepped back and waited while Aunt Marjorie settled the fare. And no doubt gave a generous tip.

'Oh, do look,' Ellie said. She gripped Thea's arm with one hand and pointed with the other.

Thea saw that she was pointing towards where the cab horse waited, its flanks gently steaming. A small girl was looking up at the patient beast. It was hard to tell her age – perhaps eight or nine, Thea guessed. The hem of her ragged dress hung down unevenly, the pinafore that covered it was grubby and, Thea noticed to her horror, her thin, dirty little feet were bare.

'Just look at her face,' Ellie whispered, 'so beautiful . . .'

The child stared raptly at the horse. The light from the nearside coach lamp illumined an oval face framed by a tangled mass of red-gold curls. The delicate features were almost ethereal in the smoky light and the blue eyes were huge with wonder.

As the two girls watched, an older boy with the same colour curly hair came up and caught her by the hand. 'Hawway in, wor Janey,' he said.

The child turned her head and stared up at him. 'Joe?'

The boy, her brother, Thea guessed, smiled patiently. 'You've got to come in now. Mrs Barrett's got some shoes for yer – good as new, they are. She wants yer to put them on afore the party starts.'

So that's why the boxes had vanished so quickly. Thea imagined the teachers unpacking and sorting swiftly so that the most poverty-stricken children could be given what they needed straight away – and each one of them would look as

7

decent as possible for the Christmas party.

For the next hour Thea and Ellie, along with two plump, friendly ladies, Miss Moffat and Mrs Shaw, who were introduced as friends of her aunt, stood in the brown- and cream-tiled cellar, dimly lit by flaring gas jets, cutting bread and making meat paste sandwiches, and piling sugar buns in sticky pyramids on large plates.

Every now and then they hurried up the stone staircase to arrange the food on the two rows of trestle tables, which had been arranged the length of the hall.

In one corner there was a large Christmas tree, and Thea saw that a young man and woman, most probably teachers at the school to judge by their plain, dark clothes, were decorating it with silver ribbons and golden stars. They talked quietly to each other as they worked and she couldn't help noticing what an attractive, if rather severe-looking, couple they made.

Couple? Were they a couple, she wondered. Were teachers allowed to form attachments? If not, then that young woman should be rather more guarded in the way she looked up into the man's undeniably handsome face.

Ellie's colour had returned and, wrapped in one of the enormous white pinafores that Aunt Marjorie had provided for them both, she looked more sweetly pretty than ever, Thea thought.

Her own dark curls were escaping all restraint as usual, and she thought it just as well that, when the party was over, they would have at least an hour in Ellie's house to change and prepare themselves before they set off for the theatre.

When the tables were ready Thea stood back and looked at them. Surely there was enough food to satisfy the appetite of even the hungriest of the ragged little guests. Almost immediately the children, directed by two teachers, an older woman and a very young man, filed in, bringing their own enamel mugs.

They must have been sitting waiting in the classrooms and now there was an air of barely controlled excitement. They hardly knew whether to look at the food on the table or the great shimmering Christmas tree in the corner with the green- and the red-wrapped parcels piled up around the base. The food won.

But before they sat down, they stood to attention in their allotted places and looked at the headmaster, the Reverend William Barrett, who stood on the platform smiling down at them. Mrs Barrett struck a chord on the piano and the children began to sing grace. They finished a few bars ahead of the accompaniment.

And then, at a nod from on high and with a collective sigh of anticipation, they sat down. In no time at all, it seemed, every scrap of food, every crust and every crumb had been eaten. Thea and Ellie had joined Aunt Marjorie and her cohorts as they hurried up and down the rows of seated children, filling up the mugs with milk until not one child asked for more.

She was glad that she had come even though she acknowledged to herself guiltily that she had agreed to Aunt Marjorie's plea for help mainly because it would give her the excuse to get ready at Ellie's house before going to the theatre. There would not be time to go home first – home where she might risk an inquisition from her father.

'Thea.' She turned to find her aunt smiling at her. 'When the tables are cleared away I want you and Ellie to help Grace organize the games. I've plenty of helpers to wash up in the basement.'

'Grace?'

'Grace Barrett, the headmaster's daughter.'

9

Aunt Marjorie nodded to where the pretty but plainly dressed young woman who had been decorating the tree now stood amidst an uneven circle of children who were looking up at her obediently. Grace Barrett didn't smile at the children as her parents did, Thea noticed. She wondered whether the poor girl had had any choice or whether her father had informed her from an early age that she was to follow him into the teaching profession.

But at least she was doing something with her life . . .

Thea studied the faces of the children gathered round the young woman. Most of them bore the unmistakable pallor brought on by poor diet and lack of hygiene. Aunt Marjorie had told her about the sort of houses that they lived in and the squalid conditions that shaped their lives. Thea found herself admiring the Barretts for choosing to live and work among such poor people. It must have been a considerable sacrifice. But the expression on their daughter's face reinforced her suspicion that Grace had become an unwilling victim of that sacrifice.

One of the boys had his hand up. Thea recognized Joe. 'Yes?' the young teacher said.

'Wharra we waitin' for, miss?' he asked.

Grace frowned. 'Miss *Barrett*, you must say, *Miss Barrett*,' she told him. 'We are waiting for the party games to begin.'

The children nudged each other and smiled.

'Will there be prizes, miss? Miss Barrett?' Joe asked, and the children held their breath.

'Prizes? Isn't it sufficient simply to play and to win the game?'

The little shoulders sagged and she relented. 'But, yes, there will be a prize for each winner – a token.' The shoulders lifted a little.

At that moment the man who had been decorating the Christmas tree with Grace glanced over towards them and

10

Thea saw the girl's demeanour change. She smiled brilliantly as she continued, 'And haven't you noticed the parcels around the tree?' The children turned to look. 'They are not just part of the decorations; there is a present for everyone there. When you go home, each one of you will be allowed to take one.'

'Hev they got wor names on, miss?' Joe asked.

'No, but the presents for the girls are wrapped in green and those for the boys in red. It will be up to you which parcel you choose.'

'Like a lucky dip?'

'Yes, like a lucky dip.'

Thea knew very well that every parcel was more or less identical. Each one contained a small tin of toffees, the only difference being that the tins in the girls' parcels were shaped like a country cottage with impossibly colourful flowers growing round the door, and those in the boys' were like a little drum. The gifts had been provided by Thea's father; identical tins of toffees were part of the Christmas displays in every one of the family grocery stores.

Thea had seen children, perhaps some of these children, stop and press their faces to the shop windows, their eyes feasting on the bright shiny colours of the tins, their imaginations savouring the delights inside.

Aunt Marjorie had coerced Samuel Richardson into his act of generosity, no doubt showing him the list of presents donated by other rich businessmen and hinting how bad it would look if his name did not appear there.

The children were smiling again. 'Hurrah for Miss Barrett!' Joe exclaimed. 'Hip, hip, hurrah!' The others joined in.

'Hush, now, Joe Roper!' Grace said, but she was smiling. 'Here comes Mr Hedley.'

The cheers subsided into excited whispers as the handsome teacher announced, 'I'm ready to start the games.'

11

It was the first time Thea had heard his voice. It was deep, with a pleasing lilt, but, in spite of his education, he had not quite managed to erase all trace of his working-class accent. Thea realized with surprise that, somehow, it made him even more attractive.

The children were looking at him expectantly. 'Behold,' he turned and gestured towards a large blackboard he had set up against the wall, 'Dobbin is waiting for you!'

At a nod from Grace the children edged over to look at the picture that was pinned to the board. It was a large pen and ink drawing of a comical donkey looking back bewilderedly towards his own rump. There was no tail. The children began to laugh and point.

Mr Hedley held up an overlarge paper tail. 'Here is his tail. Who can pin this on for Dobbin?' he asked. 'Hands up.'

All of them put up their hands. 'Easy, easy!' some of them exclaimed.

'Very well,' he said. 'Miss Barrett, will you choose who should go first?'

The headmaster's daughter took the raised hand of one of the little girls. It was Joe's sister, the little girl who had been staring at Mr McGrath's horse. The child's eyes were shining as she stepped forward and reached for the paper tail.

'Here you are, Janey,' Mr Hedley said, 'but be careful that you don't prick your finger with the pin. Oh, and wait a moment. You must wear a blindfold; it's too easy otherwise.'

'A blindfold?'

The child looked up at him and he smiled and showed her the white scarf he was holding. 'Don't worry, it won't hurt you. Miss Barrett, would you come and tie this scarf around Janey's eyes so that she can't see?'

The other children giggled in anticipation as Grace took the scarf. Thea saw her turn her head away quickly to try to

12

hide her *moue* of distaste from her fellow teacher as she tied it round the upper part of the child's face.

'I don't blame her,' Ellie suddenly leaned towards Thea and whispered. 'They stink, don't they?'

'Stink?' Thea murmured as she turned towards her friend.

'Yes, the smell wafting up from their clothes is positively cheesy. Their mothers must never wash them. I don't blame Grace Barrett for not wanting to get too near.'

Thea felt uneasy. She had once overheard a heated discussion between her aunt and her father. Her father had said something scathing about there being no need for the poor she was so fond of to be so dirty, and Aunt Marjorie had retorted that if the choice was between a bar of soap and a loaf of bread she knew which she would choose.

But Thea had no desire to risk an argument with Ellie, who might not agree, so she changed the subject.

'Look,' she whispered, 'that teacher, Mr Hedley, don't you think he's handsome?'

Ellie frowned. 'Well . . .'

'You don't think so?'

'Oh, yes, I do. I mean he's got nice brown hair and his face is well formed – but he's so, well, large. So tall and somehow forceful . . .'

Thea studied the man as he and Grace Barrett laughingly directed the children in the game of Pin the Tail on the Donkey. Or rather *he* was laughing. Thea had seen Grace Barrett's face when he asked her to take hold of the shoulders of one of the little girls and spin her round three times before releasing her. The headmaster's daughter had lowered her eyes and pursed her lips in disapproval. But once more she had taken care to hide her reaction from the man she was so obviously attracted to.

Ellie was right, Thea thought. He did look forceful, but it was a restrained inner force – it added to his attraction.

13

Suddenly she realized that he was looking at her. Their eyes met and she felt a *frisson* of – of what? Embarrassment? Unease? No, Thea realized that the feeling was excitement, but a kind of excitement she had never felt before, and she dropped her gaze in confusion.

When the game was over, and only one boy, a tall sharp-featured urchin whom Thea suspected had cheated by squinting down under the scarf, had managed to pin the tail in the correct place, the man said that as they had the blindfold they might as well play Blind Man's Buff.

'Oh, no, Robert,' Thea heard Grace Barrett protest weakly. But he didn't hear her.

'Come along, Ellie, we're supposed to be helping,' Thea said, and, holding on to Ellie's hand, she pushed her way through the excited children towards the headmaster's daughter. 'Do you want to rest for a while?' she asked. 'My friend and I will take over if you want to go and have a cup of tea.'

By now Thea's aunt, her friends, Grace's parents and the two teachers were settling themselves at a small table at the back of the hall to enjoy tea and scones. Grace glanced at the table briefly and Thea got the impression that she would dearly have liked to escape from the children for a while, but instead of appearing grateful, she looked vexed.

'No, that's all right,' she said. 'You're not needed here.' She turned her back on them.

Thea and Ellie retreated.

'She's jealous,' Ellie murmured.

'What do you mean?'

'She hasn't missed the fact that the dashing young schoolmaster hasn't been able to take his eyes off you.'

'Don't talk nonsense. He's been much too busy to notice me.'

14

'No he hasn't and you know it. Every now and then, whether you'll admit it or not, he has looked in your direction – and Miss Barrett is not best pleased.'

Thea was thankful that her aunt chose that moment to join them. 'I see that Grace doesn't need you to help her,' she said. 'In that case would you like to come and join the old fogies and have some refreshment?'

'No, thank you, Miss Gibb. I mean, if we are really not needed, would it be possible for Thea and me to leave now?' Ellie asked.

'But you haven't had anything to eat, child. I'm not in favour of young women going without meals.'

'Neither is my mother.' Ellie smiled winningly. 'She will insist that we have something to eat at home. And Thea and I will have longer to get ready for the theatre,' she added.

Aunt Marjorie frowned. 'Ah, yes, it's a pantomime, isn't it? Some piece of seasonal nonsense?'

'Yes.' Thea and Ellie replied in unison and a little too quickly, but Miss Gibb did not appear to have noticed. She was still frowning. 'I suppose I have no objection to your leaving now, Thea, but how will you get to Ellie's house?'

'We can take the tram,' Thea said, 'from outside the Central Station. It's not far from here.'

'I know that, but I can't possibly allow you to walk through these streets alone.'

Thea was tempted to say that Aunt Marjorie herself often walked through these streets alone, but she held her tongue when she saw her aunt's features begin to relax into a smile.

'You've been a great help to me today,' Aunt Marjorie said, 'not only here at the party but also wrapping all the gifts and boxing up the clothes at my house before we came. Of course you should go now and prepare to have some fun. I'll ask Mr

15

Hedley to accompany you to the station and see you safely on to the tram.'

'Oh, but that's not necessary—'

'It's quite all right. Robert won't mind.'

And before Thea could protest further her aunt strode across the floor towards him.

Chapter Two

'Have a care!'

Robert Hedley gripped Thea's arm in time to stop her from tripping over the dark shape lying on the pavement just outside the school gates. Ellie stumbled to a halt behind her.

'What is it?' Ellie whispered, peering round.

Thea looked down. The light from the nearby gaslamp was sufficient to reveal the inert body of an old woman.

The woman was lying on her back. Her clothes were ragged and filthy. A black woollen shawl crisscrossed around the upper part of her body. It was pulled up around her head to frame gaunt sallow features; her eyes were closed. Her hands were clasped across her breast. She looked strangely at peace.

'Is she dead?' Thea murmured, and she felt Ellie shiver and withdraw.

'No,' Robert replied. 'Look, she's breathing.'

Thea looked closer and saw the woman's breath frosting in the air. 'Well, why . . .? Is she ill?'

'I don't think so,' he said. 'More likely she's collapsed from sheer exhaustion – that, along with the cold.'

'Poor thing,' Ellie whispered as if she were at a deathbed. 'Fancy ending up like that when you're old.'

'She's not old,' Robert told her. 'She looks like that because she's worn out with childbearing and the way she has to live.'

'Do you know her?' Thea asked.

'There are any number of women like her living in these streets, but, yes, I do. Now, if you and Miss Parker will wait in the school yard for a moment, I'll go and get help. The sooner we get her inside the better.'

He turned and left them.

Ellie walked back into the yard obediently. She had sounded genuinely moved by the woman's plight but she was apparently satisfied by the thought that someone – someone else – would do something. Thea lingered. She found that she could not bear to leave the woman on the cold ground for one moment longer. She kneeled down to try to help, but she was pulled roughly aside.

She gasped and looked up into the face of Robert Hedley. 'I wouldn't touch her,' he said before releasing her arm.

Aunt Marjorie and Mrs Barrett had come with him.

'Robert is right, my dear,' her aunt told her. 'If you go home infested with lice, your mother will never forgive me. Mrs Barrett and I are used to this and we know how to deal with any unwelcome visitors who might take up residence on our persons.'

Thea watched as the two women roused the poor creature and hauled her to her feet. Some coins fell out of the folds of her ragged skirt and Aunt Marjorie picked them up. She showed them to Robert. They glinted on her palm in the lamplight.

'Put them back in her pocket,' he said. 'She's earned them.'

Mrs Barrett tutted but made no objection, and Aunt Marjorie did as she was bid. The woman groaned and took a step forward; Thea backed away as she caught the sour smell of unwashed clothes. Mrs Barrett and Aunt Marjorie supported her between them as they set off across the yard.

At one point the woman stopped and broke away. 'Ha'ad on . . .' she said. She sounded confused. 'Me bairns! Where's me bairns?'

'Don't worry,' the headmaster's wife soothed, 'Joe and Janey are safe inside. They're at the Christmas party, remember? Now, come, my lass, let's get you in out of the cold or you'll be no use to them.'

The woman went with Mrs Barrett without further protest.

Aunt Marjorie came back to have a word with Robert Hedley. 'Don't worry,' she said. 'I'll keep her off the streets until you get back; I know what you suspect and I think you may be right.'

The light from the school hallway spilled down the steps into the yard. There was a faint covering of snow on the asphalt that reflected the light upwards. Thea looked up into Robert Hedley's austere face. 'What will happen to her?' she asked.

'She'll be cleaned up and given a bite to eat and a hot drink,' he replied. 'When the party's over I'll take her home with her children.'

Thea frowned. Suddenly the significance of the coins and Aunt Marjorie's words were beginning to make sense. 'Home with her children? With Janey and Joe? But she's . . . she's a . . .'

Robert's look was stern. 'You can't say it, can you? You can't say out loud what you suspect the poor woman has to do to survive – to make life easier for her children. Do you blame her? Do you condemn her for walking the streets?'

Thea heard Ellie's startled gasp.

'I . . . I don't know.' Thea struggled to overcome her genuine

19

shock. 'I mean, if we hadn't found her she might have died and then what would have become of her children?'

Thea's eyes widened when she saw the change that came over his face. For a moment she thought he was angry, and she was not the only one, for she felt Ellie grip her arm. She couldn't tell how long the moment lasted but it ended when he glanced away into the shadows. When he turned to look at her again he seemed to have won control over whatever emotion it was that had so disturbed him.

'You're right, of course,' he said. 'But now we must go. I believe you and Miss Parker are going to the theatre.'

His words were polite enough but Thea imagined there was an undertone of – of what? Contempt? No, that was too strong a word. His manner was patronizing. She felt that Robert Hedley had summed her up and found her wanting. In his eyes she was merely a comfortably-off young woman who was happy to spend an hour or two helping out at the poor children's Christmas party so long as it didn't interfere with her social life.

Inwardly she raged that he should be so presumptuous as to make judgment on her, but her anger was tempered with the uneasy stirrings of her conscience – the worry that there could be some justification for his opinion.

None of them spoke until they reached the corner of the street, when Robert Hedley paused and nodded towards a narrow lane. 'This way,' he said, 'it will be quicker.'

A gaslamp fixed to a bracket on the wall revealed an alley that led between the high-walled backyards of two rows of houses. The light covering of snow looked clean and fresh but their guide said, 'I advise you to hold your skirts well off the ground. You never know what filth lies under the snow.'

Both girls complied. They were used to it. Fashion dictated

20

that even their everyday walking skirts were long enough to sweep the ground. Thea had sewn at least two and a half yards of brush braid round the bottom of most of her skirts to collect the worst of the dirt. She resented both the time spent in sewing and also the hour or more it could take to brush off any encrusted mud when she got home after an outing.

Ellie did not have to look after her own clothes. She didn't exactly have a maid of her own, but she and her mother would happily borrow an assistant from Mr Parker's dancing academy to look after their wardrobes.

Thea's parents were much better off than the Parkers. Samuel Richardson's wholesale and retail grocery business, started by his wife's family in the last century, was now established throughout the North East. But, apart from the fact that their villa in the prosperous suburb of Jesmond was both substantial and comfortable, and that they kept a good table, the Richardsons did not live ostentatiously.

Thea was sometimes ashamed of the way she and her mother appeared shabby and unfashionable. Only Imogen, her younger sister, seemed to know how to get what she wanted from their father.

When they emerged from the back lane, Thea saw that they were just across the road from the tunnel that led under the railway lines. Soon they would be back in the familiar world of wide roads and grand buildings.

Just as they were about to step into the tunnel they heard the hiss and rumble of a train overhead and Ellie gasped. Thea turned to find her friend smiling ruefully. 'I can't help it,' she said.

Thea was just about to take Ellie's arm when Robert Hedley forestalled her. 'The pavement is poorly maintained in the tunnel. Would you care to take my arm?'

Ellie slipped her arm through his gratefully and they set off, keeping close to the grubby walls, with Thea following them. She felt slighted – and angry with herself for feeling so. She didn't need help negotiating the broken paving stones and neither was she frightened of the noise the trains made, but she resented the fact that Mr Hedley hadn't even considered asking her if she also might need his assistance.

Wrapped up in her displeasure, she didn't notice the horse and cart approaching until it was too late. The other two had already stopped and flattened themselves as best they could against the curved wall, when a rag-and-bone man cantered past, flinging up a wake of cold sludge which drenched Thea from head to toe.

She gasped with shock. She closed her eyes as liquid dribbled down her face. It was not only cold, it was filthy and foul-smelling. She dreaded to think what had lain on the surface of the road.

'Thea!' she heard Ellie say. 'How awful!'

Thea rubbed her face with her gloved hands and opened her eyes. The flaring gas jet overhead revealed her friend staring at her with sympathy and dismay. But the expression on Robert Hedley's face infuriated her. His eyes were bright and his lips were held tightly as if he were keeping in a burst of laughter.

'Do you find this amusing?' Thea challenged.

'Oh, no,' Ellie breathed. 'Of course I don't!'

'Not you,' Thea said. 'I mean Mr Hedley. I could swear that he finds this amusing.'

Ellie glanced up at their companion's face and what she saw there didn't seem to reassure her. She hesitated before she said, 'I'm sure you're mistaken.'

'And I'm sure I'm not.'

She raised her chin as she stared up at Robert Hedley and

she saw the faintest flicker of something else in his eyes. Something that sparked that feeling of excitement deep within her.

Eventually, perhaps when he trusted himself to speak, he said, 'Please allow me . . .'

He stepped forward and took hold of Thea's face with one long-fingered hand. She felt a wave of shock. She stumbled backwards and came up against the wall of the tunnel. She remained there while he began to wipe her face with a clean white handkerchief. She was aware that her pulse was racing. She felt her chest constrict. It was difficult to breathe. His face came closer as he leaned forward to examine his handiwork. She closed her eyes and didn't open them again until he had done.

'Thank you,' she whispered, and she thought she heard him catch his breath.

She didn't protest when he took her arm and, with Ellie clinging on at the other side of him, they made their way to the end of the tunnel.

'Not that way,' Thea said when she saw which way he was leading them. 'The tram stop is over there.'

He stopped and smiled at her. 'If you could see yourself you would not want to go home by public transport.'

'Mr Hedley is right,' Ellie added. 'It would be too, too embarrassing.'

To you or to me, Thea wondered, but she said, 'So what shall we do? I suppose we could walk to your house in Heaton but by the time we get there and bathe and change our clothes it would probably be too late to go to the theatre.'

She saw an expression of panic cross Ellie's face but, before she could say anything, Robert Hedley asked, 'And that's important to you?'

'Oh, yes,' Ellie said. 'We've been looking forward to tonight for ages!'

Thea hated the way the man's strong intelligent features softened as he smiled at her friend. She had never been jealous of Ellie's beauty until this moment. She'd had no need to be. She was not vain but she knew that she was attractive in an altogether different way.

But now she was unsure about what was going on. When Ellie had teased her at the party about the schoolmaster not being able to take his eyes off her, she had denied it. But she knew it to be true. She had sensed that Grace Barrett might indeed have cause to be uneasy. This was what made his behaviour towards her now so puzzling.

'Then we must make sure you get home in good time,' she heard him say to Ellie. 'I'll get you a cab.'

'No,' Thea said. 'I don't think we have sufficient money for a hansom.'

'That's all right,' Ellie assured her. 'My mother will pay the cabbie when we get home.'

'No need for that,' Robert Hedley said as he raised one arm and beckoned to the driver at the head of the queue of hansom cabs. 'Tell me the address and I'll settle it with the coachman.'

'No – you can't – you mustn't,' Thea protested.

But, 'Thank you so much,' Ellie said, and told him her address.

Her friend stepped up into the cab eagerly. She held out a hand to help Thea, who saw that it was too late to protest further and climbed in.

'Don't sit too close!' Ellie wrinkled her nose. 'You're still covered in – er – mud.'

The cab had set off before Thea realized that they had not thanked the schoolmaster. She leaned forward and looked for him but he was already striding away through the crowds.

Many of the people hurrying through the snow had been Christmas shopping. Men, women and children, warmly dressed against the weather, carried intriguing parcels, boughs of holly and mistletoe, and sometimes whole Christmas trees.

Thea's attention was caught by a woman and a child – mother and daughter, she guessed – laughing as they pulled a tree along on a wooden sled. They were heading towards the grand, brightly lit portico at the entrance to the station. She wondered how they were going to get the tree and sled on the train – and how far they would have to travel before reaching home.

They were already too far away for Thea to see the expressions on their faces, but she saw that the woman had a young and graceful figure and the child, a girl of no more than six or seven, was well-dressed and sturdy. Thea watched wistfully as they disappeared amongst the crowds.

That little girl would probably always remember today, she thought. Going into town with her mother and choosing the Christmas tree – probably from a stall in the Grainger Market – taking it home through the snow. Such happy memories.

Thea had no memories to compare with that; no such easy relationship with her mother. She could only ever remember being treated with cool indifference. There had been no shared tasks, no shared laughter. Sometimes she wondered whether her mother even liked her.

She leaned back in the cab and stopped that train of thought guiltily. At least she would be going home to a house that was warm and comfortable. They would have plenty to eat and drink on Christmas Day, unlike the children she had spent the afternoon with. And what of the other children that her aunt had spoken of? Those who had no home at all but simply lived on the streets? And died there.

No, she had no right to feel self-pity, no right at all.

* * *

25

'It's all right, Mr Hedley, you can leave us now. I'll look after me mam and wor Janey.'

Joe Roper kneeled by the hearth and raked the coals together; then he pulled the damper out to draw in air. The embers glowed more brightly and flickered into life. Robert saw the lad look hard at the coal scuttle before he picked up the tongs and took out three precious lumps of coal, one by one, to place them in the smoky flames. Robert guessed the Ropers might not have any more.

Joe got up and, turning round, saw the direction of Robert's gaze. 'Divven't fret, there's more where that came from.'

Robert didn't ask where that was. He suspected that Joe, like many other children, would go over the wall and raid a factory yard or a coalman's depot. He wouldn't ever be able to condemn the practice – in fact, when he was a boy, and still living with his mother, he'd done it himself.

'Push the damper in, now, Joe. I divven't want the fire to burn away too quick.'

Lily spoke over her shoulder from the corner of the room; she was settling Janey on a filthy mattress on the bare, scuffed floorboards. The little girl was already asleep. Her mother tucked the blanket round her, then rose wearily and crossed to the table. She stared at the gifts the children had brought home. Along with the tins of toffees there were two oranges, two bright red apples and a small heap of nuts.

Lily smiled. 'I divven't think we've got a nutcracker but I suppose the heel of me boot would do.' She looked up at Robert. 'It's very kind what you do for the bairns,' she said, 'you and the other good folk.' She sighed. 'Ee, I'm tired.'

'I'll go then,' Robert said. He stopped by the door. 'Will you go to bed now, Lily? You need the rest.'

'Aye, I might. I'll try to get to sleep before me man gets yem.'

Robert made his way back to the school through the narrow alleyways. He had promised Mrs Barrett that he would round up any of the children whose parents or older siblings had failed to come for them and see them safely home.

The light covering of snow crunched under foot; he didn't think it would lie for long. The air, cold as it was, was too damp here near the river and, besides, he thought the snow would turn to rain before the night was out.

He pushed his hands in his pockets and thought himself lucky to be able to afford a good overcoat. It hadn't always been so. Once he had been a ragged urchin just like the children who had been to the party tonight.

He smiled when he thought how much the children had enjoyed themselves. Mr Barrett, suppressing his doubts about the holy time of Christmas reverting to pagan rites, had dressed up as Father Christmas. Robert suspected that the false white beard that almost obscured his face had not fooled the older boys and girls but they were happy to go along with the pretence for the sake of the little ones. And perhaps for themselves too. Heaven knows their lives needed a little magic.

They had lined up obediently and moved forward one by one to reach into the sack for the gift of a net containing one apple, one orange and a handful of nuts. He should have made a few sketches – but there wasn't really any need. He didn't need pencil drawings to remember the way the excitement and anticipation had shone in their eyes; how the pinched pallid faces had flushed with transitory joy.

But then, as he tried to compose a painting in his mind, the children's faces faded to be replaced by another face, dark and intense. Thea Richardson's. He had been taken completely unawares by her beauty. His response to her had been immediate. Overwhelmed by a surge of his senses he had instinctively protected himself by pretending a cool indifference.

27

But would it have been so wrong to let her see what he really felt?

Robert smiled self-mockingly. Of course it would. Thea came from a different world. She led a comfortable middle-class existence in a warm house with plenty of food on the table. Her Aunt Marjorie was a genuinely good woman who really cared about the people she helped and the work that she did to improve their lives. Marjorie Gibb's social conscience had steered her into a way of life that was almost classless. But what of Thea?

No doubt like many other girls of her kind she had been taught that it was her Christian duty to give to charity and visit the poor. And then to retreat as quickly as possible to her own world of parties and theatre-going.

Marjorie had told him how important it was for Thea and her friend to get home in time to bathe and change before they went to the theatre. Wash away the malodorous stench of poverty and put on clean fine garments, the like of which the children at the charity school might only glimpse in picture books. Or in Bainbridge's window when they went begging or scavenging in the city centre.

No doubt Thea and her friend thought they had done their duty by helping to fill a few bellies, by providing a few boxes of second-hand clothes and boots. But they could have no idea what poverty really did to people; not just to their bodies but to their hearts and souls.

He remembered Thea's expression when she had realized what Lily Roper might have been doing out on the street that night. Her idea of a prostitute would be of some low creature so far removed from normal life as to be beyond redemption. The idea of such a woman having children living with her had shocked her to the core.

But was he being fair? Was he allowing his own prejudices

28

to cloud his judgement? Why shouldn't a girl like Thea be shocked when she was confronted with the reality of poverty?

He saw again the distress in her face when he had asked her if she condemned Lily Roper for walking the streets.

'I . . . I don't know . . .' she had said. And then, still troubled by the fact that Lily might have died, she had asked, 'What would have become of the children?'

Her concern for the children had been genuine, he was sure of it. Not like Grace Barrett who, good teacher though she was, obviously found it difficult to empathize with her small charges.

Grace . . . The thought of her was troubling.

The headmaster's daughter was an attractive and intelligent young woman. He had enjoyed her friendship. But Robert hoped for her sake that no one else had noticed her growing infatuation with him.

Robert owed a tremendous debt to Grace's parents. When his need had been greatest they had found him a place in a spartan but well-run orphanage, and they had encouraged his education. He knew them to be genuinely proud of how he had bettered himself and of what he had achieved.

But even so, and supposing that he wished it, they would never allow their daughter to marry him.

29

Chapter Three

The hansom cab drew up outside the Parkers' large house on Heaton Road. None of the passers-by gave the two girls who emerged from it a second glance. The weather had worsened and people hurried by with their heads down, faces turned away from the large snowflakes that were too wet to lie for long. Thea and Ellie dashed across the slushy pavement, through the wide gateway, and up the curved gravel path to the porch.

'Be quick,' Ellie cried breathlessly. 'We don't want anyone to see you in such a state!'

'Whyever not?' Thea asked. And they started to laugh.

They were still laughing as they hurried up the short flight of wide stone steps, through the open front door and into the stone-tiled porch. They paused to peer through the frosted-glass panels of the inner door. There was no one to be seen in the brightly lit hall but, as usual, the sound of a piano and feet thumping a wooden floor more or less in unison reverberated through the house. The sounds came from behind the closed double doors of the room on the left. This evening's class was Scottish dancing.

Mr Parker not only ran his academy, he also took dancing classes at Thea's old school. And that was how the two girls had become friends. Ellie was also a pupil there, and the other girls, although not openly hostile, had not wanted to socialize with the daughter of 'the little dancing master'; especially because as far as Ellie's school fees were concerned, some of them suspected that her father had been allowed 'special rates'.

Thea had felt sorry for Ellie at first and had taken her under her wing. Thea, herself, although admired, was not entirely accepted. She was too individual to fit in with the other girls. A genuine friendship had developed between Thea and Ellie in spite of the differences in their interests. Thea was happy to spend more and more time in the Parkers' undemanding and cheerful household.

She could hear Mr Parker now as they hurried up the Turkey-carpeted stairs. His voice was clear but oh, so courteous as he exhorted his pupils to keep in time with the music. When he was teaching he wore a swallow-tailed dark coat, white gloves and patent leather pumps. He was small, graceful and dapper, and a complete contrast to his large untidy wife.

Mrs Parker met them at the top of the stairs. 'I saw the cab from the drawing-room window,' she said. And then, 'Gracious, Thea, what has happened to you?'

Barely pausing for an answer she led them up yet another flight of stairs to the family bathroom. For a large woman she could move quickly, Thea noticed. But, of course, she had once been a dancer, a statuesque chorus girl, who nevertheless had been able to execute the highest of high kicks – or so she was fond of telling everybody.

A cheerful young woman in a large pinafore was already running the bath. She took a jar of pink-coloured crystals from a shelf and scooped out a generous measure. Thea watched bemused as the crystals swirled under the flow from

31

the taps and the colour bled into the hot water. The rising steam was scented with carnations.

'You first, Ellie, dear,' her mother said, 'as we'll have to tong your hair. And be as quick as possible so that Susan can get the bath filled up again. Now, Thea,' she said with hardly a pause, 'you go behind the screen and get out of your clothes. Just leave them there; Susan will clean them for you.'

Behind the screen, Thea closed her mind to the laughter and bustle in the bathroom as she tried to quell her nagging misgivings about the night's enterprise. She had allowed herself to be talked into it to please Ellie and, not only did she find the whole idea slightly vulgar, she knew that her father would be absolutely furious if he found out. She only hoped that Mrs Parker was right and that he never would.

A little later, with the bathroom to herself, she pinned up her hair on top of her head and lay back in the bath. For a while she gave herself up completely to the luxurious experience of the warm scented water that came up to and covered her shoulders.

There was a bathroom at home in the villa in Jesmond, of course, and a plentiful supply of the best bath soaps. But her father considered that to linger in the bathroom was decadent. In his opinion scented bath crystals would be an indulgence. Quality was his due but luxury was a waste of good money, though Thea was sure that her mother yearned for a bit of non-essential softness in her life.

Thea sighed and sat up as she soaped the sponge. She squeezed it to release the creamy lather and began to smooth it over her body.

'The only bit soap they ever set eyes on is at school . . .'

Suddenly the coach driver's words floated into Thea's consciousness and she remembered the children she had spent her afternoon with. Janey . . . wasn't that the child's

32

name, whose eyes had filled with wonder as she gazed at the horse, her lovely face framed with tangled curls. Thea wondered if Janey had ever even seen a bathroom. Or if she ever would . . .

'There, now. Stand perfectly still, both of you,' Ellie's mother said.

They were in Ellie's large, prettily decorated bedroom. Thea stood next to her friend as requested. She felt self-conscious as both Mrs Parker and Susan walked all round them, holding their breath and staring solemnly as if she and Ellie were supernatural beings to be worshipped rather than two human girls dressed up for an evening at the Olympia Theatre.

But, of course, this would be no ordinary visit to the theatre. Rather than being entertained by professional performers, Thea and Ellie themselves were going to be on show.

'Susan, you've done wonders with those gowns,' Mrs Parker said eventually. 'They look so beautiful, I can't see how any other pair of girls could surpass them.' Ellie's mother had included them both in that compliment but her eyes were only for her own daughter, for whom she had such high hopes. 'Just look at yourselves,' she told the girls. 'Susan, turn that mirror round. No! Don't both look in at the same time – it's unlucky to share a mirror!'

Mrs Parker's piled-up baby-blonde curls wobbled danger-ously as she flung herself in front of the mirror and spread out her arms. She was already dressed for the theatre in a bright yellow silk taffeta evening gown trimmed with fuchsia-coloured ribbons and flowers. With her pink cheeks and trembling flesh she looked like an overblown rose.

'*She's fat and foolish, my dear.*' Thea remembered her Aunt Marjorie saying, the edge taken off the comment by her kindly smile. '*But your friend's mother is kindly in a careless sort of*

33

way. I can see why you spend so much time at Ellie's house,' she had added. *'And I can't say that I blame you . . .'*

Thea stood aside politely to allow Ellie to preen first. Her friend's rose-pink satin evening dress was styled to mould the curve of her figure. It had an outer layer of fine white net trimmed with creamy pearl drops. The low-cut neckline revealed a little too much of Ellie's rounded breasts, Thea thought, but it was softened and made decent by a froth of white lace frills edged with gold thread.

Her mother and Susan had swept up Ellie's hair and tonged the front into a mass of tendril-like curls. A white silk flower nestled just above her right ear. She looked truly lovely, Thea thought, if a little like wedding cake confectionery.

She turned away to hide her smile. She knew very well what Mrs Parker's hopes were for tonight: that Ellie should catch the eye of George Edwardes, who had come from London especially for this important event in British theatre history.

The very first beauty contest in the British Isles, Blondes and Brunettes, was to be held here in Newcastle at the Olympia Theatre. George Edwardes, general manager of the world-famous Gaiety Theatre in London, was to be one of the judges. Mr Edwardes had an eye for beauty. More important, he had specific ideas about the girls he wanted for his productions and Rosalie Parker was sure that her daughter would fit the bill.

Ellie, a petite shapely blonde, had a light operatic voice and, thanks to her father's teaching, could dance competently and with a certain grace. Her mother was convinced that Mr Edwardes would take one look at her and whisk her off to the Gaiety.

Then, after a respectable few years establishing herself as a beauty, she would follow in the footsteps of other famous

Gaiety Girls and marry into the aristocracy. The link between the Gaiety and the peerage was well documented by the press. Thea knew that Mrs Parker had dreams of a title for her daughter, and that was why it was so important that they should be the winners tonight.

And Ellie could not have entered the competition without Thea. The girls had to enter in pairs, one of them being a blonde and the other a brunette.

It was Thea's turn to examine herself in the vanity mirror. Her dress was the same as Ellie's except that, instead of white, a fine black net covered the shiny pink satin. Thea did not like wearing pink – she would never have chosen it for herself – but as pink flattered Ellie's milk-and-roses complexion so luminously, she'd had to agree.

But at least the contrasting black net made the effect more dramatic and more suitable for her dark looks. The pearl drops sewn into the net were smoky black and the lace that filled the décolleté neckline was black shot through with silver. The flower pinned to Thea's hair was silvery grey.

Both girls wore pink satin shoes and long evening gloves, Ellie's white and Thea's black, with a flower to match the one in her hair pinned on to the back of the left wrist.

'What do you think, Susan? Do they look about the same height?' Mrs Parker asked.

'Mm, just about.' The young maid scrutinized them with her head slightly to one side.

'Well, it will have to do. Ellie can't wear heels any higher or she will topple over, and if Thea's shoes were any flatter she would walk like a farm girl.' Mrs Parker looked troubled for a moment and then she smiled. 'I could always tease Ellie's curls up a bit. What do you think?'

'Oh, no, Mother,' Ellie protested. 'You'll give me a headache. I'll hold myself high and straight as I walk, just as

35

Father has taught me. But, please, we must go. We mustn't be late!'

'Very well.' Her mother shrugged and gave in. 'Now, Susan, fetch our cloaks – and don't forget to take your pinafore off. We can't have you sitting in the box like that.'

As Susan hurried to obey, Ellie's mother turned to the girls and smiled as if she were about to tell some children of a special treat. 'We won't be late. I didn't tell you, I've ordered one of those new motor-taxis. In fact, I think I can hear it stopping outside just now. Come along, my dears, this is going to be a night to remember!'

Thea was shocked when she saw the crowds outside the theatre in Northumberland Road. 'What are they waiting for?' she asked.

'To see the girls, of course,' Mrs Parker replied.

'But that's dreadful!'

Ellie's mother looked puzzled. 'Dreadful? Why?'

'Well . . . it's like putting ourselves on show. I mean—'

She stopped when she saw that none of her companions in the taxi understood her. Perhaps Ellie wanted to put herself on show. That would be part of the life she had chosen. For the first time since she had been talked into this escapade, Thea thought about what it could lead to. If Ellie were successful and entered the world of the theatre, could they still be friends?

Rosalie Parker, cheeks flushed with excitement, had risen from her seat. 'Come along, girls,' she said. 'Susan, help them down. Ellie, mind you don't catch your heels in your hem.'

As Mrs Parker clambered down from the motor-taxi ahead of them, Thea leaned forward and glanced up at the façade of the theatre. There was a huge, brightly painted placard over the entrance bearing the legend:

THE BLONDES AND BRUNETTES BEAUTY SHOW!
GRAND CONTEST! MAGNIFICENT PRIZES!

That bit about the prizes surprised Thea. She supposed she had known at the beginning, when they had first read in the *Daily Journal* that there was to be a Blonde and Brunette Beauty Show for girls of sixteen and over, that prizes had been mentioned, but she had forgotten that detail. Gold bangles and bracelets, she seemed to remember, but she had doubted that either the bangles or the bracelets would be made of real gold. They would hardly be magnificent.

She remembered thinking that the whole idea was somehow tawdry and when Ellie had said that she would like to enter, Thea had thought that she was joking. Well, she hadn't been joking and here they were, and for her friend's sake, she knew she ought to smile and do her best to enjoy herself.

She was glad that the theatre had provided two large men in maroon brass-buttoned uniforms to escort the arriving contestants past the waiting crowd. She kept her eyes forward and tried to avoid the leering faces and the cheerfully offensive comments.

'Ee, look at the two lasses gettin' out of the motorcar!'

'That bonny little blonde one's a proper mazer!'

'You can have her – it's the dark one fer me!'

'Haddaway, man. That one's quality. A lass like that wouldn't give you the time of day!'

It was like running the gauntlet.

They were met in the foyer by a tall, thin, elderly man in an old-fashioned evening suit that had seen much better days. He introduced himself as the assistant manager and he proved impervious to Mrs Parker's captivating smile. He would not agree to her request.

'No, I'm sorry, madam, but the young ladies will have to

wait with the other contestants; they cannot sit in the box with you.'

'Oh, but couldn't you send for them, when it is time—'

'Those are the rules.'

Thea watched as the man and Mrs Parker took the measure of each other. Uncharacteristically, Mrs Parker gave in first. 'Ah, well, I'll have to sit there all alone. I told Mr Parker that he should cancel tonight's classes but he said his pupils had paid for twelve sessions before Christmas and they should have twelve sessions. Susan, I'll trust you to see that the girls look as perfect as possible before they set foot on the stage.'

'I beg your pardon, madam, but this young woman is obviously not a contestant and therefore she will not be allowed backstage.'

Rosalie Parker looked wounded. Her blue eyes widened and her lips trembled as though she were going to cry.

Her daughter smiled at her. 'It's all right, Mother. Thea and I can manage by ourselves. We'll look after each other. Now, if Susan could take our cloaks, you two should go straight to your box and order something nice for yourselves. A cup of coffee and some pastries, or perhaps an ice-cream.'

Her mother sighed. 'Very well. I see I have no choice, but, remember, keep in time to the music, whatever they play, and look straight ahead. Never try to look for faces in the audience – even mine!'

As if I would, Thea thought, as she and Ellie followed the victor through a door that led to a maze of narrow, dimly lit corridors. I would rather believe that there was no audience there at all!

Soon they were standing with many other pairs of girls in a large, echoing area backstage. It was cold and the girls seemed to have huddled close to each other for warmth. The sweet smells of the perfumes and powders they wore mingled unpleasantly with the musty smells coming from the painted canvas backdrops and battered stage props.

Thea looked around surreptitiously at the other contestants. They were all pretty girls, otherwise presumably they wouldn't have entered the competition, but there had been some very generous interpretations of what constituted a 'blonde' or a 'brunette'.

In fact one pair, who looked like sisters, had hair colouring that was hardly any different from each other. Thea imagined that one of them would say that she had light brown hair and the other that she was a dark blonde. At a quick estimation, Ellie and herself at least provided the best contrast.

But she was sure that it would also be a matter of beauty and style. Some of the dresses were copies of gowns from the fashion magazines. They were obviously home-made, from inferior fabrics, but that didn't matter if they were worn by girls with beautiful faces and stunning figures. And some of them were.

No, Thea didn't think that the result of the competition was a foregone conclusion. She glanced round to find her friend frowning. She took Ellie's hand and squeezed it. 'Don't worry,' she whispered. 'Not one of those girls is as lovely as you. You are bound to catch Mr Edwardes' eye.'

And, as for me, Thea thought, I don't want to catch anybody's eye. In fact I wish I could slink away right now and pretend that none of this is happening!

The other girls had been glancing round too, and whispering to their partners, but they all stopped talking obediently when the assistant manager reappeared, bringing with him a much better dressed and younger man whom he introduced as Mr Howard Cassell, the theatre manager.

Mr Cassell told them what an important occasion this was, and how they could bring honour not only to themselves, but also to the theatre, and to the city of Newcastle, if they conducted themselves properly.

There were to be no attempts to draw attention to themselves individually by use of any trickery; no prima donna behaviour. They must be dignified and ladylike. And there must definitely not be any hysterics if they were tapped on the shoulder and led off the stage.

For that was how the competition was going to be conducted, like a children's party game, until the judges were satisfied that they were left with the three best pairs of girls for the final judging.

They were asked to line up with their partners – just like a 'crocodile' of schoolgirls, Thea thought. Only rather than being led to Jesmond Dene for a nature ramble, she felt as though she was being led to the scaffold.

However, once the orchestra started to play and they began to move, it wasn't too bad. In contrast to the backstage area the stage was warm, probably because of the footlights, and Thea couldn't have seen the faces of the people in the dim auditorium even if she'd tried. But she could hear them.

The contestants had been directed to walk round in a grand circle and there were cries of 'Ooh!' and 'Aah!' as each pair of girls approached the front of the stage, paused briefly to face the audience and then walked on again. Soon she became aware that the space between Ellie and herself and the couples before and behind was becoming larger. The circle was thinning out.

She saw that this was because a band of pretty children dressed as pantomime fairies and elves seemed to be obeying directions from someone standing in the wings as they approached first this couple and then another and led them away; a fairy and an elf to each couple.

'The children are from a theatrical dancing school,' Ellie

40

whispered when she saw them. 'I recognize two of them who started off at my father's academy.'

Soon it became obvious that the audience – now proving to be partisan – did not approve when some of the girls were led away. Thea could hear hisses and boos and much shushing going on. One of the unfortunate losers broke down in tears before she left the stage. Her partner put her arms around her and there was a call of 'Shame!'

Thea was so taken up with the drama of it all that she was surprised when the orchestra stopped playing and she heard Ellie say, 'Stop, Thea, there are only three couples left on stage!'

The orchestra struck up a cheerful medley of Christmas carols in keeping with the season. The elves and fairies brought six red velvet and gilt chairs on to the stage and arranged them across the back. Then they led the remaining contestants to the chairs and indicated that they should sit.

Meanwhile a table and three chairs had been placed to the front and at one side of the stage. The theatre manager appeared, to introduce the judges to the audience. They came on one by one, to applause and cheers: first a striking dark-haired woman introduced as Madame Cora Levey, the director of the stage school that had provided the little dancers; then a blond, good-looking man who was introduced as Vernon Gray, a photographer, and finally, Mr George Edwardes, the general manager of the famous Gaiety Theatre in London.

George Edwardes proved to be a big handsome Irishman, who quickly took charge of the proceedings. When the manager left the stage, Mr Edwardes invited the other two judges to sit at the table and then he strolled centre stage to address the audience.

'As you know,' he said, 'the Gaiety is reputed to have the most beautiful chorus girls in the whole world.' He paused

41

and Thea could sense the audience holding its collective breath. 'But tonight in this theatre in Newcastle,' he continued, 'I have seen some of the loveliest girls – no, I should say *bonniest lasses* – it has ever been my privilege to clap eyes on!'

The audience rose to their feet. They stamped and cheered. They laughed in appreciation of the great man's attempt to speak in the local accent.

George Edwardes allowed the clamour to continue for a while but when he raised a hand, it stopped. He waited until everyone was seated again and he smiled down into the orchestra pit.

'And now,' he said, 'if my friends in the orchestra will strike up again, I'm going to ask these young ladies,' he turned and took them in with a wide gesture, 'to resume their perambulation around the stage. Ready, girls?'

The three couples rose to their feet and Mr Edwardes sensed how nervous they must be because he reassured them before he sat down at the table. 'Don't worry,' he said, 'this won't take long.'

But it was too long for Thea's liking. She hated the way that Mr Edwardes and Madame Levey looked them up and down as they walked past the table. Like cattle at a show, she thought. She hated the way they scribbled notes on a sheet of paper and leaned in to confer with each other in whispers.

She noticed that the photographer, Vernon Gray, was neither writing nor conferring. To her embarrassment, she caught his eye and she saw that he was smiling at her. Is he laughing at me? she wondered. How dare he? She felt herself stiffen with rage and she knew that, for a moment, her glare was ferocious.

But then she saw him shaking his head gently. Had he read her mind? How could he? But in any case, she saw now that his smile was sympathetic and it was directed just at her – as if they shared some kind of secret. She couldn't help but smile back.

During their sixth perambulation Thea noticed the judges glancing at each other and nodding their heads. George Edwardes rose to his feet and with one grand gesture he indicated both that the orchestra should stop playing and the girls should stop walking. The judges had made their decision.

The audience had gone, the curtain had fallen and they were waiting on the stage as they had been told to do for further instructions. The other two pairs of girls had been joined by their parents and friends but they stood in a closed group, talking and glancing occasionally at Thea and Ellie.

Mrs Parker suddenly hurried towards them from the wings. She was flushed with triumph. Her cheeks matched the fuchsia trimmings on her evening gown. 'I've sent Susan home in the motor-taxi,' she said. 'She will tell Mr Parker the good news, and that we will be delayed.'

Ellie smiled at her questioningly.

'My dears, we are invited to a party – all of us.' She smiled graciously at the other girls and their companions. 'But of course, as the winners of the contest, you and Thea will be the guests of honour. Mr Edwardes is hosting the party in the green room. You can follow me. I know the way, I once played at this theatre.'

'What is the green room?' Thea asked.

'A sort of actors' common room, a room near the stage where the performers can wait until it is time for their entrance.'

'But why green?'

Mrs Parker didn't answer her for she had gone, leading the surprised and excited group off stage and into the shadowy wings. Thea found herself alone.

'Green because originally they used to paint the walls green to relieve the eyes from the glare on the stage.'

She turned to find that she was not alone after all. Someone else had been hanging back and now he walked towards her. It was the photographer, Vernon Gray. As he spoke the overhead lights dimmed and Thea found herself staring at him uncertainly in the semi-darkness.

'Oh, I see.'

She closed her eyes and opened them again, hoping that her vision would adjust and that she could make out his expression. He was about the same height as she was and he was standing very close.

'Aren't you coming to the party?' he asked. 'Don't you want to celebrate your triumph?'

'Certainly not!' She saw that he was taken aback and she wished she hadn't sounded so forceful. 'I mean, I suppose I will have to go to the party – I came here with Ellie and her mother – but as for wanting to celebrate my triumph . . .'

'So I was right. You hated every minute of it, didn't you?'

'Yes.'

'Then why enter the competition? For the sake of your friend?'

'Yes.'

'Then the truly lovely Miss Ellie Parker is lucky to have a loyal friend like you.'

Thea felt uncomfortable. 'Please don't make me sound so noble. I love Ellie, and her parents are warm and kind . . .' She stopped, not wanting Vernon Gray to know why she might have been in need of warmth and kindness.

But if he had noticed her discomfort he chose to ignore it. He took her right hand and lifted it up between them so that the remaining light shone on the gold bangle she was now wearing. 'And what do you think of your magnificent prize?'

She could feel the warmth of his hand through the thin silk of her glove. She caught her breath before she answered, 'I . . . I think . . . I mean it's pretty, I suppose, but I don't think it's real gold.'

Vernon Gray laughed and squeezed her hand more tightly. 'Of course it isn't, and neither are the bracelets that the other girls were given – they are just cheap little chains. But when those girls are wrinkled old grandmothers they will have something to remind them that they were once young and beautiful. And, as for your friend, I shouldn't think she cares one jot about her winners' bangle. That's not the prize she's after, is it?'

'No.'

'And she stands a good chance of achieving what she wants. Except . . .'

'What is it?'

'Is it Ellie or her mother whose ambition is the driving force?'

'I'm not sure.'

'Well, whatever the case, they are both happy tonight and you should try to be happy for them. Now, allow me to escort you to the party.'

Chapter Four

Thea looked around her. It would have been hard to say what colour the walls of the green room were. Whatever they might have been originally, they were now an indeterminate neutral shade, and mostly obscured by framed sketches and photographs of performers who had appeared at the Olympia over the years.

Old sofas and chairs sagged forlornly round the edge of the room, along with badly scratched and stained occasional tables. The faded rug that covered most of the floor was threadbare. There was a faint musty cheesiness in the air, something like the smell backstage. So, in spite of the clean damask cloth covering the long table at one end of the room, and the generous refreshments set out there, the overall effect was shabby.

'A brave attempt but it's a trifle down at heel, isn't it?' Thea turned to see Vernon Gray smiling at her as if he had read her thoughts again. Inconsequentially she noticed that his eyes were grey and that his fair hair waved softly and was just a little too long. Also that he looked very handsome in evening clothes. 'Do you want to join in the bun fight, or will you wait here while I go and fill a plate for you?' he asked.

Thea glanced at the lively crowd surrounding the table and smiled. 'I'll wait here, if you don't mind.'

She was grateful for his offer. In spite of Ellie's assurance to Aunt Marjorie, Mrs Parker had not insisted on them having something to eat before they set off for the theatre, and Thea was hungry.

She watched him ease his way through the guests. She had no idea who they all were but she thought that some of the older couples were business people and city worthies. An untidily dressed young man with a pencil and notebook seemed to be taking their names. She frowned. For some reason this worried her.

Everybody was talking at the same time, barely stopping to listen to each other. Even the runners-up seemed to have cheered up a little. Thea saw that Ellie and her mother were talking to George Edwardes, or rather Mrs Parker was talking, Ellie seemed subdued. Perhaps she had just realized what this win could mean to her. Thea recalled something that Vernon Gray had said before they left the stage.

'*Is it Ellie or her mother whose ambition is the driving force?*'

Thea had never thought about it before but now she realized that the two women's aims might be different. Mrs Parker was seeing this contest as an opportunity to launch her daughter's career.

But what of Ellie? Much as Thea loved her friend, she had to admit Ellie was vain. To win such a contest would be to have her beauty acknowledged, but although Ellie had been taken up with the idea of winning, she had never spoken of any burning ambition to go on the stage.

So now Ellie stood demurely as her mother talked with great animation to Mr Edwardes. He was listening politely but Thea noticed that he kept glancing away. She suppressed her laughter as she wondered whether Mrs Parker was boring the poor man with anecdotes from her own theatrical career and her famous high kicks.

'What has amused you?' Vernon Gray had returned carrying two plates of savoury pastries and tiny iced fondants. He glanced back the way he had come and apparently saw immediately why Thea was smiling. When he turned to look at her, his answering smile once more drew her in to some kind of intimate understanding with him. Thea felt as though they were conspirators, although she had not sought to join forces with him.

At Vernon's side there was a smaller dark-haired man who carried two glasses of wine. 'Put those down here, Lewis,' Vernon said, indicating a small table just behind Thea, 'and then go and fetch your own refreshments.'

'Yes, Mr Gray,' the man said politely. But as Thea moved aside to allow him to place the glasses on the table, he smiled at her and said, 'I'm not a waiter and neither am I Vernon's servant. He forgets himself because I'm so agreeable.'

'And that is because you want a favour,' Vernon said under his breath as the dark man walked away.

Thea looked at him. 'He wants a favour? What do you mean by that?'

'Ah, you heard me.'

'Didn't you intend that I should?'

Vernon laughed. 'I like you more and more, Thea. Yes, I suppose I did want you to hear that remark because, if I am to grant Lewis this favour, I need your co-operation. But here, do take one of these plates, or people will mistake *me* for a waiter.'

Thea took a plate but immediately put it down on the table next to the drinks. 'If you want me to co-operate with you, you had better explain what you mean.'

48

'Don't frown like that, it mars your beauty, and please don't look so suspicious. Lewis Sinclair simply wants an introduction to your friend, Miss Parker, and I said that I could arrange it, that's all.'

'*What* did you say?'

'Why the outrage? I said I could arrange an introduction to Ellie – and, as she is your friend, it will all go easier if you are present. But why are you looking at me like that? That's not so dreadful, is it?'

'No, not dreadful . . . it's just, *who* did you say he was?'

Vernon relaxed. 'I see you have heard of him.'

'Of course I have. I've read every one of his books. Why do you look surprised?'

'Lewis's books are very – shall I say – masculine, and you – you are so young.'

'That is a *non sequitur*. I think you meant to say that women have not enough brains to read detective stories!'

Vernon burst out laughing. 'Thea, Thea, I think I could very easily fall in love with you. You look absolutely delicious when you are fired with indignation.'

'Please don't talk like that. I'm not used to it.' For a moment, she could not meet his gaze. She felt uncomfortable. She wasn't sure why. There was nothing threatening in his manner, nothing to give offence. Unless the threat lay in his assumption that he could tease her this way.

Teasing? Is that what Vernon was doing? She was aware that his laughter had subsided. She looked up to find him observing her intently. It was as if there was no one else in the room. He was drawing her in, the look in his eyes stripping her of conventional defences. Thea caught her breath. He desired her.

Robert Hedley had looked at her like that . . . he had been standing just as close . . .

49

She remembered that moment in the tunnel under the railway track. She had been excited without at first knowing why. She remembered her pulse racing . . .

It was racing now as she held Vernon's gaze, but not with excitement. What then? Fear? No, that was too strong a word. Unease . . . that was it.

Vernon blinked and suddenly the expression in his eyes was merely affable. When he spoke she had to concentrate to remember what they had been talking about.

'I'm sorry,' he murmured, 'and forgive me if I've insulted you. I should have realized at once that you have brain enough to deal with any of Sinclair's complicated plots. In fact I'm sure that you have solved many of the cases at least one page, if not a whole chapter, before the hero of the books, himself; Hugh Martin, the great detective!'

He was smiling. The moment of intimacy had passed. Thea relaxed. 'There is one mystery I haven't solved,' she said.

'What's that?'

'I can't imagine why such a successful author should choose to leave London and come to live in Newcastle.'

'Is that a question?'

'Do you know the answer?'

'No. Now pick up your plate and taste some of these delicious refreshments. I'm told they had them sent along from Alvini's. Ah,' he turned and smiled at the man who was walking towards them, 'you're back, Lewis.'

Thea was left with a feeling of discomfiture. She had been made to feel that it was impolite of her to have enquired about Lewis Sinclair's reasons for leaving London. But she also had the feeling that Vernon Gray might not have told the truth. She suspected that he knew more about the detective novelist than he was prepared to tell her.

The food was as good as Vernon had promised. She sipped

the wine experimentally; it was delicious. She glanced up at her companions and wondered whether they could tell that she had never tasted any before. For, although her father was happy to sell wine and spirits in some of his shops, he would not allow any in the house. Thea had never understood how he could reconcile the fact that he would sell alcohol to others and yet have taken a personal pledge to the Temperance Movement.

'Is your friend trying to attract your attention?' Vernon asked suddenly. Thea looked across the room and saw that Ellie was glancing in their direction. 'Why don't you beckon her over?'

At that moment Ellie caught her eye and raised her own heavenwards as she inclined her head slightly towards her mother. Mrs Parker was still talking to Mr Edwardes who, by now, was hardly concealing his desire to move on. Thea saw that his attention had been taken by the pair who had come third in the contest, the girls whom she thought must be sisters and whose hair colouring was so very similar.

Thea smiled at her friend and raised one hand to make a beckoning gesture. But at that moment George Edwardes finally made his escape, so it was not just Ellie but her mother as well who came across the room to join them.

Thea made the introductions and was amused to see Rosalie Parker frown as she tried to recall why Lewis Sinclair's name should be important. 'Ah, yes, the writer of detective stories,' she said at last. 'My husband, Mr Parker, brought one of your books home from the library. He said it was very clever and he wondered where on earth you got all those ideas from—'

'Mrs Parker,' Vernon interrupted her with a smile, 'may I escort you to the refreshment table? Thea, would you come with us? Perhaps you would like to fill a plate up for your friend?'

Thea saw how deftly Vernon had arranged that Lewis

Sinclair should be left alone with Ellie. He kept up a flow of conversation as he escorted Mrs Parker through the crowd of guests and when he saw Thea looking askance at him he gave that now familiar private smile.

Thea glanced back to see her friend and Lewis Sinclair looking at each other silently. They were about the same height. He was thin, dark, and his black evening clothes added to his intensity. She was all soft curves, fair, and unashamedly frivolous in pink. They couldn't have been more different. And yet Thea imagined that each had sensed in the other something he or she desired. She wondered if even they knew what it was.

The motor-taxi returned for the girls and Mrs Parker one and a half hours later, as instructed. One of the maroon-uniformed gentlemen brought their cloaks and escorted them along the dusty passages to the foyer. The sleet had turned to rain, and the road and pavement just outside the theatre shone wetly. Their escort held a large umbrella and took them one by one to the waiting taxi, Mrs Parker first.

As she waited, Thea glanced out into the street. The admiring crowd had gone. There was no one waiting to see them leave. But she could see other figures huddled in the doorways of the shops opposite. She knew they were not there for any other reason than to find shelter on a cold December night. She was chilled by the knowledge that they would be there until morning.

The motor-taxi drew away, and as they turned into the Haymarket, Thea watched through the window. She saw that many of the ragged figures were small – merely children. Children who were even worse off than those she had met at the Charity School that afternoon. No wonder her aunt was so concerned.

Even as she thought of Aunt Marjorie, she saw a familiar figure making her way from doorway to doorway. A figure wearing a flat tweed hat. The children were rising to their feet and following her. Her aunt was like the Pied Piper, Thea thought, but where could she be taking her tattered band? And was it safe for her to be out in these streets alone so late at night?

But then Thea saw another figure, a man, following them, rounding up the stragglers. He was tall and wide-shouldered. As she watched she saw him stoop to gather up one of the smallest children. He held the child in his arms. The light from a nearby streetlamp shone on the wan face of the child and on the strong, compassionate features of the man. It was Robert Hedley.

Thea shrank back into her seat. He couldn't have seen her, of course, but she found that it mattered dreadfully to her that he might have done. She recalled the moment when their eyes had first met during the Christmas party at the school only that afternoon.

She had been stirred by a strange excitement and, if Ellie was to be believed, Robert Hedley was not indifferent to her. And yet later, when he had been walking them to the tram stop, he had been patronizing, even dismissive.

Not patronizing in the way Vernon Gray had been in the green room of the theatre. Vernon had been teasing her, laughing with her, perhaps flirting with her. In spite of the fact that she had no experience in dealing with such a man, she had found herself beginning to warm to the game, to enjoy his company. But Robert Hedley . . .

Thea drew her cloak more tightly round her. What did it matter? Why should she care what the schoolmaster thought about her? She would probably never see him again.

'Thea, do you think it can be true?'

'Mm? Oh, sorry, Mrs Parker. What did you say?'

'Do you think Mr Edwardes is really interested in those two sisters?'

'Sisters?'

'Oh, my dear, you are tired. I shouldn't bother you with my concerns.'

'No. Please, tell me.'

'The pair who came third in the contest. I was talking to Cora Levey and she is under the impression that Mr Edwardes wants to introduce them as a sister act at the Gaiety.'

'I suppose it's possible.' Thea sensed immediately that this was not the answer Mrs Parker had hoped for, and she added, 'But that doesn't mean that he will not also be interested in Ellie.'

'No, I suppose not. He did ask me to send him some photographs.'

'Photographs?'

'Yes, in different costumes, theatrical poses; you know the kind of thing I mean. Well, anyway, I've already arranged it with that young man you were talking to, Vernon Gray. He said he'd be delighted to take Ellie's photograph and that you should come to his studio too.'

'Me? Oh, no!'

'Whyever not? Mr Gray has offered to do the sitting free of charge although, of course, we shall have to pay for the actual photographs.'

'But I don't want any. I mean, there is no need—'

'But, Thea, it will be such fun! And nice for Ellie to have you there as well.'

Thea glanced at her friend, who had not said a word. She seemed subdued. No, that was not the word – Ellie was distracted. But her smile was dreamy, secretive, as if she were thinking about something that she didn't want to share. Thea remembered how Ellie and Lewis had talked quietly to each other, scarcely touching the food.

But she had watched the way Ellie sipped her wine, never taking her eyes from Lewis. And he had concentrated only on Ellie, leaving Vernon to entertain the voluble Mrs Parker. After a while Vernon had shot Thea one of those smiles and murmured politely to Mrs Parker that he was being selfish in keeping her away from the other guests.

He had led her across the room, talking all the while, and left her with Madame Levey. Thea supposed that that was when the two ladies had speculated about Mr Edwardes' plans for a sister act.

And it must have been while they were walking across the room that Vernon Gray had offered to take Ellie's photograph. And Thea's too – although he had not mentioned it to her when he'd come back to join her.

It was past midnight when Mrs Parker stretched up to pull the cord that would extinguish the overhead gaslight in Ellie's bedroom. She bid the girls good night and left the room. A cinder guard had been placed in front of the fire, which had been banked up to last the night. Thea watched the warm shadows thrown up on to the ceiling and the walls, and tried to compose herself for sleep.

She was sharing Ellie's large bed and her friend was already snuggled into the feather mattress and the mound of pillows, her eyes closed. The curling rags tied into her hair somehow made her look even prettier – like a child with a riot of ribbons.

Thea had no need of such tricks. Her own, almost black, hair had a wave of its own that would not be tamed. The most she could do with it was to tie it back at the nape of her neck with a broad ribbon, like a schoolgirl, or pin it up. But when it was pinned up wisps would escape and curl around her face so that she was constantly having to deal with them.

Thea didn't think that Ellie was asleep. But, for some reason, she didn't want to talk. Her friend was content with her thoughts and didn't want to share them. She remembered other times she had stayed here – the whispered gossip, the smothered laughter, the sharing of hopes and dreams. But now, when Ellie might at last have something to hope for, she was silent.

But what exactly *was* her friend hoping for?

Thea turned away from Ellie and her movement released the smell of lavender from the bed linen. Lavender was supposed to be soothing, to induce relaxation and sleep, but there was some part of Thea's mind that prevented her from yielding.

She remembered the way Ellie and Lewis had looked at each other when they had been introduced. She wondered if her friend had felt the same charge of excitement she had felt when she looked at Robert Hedley . . .

But Ellie had the satisfaction of knowing that, whatever it was she felt for Lewis, he seemed to feel it too. Whereas the schoolmaster . . .

Thinking about him was too disturbing and Thea tried to empty her mind, only to find his image replaced with that of Vernon Gray. Reluctantly she allowed Vernon's image to remain while she tried to discover what it was that had unsettled her. She considered his eyes, grey like his name; now, in repose, their gaze was neutral. She relaxed a little. His blond hair, shining and clean as any girl's, curled softly on his collar.

His skin was soft too. She remembered the touch of his hand when they said goodbye. He had held her hand just a little too long and smiled only at her. 'Until we meet again,' he'd murmured, and she'd laughed, safe now, not really thinking that they would.

And yet Vernon had already arranged with Mrs Parker that they should. Why hadn't he told her? Did he think she would have refused his offer to take her photograph? Would she have done? Thea sighed. In any case the decision would not be hers; she thought it unlikely that her father would allow it. Vernon's image faded.

A movement at the window caught her eye. She eased herself up and watched the floral-patterned curtains waft backwards and forwards. Now that she was sitting she could feel a draught. She wondered if the window was open.

Ellie's soft, regular breathing told Thea that her friend was now asleep so she moved as gently as she could to the edge of the bed and lowered her feet to the floor. She had no slippers with her and when she stepped off the rug on to the cold linoleum near the window she shivered.

She pulled the curtain aside and saw that the bottom half of the window had not been closed properly so she pushed it down. Then she paused and looked out into the street. It was a place of shadows.

The gardens in front of the houses were pools of blackness edged with the frosted tops of privet hedges reflecting the light from the streetlamps. Beyond the hedges and the garden walls the street was starkly black and white, like a photograph.

Thea shivered at the chill coming from the cold glass. She was about to turn and go back to bed when she noticed a shape detach itself from the shadows at the other side of the street. She leaned forward and watched as the figure moved out into the centre of the pavement. It was an old woman. Or rather it was a woman stooped with either age or ill health. The woman staggered but righted herself just in time to prevent herself from falling. Was she drunk?

Where was she going? Did she have anywhere to go? The woman vanished into the shadows once more.

Thea returned to bed and pulled the bedclothes round herself. She remembered that today was Christmas Eve.

Chapter Five

Thea returned to her father's house in Jesmond later that day. It was Christmas Eve, but it was also Sunday, so her father was at home. In spite of the Christmas tree in the large oak-panelled hallway, and the garlands of evergreens, and red and gold ribbons decorating the downstairs rooms, the atmosphere was cheerless. Her mother seemed determined to fade into the background of any room she inhabited, and her sister, Imogen, a younger version of her small, fair-haired mother, sat quietly embroidering, as usual. She could sit like that for hours.

Samuel Richardson had shut himself away in the library, although Thea doubted that he ever read any of the books that lined the shelves from floor to ceiling. They were for show. In there her father would read the newspapers that he had delivered daily or spend hours poring over the ledgers and papers that, when he was not there, were kept locked in his desk.

Thea cheered up a little when her aunt arrived in time to go with them to evensong. Better still, her father decided not to join them, and everyone's spirits were noticeably lighter when the four women, wrapped up against the cold, set off to walk the short distance to church.

Warm light streamed from the windows of the substantial houses they passed, illuminating well-kept gardens. Frost sparkled at their feet. They heard the occasional burst of conversation and laughter as guests arrived and were greeted at the doors.

Thea's mother walked ahead with her older sister. 'Are you coming to join us tomorrow, Marjorie?' Thea heard her ask.

'You know I would love to come to you on Christmas Day, but I have other duties.'

'Hardly duties,' Amy Richardson replied. 'At least if they are, they are self-imposed. But, in spite of the feast we shall provide, I see I shall not change your mind.'

'No, dear, I'm sorry. The Board of Governors of the Charity School has been good enough to let us use the building over Christmas, and the Reverend Mr Barrett and his wife are giving up their free time in order to supervise. We shall house and feed as many homeless children as we can for these few days and, you never know, perhaps time spent with them will bring more simple joy than a feast would do. 'Now, Amy, don't be offended,' Aunt Marjorie added quickly, 'I didn't mean to belittle time spent with my family.'

Thea's mother laughed gently. 'I'm not offended, Marjorie. To tell you the truth, I was being selfish. I'll miss your company.'

'But you have your daughters.'

'Yes.'

Thea wondered if Aunt Marjorie knew how distant her sister was from her daughters. Imogen was devoted to their father and, having seen at an early age what little regard he had for his wife, she treated her mother accordingly.

Thea would have loved to have become her mother's friend but she was held at a distance. Her mother never defended nor even consoled her when her father berated her, even though she must have known that most of the time his complaints were unjustified.

Imogen, who was much smaller than Thea, took her arm and pulled her down so that their heads were close as she murmured, 'Anyone with any sense can see that it's their own fault that those people live the way they do. They're dirty and they're smelly, and I don't know how Aunt Marjorie can bear to spend her time with them!'

At her sister's words Thea had a vision of her aunt's indomitable figure leading the little group of children the night before. So that was where she had been taking them – to the Charity School for a few days' warmth and comfort. And she had been helped in her task by Robert Hedley.

Thea wondered if he would be staying at the school on Christmas Day – and whether that would please Grace Barrett. She realized that the thought of those two together aroused a feeling in her that was akin to jealousy, and she was angry with herself. That was probably why she answered her sister the way she did.

'Me, neither. I'm glad that I won't be there!' she said.

Imogen was surprised. 'Why should you be?'

'Oh, no reason. Just perhaps that Aunt Marjorie might have asked me to help, as I did yesterday.'

Thea was flustered. Was she disappointed that her aunt had not asked her to help? Would she have gone if she had been asked? She was glad that they had reached the church. The choir was already singing. After greeting other members of the congregation at the door they hurried in and took their places. There was no more time for conversation.

* * *

After lunch on Christmas Day the family sat together in the drawing room. There was a good fire and Samuel Richardson had eaten well, as he always did. Thea hoped that the warmth and the food would make him content to sit quietly and leave them all in peace. But it was not to be. She suppressed her look of dismay when she saw him get up and walk towards her.

'Don't you like your present, Thea?' he asked. 'I can assure you that everything is the very best that Bainbridge's can supply.'

And supplied to you at trade price, no doubt, Thea thought. But she kept her head down so that her father could not see the scorn in her eyes.

They had not been allowed to open their presents until after lunch and now she stared down at the work basket full of colourful embroidery silks. The basket contained not only the silks, but packets of needles and pins, thimbles and scissors, and tiny metal implements she did not recognize. Unlike her sister, she hated embroidery or any kind of sewing, and her father knew this very well.

She could sense him growing impatient. He was a big man and to have him standing over her was intimidating. She could smell the tobacco on him and hear his breathing getting shorter. She forced herself to look up.

'It's a beautiful present. Thank you, Father.'

He didn't move away. He stood as if he were waiting for her to say something else. Or was he disappointed at her correct response? Had he sought a confrontation? When she was younger Thea had always been in trouble for contradicting and arguing with her father.

Eventually it had dawned on her that he was the one who was keeping the arguments going. He knew how to manipulate her until her behaviour was such that he could punish her; and his punishment was harsh. From the day she had realized what was happening she had made every effort not to let him provoke her. She knew it angered him even more and this gave her a quiet satisfaction.

'You see, I have given Imogen exactly the same present,' he said at last. 'There is no difference between you.'

Thea glanced across the room to where her sister was sitting by the window. It was true that the padded wicker baskets were identical. And no doubt they contained exactly the same quantities of silks and pins and needles, and whatever else would give a needlewoman joy.

But Thea had watched while Imogen delved urgently amongst its contents, almost as if she were expecting to find something else hidden amongst them, and she had seen the quiet smile as her sister's fingers found what she was looking for. No doubt a piece of jewellery.

Thea remembered the days when she hadn't been so wise; hadn't been so guarded. 'It's not fair!' she had exclaimed so many times when she had perceived that her younger sister always got preferential treatment, was loved better than she was. She didn't know why this was so, but she had learned that her only way to triumph was to pretend that she hadn't noticed.

Thea held the work basket with both hands and rose to her feet. She was dismayed to find that her father didn't step back and they stood uncomfortably close. She was almost as tall as he was and she forced herself to look into his eyes. He stared back; his face was flushed and his breathing irregular. She wondered if he truly hated her. She asked him, 'May I go and show Mother my present?'

From the corner of her eye she saw her mother glance up in surprise. She had been staring into the fire and she looked distracted, reluctant to be drawn back from wherever her thoughts had taken her.

Her father stepped aside. 'Yes, why not?' He sounded disappointed.

As Thea crossed the room she glanced at the clock on the mantelpiece and thought wearily of all the hours before bedtime.

The next morning the family took breakfast together at the same early hour as any working day. Even though it was Boxing Day, many of the shops would be open and Thea's father would go to his office in the city as usual. Apart from wishing each other good morning, no one said much as they served themselves from the warming dishes laid out on the sideboard.

Thea helped herself to scrambled eggs, toast and coffee, and took her place opposite her sister. Her mother and father, separated by the length of the dining table, might as well have been in different rooms, they seemed so unconnected with each other.

Samuel Richardson, after devouring a plateful of herrings broiled in mustard sauce, went back for eggs, bacon, kidneys, mushrooms, tomatoes and toast. When he had done, he picked up his cup of coffee and, without excusing himself, he took it to the library where his newspaper would be waiting for him.

When he had gone, Thea noticed that her mother relaxed as usual. Thea could not remember a time when her parents had smiled and talked to each other as Ellie's parents did.

She often wondered why on earth they had married in the first place. She knew very well that when they had been young – and even now among certain classes – people did not always marry for love. Sometimes a marriage could be an arrangement between two families.

But if that had been the case, her mother, as the daughter and granddaughter of successful businessmen, could have done much better for herself than one of her father's employees. For that was what Samuel Richardson had been. A hardworking, clever young shop assistant.

Her mother and Aunt Marjorie had no brother, and as Aunt Marjorie had not married and declared that she never would, Amy Gibb's husband had become head of the family firm when Nathaniel Gibb had died. He had even changed the name of the firm to Gibb and Richardson. And, after a while, he'd dropped the Gibb.

So had her mother loved him? He must have been a fine-looking man. He was tall and well made. His face had broad, open features, although now broken veins traced a pattern across his cheeks and he was becoming heavy-jowled. He had a good head of reddish blond hair that, even now, had kept its colour. His eyes were blue.

So were her mother's eyes, and her sister's, while Thea's were brown. They were white-skinned, fair-haired and small-boned, whereas she was tall and vibrantly dark.

As Thea sipped her second cup of coffee the door to the dining room burst open and her father strode in. His face was mottled with rage. In one hand he clutched the morning paper and the other was clenched into a fist. He brought it down on to the table and the crockery rattled.

'Thea!' he thundered, and even in her fright she saw her mother relax when she realized that his anger was not directed at her. Imogen remained calm. She looked up from her breakfast with interest.

Thea put her cup down and sat back in her chair. 'Yes, Father?'

He didn't reply immediately but came towards her, waving the newspaper angrily. She was transfixed by the rustling pages of print and as she watched them her eyes widened in horror. She remembered the untidy young man with the pencil and notebook going from group to group in the green room. Now she knew what was to follow.

Suddenly her father grasped her arm and yanked her to her feet. She winced with pain but he held on; she could feel his fingers burning into her flesh through the thin material of her blouse. He pushed the paper roughly in front of her face.

'Take it,' he hissed, and his face was so close to hers that she could smell the coffee and tobacco on his breath and feel the hot spittle on her cheeks. 'Take it and read what you have done!'

Thea clutched the newspaper and was grateful to find that he let go of her arm. She could still feel the pain. She knew that the imprint of his fingers would leave bruises as they had in the past.

'Read!' he bellowed.

Thea brought the paper up so that she could see it. 'What shall I read?' She regretted her words immediately and she flinched, expecting his blow.

But instead he said quietly, the menace all the more terrifying for being controlled, 'I think you know.'

She stared at the close print on the page in front of her. Two headlines, the higher slightly bigger than the one below, dominated one of the columns. The larger headline, in bold print, read:

Visit of Mr George Edwardes to Newcastle

Then below that in smaller print but just as bold, there was a smaller headline reading:

An Important New Contest!

'We're waiting, Thea,' her father said quietly.

Thea drew in her breath and glanced quickly at her mother. Her mother's eyes were wide with apprehension. It was obvious that she was both puzzled and terrified. Across the table Imogen was observing the scene as if it were an interesting experiment in the science laboratory at school. Thea could not help feeling that Imogen was enjoying the spectacle of her older sister in trouble again.

From the corner of her eye she saw her father close the distance between them even further and she heard him catch his breath. She began to read:

> 'On Saturday evening Mr George Edwardes, the general manager of the world famous Gaiety Theatre in London, visited Newcastle to officiate as chief judge at the Blondes and Brunettes beauty contest held at the Olympia Theatre. The other judges were Madame Cora Levey, proprietor of the celebrated Northern School of Dance and Theatre, and Mr Vernon Gray, the acclaimed photographer.
>
> 'The contest, the first of its kind to be held in the British Isles, was won by Miss Eleanor Parker, a beautiful blonde—'

Thea heard Imogen's slight gasp and sensed her air of speculation. She did not dare glance at her mother. She went on reading—

> 'and her friend, Miss Dorothea Richardson, a bold brunette—'

Her mother cried out in terror and her father's fist came crashing down on the table once more. He caught the edge of the saucer of Thea's coffee cup and both cup and saucer fell to the floor.

Thea's eyes raced ahead. The report went on to name the runners up and then there was another small headline: 'Reception.'

Her father stabbed at this with his finger. 'There,' he said, 'read from there.'

Thea began to read again:

'After the contest there was a reception for the honoured guests in the theatre's green room. Amongst those present were—'

Her father snatched the paper from her before Thea could read out the names of any of the city worthies and local trades-people who had been at the party.

'All those people there to see your shame, Thea! City councillors, important tradespeople, customers – they know me! Respect me! What will they think of me now when they have seen you flaunting yourself on the stage in such a manner?'

'Manner?'

'Offering your body for men to ogle!'

'No!' her mother cried.

'Dressed like a woman of the streets!'

'Stop!' Her mother rose to her feet, sobbing.

In spite of his rage Thea could not help defending herself. 'Where does it say that I was dressed in such a way?'

Risking his wrath she snatched the newspaper from him and read the rest of the report feverishly. There was nothing about the way she was dressed, but when she came to the bottom of the report she groaned; a knot of fear tightened within her. There was a request to turn to the regular Fashion Notes column for a full description of what the contestants were wearing.

Her father stood back and allowed her to turn the pages. The description of the winners' dresses came first.

'Well, Thea,' her father said, 'do you want to read it aloud and let your mother and your sister know what kind of woman you are?'

'That's not fair!' Thea half sobbed, echoing herself as a child. 'The dress I wore was not . . . was not—'

'Not what, Thea?' Her father took the paper from her and began to read it himself. 'Not, "a delightful confection of pink satin and black lace which clung to Miss Richardson's figure outlining her womanly curves"?' He paused and looked at her with scorn in his eyes. But there was something else reflected there, Thea didn't know what it was. If he hadn't been her father and so angry with her she would have said it was excitement.

'And wasn't the neckline "cut daringly low in a delightful décolletage which was only made decent by a froth of black lace"?'

Her mother's sobs grew louder; she was clinging to the back of her chair. Imogen was wide-eyed with genuine surprise. Samuel Richardson lowered the newspaper. 'Well?'

'You have made it sound . . . sound . . .'

'What?'

'You have made it sound indecent. The dress I wore was not indecent.'

'Would you like to put it on and show us? Let your mother and sister be the judge? For heaven's sake, Amy,' he glared at his wife, who was sobbing softly as she clung to the back of her chair for support, 'either leave the room or sit down again.'

Her mother whimpered and sat down – like a whipped puppy, Thea thought. Her father turned his attention to her again.

'It is not I who have made it sound indecent,' he said. 'If that's the word you choose then it is because you have read the same words that I have read, in the newspaper that will be read by all our friends and acquaintances.'

'And your customers, don't forget your customers!' Thea said.

'Thea – please!' her mother cried.

But, for once, her father didn't rise to the taunt. 'Well, then,' he said. 'Are you going to put the dress on and show us?'

'I can't.'

'Can't or won't?'

'The dress is at Ellie's house. It was made for that one occasion. I doubt if I shall ever see it, let alone wear it, again.' And I don't even like it, she could have added, but she knew that to do so would be pointless.

'I see. I have long suspected that I should have forbidden you to go there. It seems to me that the Parkers and their like lead a completely worthless existence. The girl knows of no better way to spend her days than in pointless frivolity. But no doubt that was what attracted you.'

'How can you say that? I begged you to let me go to university. That would have been neither pointless nor frivolous. I don't know what you expect me to do with my time. Sit at home and embroider all day like Imogen? It seems to me that that could also be described as pointless!'

Again he didn't respond to her challenge and Thea found this frightening but, nevertheless, she continued, 'And if I like going to the Parkers' house it is because they are warm and they love each other. Unlike my own family . . .' She faltered when she saw his eyes narrow.

'So,' he said, 'you dislike living here?'

'Can you blame me?'

'I take that as an affirmative. Now, go to your room and stay there while I decide what to do.'

Her father moved back only slightly to allow her to pass him. She held her breath until she had left the room but, when she began to go upstairs, she was dismayed to hear his footsteps following her. She didn't look round, neither did she quicken her step, but she sensed that he was closing the gap between them.

When she reached for the handle of her bedroom door she gasped with fright to feel his presence right behind her. He snatched at the door handle ahead of her. She could feel his breath on her neck and, as soon as he opened the door, she fled into the room and turned to face him. Contrary to her expectations, her father remained standing in the doorway. His eyes were glittering and he was breathing heavily.

'You have behaved like a common slattern. Just like – just like . . .' He faltered as if his rage made him choke on his words. Then, puzzlingly, the look he gave her was almost one of satisfaction. 'No decent man will want to marry you now,' he said, and with great deliberation he removed the key, closed the door and locked it from outside.

When she heard the key turn in the lock Thea sank on to the floor, weak with relief. She tried to push away the memories that came crowding in. Memories of the other times, when she had been younger, when her father had followed her to her bedroom in order to punish her.

'No! Papa, no!' she had screamed when he had chastised her bare flesh with the cane. Her calls for mercy had echoed through the house.

But no one had ever intervened. Her mother had never come to put an end to what was going on. How could she have done? But neither had she ever come to comfort her.

Chapter Six

After prowling round her room for a while, fists clenched with frustration, Thea flung herself on her bed and lay staring at the ceiling. Outside the sky was grey and overcast; not much daylight filtered in through the cream lace curtains. Inside a fire burned in the grate, giving a false illusion of comfort.

Her bed was made up with the best Yorkshire linen, the wardrobe and dressing table were solid mahogany, the rugs were Persian; but there were none of the pink and white frills and ornaments and light-hearted feminine touches such as could be found in Ellie's room in the house on Heaton Road.

Thea wouldn't have wanted a room like Ellie's even if her father had been prepared to indulge her, but she did wish that the overall effect of her own room was not quite so sombre. She had at least made it more personal by adding a desk and a bookcase filled with her favourite books.

She wished that she could concentrate on one of those books right now. She'd made a half-hearted attempt to read one she'd borrowed from the library, *The Riddle of the Sands*.

She liked tales of spies and secret agents as much as she liked detective stories, but she couldn't concentrate. She wondered how long she was going to be kept locked in like this and she tried to stop herself from glancing every now and then at the clock on the mantelpiece.

It was almost three o'clock when the door opened and the housekeeper appeared carrying a tray. Mrs Bostock was nearly as tall as Thea and her long, sad face and black clothes gave her an air of perpetual mourning. Thea had often wondered who it was she could be mourning; her only son was alive and prospering in Australia, and her husband lived here with her and looked after the gardens and chauffeured their employer in his new motorcar.

The housekeeper glanced at Thea but she didn't speak; she simply put the tray down on a small table near the hearth, then kneeled down to tend to the fire. It wasn't a job that she usually did and her expression showed her distaste for it.

She had left the door ajar and Thea wondered what would happen if she were to leap off the bed and make a break for freedom, but she decided that it wasn't worth it. Where would she go? To her mother? She would get no support from her, and she would only cause trouble for Mrs Bostock.

'Shall I put the light on, Miss Richardson?' The woman hesitated by the door. 'It's dark enough.'

Thea sat up. 'Yes. Thank you.'

Mrs Bostock switched on the overhead electric light and then crossed to the windows to draw the curtains. When she had gone Thea gave in reluctantly to hunger and went to examine the tray. There was a plate of cold meats, cheese and bread and a cup of tea. At least her father didn't mean to starve her.

Later, when the housekeeper came back for the tray, she asked Thea if she wanted to go to the bathroom. Thea stared at

73

her, aghast. 'Do you mean that you have to take me?' she asked.

'Yes, Miss Richardson. I'm sorry.'

Thea was furious. She felt humiliated. But there was no help for it, she did want to go to the bathroom, so she had to go along with Mrs Bostock. At least the woman didn't insist on coming in with her, so Thea locked the door and took a small revenge by staying in there much longer than was necessary.

Once back in her room Thea sat by the fire and stared moodily into the flames. She imagined that she would not see anyone else until her father came home for his evening meal. No doubt he would have spent all day thinking about how he was going to punish her. When, eventually, she heard the key turn in the lock there was a tight knot of fear within her. She rose from her chair and stood with her fists clenched.

But when the door opened it was not her father who stood there.

'Well, Thea,' her Aunt Marjorie said as she came into the room. 'It seems that you are to come and live with me.'

Ellie sat at the table in the furthest corner of Alvini's Coffee Shop and savoured the rich smell of coffee and almond pastries. It was warm here at the back, and Ellie first of all had to loosen her fur tippet and then open the buttons of her coat. Her fur hat was warm and growing heavy and she wished she could take it off, but apart from the fact that it simply wasn't done, she knew how flattering the silver fox fur was to her complexion.

She drew her gloves from her hands and laid them on the table before looking at the menu. But she shook her head and smiled when a young waiter approached her. He understood that she was waiting for someone and retreated again.

Ellie was aware of the hiss of the coffee machine, the clink of cups and saucers and the animated chatter of the people at the nearby tables. She felt isolated, sitting here all by herself; surrounded by a small area of inactivity – and expectation.

She knew that she looked flushed and it wasn't simply because of the heat from the nearby kitchen. She was exhilarated – but ill at ease. When she and Thea met here they would sit near the window in order to look out on the bustling scene in the Haymarket, but today Ellie wanted neither to see nor be seen.

She had never been here as late in the day as this before. Instead of the daytime customers of clerks and shop girls taking a break, or housewives having a day in town, the people at the nearby tables looked as though they might be meeting before going on to the cinema or theatre; perhaps some of them were going to see the pantomime at the Palace next door.

Usually Ellie and Thea would meet and gossip over coffee in the morning, or call in for hot chocolate and pastries after an afternoon shopping trip. But today it was not Thea Ellie was to meet. Thea would never have been allowed to come into town as late as this. And Ellie doubted if her own mother would have allowed it. Which was why she hadn't told her she was coming.

She had not lied to her parents, she had simply not told them the truth. But she had made sure that she had helped as much as possible with the Boxing Day Entertainment in the church hall.

The Boxing Day Entertainment was an annual event. All her father's pupils, from the smallest girls learning ballet to the retired gentlemen taking ballroom dancing lessons, took part if they wanted to, whether they were talented or not. It was marvellous fun. The pupils and the parents all adored

Henry Parker and after the show they would arrange a 'surprise' party for him and his family.

It was this party that Ellie had slipped away from, knowing that it would be at least three hours before her parents returned home. She would have left straight after the final encore except that she knew that her mother wanted to show her off, to parade her before the admiring audience as the winner, or at least one half of the winning pair, of the famous Blondes and Brunettes beauty contest.

So she had dressed up once more in her beautiful pink dress and taken a bow on the stage in the church hall to rapturous applause, led by her mother. Then, while she was changing back into her everyday clothes, she had yawned and put her face in her hands and said that she was exhausted. She had hinted that she really should get as much beauty sleep as possible now that her whole future might be about to change, and her mother had insisted that she should go home. Ellie had hugged her and slipped away without a word.

She was aware that she was attracting glances. She suspected that a respectable young woman should not be here alone at this time in the evening and she hoped that he would come soon.

Would he come? Had she imagined those whispered words as she took her leave from him at the party in the green room? He had captured her hands in his and pressed them, never taking his dark eyes from hers.

'*Meet me at Alvini's on Boxing Day, seven o'clock,*' he'd urged.

'*Yes . . .*' She had hardly been able to breathe. '*But . . .*'

'*But?*'

'*I may be late . . . Wait for me . . .*'

'*For ever!*'

There had been a smile in his eyes as he breathed that word but she had not doubted his emotion.

But now, where was he? She had not been late. For once in her life she had been exactly on time and it was Lewis who was late. Suddenly her eyes widened in alarm.

'*Alvini's* . . .' he'd said. He hadn't specified the coffee shop. Surely he couldn't have meant the restaurant on the first floor? The restaurant was fashionable and popular with well-to-do gentlemen, but it was rumoured that they seldom took their wives or respectable young women there.

Now she half regretted that she hadn't confided in Thea. Her friend would have advised her what to do, but Ellie had lain feigning sleep that night after the beauty contest, hugging her secret to herself, not wanting to share it with anyone. Not even Thea.

'Ellie.' He spoke her name so quietly that at first she thought she'd dreamed it.

She looked up to find him standing over her table. His overcoat had an astrakhan collar and he was wearing a bowler hat. His dark good looks were enhanced by the expensive clothes. He removed his hat and gloves and placed them on one of the chairs. He looked concerned. 'Is anything the matter?'

'No.' Her previous mood of exhilaration returned. 'Why should there be?'

'You looked so far away, so worried. I wondered if you had regretted agreeing to see me. Whether you were having second thoughts.'

'Oh no!' She knew that she sounded too eager and she felt the heat rising.

Lewis pulled out the chair opposite to her and sat down. 'What then?'

'I was . . . I was thinking about Thea.'

77

He raised his eyebrows and half smiled. 'Your beautiful friend? Why should that make you look so anxious?'

She suffered a moment's irritation at his description of Thea but she told herself that she had no reason to be jealous. Lewis had not asked Thea to meet him, he had asked her. 'I haven't told her, I mean she doesn't know . . .'

Lewis laughed softly. 'You haven't told Thea that we are meeting here, tonight. It is the first time that you haven't confided in your best friend and you're feeling guilty. Is that it?'

'Yes.'

It was a half-truth. Ellie did not feel guilty about keeping her secret from Thea. Why should she? Thea might have counselled her to be cautious. She might even have advised her not to come. But it was better to let Lewis think that that was the reason for her concern rather than have him guess the real reason: that she had doubted him even for one moment.

'Well then, let me have a look at this menu.' Lewis picked it up but before looking at it he smiled apologetically and said, 'By the way, I'm sorry that I was a little late. First of all the train was delayed and then I had to fight for a cab at the Central Station.'

The last vestige of Ellie's doubts vanished. 'You should have taken the tram from the station,' she said, smiling at him.

'How wise you are.' He reached for her hand and kissed it.

She knew he was making fun of her but she could not respond. As he turned her hand over and began to move his lips across her soft palm she felt a stab of feeling deep inside that completely overwhelmed her. All she could do was sit speechlessly until he let go of her hand and picked up the menu again.

The young waiter, who had been hovering nearby ever since Lewis had arrived, came as soon as he was beckoned. Ellie was not really surprised when Lewis, without asking her, ordered hot chocolate and her favourite cherry tartlets. Earlier that day she had let her mother believe that she wanted to be prepared for a new life, but her mother could have no idea of what Ellie now hoped that future would be.

Robert Hedley pulled out his fob watch and leaned nearer to the meagre fire to study its face. It was nearly eleven o'clock and Lily Roper had not yet returned to mind her children. Janey slept, fully clothed, on the mattress against the wall, and Joe had fallen forward off the cracket and lay asleep on the greasy hearthrug. He had been determined to sit on the little stool and remain awake until his mother came home.

Robert replaced the watch in his waistcoat pocket and knelt down to pick the lad up. He placed him as gently as he could on the mattress beside his sister. There was nowhere else to put him. He arranged the ragged blanket over both of them; the foisty smell of unwashed wool sickened him; he supposed the children were used to it. Then Robert took his place again at the table by the fire.

He had called in on his way home from the Charity School. When the last of the homeless children who had spent the previous three days there had gone back to their miserable existences on the streets of Newcastle, Robert had gathered up some of the food that was left to bring here to the Roper household. He had found Joe and Janey alone there.

There were two older brothers, Matt and Luke. But Matt had already moved out to live with his young pregnant wife in a couple of rooms in a tenement only a little better than this one. He worked as a general labourer laying the new tramlines, and the wages he took home were barely enough to keep the two of them.

As for Luke, Robert frowned as he thought of him; Luke led a shadowy existence on the streets. Sometimes he would appear with money in his pocket and stay until the money ran out, when he would have another violent argument with his father and disappear again.

The children's father, Patrick Roper, was a drunken, violent man who drifted from job to job. He was strong enough and intelligent enough to have bettered himself, but the combination of drink and temper had spoiled his chances; blighted his life, and that of his family. Patrick would be at the Keelman right now drinking himself senseless.

And, as for Lily, Robert had suspected that for some time now she had eked out Patrick's wages with earnings of her own. And that was why she was out tonight, in some dark alley or dank basement, trading the only goods she had. Herself.

'What the hell are you doing here?'

Robert got up and turned swiftly to find Luke Roper glaring at him from the doorway. Luke was only seventeen years old but he was big, like his father, and his fiery hair and the glittering eyes set in his pale face seemed to hint at a barely controlled fury. He had a brown-paper parcel tucked under one arm.

The gaslight dipped and flared in the cold draught as Luke slammed the door shut behind him and advanced into the room. He stood facing Robert across the table. Then he looked around suspiciously.

Without giving Robert a chance to answer the first question, he snapped, 'Where's me mam?' He inclined his head towards the door which opened on to the small scullery. 'Is she—'

'Your mother is out. I don't know where.'

'Then I'll ask you again. What are you doing here?'

'I brought this.' Robert indicated the wrapped parcels of food on the table. 'Some bread, cold meats, a bit of cake. I found the children alone.'

Luke glowered at him. 'There's nowt wrong with that. Joe's old enough to look after wor Janey.'

'Perhaps.'

'So why did you stay?'

'To see your mother.'

'Why?'

'To offer her some work.'

'Work? Work for you, do you mean?' Robert nodded and Luke's eyes narrowed. 'And exactly what kind of work do you want her to do?'

'Some cleaning.'

Luke smiled cynically. 'Aye, I didn't really think you'd want her for anything else. She's no oil painting, is she? And I've heard that you hev your pick.'

Robert ignored the jibe. 'I'll pay her well and she'll get a bite to eat.'

'Aye,' Luke sighed, 'I know that often as not me mam gives her portion to the bairns and makes do with gravy. You would have to make sure she didn't wrap up what you gave her to bring yem with her.'

'I would.'

'So it's skivvying you want her to do? At your place down by the river? I'll tell her. You can gan yem now, I'll stay with the bairns.' At last he seemed to relax and he put his parcel down on the table.

Robert had been dismissed but he lingered to watch as Luke opened up the paper to reveal some bones with a bit of meat on them.

'Shin,' Luke said, and he grinned up at Robert. 'If you gan to Donkins' just on eleven when he's closing, and if he's in a good fettle, he'll give you what he might hev sent to the bone man.'

While he was speaking Luke reached into his pockets and brought out an onion, a small turnip and a couple of large carrots and laid them on the table.

'Fell off the stall,' he replied to the question in Robert's eyes. Then he continued. 'I do this when I can. I'll make a pan of broth right away, and then I'll wake the bairns and try to make them eat it before me dad staggers yem. Sometimes he doesn't make it and lies like a dog in the street. But even if he does turn up he's usually too mortal to figure out what time of day it is or what's going on.'

'And your mother?'

The angry expression returned. 'She used to be here when I called,' he said. 'But lately she's been going out . . . I divven't know where to.'

But Robert could tell that Luke did know, or rather he had guessed. He took his leave as the younger man gathered up the bones and the vegetables and went through to the scullery.

Although it was late, there were plenty of people about as Robert walked down the steep streets to the riverside. Many of them, on their way home from the public houses, slipped and staggered on the wet cobbles, calling out drunkenly as they did so. Some, beyond shame, relieved themselves in the gutter. Others, grimly sober, materialized from the shadows whenever one of the drunks fell, and crouched over the inert figure urgently, going through his pockets.

The poor robbing the poor, Robert thought.

And then there were the women, waiting in the alleyways, some of them no more than girls, not much older than Janey. He quickened his pace, fuelled by anger, and then, without warning, the image of a different kind of woman sprang into his mind.

Tall and dark and breathtakingly beautiful. Thea Richardson. It was no use telling himself that such a woman had no place in his world. No use trying to dismiss her from his thoughts . . . from his dreams. As soon as he had seen her he had wanted to reach out and take the pins from that raven-black hair and see it cascade down around her shoulders . . . her naked shoulders . . .

Chapter Seven

'I'm sorry, Aunt Marjorie, I've caused all this trouble for you.'

Thea faced her aunt across the breakfast table in the dining room of the modest terraced house in North Jesmond. It was early, the fire had not had time to take properly, and the room was cold.

Nancy, the maid, had just placed a plate of bacon and eggs on the table in front of Thea, while it seemed that her aunt was going to make do with toast and marmalade.

'Oh, Nancy doesn't mind the extra cooking, do you, Nancy?'

Aunt Marjorie smiled up at the tall, spare woman and Thea found herself willing the maid's expression to soften but her answering smile was tight-lipped.

'No, Miss Gibb,' she said, and she left the room.

Aunt Marjorie poured them each a cup of tea. 'And it's no trouble for me to have you here, Thea. In fact I shall enjoy your company.'

'And I'm grateful that you've agreed to have me. I'd much rather live with you, anyway. If only I knew why my father hates me so.'

Aunt Marjorie looked troubled; she concentrated on stirring a spoonful of sugar into her tea. But then she looked up and

84

said, 'He doesn't hate you. He's just extremely angry. And, to be fair, you've given him cause.'

'I know. I should never have entered the beauty contest. I didn't even want to.'

'Then why did you?'

'To please Ellie. She wanted so much to win and she needed a partner.'

'But why did it have to be you?'

'Well, you know, I'm a brunette.'

Aunt Marjorie smiled as she buttered a second piece of toast. 'Oh, yes. "Blondes and Brunettes!" That was the theme, wasn't it? But didn't Ellie have another friend with dark hair?'

'Ellie doesn't really have any other friends.'

It was only as she said it that Thea realized the truth of this. Taken away from girls she might have made friends with when she was sent to the private school in Jesmond, and once there isolated by the other girls' snobbery, Ellie might not have had any friends at all if it had not been for Thea.

'Could she not have asked one of the pupils from her father's dancing school?'

'Well, I suppose she could. But both Ellie and her mother were set on having me. I don't know why.'

Her aunt laughed. 'Come now, no false modesty. Of course you know why. You are very beautiful. Ellie wanted to win the contest and she knew that, together, you would stand a very good chance. Unfortunately, neither Ellie nor her mother considered what the consequences might be for you. Nor cared.'

Thea was startled. 'Why do you say that?'

'They both know what your father is like – how strict he is. They knew he would not allow you to enter, so they encouraged you to deceive him.'

'Deceive him?'

85

'Thea, don't dissemble. I don't know exactly what you said to your parents but I imagine it was the same kind of thing you told me – that you and Ellie were going to the theatre. You have been to the theatre with Ellie and her mother before. And this time you allowed your parents to think that it was a pantomime or Christmas entertainment of some kind. Was that the way of it?'

'Yes.'

'And whose idea was it?'

'Idea?'

'Who prompted you to behave in such a deceitful manner?'

Thea had never seen her aunt look so stern. Her half-eaten breakfast lost its appeal. 'Well, Ellie, I suppose . . . and her mother.'

'So you allowed yourself to be persuaded by those two frivolous, empty-headed women to do something you really didn't want to do. Thea, I just don't understand it.'

Thea looked up from her plate and found that, in spite of her harsh words, her aunt was smiling. She was encouraged to say, 'Ellie's mother has been kind to me, you know. I go to their house just to get away from the grim atmosphere at home, and they have always made me welcome.'

'I know, dear. And I know how upset you were when your father refused to allow you to go to university—'

'He has always opposed anything I want to do!'

Her aunt ignored her interruption and continued, 'And I think I can guess how miserable you've been since leaving school—'

'Not just since leaving school. All my life!' She was aware that she was being dramatic but she could no longer contain her emotion. 'I told you he hates me and I just don't know why!'

'Thea—' Her aunt looked distressed. She got up, came

round the table and laid one hand on her niece's shoulder, but she didn't seem to know quite what to do. 'Your mother . . . your mother . . .'

'She never came to my aid, never supported me when . . . when . . .'

Thea couldn't go on. She couldn't bring herself to tell her aunt about the beatings when she was a child. Her father had always locked the door of her bedroom when he chastized her. Always insisted on exposing her buttocks. She would never forget the angry rasp of his breath as he pulled down her underwear and pushed her face down on her bed. Then the drawn-out moment of silence – the fearful waiting, not daring to turn and look at him, until the cane bit into her flesh.

Did her mother even know what went on behind that locked door? Or care? The beatings had stopped when she had reached her teens but the threat was always there and, in spite of all reason, the lingering feeling that it was all her own fault, that she had invited his behaviour.

'Your mother's life has not been easy,' her aunt said. She stepped back a little and clutched her hands together. 'You couldn't know . . . Perhaps one day . . .'

Thea stared at her aunt wonderingly. She suddenly sensed that she was close to finding out something very important about her parents. She held her breath, knowing that she must keep quiet. But then her aunt shook her head slightly, as if she had made a decision. She sighed and reached over the table for the teapot.

'Here,' she said, 'let me top up your cup and put an extra spoon of sugar in.' Thea noticed that her aunt's hands were shaking. Tea splashed over on to the clean white tablecloth and Thea was distracted by the thought of Nancy's displeasure. Aunt Marjorie seemed not to have noticed the brown stains. 'Oh dear,' she said, 'your breakfast has gone quite cold. Just leave it. I'll ask Nancy to make some fresh toast, nice and hot.'

'No! I mean there's plenty left, and I don't mind if it's cold, really.'

But her aunt took no notice. Not only did she ring for Nancy to make more toast and a fresh pot of tea, she also asked her to build up the fire, and to make sure that the fire in the sitting room was built up too. Nancy nodded her head to each new order, but she kept her eyes down and didn't say a word. Thea was left with the distinct feeling that the woman resented her presence – and all the extra work it would mean.

'By the way, don't take any notice of Nancy's sulks,' Aunt Marjorie said as the maid closed the door forcefully behind her.

Thea was bemused. She wondered how a servant who sulked would fare in her parents' house.

'Nancy has a good heart,' her aunt continued, 'I imagine she's behaving like this because she has grown protective of me. But as soon as she sees how happy it makes me to have you here she'll remember her manners.'

Thea was puzzled. 'Protective of you? Why?'

Aunt Marjorie looked embarrassed. 'Well, you know, I gave her a job when – when others might not have done.'

'I see. No I don't. Why couldn't she have got a job somewhere else?'

'Her husband had died and she was finding it difficult to manage. She wasn't trained to do anything. Nancy was faced with either the workhouse or the streets.' Aunt Marjorie paused and looked grim. 'You know what I mean, don't you?'

'Yes, I do.'

'Well, I found her and her daughter lodgings in a house owned by the parish. She shares it with other women who have fallen upon hard times. They help each other look after

88

any children or old folk they have, and they all go out to find respectable employment, however menial it might be. It's a sort of community.'

'No wonder Nancy is grateful.'

'Well, I'm grateful too. She may be a little rough and ready but she looks after me better than a more superior sort of housemaid would. So don't be put off if she seems a little fierce. She'll come round, I'm sure of it.'

'I hope so,' Thea murmured, but she wasn't convinced.

After breakfast Aunt Marjorie had to go out. She was on the committee of one of the soup kitchens run for the benefit of the unemployed and the homeless. Aunt Marjorie made no distinction between the 'deserving' and the 'undeserving' poor. She thought that it was society that was at fault, not the poor denizens at its lower reaches.

She also had strong views about the place of women in society, all women, no matter what social class. Thea realized that by enabling women like Nancy to help themselves rather than accept charity, her aunt was encouraging them to take up her other passion – women's rights. But at heart she was a good woman. Today, she would not just be organizing meals for the poor, she would go on to collect still wearable second-hand clothes, arrange for other good women to wash and mend them, and then distribute some of them. And Thea knew that her day would probably not be over even then.

She called to mind the brave figure striding through the dark streets that night. Then, completely unbidden, another figure strode into her mind's eye, tall and powerful, a mysterious silhouette, until he had stopped under a streetlamp to pick up the child. Robert Hedley.

'Can I clear this table now, Miss Richardson?'

Thea looked up to find Nancy looking down at her coldly. She hadn't heard the maid enter the room and she wondered how long she had been standing there. She dismissed the foolish notion that the woman could have read her thoughts.

'Of course. I'm sorry if I've delayed you.'

Nancy made no reply; she simply set about clearing the table. Thea left her to it and went upstairs to begin sorting out her things.

The night before, she and her aunt had packed as many of her clothes and books as they could into the cabin trunk that Mr Bostock had carried into Thea's bedroom just after her aunt had arrived at her father's house. They had been left alone, and when the trunk was full, her aunt had looked around to see if there was anything else they could use. Eventually they'd decided to make up as big a bundle as could be tied up into a sheet from the bed.

'My father will send after us to say that I've stolen it,' Thea said. She was only half joking.

Aunt Marjorie studied her face for a moment then said, 'I'll write a note and leave it, telling him what we've done and that I'll have the sheet washed and sent back!'

They laughed like schoolgirls at their plan but Thea sensed an underlying note of hysteria in both of them.

'What exactly did my father say to you?' she asked at last.

'I haven't seen him.'

'Then how...?'

'He sent Bostock with a letter. He told me what you had done and how you had shamed him. And that he was afraid you would be a corrupting influence on Imogen.'

'What!' Thea exclaimed angrily, and her aunt held up her hand to silence her.

'He said...' Suddenly Aunt Marjorie was unable to meet her eyes but only for a moment. Then she smiled at Thea sadly. 'He said that in spite of the fact that you had neither married nor reached your majority, he was no longer prepared to treat you as a daughter and that I must come and get you.'

When they were ready to leave Thea asked how they were going to get the trunk downstairs and her aunt said, 'Mr McGrath is waiting with his coach in the drive. I'll go and get him while you put your hat and coat on. Say your goodbyes, Thea.'

'Goodbyes? Do you mean I should go and see my mother . . . and Imogen? Are you not worried that I will corrupt her?' Thea was still smarting from the words in her father's letter and her aunt sighed.

'No, dear. I'm not worried about that. But I didn't mean that you should go and see them. In fact your father has forbidden it. I meant that you should say goodbye to your home. I don't think you'll be coming here again.'

So Thea left the house she had lived in all her life. Mr McGrath was a big man and he grasped the handles at each side of the trunk and carried it down the stairs easily. Thea and Aunt Marjorie followed, carrying the unwieldy bundle of belongings wrapped in the sheet between them.

'We must look like burglars!' Thea had said, and they'd both laughed. They'd been still laughing as they crossed the hall. Thea had wondered if her mother could hear them.

Now, as Thea unpacked her clothes and tried to fit them into the small wardrobe and chest of drawers in her new bedroom, she realized there was not room for all of them. It was easy enough to decide that she should take out her warmer clothes and leave her summer dresses in the trunk.

When that was done she arranged her books in stacks on the top of the chest of drawers and then closed the trunk and pushed it along the wall at one side of the bed. There was just sufficient room left to squeeze past.

Thea folded the sheet they had used and sighed as she realized she would have to ask Nancy to launder it. She hesitated by the door for a moment and then she frowned. She remembered something her aunt had said while they were piling her belongings on the sheet the night before. Or rather something that was not said. Thea frowned as she tried to focus on what was bothering her.

It was the way her aunt had paused for a moment when she was telling her what her father had written in his letter. Was it because she was saddened by what she had to say, or was it because there was something more – something she could not bring herself to say? Thea could not decide.

Thea took the sheet downstairs but stopped at the foot of the stairs. Should she go into the front parlour and ring for Nancy, risking her displeasure, or should she take it into the kitchen herself? Neither option appealed to her.

Eventually she chose what she considered the coward's way out and made her way along the dark passage that led to the back of the house. Then she paused again. She realized that she had no idea what was the proper thing to do. She stared at the door which led into the kitchen. Should she knock or just open the door and go in?

Her mother would not even have come this far. She would simply have walked to the nearest bell pull. But this household was much more informal; it seemed sometimes that her aunt regarded Nancy almost as an equal. She compromised by knocking smartly and opening the door without waiting for an answer. She walked in to be confronted by two faces staring up at her in surprise.

Nancy put down her cup of tea and rose quickly from her seat at the kitchen table, her eyes narrowing into a scowl, the lines of her body defensive. 'It's me daughter, Ellen,' she said with a sideways nod, although Thea had not asked who it was who sat at the other side of the table with her back to the range.

Thea looked at Nancy's daughter. She was small and thin, about twelve years old, she guessed when she looked at the pinched, knowing face. Ellen scowled up at Thea with an expression as hostile as her mother's. On the table in front of her there was a thick slice of bread spread with something that looked like set honey, but not quite. The girl saw Thea's glance and moved her hands round her plate protectively.

'Miss Gibb doesn't mind if Ellen has a bit breakfast,' Nancy said, 'a slice of bread and dripping and a cup of tea, that's all.'

'I'm sure she doesn't.'

'Especially as the lass stays and helps with the housework sometimes, and no pay given.'

Thea wondered about that last statement. She couldn't believe that her aunt was mean, but she was beginning to realize that she might be, not exactly poor, but certainly not comfortably off. In fact, she wondered if Aunt Marjorie could afford a full-time housemaid at all and was just keeping Nancy out of kindness.

'Look, I'm sorry I interrupted you,' she said. 'It's just – just I've sorted my room out and I wondered if – I mean – this sheet has to be laundered . . .'

Nancy's features relaxed a little. 'You needn't hev bothered. Your aunt told me about the sheet. I would hev got it later. Here, give it to me.' Nancy took the sheet from her and Thea felt herself dismissed.

But she lingered in the doorway as the woman hurried through a door at the back of the kitchen into what was obviously the scullery. Ellen had already forgotten her presence, it seemed, and she was taking great bites of the bread and whatever-it-was . . . dripping, Nancy had called it, and washing them down with gulps of tea. She became aware

93

that Thea was still standing there and looked up.

'What's the marrer?' Her tone was belligerent but the thin voice was that of a worried child.

Thea smiled at her. 'Nothing's the matter. I just wondered what that is – what you're eating?'

Ellen stared at her slice of bread for a moment and then grinned. 'Hevn't you ever seen bread and dripping? Look,' she reached for a white bowl on the table before her and tipped it over slightly so that Thea could see its contents. 'It's the juices from the roast. You pour it into a bowl and let it set. It's grand spread on a piece of bread, with salt and pepper – especially if you mix in a bit of the jelly. See?'

Ellen took a knife and dipped it into the bowl of dripping to bring up something from the bottom, a wobbling portion of dark brown jelly. She registered Thea's expression of doubt and she grinned. 'Do you want to try a bit?'

'Er – no, thank you. I've had my breakfast.'

'Was there something else?' Nancy had returned and Thea looked up to find her staring at her impatiently.

'No, that's all, I mean . . .'

'Would you like a cup of tea? Is that it?'

'Well, yes, but—'

'I'll bring you one through to the front room. Just go along, there's a nice little fire.'

Thea did as she was told. That was not what she had been going to ask Nancy for but she sensed that the woman was uneasy having her in her kitchen. And, besides, she must want to be alone with her daughter. For all her hard-edged ways Thea sensed a closeness between the two such as she had never experienced with her own mother.

The sitting room was clean but somehow cheerless. Thea guessed that her aunt did not spend much time in here. She sat in an armchair by the hearth and put her feet up on a red velvet-covered footstool in order to escape the draught that came under the door. In a matter of minutes Nancy knocked and entered. She was carrying a tray; she set it down on a small table, placing the table within Thea's reach. She had brought not only the promised tea, but also a plate of scones. Thea was embarrassed.

'I'm sorry – you've gone to so much trouble.'

'No trouble.' Nancy turned abruptly to go.

'Nancy . . .?'

'Yes?'

Thea heard the slight sigh and she bit her lip. 'What I was going to ask you . . . well, it's just I seem to have left my writing paper behind. And I have a letter to write.'

'In a folder on that little table by the wall,' the maid said, hardly bothering to turn round, 'pens, ink and paper and stamps as well. I'm sure Miss Gibb won't mind. And if she's still here, our Ellen'll post it for you on the way home.' She left the room without a backward glance.

Thea drank her tea and had one of the scones. Then she wiped her hands on the napkin Nancy had laid on the tray and went over to the table. She sat there and thought for a while before she started writing her letter. It was to Ellie and she didn't know quite what to say. She would have to tell her friend that she was living with her aunt, but she didn't know how to explain it. She didn't want Ellie and her mother to think it was their fault in any way, in spite of what Aunt Marjorie had said.

In the end she decided not to give a reason. She tried to make a joke of it.

Dear Ellie, *she wrote*,

Exciting news! I have run away from home and have taken refuge with my Aunt Marjorie. I'm (half) joking,

95

of course, but please call and see me as soon as you can and everything will be explained!

Love
Thea

She had decided that it was better to invite her friend here than to go to the Parkers' house on Heaton Road. There were too many distractions there, too many comings and goings and, more importantly, she didn't know if she could face Ellie's mother feeling sorry for her.

She didn't feel sorry for herself, she realized. She felt angry. But she wasn't quite sure where to direct her anger. She supposed that her father's action, although cruel, had been predictable. She knew that she had acted unwisely. It would have been a miracle if her mother had, for once, taken her part. So who should she be angry with? Everybody? Nobody? Life itself? Thea sighed as she sealed the envelope.

She looked around for the stamps. Nancy had said there would be some on the table. Perhaps they were in one of the drawers. Thea sat back a little and opened one of the two drawers set under the table top. The first contained what looked like photograph albums. Thea shut it again and tried the second. This drawer contained more stationery, blotting papers, a sheet of stamps and a few loose coppers. Thea tore off one of the stamps, resolving to tell her aunt what she had done as soon as she came home. She had just stuck the stamp on the envelope when someone knocked at the door.

It was Ellen. The child had her coat and hat on, obviously ready to leave.

'Me mam says I've to post a letter.'

'That's right. Here it is. Er – thank you.'

Thea was embarrassed. She wondered if Ellen would expect some kind of reward for posting this letter for her, a penny or two? Did she post letters for Aunt Marjorie? Is that what the pennies in the drawer were for? She pulled the drawer open and took tuppence out. She would replace them from the money that she had left in her purse upstairs.

'Here you are, Ellen.'

'Thanks, miss.'

The girl took the pennies readily and grinned. The sharp smile somehow made her look less of a child, more knowing. But Thea felt relieved. It had been the right thing to do. But after Ellen had gone Thea sat down again and, resting her elbows on the table, she dropped her head into her hands.

The simple task of writing a letter to her friend had brought home to her how much her life had changed. Yesterday she had lived in a large comfortable villa with servants to take care of all her needs, and an allowance, which although it was begrudged, nevertheless meant that she had never had to think about not taking the tram into town or even catching the train to the coast if she and Ellie fancied a walk by the sea.

Now she probably didn't have enough money left in her purse to go anywhere. What was she going to do? She supposed that her allowance would be stopped. What was it her aunt had said last night? That her father had said he was no longer prepared to treat her as a daughter? Did that mean that he was no longer responsible for her upkeep? She sighed. It was more than likely.

Thea groaned. She should have thought more about what this meant to her aunt. She supposed she had always known that Aunt Marjorie had probably used up her inheritance by pouring her resources into what Thea's parents called 'Marjorie's good works'. But it had never touched her own comfortable existence and, to her shame, she had never really thought about what that meant.

Now her aunt would have to be responsible for Thea. She

couldn't possibly ask her for an allowance. She supposed she would have to seek employment. But what could she do? Her expensive education had left her fit for nothing – unless she undertook further training. And that would cost money. She could always work in a shop, she supposed.

And then she raised her head and smiled as the idea came to her of applying, anonymously, of course, for a job in one of her father's grocery shops. That would shame him. That would set his fine customers gossiping! But, of course, the job would probably last only as long as it took her father to find out about it. And then she might be responsible for whoever it was who had taken her on losing his job too.

Perhaps she could work for a rival chain of grocers? That would really annoy her father!

She thought about it for a moment and sighed. She knew that whatever kind of job she applied for she ought to get Aunt Marjorie's approval. She didn't want to cause any more trouble for her kind-hearted relative.

But now, what was she going to do with the rest of the day? She could wrap up warmly and go for a walk across the Town Moor; it wasn't far away. She glanced towards the window. The sky was leaden and there was enough wind to rattle the panes and toss the occasional shrivelled leaf against the glass. No, she didn't think that it was weather for walking.

She had brought her books with her, including her library book. She supposed that she could settle down by the fire and try to escape into a different world for a while. She was just about to get up when she remembered the photograph albums. She opened the drawer and took them out.

There were two of them; the larger one was covered with dark red padded leather and had gilt corners, the smaller was covered in dove-grey silk with a small bouquet of pale pink roses painted in the centre of the front cover. Thea placed them on the table.

She opened the larger of the two first. It was only half-full but each photograph was mounted on a separate page, and each was of a group of children. Poor children. That was easy to see from the shaved heads of some of the boys, the shabby clothes and the pinched faces. One or two of the children were smiling, but most stared at the camera apprehensively as though they were not quite sure what was happening.

What was happening, in each case, was that they had been taken on a trip – some kind of treat.

One of the photographs, Thea guessed, had been taken in Leazes Park. The children were lined up before the lake, the back row standing, the middle row kneeling and the front row sitting cross-legged on the grass. It was hard to tell the season; the trees were in leaf but the children were not dressed for summer. But perhaps they had only one set of clothes that had to make do all year round until the time they outgrew them – and sometimes beyond.

Had the children been running around, playing and laughing just before the photograph was taken? Impossible to tell. The whole business of keeping still for the camera had quelled any spontaneity. But then Thea spotted one smiling face. Her Aunt Marjorie was standing at the centre of the back row. She was not much taller than the children at each side of her, two solemn-faced lads. Unlike theirs, her expression was one of pure enjoyment.

The photograph on the next page was slightly smaller. The children – were they the same children? – it was impossible to tell – were standing on the deck of a Tyne Ferry. One or two of the bigger boys were grinning, arms folded like sailors about to do a hornpipe, but some of the younger children looked terrified. Thea spotted one of Aunt Marjorie's friends, Miss

Moffat, kneeling to comfort a small girl who looked as if she thought her last days had come.

On the page below the photograph Aunt Marjorie had stuck a piece of card which announced:

TRIP TO THE SEASIDE
Admit bearer to train, ferry, lunch and tea.
(For children 7 to 13 years)

A line of print along the bottom of the ticket informed that it had been issued by the 'Poor Children's Holiday Association'.

The next picture had been taken on a beach. From the wide curve of the low cliffs behind it looked like the Long Sands at Tynemouth. Thea wondered if it had been taken later the same day. If so, then the magic of sand, sea and sunshine had driven away all the tears. Every single child was smiling.

When she had looked at all the photographs Thea replaced the album in the drawer and turned to the smaller one. Here there were also photographs of children but only two of them, and they were quite different. The two little girls belonged to an earlier age and their frilled, old-fashioned dresses and pinafores, the ribbons in their abundant ringlets, their happy, confident faces, declared them to be very fortunate children indeed.

As Thea turned the pages the girls grew older. And soon she saw with wonder that this was a loving record of the lives of two sisters: her own mother and her aunt.

She turned back to the first photograph, taken when they were little more than babies sitting together on a rug in a garden. She supposed they looked similar, although the older child was more rounded, more robust. They still bore a family resemblance in later pictures, although the older one, Marjorie, grew even sturdier while the younger child, Amy, remained more delicately pretty.

As she grew Amy Gibb became prettier and prettier, and her smile was both natural and joyous. Thea had never seen her mother smile like that – in fact she had hardly ever seen her smile. And she had certainly never seen her mother face the world with such confidence and trust.

The last few pictures must have been taken when Amy was in her late teens and Marjorie in her early twenties. Marjorie had already lost any promise of prettiness but she looked wholesome and agreeable; the type of young woman that girls at Thea's old school would have called 'a good sort'.

Amy, on the other hand, was beautiful. Thea stared at the photographs, hardly believing what she saw. Why had she never realized that her mother was beautiful? Because she had never seen her look like this? Because years of misery could make you ugly?

The last photograph in the album must have been taken when the family were on holiday. Marjorie and Amy were dressed in pale summer dresses and flower-trimmed straw hats. They carried parasols. They were standing on a promenade by the sea and there was something about the scene that suggested that they were in some foreign country. Perhaps it was the extravagantly carved stone balustrade that looked like part of a stage set, or the cut of a fishing boat that looked nothing like the cobles that fished the North Sea.

A holiday abroad then? But, wherever and whenever it was, the sisters were obviously enjoying themselves. Marjorie smiled broadly at the camera and Amy – Thea held her breath as she looked at the younger sister.

Surely her mother had never been as beautiful again as she was on that long-ago summer's day. And Thea half understood that there must be a reason for all that beauty to survive in this sepia image printed on a piece of card perhaps twenty years ago.

She saw the way her mother's head was tilted so that she was glancing upwards through her lashes as she smiled at the photographer. But how should Thea describe that smile? Secretive? Well, perhaps. But if there was a secret – and she was sure there was – it was shared by one other.

Her mother's smile reached out so strongly that Thea almost felt as if there were a third presence in the photograph. The person who held the camera.

Chapter Eight

January 1906

'Many Happy Returns, my dear.'

Aunt Marjorie placed the small brightly wrapped parcel on the table. They had just finished breakfast. Thea looked up in surprise.

'Did you think I had forgotten?' her aunt asked.

'No . . . I mean, I wasn't really expecting anything.'

'Have I ever forgotten your birthday?'

'No, but this year . . .'

'Oh, go on, open it. I'm going to pour myself another cup of tea.'

Aunt Marjorie busied herself with the teapot and Thea suspected that her aunt was probably as upset as she was that the postman had been and gone and there had been nothing from her family, not even a card.

From the size and shape of the parcel Thea guessed her present to be a book. She picked it up. The paper was bright red. She guessed it was the same paper that her aunt had used to wrap the Christmas gifts for the children's party at the Charity School.

For a moment she allowed herself to feel the same

excitement a child would feel as she carefully untied the string – Aunt Marjorie saved all paper and string to be used again. She half imagined the book would be something worthy and educational, such as an account of some good woman's efforts to achieve justice for the inhabitants of some distant outpost of the Empire.

But it wasn't. She stared at the cover of *The Scarlet Pimpernel*, a recently published novel by Baroness Orczy, with delight. 'Thank you,' she said, 'how marvellous.'

Her aunt smiled. 'Mind you, it's all nonsense. For a start I don't know if some of those French aristocrats deserved to be rescued, but I've heard that it's a jolly good yarn. Just the sort of thing to take you out of yourself for a while – forget your troubles. Oh dear, have I said the wrong thing?'

'No, no, of course not. How could I have troubles when I've been fortunate enough to come and live with you?'

Aunt Marjorie looked thoughtful as she took a sip of tea. She put the cup down, watching as she placed it carefully in the saucer, and then she looked up at Thea. Her smile had gone.

'Nevertheless,' she said, 'we cannot altogether forget your situation.' She sighed. 'When you asked me just after Christmas whether you should seek employment of some kind, I said there was no need because I was convinced that your father would not stop your allowance.'

'And has he?'

Her aunt gave a half-smile. 'No, my dear, he hasn't. If he had he would have been breaking a promise.'

'Promise?'

For a moment Aunt Marjorie looked flustered but she hurried on, 'I've had a letter from him. Your father has paid a lump sum into my bank account; it is to cover your allowance for the next two years. He trusts me to administer it.'

'Of course he would trust you!'

Her aunt laughed. 'Oh, I don't know. He took this letter as another opportunity to lecture me on how improvident I have been with the money my father had left me – giving it all to the poor whether deserving or not. You know the kind of thing he says.'

Thea laughed too. 'I do. And my sister expresses the same sentiments.'

'Well, anyway,' her aunt continued, 'he said that your allowance should be exactly the same as it was before, the difference being that you will have to live off it.'

'Live off it? But the amount I get is hardly enough to—'

'Don't worry, dear, I shall look after you.'

'No! I can't expect you to feed and clothe me. I know how—' Thea broke off. She had just been about to say that she suspected her aunt had to scrimp and save enough as it was. 'I mean, I want to contribute my share to this household. That's what a New Woman would do, isn't it? I shall have to seek employment.'

'Well said, Thea, but no you shan't. In fact I don't want you to. I want you to help me with my charity work.'

'Of course I shall. Haven't I been asking you if I can do just that?'

'Yes, dear. So you see I can't have you going off to some kind of job every day. We'll manage very well for the next two years.'

'Why two years?'

'Then you will be twenty-one. Two years today, in fact. And when you reach your majority you will receive a family inheritance; money that is owing to you.'

'I don't understand.'

'My father, your grandfather, left you provided for, a small sum of your own in case . . . well, in case your father didn't . . . oh dear . . .'

'In case my father cut me out of his will. Is that what you're trying to say? But why should my grandfather imagine that my father wouldn't provide for me? Why did he feel he should make special arrangements?'

'Well, it's hard to explain – lawyers you know, something to do with women inheriting money and business interests.'

Her aunt looked at her helplessly but Thea did not for one moment believe that she couldn't have explained the legal niceties of the situation if she'd wanted to. Her aunt, of all people, was actually pretending to be a feather-brained female. And that was far from the truth. However, Thea didn't feel that she could question her further.

'So what can I do to help you today?' she asked.

'It's your birthday. Why don't you just curl up with your book? I've asked Nancy to prepare you something nice for lunch and I'm going to make every effort to be home by teatime so that we can eat together for once.'

Her aunt looked rueful and Thea smiled. Aunt Marjorie hardly ever enjoyed the comfort of her own home. Thea worried that she didn't seem to eat regular meals during the day, and in the evenings, more often than not, she would come home to something cold left out for her, after Nancy had gone.

In the short time that Thea had been living here, she had started venturing into the kitchen to make at least a pot of tea the moment she heard her aunt's key in the lock. She had also decided to borrow a copy of *Mrs Beeton* from the library and try to teach herself how to cook.

She was still too much in awe of Nancy to ask her advice, uncomfortably aware that her presence here was making extra work for her. For example Nancy had probably hardly ever had to cook meals at lunchtime before.

'Oh, do try to come home early,' Thea said. 'Or better still, why don't I come with you today?'

Her aunt coloured. 'Not today. I'll be spending most of it at a refuge for – well, how shall I put it? – for what society calls "fallen women" and their children. I don't think you should come there, Thea. An unmarried girl.'

Thea knew what was meant by that expression and she knew that people like her aunt tried to help and rehabilitate those women. She felt awkward, but nevertheless she said, 'But, Aunt Marjorie, you are not married.'

Her aunt laughed. 'Nor likely to be. Don't worry, you haven't offended me. I think I knew from the start that married life would not be for me. But, Thea, there's a difference between us. You are a very young woman, still a girl, really, whereas I am now thought of as an old maid. I'm past forty, I've reached the age where I can be safely allowed out to do good works and nobody will worry that I might be corrupted by the harsh facts of life.

'And if you really want to work today, birthday or not, there's a large pile of darning and mending to be done of the second-hand clothes my friends have collected and washed for me. I hate sewing of any kind, you know, so it would be a real help. Why are you laughing?'

'Because I hate sewing too. I hate it so much that my father gave me a sewing box for Christmas! I was going to leave it at home but you seem to have packed it.'

'Well, then . . .'

'Of course, I'll mend and darn, and I will feel all the more virtuous for having done something I hate so much.'

They smiled at each other and began to laugh. 'I'm so glad you're here with me, Thea,' her aunt said.

'Me too.'

But after Aunt Marjorie had gone Thea wondered if this

kind of life was going to be enough for her. At least she would be doing something useful but, no matter how worthwhile it might be, she hoped she wasn't destined to be another spinster, giving her life to good works.

She spent the morning by the window in the sitting room, doing as good a job as she could in the cold winter light with the darning and mending. Her fingers were thoroughly pricked and sore before she remembered that she could have used a thimble.

After a lunch of lamb chops followed by apple pie and custard, she went back to the sitting room with her coffee. She decided she would read for a while. When she opened the book her aunt had given her, a pretty floral card fell out and she picked it up and placed it on the mantelpiece. Her only birthday card. She had not really expected anything from her family; the break with them seemed to be so final. But what about Ellie?

The girl Thea thought of as her friend not only seemed to have forgotten her birthday, she seemed to have forgotten her very existence. She had neither called to see her nor answered her letter. Thea wondered if, perhaps, Ellie had been whisked off to London by Mr George Edwardes to become a Gaiety Girl. But surely she could have found the time to write a letter.

Thea tried not to feel bitter. If she wanted to, she could say that it was Ellie's fault that she had been cast out from her home. But she was too honest to blame Ellie entirely. She could have refused to take part in the beauty contest, and perhaps if she had been feeling less bored and dissatisfied with her life she would have done.

It was only just past noon but the light was fading. She took a spill from the fire and lit the reading lamp, placed it on a small table beside the armchair and sat down with her book.

Paris: September 1792, she read, and soon she was transported into another place, another time, where people had much more to worry about than an inconstant friend.

Ellie hurried into the Grainger Market. She'd told her mother that she was going to town to buy gloves but, on seeing the bookstall, she paused, wondering if perhaps she should buy one of *his* books.

She had never bought a book in her entire life but she had visited the lending library with Thea so she guessed that the books would probably be arranged alphabetically according to the names of the authors.

She ran her eye along the rows of books and frowned when she realized that they were all old. Their black, brown, and red leather spines illuminated by the lamps hanging along the front of the stall were cracked and stained. The gold lettering was so faded that she could hardly make out the titles or the names of the authors.

She glanced quickly at the other customers. One was an old stooped man, as faded as the books he was fingering lovingly with his arthritic fingers. The other was young, pale-faced and so shabbily, although decently, dressed that she guessed him to be a student.

'Can I help you, madam?' The stall-holder appeared at the entrance to the inner room. He was small, even smaller than she was, with old-fashioned shoulder-length white hair. He wore gold-rimmed spectacles and an embroidered velvet brimless cap; his clothes looked as dusty as his shelves of books. 'Is there something particular you're looking for?'

Ellie smiled at him. 'Do you have anything by Lewis Sinclair?'

'Any particular title?'

'Er, no, anything will do.' She didn't want to admit that she did not know any of the titles so she smiled brightly and said, 'Actually I haven't read any of Mr Sinclair's books so I'd be grateful if you would recommend which one I should start with.'

'Well, I suppose you should begin with the first, *The Murder in the Hansom Cab* – that's when Hugh Martin makes his first appearance – but I'm not sure if we have a copy. Mr Sinclair's books go out as fast as they come in, as you can imagine.'

Ellie had no idea what he was talking about. Or rather she knew Lewis wrote detective stories, so she guessed that Hugh Martin might be a detective, but as for the last part of the bookseller's statement . . . She frowned in puzzlement.

The man peered at her over the top of his spectacles. 'You do realize that I deal in second-hand books, don't you?'

'Oh!' Her frown vanished. 'I see! I mean, of course.'

'Well, let's see what I can do for you.' He stepped back into the inner room, talking over his shoulder. 'I keep the popular fiction inside here. Sad to say, it's too tempting to leave on the shelves outside.'

Ellie followed him in. 'Tempting?'

'They get stolen, my dear.' The bookseller was searching along one of the shelves.

'Books? Stolen?'

The man straightened up. He was holding a slim volume in his hand. He smiled. 'Why are you surprised? Books are valuable, you know. I don't just mean the rare books and first editions. Any book is valuable to someone who wants to read it badly enough.'

'But surely the kind of person—'

He shook his head sadly. 'You would believe so, wouldn't you? Students, university lecturers and even gentlemen of the cloth. For some reason they all stoop to the level of the criminal classes when it comes to books. And talking of criminal

110

classes, I don't have a copy of *The Murder in the Hansom Cab*, but I do have this, *The Mystery of the Single Glove*. Very nice, the dust jacket as good as new.'

Ellie took the book he proffered and smiled with pleasure as she examined the illustration on the cover. As well as the title and the name of the author, there was a drawing of one glove, lying as if it had been dropped at the foot of what seemed to be a grand staircase. A single flower, perhaps a buttonhole, lay on the third stair.

'I think you'll like this one. It involves a grand house and a dinner party. Fashionable people – the leaders of society!' the bookseller said.

'Oh, I'm sure I shall.'

Ellie counted out her money while he wrapped the book in brown paper, making a neat parcel. She couldn't help thinking how apt the title of the book was – after all, she was supposed to be here to buy a pair of gloves and she had. Well, at least one glove!

She was still smiling as she hurried through the market towards the tearoom where they had arranged to meet.

Lewis was waiting for her. He rose politely as she approached and his welcoming smile, the way he seemed to devour her with his eyes, made her pulse race. He took the parcel from her hands and placed it on the table before settling her in her chair.

'That looks like a book,' he said.

'Er – yes.' She knew she was blushing.

'You needn't have bought it. I would give you any one you wanted.'

She raised her chin. 'How do you know it's one of yours?'

'I guessed.' His eyes widened as she continued to regard him coolly. 'Have I been vain?' he asked.

'Oh, Lewis . . .' She couldn't tease him any longer. 'Yes,

you have been vain, but I admit, it is one of your books. But look, the waiter is hovering, he wants to take our order.'

Ellie watched contentedly as Lewis gave the order for tea and toasted teacakes, a speciality of the establishment. She hoped he would forget the subject of the book. She hadn't wanted to get into a discussion about which book she had bought. She hadn't exactly lied to Lewis – she had not claimed to have read any of his detective novels, but neither had she admitted that not only had she not read even one of them but she hadn't even heard of him until the day she met him in the green room at the Olympia.

When their order arrived they were silent for a while as they enjoyed the buttery teacakes. Ellie glanced around at the other customers. It was a cold day and everyone was muffled in scarves and furs. The temperature inside the tearoom was only a little warmer than it was outside in the aisles of the large covered market, and none of the people at the other tables lingered long after they had finished their refreshments.

The place was clean and cheerful enough, with red and white checked tablecloths, and a small vase of flowers on every table. At the moment each vase contained evergreen leaves and a single Christmas rose, and the food was good. But it was hardly romantic, hardly an intimate little rendezvous with the bustle of the market only a few feet away, and the ever-present racket of the traders calling out their wares. She supposed Lewis chose to meet her here – this was not the first time – because it was convenient.

It was only a brisk five-minute walk up from the Central Station for him and much less for her from the nearest tram stop. And it wasn't very likely that anyone who knew either of them would see them here. She glanced at him uneasily. She could think of no reason why Lewis would want to hide from

112

society. Was he being considerate? Did he want to protect her, knowing that she had not told her parents about him? Ellie frowned. Or was there some other reason? Did he not want his clever and fashionable friends to know that he was meeting someone they might consider to be his mental and social inferior? No, it could not be that; Lewis was surely the least snobbish of men . . .

'What is it, Ellie? Is something the matter?'

'Oh, it's nothing.' She tried to shake off the far-fetched notion that Lewis was avoiding being seen and hid her confusion by picking up her cup: it was nearly empty. She smiled at him. 'It's just that I'm a little cold.'

'Here, let me fill up your cup. A warm drink and then we shall walk a little, get the circulation going.'

'Walk?'

'Yes, around the market. Don't you love this market, Ellie? Isn't it so full of atmosphere?'

'Well . . . yes, I suppose so.'

Lewis did not notice her hesitation. He hurried on, 'I love walking around here savouring the sights, the sounds, the smells. The fruit and vegetables, the cheese stalls, the coffee stalls, the poultry sellers and the butcher's stalls with those great carcasses hanging.'

Ellie wrinkled her nose. 'And the blood dripping into the sawdust!' she said.

He laughed and reached across the table for her hand. 'Well, all right, I admit that butchers' alley would not appeal to you, but what about the flowersellers, the toys, the jewellery? And I know that you cannot resist all those pretty ribbons, laces and trimmings at the haberdasher's.'

At the mention of the haberdasher's Ellie remembered the reason she had given to her mother for coming here today. 'Actually I would like to go to the haberdasher's now, the little

113

shop under the gallery at the Nun Street end. I want to buy a pair of gloves.'

Lewis stood back and watched as Ellie chose her gloves. He smiled to see how serious a matter it was for her. She frowned and chewed on her lip as she compared two pairs of wrist-length kid gloves. One pair was plain and unadorned, the other an inch or two longer, and slim-fitting, with an opening at the back which fastened up with a row of tiny pearl buttons.

He caught his breath as he saw her look at the price tag and her expression of disappointment as she replaced the buttoned gloves on the counter. She was so childlike – but an enchanting child, a beautiful child – and yet she had the delicious body of a woman. At that moment his desire for her threatened to overwhelm him and he stepped forward quickly and snatched up both pairs of gloves.

She looked up, startled. 'Have I been too long? I'm sorry.'

Her blue eyes were wide with shock. She thought he was angry with her and he felt wretched to have caused her even a moment's distress. But, at the same time, there was another part of himself that could stand back and observe the way he was behaving – and be amused.

The wiser self reminded him that, no matter how deep and true his feelings were, they could come to nothing. And yet he was helpless. He couldn't deny himself.

'No, not too long, it's just that you must have both pairs.'

'No, I can't. Oh, please don't—'

She placed a hand on his arm to try to stop him paying for the gloves, but after he had handed over the money, he turned and clasped both her hands in his.

'My first gift to you.'

'But I'm not sure if I should accept.'

'Whyever not?'

114

'I don't think it's proper.'

'Oh, Ellie, Ellie, when you are a famous beauty you will be given much more valuable gifts than kid gloves. And I'm sure you will think it quite proper.'

Lewis took the wrapped parcel from the shop assistant and tucked Ellie's arm in his as they went back out into the market. But they had only gone a little way when she stopped. He turned to look at her.

'What's the matter?'

'What did you mean by saying that I will be a famous beauty?'

'You know what I mean. You are hoping that Mr Edwardes will ask you to appear at the Gaiety Theatre in London and that you will become one of the fabulous Gaiety Girls.'

'Who says so?'

'Your mother. Surely that is why Vernon is to take some photographs of you? To send them to Mr Edwardes?'

'Have you spoken to him? To Mr Gray?'

'I have. He tells me that your mother has telephoned him at his studios and you are to go next week. With your friend, with Thea.'

'Thea.' Suddenly Ellie could not meet his glance.

'Are you going to go?'

'Where?'

'To Vernon's studio?'

'I suppose so.'

'And if Mr Edwardes wants you to go to London?'

Ellie didn't answer; she simply shook her head.

Lewis sighed. 'Ellie, you should.'

'Why?'

'Your mother will be disappointed if you don't.'

'And if I do? If I do go, will you be disappointed?'

He took hold of her upper arms and, together, they stepped

back into a shadowed archway under the overhanging gallery. 'My darling,' he said, 'this has all happened so quickly.' He saw her eyes light with joy at the endearment. 'You took me by surprise,' he said, 'I shouldn't ... I mustn't spoil your chance of success ... of fame.'

'You haven't answered me.' She looked more confident now. 'Would you be disappointed if I go to London?'

He looked into her eyes a long time before he answered. Then, 'Yes,' he said softly, and she leaned forward and raised her face for his kiss.

Ellie watched Lewis walk away down Grainger Street towards the Central Station. He had told her that he must go; he had done no writing that day and he had a deadline to meet. When she'd frowned he explained that meant his publisher was waiting for the manuscript of his next book.

She'd told him that she was quite happy to be left near the tram stop, but when she could no longer see the slim, dark figure, she slipped back into the market.

The assistant, a sallow-faced woman with prominent teeth, recognized Ellie and was happy to undo the parcel, replace the plain pair of gloves with an identical pair one-half size larger, and then wrap each pair separately. She didn't complain. After all, the pretty young woman had a rich admirer, and she didn't ask why.

So there was no need for Ellie to tell her that it was only just a short while ago that she had remembered it was her best friend's birthday.

Chapter Nine

'Ellie! How marvellous. Come in!'

Thea was angry with herself for feeling so pleased, so grateful. She held on to the door and moved back quickly as her friend stepped into the small entrance porch; she did not want her to see the tears that had welled up in her eyes.

Ellie brought the cold air in with her; it clung to the trembling fur strands of her hat. Her cheeks were flushed – whether because she'd been hurrying or because of some inner excitement, Thea couldn't tell. She brushed past Thea and stood waiting in the narrow passageway, clutching some packages against her green velvet coat.

'I don't know whether I should be insulted that you seem so surprised,' she said. 'After all, it's your birthday, isn't it? You must have known that I would come and see you.'

'Yes . . . well . . . of course. Go ahead into the sitting room – the first door – it's open.'

Thea closed the front door, then the half-panelled glass door, and then paused for a moment to compose herself. When Thea entered the sitting room, Ellie was already standing by the fireplace. She had put her packages down on the small table under the reading lamp and was taking off her gloves.

'I don't suppose you could get your aunt's maid to make a hot drink of some sort, could you? Chocolate would be lovely.'

'I'll see,' Thea said.

'But where are you going?'

'To the kitchen, to ask Nancy to make us some chocolate.'

'But why don't you just ring for her?' Ellie stepped towards the bell pull at the side of the fireplace.

'No!'

Her friend turned to look at her, startled. 'Whatever's the matter?

'Nothing. It's just that the bell is broken.'

'Oh, I see.' Satisfied with the explanation, Ellie removed Thea's book from the armchair and placed it, with her gloves, next to her parcels on the table. Then she sat down and leaned towards the fire to warm her hands.

Thea fled along the passageway to the kitchen. She hadn't liked to admit that she did not have the courage to ring for Nancy, even though her aunt did when she was at home. She was glad that Ellie had not questioned the fact that she had answered the door herself.

That was not too surprising as the Parkers' household in Heaton was cheerfully haphazard and informal. But, neverthe-less, if Ellie did mention it, Thea planned to say that she had glanced out of the window and seen Ellie coming and had told Nancy not to bother.

She knocked hesitantly on the door, as she always did, and went into the kitchen to find her aunt's maid dressed and ready to leave. Nancy stood at the kitchen table wrapping something into a parcel in a sheet of butcher's paper. She looked up and for a moment she looked discomforted. But if she was, she soon recovered.

'Just a bit of scrag end that came with the chops,' she said.

'Most of it's in that broth there,' she nodded towards a pan that was simmering on the range. 'Your aunt doesn't mind if I take any leftovers home for myself and the bairn.'

'No, I'm sure she doesn't.'

Thea wasn't quite sure how the scrag end could be 'leftovers'. Surely you used it all in the broth or you didn't? But she was sure that her aunt would have wanted to help Nancy in this way.

'That broth'll be just what Miss Gibb needs when she gets back tonight. And I've made a raisin cake – it's in that tin on the dresser.'

'Oh, thank you.'

Thea was never sure how to talk to Nancy. Her mother or her sister would probably not even have looked at her properly; they would have simply given their orders – and Imogen didn't even say thank you. But she had observed very quickly that Aunt Marjorie was much more informal.

'So what did you want?'

Nancy's brusque question reminded her why she had ventured into the dragon's lair. 'I'd like . . . I mean, is it possible to have a cup of hot chocolate . . . two cups? A friend of mine has called to see me. I could make it myself if you want to go.'

Her last statement actually brought a hint of a smile to the vinegary features. 'And have you burning me milk pan? Not likely. I'm not sure about hot chocolate but will cocoa do?'

'Of course – thank you.'

Nancy took the tin of Fry's down from a shelf on the dresser and hurried into the back pantry to fetch the milk. When she came back she looked surprised to see Thea still standing there. 'Gan on then,' she said, 'I'll bring it in to you.'

Thea hurried back to the sitting room to find Ellie staring into the flames dreamily. She had loosened her coat and the firelight illumined her pretty face and the white lace flounces of her high-necked blouse. When she turned to watch Thea drag the other, smaller, armchair nearer to the fire her smile was unfocused. Thea could see that it was an effort to bring herself back from whatever it was that she had been contemplating and ask, 'Well, now, what is all this about you running away from home?'

Thea found that she could not tell her. How could she say that, because she had agreed to Ellie's proposal to pair up with her in the Blondes and Brunettes beauty contest, her father had thrown her out? She did not want Ellie to feel responsible and perhaps guilty. It was her own fault. She had agreed to Ellie and Mrs Parker's plan and she must take responsibility. She decided all that in a moment as she looked into her friend's happy and unsuspecting eyes.

'Oh, it's nothing dramatic,' she said. 'It's just that my father and I – who have never agreed about anything – have at last agreed that it would be better if I live with my aunt.' She felt pleased to have made it sound as if it was her decision too. It was less humiliating.

'Well, I know that you and your father don't get on very well, but won't you miss your mother and your sister?'

Thea paused a moment before she replied. She imagined that Ellie, like many only children, would be surprised to hear that sisters were not necessarily friends, and as for not being close to her mother – to Ellie, that would be unthinkable.

'I'll miss them,' she said.

And that was true. She would miss her sister's complacent acceptance of the place of favourite in their father's affections and, even in this short time, she was learning to let go of the burden of pain caused by not being able to understand her mother's seeming indifference. No, her life might have changed for the worse as far as material comfort was concerned but her friend's question had made her realize that,

120

emotionally, this could have been the best thing that had happened to her.

She smiled at Ellie, the unsuspecting cause of her liberation. 'But I know that I shall be happier here.'

She acknowledged silently her own choice of words. She had said 'happier', not 'happy' – for she knew that she still had not solved the problem of what to do with her life.

'We-ell, if you say so . . .' Ellie looked doubtfully around the solidly furnished and yet shabby room. Her glance fell on the occasional table and she smiled again. 'But here is your birthday gift – the reason I am here.'

She took up one of the packages and then frowned and took up a nearly identical one. Thea watched as her friend seemed to rub her thumbs over the paper as if feeling for something inside and then she smiled and held it out. 'Many happy returns, Thea, dear.'

'But, Ellie, these are beautiful!'

Thea had opened the package to discover a pair of kid gloves, beautifully cut and quite plain and unadorned – just the way she liked them. She found that her eyes were moist again and actually had to wipe a stray tear from her cheek with her fingers.

'For goodness' sake, don't blub, Thea, or you'll have me crying too!'

But Ellie sounded far too happy to be about to burst into tears. However, she turned her head quickly to hide her expression as she returned the other package to the table. Thea got the impression that she was embarrassed.

She tried to lighten the moment by saying, 'What else have you been buying?'

Ellie shot her a startled glance. 'What else?'

'That looks like a book.'

'Oh – yes! Thea, it's one of *his* – one of Lewis's books!'

'Lewis? You mean Lewis Sinclair? But, Ellie, you've never read detective stories before. In fact you told me once that you considered them tedious.'

'Did I say that?' Ellie looked stricken.

'Yes, you did. You told me once that I was wasting my time reading such rubbish. In fact I couldn't persuade you to even read half a page.'

Ellie shook her head and smiled as if she were remembering a younger and foolish self. 'Ah, yes. I should have listened to you.'

'So what has persuaded you to change your mind?'

'Well, I've met him, haven't I?'

'And that's it?' Thea was puzzled. 'You're going to read one of his books simply because you've met him?'

'Yes, and I shall read every one of them!'

'I see.' And Thea did see. She saw how her friend's eyes were shining, how they were brimming over with happiness and – what was that other emotion that had made Ellie clasp the brown-wrapped parcel to her breast in a theatrical but unmistakable gesture? 'I think you'd better explain,' she said.

They were interrupted when Nancy brought in a tray with two cups of cocoa and two slices of raisin cake.

'I thought the cake was for my aunt's supper,' Thea said.

'There's plenty. And as a matter of fact I made it for your birthday,' she said as she placed the tray on the table that Thea's aunt used as a desk at the back of the room.

'Thank you . . . thank you, Nancy. How kind of you.'

'Miss Gibb asked me to make it.'

'Oh . . .'

'But I didn't mind.' The housemaid's thin lips stretched into the closest she had ever come to a smile before she turned and left the room.

Thea was relieved that Nancy had removed her coat and

hat before bringing in the tray and also that Ellie had not seemed to notice that her manner could be thought eccentric. Her friend was sitting very still, staring into the fire with that same unfocused gaze as before. Thea placed her cocoa and slice of cake on the small table beside her and she smiled her thanks distractedly.

With her own plate balanced on her knee she sipped her cocoa as she gently prompted Ellie to explain her determination to read all of Lewis Sinclair's books. Ellie seemed relieved to be able to talk to someone and, after a while of listening to her outpourings, Thea asked wonderingly, 'How often have you met him?'

'As often as possible. Nearly every day!'

'And do your parents know? Have you told your mother that you're going into town to meet this man?'

'*This man!* Don't say "*this man*"! That is something your father might say! But, no, as a matter of fact, I haven't told them.'

Thea was annoyed to be likened to her father and she frowned. 'So what have you told them? Where are you supposed to be when you go to meet this— to meet Mr Sinclair?'

'Thea, don't scowl! Oh, now I know you're going to be angry... Oh dear!'

'Why am I going to be angry?' Thea asked, but she had already guessed what Ellie was going to say.

'Because... because I told my mother that I was meeting you.'

Ellie stared at Thea, her blue eyes wide with apprehension – but there was also a kind of excitement there, and confidence too, as if she could not possibly conceive that Thea might be really angry with her.

But Thea was angry – angry and hurt. She waited for a

moment until she could say quite calmly, 'Then not only have you lied but you have involved me in your deception.'

Instead of being ashamed of herself Ellie retorted angrily, 'Listen to yourself, Thea. I can't believe you would be so . . . so pompous! I haven't really done anything very wrong. I thought you would believe it to be romantic – meeting someone and realizing that it's important. I mean, that's what friends are supposed to be for, isn't it? To help one another when something like this happens?'

'Romantic? Important? He means so much to you?'

'Yes. Yes, he does.'

'But, Ellie, this has happened so quickly.'

'I know, I know.' Ellie sighed and sat back in her chair. 'That's just what Lewis said. But he called me "my darling" when he said it and he took hold of my arms and looked into my eyes and it was as though the crowds in the market had disappeared and we were completely alone. Oh, Thea, I know he must feel the same way as I do!'

'I see.'

'So, if my mother mentions anything – asks you about our shopping trips, although I don't think she will – you will say that we went together, won't you?'

'I – I don't know . . .'

'You know I'd do the same for you!'

Ellie looked so indignant that Thea was forced to smile. 'Of course you would – and of course I will – but only if you promise to tell your mother as soon as possible that you and Mr Sinclair have formed an attachment.'

'*Formed an attachment!* Goodness, Thea, sometimes you sound just like those boring books we had to read at school – Jane Austen and the like. This is the twentieth century, you know. Perhaps you should get your nose out of your books and start living!'

The sting was taken from Ellie's words by her smile and Thea couldn't help responding, 'Whereas you are going to do the opposite and start reading books.'

'What?'

Ellie looked genuinely puzzled until Thea pointed to the neatly parcelled book on the table beside her and then she laughed. 'The difference being that I shall read all of Lewis's books because they are part of him. He has created them and I want to know more about him.' She saw that Thea's eyes had widened in astonishment and she said, 'There, now. You didn't know that your friend could be so profound, did you? That's what love does, I'm afraid.'

'Love? Are you in love with him, Ellie?'

'Yes. I think I knew it the moment I saw him.'

'Love at first sight?'

'Don't look so cynical. It can happen to anyone, you know. It could even happen to you. You look at someone and there's this feeling – this tug inside you. Oh, I don't know how to describe it – in fact I don't think it would be delicate if I could because it's a physical feeling . . . a sort of delicious shiver . . .'

Ellie blushed and looked away, and in the short silence that followed Thea thought about Ellie's description of what she had felt when she had first seen Lewis and recognized what her friend had been trying to say. For hadn't she felt that same shiver of excitement when she and Robert Hedley had first looked at each other across the heads of the children at the Christmas party?

But the books which Ellie so despised had taught Thea enough about human emotion to be able to recognize that reaction as physical attraction. That did not always have to be the same thing as love.

'. . . but now I have this problem . . . Thea!'

She looked up to find Ellie glaring at her. She looked cross.

'Thea, you're not listening!'

'I'm sorry. What did you say?'

'My mother is still keen on my going to London. She hopes that Mr Edwardes will send for me to become a Gaiety Girl the minute he sees my photographs and—'

'And now you don't want to go to London. You want to stay here to be near Lewis.'

'Of course. But how can I tell my mother when Lewis hasn't actually said anything – hasn't actually asked me to marry him, yet.'

'Yet? You are sure that he will?'

'We-ell . . .' Ellie looked uncomfortable. 'Actually he said that I should go to London. He is sure that I will be an acknowledged beauty and he doesn't want to spoil my chance of becoming rich and famous.'

'Then, Ellie—'

'Oh, don't look so alarmed. He's only saying that because it's the right thing to do. He's probably testing me.'

'Do you think so?'

'Yes.'

Ellie sounded certain but Thea wasn't so sure. Nevertheless, she asked, 'So what are you going to do?'

'I shall do exactly as my mother wants and we'll go and have our photographs taken next week. She mustn't suspect anything until Lewis has asked me to marry him and I can say that we are engaged.'

'*What* did you say?'

'I'll tell her that we are engaged and that I can't go—'

'Not that. What did you say about having photographs taken? You said *we'll* go. You mean you and me?'

'Of course. It's all arranged. My mother has already telephoned Mr Gray.'

'But why do I have to go? I don't want any photographs to

126

send to Mr Edwardes. I don't want to be a Gaiety Girl.'

'Of course not!' Thea was not sure if she liked the way Ellie was smiling – as if the idea was ridiculous. 'It's just that when he spoke to my mother, Mr Gray made her promise to bring you too. He was most insistent. Naturally Mama asked why, and he said that he would like to take one or two pictures of us together – to show the contrast of our different looks. He said it would be flattering for me.'

'But not for me, I presume.'

'Oh, Thea, don't look so sour. I'm sure he didn't mean it that way and it's not important for you anyway, is it? Well, obviously my mother agreed.'

'Obviously.'

If Ellie noticed that Thea's feelings were ruffled she chose to ignore it. 'So you'll come?'

'I'm not sure. I'll have to ask permission.'

'Of your father? But surely if you have left home—'

'No, of my aunt. After all, I'm living under her roof and I don't want to do anything that will annoy her.'

'But why should it annoy her? You're just being difficult and I don't know why!'

Ellie did her best to persuade Thea to agree to accompany her to Vernon Gray's studios and they came the closest they had ever come to having an argument. Thea knew that Ellie could not understand why she was being 'difficult' – she couldn't understand because Thea had never opposed her before.

Often Thea had agreed to something that she really didn't want to do – the endless window shopping, walks in the park when the object was to be seen rather than to see anything interesting – simply because Ellie and her mother were charming and easy-going and more fun to be with than her own dismal family.

127

But now she realized that under the charm there was a degree of self-interest. It had suited Ellie to have Thea for a foil, a friend whose looks were so different from her own – and unfashionable in a world that seemed to prefer engaging little blondes – that Ellie's beauty stood out all the more.

Agreeing to enter the beauty contest had had serious consequences. Ellie should have guessed that Thea's removal to her aunt's house might not be a coincidence but she had been too full of her own concerns to wonder about it. Now she needed Thea again – and Thea didn't see why she should oblige.

But in the end she promised Ellie that she would ask her aunt's permission, safe in the knowledge that her aunt would find the idea too frivolous even to consider, and Ellie went home vowing – or threatening – to call the very next morning to hear the verdict.

Aunt Marjorie kept the promise she had made that morning and came home much earlier than usual so that they could have their evening meal together.

They had taken to eating in the kitchen in front of the range at night because it was so much cosier and more practical besides. Thea suspected that her aunt had neglected herself before she came to live with her, carrying a bowl of broth and some sandwiches through to the dining room and leaving most of it because she was simply too tired to take the sustenance she needed.

So now she would cover the wooden scrubbed table with a gingham cloth, slice the bread as expertly as she could – 'My goodness, they're like doorsteps, child,' her aunt had exclaimed the first time – and have the pot warmed to make the tea.

Tonight they had the broth followed by slices of raisin cake and a glass of Madeira wine in honour of Thea's birthday.

When they had finished Thea cleared the table, leaving the dishes stacked neatly on the bench for Nancy to deal with the next morning. Then she made the tea and carried the tray through to the sitting room.

When her aunt was settled by the fire she decided to broach the subject of the trip to Vernon Gray's studio, but only because she had promised Ellie that she would.

'But of course you must go,' her aunt said. 'Why do you look so surprised? Did you think I would refuse?'

'Well, yes, I did.'

'Why? It's perfectly respectable to have your photograph taken, you know.'

'But that depends on the photograph, doesn't it?'

'Oh, if you're worried that the poses will be in the least provocative, you needn't be. Mrs Parker will be there like the fiercest of theatrical mothers to make sure that her darling is shown as a sweet innocent. After all, I suspect the real reason that she wants Ellie to go to the Gaiety is to attract the right sort of husband – a peer of the realm perhaps – therefore she must remain respectable; not like the girls who are content to be some rich man's mistress.'

'But what about the costumes she will wear for the photographs?'

'Let her wear whatever she wants. You don't have to wear the same if you don't want to. Make Ellie and her mother respect your choice – for once,' her aunt added, and looked at Thea keenly.

'And you know, Thea,' she continued, 'even though you tell me that Mr Gray wants you to pose with Ellie as a contrast or a foil or whatever, I'm absolutely sure that Mrs Parker will not send any of the pictures of the two of you to London. You are too beautiful—' She held up her hand as Thea started to interrupt. 'No, your beauty is of an entirely different and more lasting sort. Rosalie Parker will send Mr Edwards photographs of Ellie alone.'

'So it's a waste of time my going, isn't it?'

'No it isn't, because I would like some photographs of *you* alone and I shall ask Vernon to make sure that they are as tasteful as only he can make them.'

'Vernon? As only he can make them? You know him?'

'Indeed I do. Thea – I'm so comfortable here – would you mind opening that drawer in the table and bringing me the two albums you'll find there?'

Thea brought the photograph albums to her aunt. She had not told her that she had already looked at them: she hadn't wanted to be seen to be prying into something her aunt might want to keep private.

'Now sit on the little footstool beside me. I want to show you something.'

Thea balanced on the footstool and moved close so that she could see the albums on her aunt's knee. It felt good to be sitting near like this with only the sound of the coals shifting and settling in the hearth. Her aunt's clothes gave off a faint scent of her favourite eau-de-Cologne, which was her only indulgence. With a slight catch in her throat Thea realized that she had never had a moment of closeness like this with any other human being. Certainly never with her mother . . .

Aunt Marjorie opened the larger of the two albums, the first that Thea had looked at, and explained that Vernon Gray had taken every one of the photographs of the groups of children.

'He's been so good to me, my dear . . .'

'Good to you?'

'Do you know he comes whenever and to wherever I ask him and he never charges me a penny? And he will make extra copies to help me when I go begging.'

Thea looked up at her aunt's kind face, softened and made attractive by the gentle firelight.

Aunt Marjorie smiled as she continued, 'I take these photographs with me when I call on the rich gentlefolk and tradesmen to show them what happiness a very small contribution from them can bring. Small in relation to their own wealth, I mean.

'And sometimes one of the local newspapers will print one of the photographs and send a reporter along to get the facts from me. Something like that brings in more contributions. Yes, I have a lot to thank Vernon for.'

'You like him,' Thea said wonderingly.

'Of course I do. He doesn't just take the photographs. He's good with the children and will explain to any of the older ones who show an interest the principles of photography. He often asks me about what I'm doing and what has become of the poor little mites. Why shouldn't I like him?'

Thea averted her gaze and stared into the fire for a moment. She thought about the man who had been one of the judges of the beauty contest and whom she had met later at the party in the green room. He had been kind to her, he had gone out of his way to put her at her ease, and she had been drawn instinctively to his humorous assessment of the place and people which had seemed to match her own. And yet nothing he had said and done that night had led her to believe that there was this other more serious side to him.

She tried very hard but she could not see Vernon who, even to her inexperienced eyes, gave the impression of enjoying life's more hedonistic pleasures, caring for poor and homeless children.

She heard her aunt sigh and she looked up to find that she had opened the smaller album, the one covered in grey silk. Thea waited to hear what she would say. But Aunt Marjorie didn't say anything. She turned the pages one by one and they looked at the photographs together in silence. When she came to the last photograph she seemed to linger a little longer and then she closed the album and placed both her hands on it firmly, as if preventing the memories from escaping.

'Well, Thea,' she said at last, 'you know who the two girls are, don't you?'

'Yes, you and my mother.'

'We had such a happy childhood, you know.' Her aunt leaned back until her face was shadowed by the wings of the chair. 'Our parents – your grandparents – were so delighted with their two little daughters that they wanted some kind of record of their lives. Of course there are other photographs – photographs of our parents, the four of us together, the house, the gardens, the servants even, and I shall be happy to pass them all on to you one day. But this was your grandmother's special album. Can you guess who the photographer was, Thea?'

'How could I?' Thea was puzzled. She looked up to find her aunt smiling. 'I know – my grandfather.'

'Nearly right. It was your grandmother. She had seen photographs taken by Julia Margaret Cameron, who became quite famous, and your grandmother reckoned that if one woman could do it then so could she. So she persuaded your grandfather to buy her whatever was needed. Every photograph in this album was her work – every photograph bar one, that is . . .'

At these words her aunt's smile vanished and she stared down at her hands. She spread her fingers and gripped the edges of the album but she didn't open it again.

Thea knew without asking which photograph had been taken by someone else.

Chapter Ten

Lily Roper filled the kettle and placed it on the gas stove. She had been here for a couple of hours and she was going to stop and have a cup of tea and a bit bread and cheese. It wasn't that she was tired – it was easy to clean a place when there was plenty of hot water and soap – but Mr Hedley had said she should have a break, a sit-down and a bite to eat; that it was part of her duties here.

While she waited for the kettle to boil she stood by the window and looked out across the river. The top floor of this tall, old building was a good vantage point, and whichever way she looked, up- or downstream, she could see a forest of masts and rigging. There were sailing ships and also steam ships from all over the world – and many of them had been built right here on the Tyne.

Mr Hedley worked at the yards, but he went to work dressed. Lily smiled at the expression. It meant that Mr Hedley wore a collar and tie and a proper suit and gentleman's shoes, instead of worker's overalls and hard-toed boots. But he still worked six days a week in the drawing offices, even though he started at nine o'clock instead of six o'clock like the men.

Lily sat at the table with her cup of tea and stirred two spoons of sugar into it – he'd said to help herself. While she nibbled at her slice of bread she found herself wondering guiltily what Robert Hedley would be like undressed . . . with nothing on at all, she meant. He was a big man . . . his hands were large but his fingers and nails were clean and well-kept . . .

She glanced down at her hands; the skin was rough and calloused but they were grime free. He'd said that she could use his nice toilet soap for her hands and not the carbolic. Had that been a gentle way of telling her that she was dirty? But he wasn't being unkind. He knew what it was like to be poor – to have to choose between buying soap or milk for the bairns.

She wondered what it would be like to get in that bath of his and wash her body all over with sweet-smelling soap, then dry herself on one of his big, soft towels . . . wrap herself up in it and, wearing nothing else, to sit by the fire and wait for him to come home . . .

'I thought you came here to work, Mam, not to sit dreaming like this.'

Lily looked up in fright to find Luke standing in the doorway. 'Luke! How did you get in?' She'd stood at the top of the stairs and watched Mr Hedley set off for work as she usually did and she was sure that he'd slammed the outer door shut. She'd heard the lock click into place.

'There's ways.' Her son closed the room door behind him and came to sit opposite her. 'Pour us a cup of tea, then.'

Lily got up obediently. Her middle son had never been violent towards her like his father had, but there was always a sense of menace. Even though he was only seventeen, Lily afforded him all the respect – bred by fear – that she would give to any grown man.

'Here you are.'

She placed the cup before him and left him to help himself to sugar. She watched his great clumsy hand reach for the sugar bowl and she would have liked to tell him to be careful with Mr Hedley's nice pots but she didn't dare.

'Is there owt to eat?' he asked, just as she sat down again.

She sighed. Her chance of a few moments of peace had gone. Perhaps it was a punishment for thinking about Mr Hedley like that. 'You can hev a bit bread and cheese,' she said, and pushed her plate across the table towards him.

'No, Mam, I'll not take yours.'

'Well, it's that or nowt at all,' Lily was surprised to find herself defying him. 'I'm not going to steal from Mr Hedley.'

Luke looked at her in surprise. And then he grinned as he pushed the plate back across the table. 'Then it's nowt,' he said.

Lily was worried. She didn't know if he was playing with her – just as his father would have done. Often with Patrick a smile like that was followed by a clout across her face with the back of his hand.

'You see . . .' she began uneasily, 'you see, I don't want to lose this job. We need the money . . .'

'It's all right, Mam. I know you do, and I don't want to spoil things for you. I'd much rather you worked here than . . . than . . .' his face darkened and he stared down into his tea, 'than anything else,' he finished. 'So how many days do you come here, then?' he asked after a pause.

He was smiling openly now and Lily remembered what an affectionate bairn he'd been. He'd like to cuddle up to her long after he'd been weaned, and it was only his father's scorn and ill treatment that had finally driven him from his mother's side. Luke had left home as soon as he'd left school – and God knows how he'd survived. But he'd always called to see her when he thought his dad would be out. And he brought her whatever he could.

'Three times a week,' she said, 'sometimes four, although I often think he's inventing jobs for me to do. But there's cleaning and washing and ironing and, do you know, Luke, he says I can bring me own washing and use his poss tub if I want.'

'And you do a bit cooking for him too, from the smell of it.' Luke nodded towards the stove where a large pan was steaming softly on the back ring.

'Aye, there's stew cooking, potatoes an' all,' Lily said. 'All he'll hev to do is warm it up when he gets in from work.'

'Lucky man.'

Luke was glowering again and Lily reached across the table timidly to take his hand. 'Don't begrudge him owt, Luke. Robert Hedley's worked hard for anything he's got.'

'Aye, I suppose so.'

'And he's not mean. Look at the way he treats me. And you know he gans up to the school after work some nights to teach the bairns drawing and painting – any that want to stay and learn, that is.'

'I know. Our Joe goes, doesn't he?'

'Aye, and Janey too, although she can't draw for toffee. And, remember, Mr Hedley came from nowt – from the orphanage – and there's not much love in them places.'

Luke snorted. 'And is it any better where I grew up? Where was the love in our house, Mam?'

'Luke!' Lily was cut to the heart. 'Luke, me bairn, how can you?'

'Mam, I'm sorry.' He took hold of both her hands across the table and squeezed them. 'I know the life you've had with me dad and I know you've done your best. And I don't begrudge Robert Hedley owt, and I'm glad you're working for him. Now how about filling me cup up? All this blether's made me parched.'

As well as topping up his tea and her own, Lily went to the bread bin and cut one more slice of bread. Luke raised his eyebrows and she smiled. 'Just this once,' she said. 'Mr Hedley's always saying I don't take enough. But you'll hev to make do with a bit of my cheese.'

They ate their bread and cheese and drank their tea in companionable silence and then Luke said, 'Are you going to show us around, then?'

Lily looked at her son suspiciously. 'Why?'

He grinned. 'Divven't worry. I'm not going to pinch owt. How could I when you're here?'

'But what about when I'm not here?'

'Are you still worried about how I got in?'

'Yes.'

'Well, I'll tell you – and you can tell Mr Hedley so's he can see to it. But first will you show us round – just to satisfy me curiosity?'

Luke leaned across the table and took her chin in one of his big hands. He was gentle but firm and he tilted her head so that she had to look at him. He was grinning and, in that moment, she could see how like his father he was. But not Patrick as he was now, with his once-handsome features bloated with the drink. This was Patrick as he used to be: big and raw-boned but bonny with it – and with that roguish twinkle in his eye. She had never been able to refuse Patrick anything when he looked at her like that – and she couldn't refuse her son now.

'All right,' she sighed, and he let go of her and sat back, laughing softly. 'But first I'll wash these pots.' This was said more to assert her position of authority here than because she couldn't wash them after he'd gone. 'And I'll wipe the table down.'

Luke watched his mother, her sleeves pushed up over her skinny arms as far as her elbows. He didn't know how old she was and he realized that he had never wondered before. He knew she'd been very young when she'd had Matt, and his older brother was twenty now. So his mother wouldn't be forty, and yet, God help her, she looked years older than that.

He remembered her having two more bairns in between him and Joe, and another between Joe and Janey. But they hadn't lived long. And in all probability there could have been more between Matt and himself. Luke knew enough about life to realize what childbearing could do to a woman – childbearing and poverty. And in his mother's case, a drunken violent husband. Why in God's name had she married Patrick Roper?

Luke smiled wryly. Of course if she hadn't married him, he wouldn't be sitting here now. So, the least he could do would be to try and help his mam whenever he could – and to make sure that his little sister, Janey, didn't end up like her mother, a dried-up old bag of bones before she was forty. And also to make damned sure that no man like his father ever got his hands on her.

Luke was touched when he saw his mother's pride as she showed him round Robert Hedley's living quarters. Hedley had fashioned them himself out of the offices on the top floor of a deserted warehouse. The gossip had it that the draughtsman was renting the place cheap on condition he looked after the property. So Luke'd be doing him a favour if he told him about the window at the back of the building in the lane.

The ancient stonework had crumbled so that it was possible to lift the frame clean out and scramble in, then, when you left, replace it after you. Judging by the smart kitchen Hedley had fitted out for himself, he was handy, it would be no problem for him to fix the window.

'What do you think of this, Luke?'

His mother had opened the door to the bathroom. He thought of the arrangements in his parents' home: they had a sink of their own, at least, but they shared a privy across the yard with five other families. He looked at his mother's face and saw the yearning in her eyes. He grinned.

'I bet you'd like to get into that bath, wouldn't you, Mam? Hev you ever been tempted to try it out before Hedley comes home?'

'Of course not!'

She pushed him aside and closed the door. Something had made her blush but he guessed that whatever it was, wild horses wouldn't drag it out of her.

The bedroom was comfortable but sparsely furnished – like a monk's cell, Luke thought – the only luxury being a shelf of books. And the small sitting room looked as if it was seldom used.

'And where does that lead?' Luke asked, pointing to the door at the end of the passage.

His mother had turned to lead the way back into the kitchen. 'I divven't gan in there,' she said.

'Why not?'

'It's where he works. He calls it his studio.'

'Does he keep it locked?'

'I divven't know. He told me not to bother with that room, that he'd keep it in order himself.'

'And you've never even opened the door to look inside?' Luke was incredulous. His mother shook her head. 'Mam, you're a mazer. Hawway, let's have a look.'

'No, Luke, no . . .'

But he pushed past her and strode towards the door. 'Divven't fret – I won't harm anything.'

The door wasn't locked and he heard his mother's soft cry of distress as he opened it and stepped inside. This room was

139

as big as two of the other rooms put together. It had windows just like the others, those on the front of the building giving a fine view of the river and across to the south bank. But what was unusual about it was the fact that the sloping roof on the back, the north side, had been almost completely replaced with glass.

His mother had crept in and was standing beside him, looking up wonderingly at the expanse of cold grey sky.

'That must have cost him a bonny penny or two,' Luke muttered. 'I didn't think draughtsmen were that well paid.'

'It's his pictures,' his mother said. 'Mr Hedley told me that every time he sells a picture, he can afford to do something to make his quarters more to his liking.'

'Oh, yes, his pictures . . . I've heard folk pay good money for his pictures.'

Luke glanced around the room. In truth nothing he saw meant much to him: the long workbench under the windows; the shelves with pots and jars and brushes; the easel – he knew that's what it was because it was like the blackboard easel at school. It was facing away from him but there was a canvas on it. There were several other canvases stacked with their faces against the walls. Everything was clean and shipshape. There was a faint smell about the place, an oily smell, but it was not unpleasant.

Luke's eye was caught by a large sheet of paper on the workbench. He walked over to look at it and what he saw made him catch his breath.

'Divven't touch, Luke! Your hands'll be dirty – you might mark it.'

'It's all right.' Luke stepped back quickly. He didn't want his mother to come any closer. He didn't want her to see what he'd just seen. 'But I'll just have a look at that,' he nodded towards the canvas.

140

'Luke!'

'Whisht, woman! Divven't shriek like that. Just one peek and I promise you I'll be off. Wait there now.'

But when he saw what was on the canvas his eyes widened and he smiled with pleasure. 'Mam, come and see this!'

They stared at the painting together and Lily Roper laughed out loud. 'Ee,' she said, 'isn't it grand? Isn't it just . . . just . . . so real?'

Luke realized that neither he nor his mother had the words to describe exactly what it was that was so good about Robert Hedley's painting.

It showed three little girls with dirty faces and ragged clothes sitting on a cracked pavement beside an open doorway, arranging little bits of broken glass and china on a counter made from a bigger stone. Somehow, in spite of the dust and the grime, Hedley had made the sunlight sparkle on the coloured glass and shine in the golden hair of one of the children. A few bright green weeds straggled up through cracks in the paving stones.

'They're playing shops,' Luke's mother said, 'with bits o' boodies – that's what we called broken pots. Those little uns are just like me and me pals when I was a bairn. Janey plays like that now.'

'And look at those two lads,' Luke said. 'Look at their faces.' Two slightly older urchins, with their caps pushed to the back of their heads, leaned against the brick wall with their hands in their pockets and grinned down at the girls in a superior way. But there was no malice in their smiles. All the bairns were as happy as they could be – and probably happier than they would ever be again.

Luke's smile faded. 'Aye, Mr Hedley's very good,' was all he said. 'Now, hawway, let's get out of here.'

Before Luke left, he took his mother down the steep wooden

stairs to the warehouse. It was dark in there with only the faintest light filtering through the grimy windows high on the back wall. Lily followed him, sniffing curiously at the lingering smells of long-ago cargoes of tea and coffee and spices. They were not unpleasant.

She was shocked when she saw that one of the windows had been lifted clean out. 'Where've you put it?' she gasped.

'Calm down. It's on the bank behind, covered up with a bit of old sacking. There's so much rubbish there that no one would notice unless they were looking for it.'

'You'll put it back?'

'Of course I will – you can stay and watch. And you'd better tell Mr Hedley that I noticed it when I called by to see you. He wouldn't believe you if you tried to say that you'd noticed it yourself.'

'But what shall I say you were doing – skulking about in the back lane like that?'

'He won't ask questions, believe me, Mam. He has a pretty good idea how I live – and the company I keep.'

He hated the expression of pain that filled his mother's face at his words but there was nothing he could do about it. He made her promise to go back up to Hedley's diggings as soon as he'd gone and try not to worry too much. He climbed on an old cask and heaved himself up on to the window ledge, looked quickly around to see if the coast was clear, then turned to drop backwards on to the stack of old timber he'd used when he climbed up to ease the frame out.

His mother was still standing with her arms grasped tight about her skinny body, her upturned face pale in the dusty light. He knew she would stand there until he had replaced the window frame. That was easy. The frame was still there, covered by the sacking on the steep bank. He took care to make a good job of replacing it and waved at his mother through the streaked and filthy glass before he jumped down again.

He was glad he'd come here today, eased his mind about his mam working for Robert Hedley. And yet he realized that he wasn't completely at ease about the draughtsman. Hedley was a good man – to all appearances, he was straight – and yet Luke hadn't been able to ignore the rumours about a working man who was so different from his fellows. And now he'd seen that drawing, the pencil drawing on the workbench, he wondered if there was some substance to them.

For all his clever ways and his good works amongst the poor, Hedley was a man like any other man, wasn't he? No, not like any other man, for there was no one else that Luke had ever met who could have created a woman like that.

He was amused to feel a tug at his loins as he brought the drawing to mind and lingered over the detail. The pencil strokes had created on cold, white paper a tall, graceful, living woman, shapely and desirable – and completely naked except for the long dark hair that cascaded down over her shoulders and covered her – allowing only the most tantalizing glimpses of her body.

Luke wondered if she was a real woman or just someone that Hedley had dreamed up. There was no way of knowing. But if she was real, Luke would certainly like to meet her.

Chapter Eleven

'Take those pins out and let your hair fall down over your shoulders,' Vernon told Thea. 'I want the next pose to be quite different.'

She looked at him in surprise. 'I thought that we were finished.'

Mrs Parker, Ellie and Susan were packing up all the dresses they had brought to the studio. Vernon glanced at them and put a hand on Thea's elbow. He drew her away and spoke quietly. 'I have promised your aunt that she shall have a portrait of you.'

'But you've already taken one.'

He smiled that secret personal smile that seemed to include just her. He lowered his voice. 'But at the time Mrs Parker made it impossible for me to concentrate. She was concerned that I might have forgotten the purpose of the visit here today – to enhance her daughter's hope of a dazzling future.'

That was true, Thea thought. When she had posed alone, they couldn't help but be aware of Mrs Parker's restless movements at the back of the studio, fidgeting and whispering and endlessly fussing with Ellie's hair or the frills and flounces on her costume.

'So, if you will return to the dressing room,' Vernon said, 'Adie will bring you the dress I'd like you to wear and help you comb out your hair.'

'But they won't want to wait for me.'

'Then they needn't. Your aunt knows Adie and I'm sure that she would consider her a suitable chaperone.'

Vernon's assistant, Adie Hall, had been present throughout. She was a small, slender young woman who might have been attractive if it had not been for her unusual complexion. Thea had never seen anyone with such white skin. But it wasn't attractively pale; Adie looked almost bloodless, and her light blue eyes, rimmed with gingery lashes the same colour as her hair, protruded slightly.

Thea was sure she'd heard Vernon address Adie as 'little frog' when he'd been giving her instructions, but his tone had been affectionate and she hadn't seemed to take offence.

Adie came towards them now, carrying a white dress; although it wasn't quite white, Thea noticed, it was what you'd call ivory. She stood just behind Vernon, waiting patiently.

'I'll have to tell Ellie,' Thea said.

'I'll tell her. Now off you go with Adie and get ready. Just one more pose, I promise you. I also promised Miss Gibb that I wouldn't tire you.'

Thea followed Vernon's assistant to the dressing room. She'd had no idea how tiring it was posing for photographs and she wished she had refused to stay. But he'd been so persuasive, and if her aunt really wanted a good portrait of her then how could she refuse?

Aunt Marjorie had come into town with Thea on the tram. They'd arrived at Vernon Gray's studio in Ellison Place at ten o'clock that morning just as the motor-taxi bearing Mrs Parker, Ellie and Susan had drawn up. Aunt Marjorie had stared unbelievingly as the poor young maid carried armful after

145

armful of colourful silks, satin and velvet dresses from the taxi, up the entrance steps and into the house where a young woman waited at the foot of the stairs to relieve her of each burden.

Mrs Parker saw Aunt Marjorie's expression and smiled. 'I've brought them all because I want Mr Gray to decide which colour will show Ellie to her best advantage,' she explained.

'Doesn't the silly woman know that it doesn't matter what colour the dresses are?' Aunt Marjorie whispered to Thea. 'On the photographs they'll all be white or black with shades of grey in between.'

When they climbed the stairs to the studio on the top floor of the house, Vernon explained this tactfully to Mrs Parker and he pleased her by saying that he'd go for the most flattering line, rather than the colour.

Thea had brought only a few changes of clothes with her. Mrs Parker shook her head when she saw them and told Thea that, for the photographs taken together, she could wear one of Ellie's outfits. It wouldn't matter if they were a little short as Thea would be standing behind Ellie and the hemline wouldn't be seen.

Aunt Marjorie looked as if she were going to explode when she heard this – whether with mirth or with outrage, Thea didn't know. But before her aunt left to go to one of her committee meetings, she'd had a private word with Vernon. That must have been when she'd made her request.

For, in fact, as Aunt Marjorie had predicted, there had been very few shots taken of them both together and not quite so many of Thea alone. Mrs Parker had made sure that the photographic session was devoted to her daughter. Thea had very soon begun to wonder why she had bothered to come. Now it was over she realized that she was cold as well as weary.

Vernon had explained that he used natural light to take his photographs. One wall of the studio was virtually one vast window, and the sloping roof was also glassed. There were movable blinds on both the window and the roof so that he could adjust the amount of light to the time of day, Vernon explained, but today, none of the blinds had been drawn. There was not going to be enough sunlight on a morning in mid-January to warrant their use. And, because of all the glass, the room had been cold.

At one end of the large room, which extended for the entire top floor, there was a collection of backdrops on rollers, and various props ranging from imitation masonry to potted plants and toys for children. There were also posing chairs with neck rests to help you keep your head still. At the other end, in the remaining fireplace, there was a gas fire but it hardly gave off enough heat to warm the whole studio.

The dressing room was surprisingly luxurious. When they had first arrived, Adie had explained that Mr Gray had some illustrious clients, a duchess, even, and quality folk expected to be pampered. The room was softly carpeted and furnished with plush sofas, cushions, occasional tables and rails to hang the clothes. The dressing table was laid out with a collection of silver-backed brushes, combs and hairpins.

But now that the room was empty of Ellie and her mother and all the clothes and paraphernalia, Thea would have liked simply to sink on to one of the sofas and rest for a while. Adie saw her expression and smiled at her.

'Look,' she said, pointing to a small table set with a damask cloth. 'There's a pot of coffee; I've just made it. Mr Gray told me to wait until the others had gone; he wanted you to have a few moments to yourself.'

'Thank you, how kind,' Thea said.

'But don't be too long.' Adie smiled to take the edge off her

147

peremptory tone, 'Mr Gray is worried about the light. If it clouds over he might not be able to take any more pictures today.'

As Thea sipped her coffee and nibbled on a ratafia biscuit, she wondered about Adie. She did not exactly speak like a lady, but neither did she have a local accent. Her speech was a little like that of the secretary at Thea's old school, she decided, and Miss Arnold had come from London. 'From Wimbledon, to be precise,' she had liked to tell the girls. Thea wondered if Adie came from somewhere like that – and, if so, how she had first met up with Vernon Gray.

When she'd finished her coffee and biscuits Adie helped her into the dress she'd brought for her and asked her to sit at the dressing table while she arranged her hair. First she took out all the pins, as Vernon had requested, and combed it through. But, rather than letting it hang loose, she tied it at the nape of Thea's neck with a white satin ribbon which she arranged into a large floppy bow.

Adie must have caught Thea's look of surprise in the mirror for she smiled and said, 'Come and stand by the cheval glass; you'll see why.'

Thea stared at herself wonderingly. The gown of ivory satin trimmed with tulle was an evening dress, but an evening dress that a very young woman would wear. The neckline was shaped into a vee both back and front, and the full sleeves puffed out where they were gathered onto a satin band just above the elbow. A deep frill hung from the neckline to hide the swell of Thea's breasts. Further frills, starting just below the knee, fell in tiers almost to the floor, giving just a glimpse of the white stockings and white satin shoes.

'What is it?' Adie asked. 'Aren't you pleased?'

'I look so . . . so . . .'

'Virginal?' Adie offered.

148

'No – I mean yes.' Thea felt uncomfortable with the other girl's easy use of a word that she had so recently only whispered about with other girls at school. 'I meant to say that I look so young. In fact I wore a dress similar to this at the reception after my last school prize-giving ceremony.'

'Perhaps Mr Vernon thinks your aunt will want to see you that way – as a girl rather than a young woman?'

'Perhaps . . . but I'm not sure.'

'Is your aunt not sentimental?'

'No—' Thea began, but then she remembered the photograph albums. Her aunt kept records not only of her own family but also of the children she worked with. Perhaps there *was* a sentimental side to her practical aunt. She decided not to complain.

Adie picked up a wide satin sash. 'Here,' she said, 'virginal or not, it would be a sin not to emphasize that tiny waist of yours.'

After tying the sash, Adie brought a comb and adjusted Thea's hair. She pulled the bow slightly off-centre and, moving round to stand between Thea and the looking-glass, she brought one thick strand of hair over her shoulder so that it curled down over her breast.

'Now, put these on,' she said, handing Thea a pair of long white evening gloves, 'and come with me.'

Vernon had been setting up the studio. In front of a backcloth representing a formal garden there was now a plaster balustrade.

'Stand there, Thea,' he said. 'Facing me but with your right arm resting along the balustrade and your head slightly turned as though you are looking out over the garden – no, not so much. It doesn't matter that you can't really see anything – it's the illusion that counts.'

When she had taken up the pose he wanted, Adie hurried

149

forward and arranged her skirt so that the folds fell gracefully, then combed the strand of hair that was falling over her shoulder, adjusting the ribbon so that the bow showed in the curve of her neck.

'Now, you know from before that you must stand very still,' Vernon said.

Thea stood as still as she could and from the corner of her eye she saw him go back to the camera which stood on a heavy wooden stand about ten feet away. He stood behind the large brass and mahogany box and pulled a black cloth over his head as he had done before. He had explained that when he did this he was looking through the camera on to the glass viewing screen.

'Be patient,' he said. 'This will take a few moments while I focus properly.'

After a short while, Vernon called out, 'Can you bring your other hand up across your body a little? Adie, get a fan from the prop box and give to Thea – that's right. Thea, hold the fan so that it's half open. Perfect. I'm going to put the plate in now.'

Vernon came out from under the cloth and Adie hurried across to take it from him. Thea knew that now he would place the heavy glass photographic plate inside the camera and withdraw its cover. He stood behind the camera holding the shutter bulb.

'Now, Thea, even though you're in half profile, we can see your expression,' he said. 'I want you to imagine that this is your first ball. The ballroom, the gardens of the grand house, the guests, the young men, particularly, are everything that a romantically inclined young girl has ever dreamed of.' He paused, and even though she couldn't see him, she knew he was smiling. 'All right,' he said, 'if you've never had dreams like that personally, imagine that you are a heroine in one of the books you've read . . . that's it. Oh, Thea, that's perfect.'

She heard the mechanical click of the shutter and Vernon said, 'You can relax now.'

She turned to find him smiling at her. Her neck was aching and her shoulders felt tense. She lowered her head and raised her right hand to rub the nape of her neck gently.

'Adie, get a chair,' Vernon said.

His assistant hurried forward with a small armchair and Thea sank into it gratefully.

'That was beautiful,' Adie said. 'So much more tasteful than the studies we made earlier with your friend.'

'Do you mean the other photographs were distasteful?' Thea asked.

She was alarmed, for although she was no longer living in her father's house, and although he seemed to have washed his hands of her, she still felt uneasy about doing anything that might anger him. She remembered his rage when he had read the newspaper account of the dress she had worn for the competition. If he were ever to see 'distasteful' photographs of her, there was no knowing what he might do. Thea did not want to cause trouble for Aunt Marjorie.

Adie sensed her anxiety. 'No, not distasteful in the way you are imagining,' she said. 'Certainly not indelicate. How could they have been with that dragon of a stage mother hovering over her little chick every moment? No, what I meant was that they were more obvious in their appeal – not so subtle.'

'I see,' Thea said.

And she supposed she did. Ellie had been content to pose as prettily and as vivaciously as any of the soubrettes to be found on the picture postcards sold in theatre foyers. Her mother had enthusiastically struck up the poses that she used to be famous for when she was on the stage – or so she told them – and entreated Ellie to copy them.

151

Vernon thanked her for her suggestions and managed to change the pose to suit himself while still bamboozling Mrs Parker into thinking he was following her instructions – and praising her for her sense of artistry.

The pictures of the two of them, as Aunt Marjorie had predicted, had Thea standing behind Ellie. She'd done her best to enter into the spirit of it all and had smiled until she felt her face aching. By the time the session was over she had found herself half hoping that, as a result of these photographs, Ellie would be snapped up by the Gaiety and she would never have to accompany her friend on any of her scatterbrained enterprises again.

She rose from her chair and began to walk towards the door that led to the dressing room. 'Wait, Thea. I'd like to take one more,' she heard Vernon say.

'But I thought you said—'

'That last pose was for your aunt. The next – and the last, I promise – is for me. Please.'

The request was unexpected and something about it made her feel uneasy. She looked at him; his smile was friendly, open, matter-of-fact. There was no trace of that private smile, the smile that excluded any but the two of them.

'Oh – all right,' she said. 'Do I have to change my clothes again?' She was tired so she was pleased when he shook his head.

'No, you don't have to change. We'll just make a few adjustments. Would you mind sitting down again?'

Thea sat down and Adie immediately took the ribbon from her hair and began to brush and comb it. It was as if she had been told in advance what Vernon wanted.

'That's it,' he told her after Thea's hair had been coaxed to fall softly round her face. 'Now the shoulders.'

'Lean forward a mo,' the girl said, and when Thea had done

152

so, she could feel Adie begin to open the buttons at the back of her dress.

'What are you doing?' she asked.

'Don't worry, just the top two or three buttons, and that's so's we can ease the neckline down a little over your shoulders, but not too far. That's fine.'

She stood back to observe the effect, and then she tucked a white silk flower in the vee of the neckline and another in Thea's hair, just above her left ear.

'Bring Miss Richardson a hand mirror,' Vernon said.

Thea stared at the unfamiliar image. Not since she had been a small girl had her hair been so unrestrained. It framed her face giving her an altogether different look, a look so alien to the sensible bookish girl she had thought herself that she felt as if she'd been cast adrift from reality. Her eyes widened as she took in the whiteness of the silk flower against her dark tresses. How was it that it also seemed to emphasize how dark her eyes were?

'Mascara, do you think?' she heard Adie ask softly, and looked over the mirror to see Vernon nod.

'But I've never—' she began.

'No one will ever know,' Vernon said. 'And, believe me, some of the great beauties who are famed for the naturalness of their appeal rely on much more than mascara when they have their photographs taken.'

By now Thea was fascinated with the image of herself she had just glimpsed and she sat uncomplaining as Adie applied the mascara to her eyelashes and then gave her face a faint dusting of powder.

'To stop your nose shining,' she explained.

'But you didn't do that for the other photographs.'

'This one is to be head and shoulders. Look, Mr Gray is already moving the camera.'

The camera's three-legged stand was fitted with castors and now Vernon wheeled it forward until it was about six feet away, then he adjusted the height, bringing the camera down a little. From under the camera cloth he gave her more directions.

'Don't sit straight like that, Thea,' he said. 'Turn your right shoulder away from me slightly but keep your head facing forward – towards the camera.'

'Should I smile?'

'No, don't smile. Remember the way you looked at yourself in the mirror just now? Your eyes were full of wonder, your lips were very slightly parted . . . that's it. Stay just like that. That's perfect.'

The only sound in the studio was the faint hiss and pop of the gas fire, but it was a comforting sound. Thea looked up through the glass roof. Dark clouds filled the sky; she thought they looked like rain clouds. It was strange sitting in an armchair by the fire and at the same time, having such a panoramic view of the world outside.

She watched as the first drops of rain spattered against the glass and smiled at the noise they made. She walked across to the window and looked out. The rooftops she could glimpse were soon wet and glistening and, even though it was barely teatime, lights began to appear in the upper windows of the nearby houses. All the chimneys she could see sent columns of smoke up into the darkening sky.

She turned to look at the studio behind her. Deserted and strange in the dim light, it looked as though it were waiting for something to happen, for other people to come and stand and look at the pretend woodland scenes, or sit in chairs in the pretend living rooms. This was a room where people became someone else for a while, or rather they became an idealized

154

version of themselves: girls posing for photographs to send to their sweethearts; young men in uniform posing for pictures that would break their mothers' hearts; family groups in their very best clothes, wanting a picture to record the fact of their existence for posterity.

She wondered how Vernon coped with all these people, with their hopes and expectations, with their dreams. She shivered as she imagined these dreams, too insubstantial to be taken to the world outside, lingering wraithlike in the shadows . . .

Only the area near the fire looked real and inviting, with its thick rug and comfortable armchairs. Thea went back and curled up in her chair again. She wondered how long she would have to wait.

After the photographic session was over, Adie had helped her to change back into her own clothes but they had laughed and given up trying to put Thea's hair up again. Adie said she was unaccustomed to dealing with such wayward tresses and Thea, for once, couldn't face the usual struggle with brush, comb and hairpins, so they settled for tying it at the nape of her neck once more. That was the way she had worn it at school.

Then Vernon's assistant had taken her back into the studio and told her to sit by the fire and wait for Mr Gray. Thea had not seen her again.

The drumming of the rain on the glass roof was so heavy now that Thea did not hear Vernon come back. A slight movement in the dark space beyond the light cast by the fire made her turn around, and she saw him coming towards her carrying a large tray. He set it down on a low table between the two armchairs and Thea stared at the contents.

Vernon smiled. 'Your aunt said that I was to look after you until she returned. I take that to mean that I should give you something to eat. After all, you've had no luncheon.'

'What time is my aunt returning?'

'I'm not sure. She had much to do today. I told her that I had no other clients booked so I would be happy to entertain you until she could return, then I'll see you both home safely.'

'I could have gone on my own – I still could. I could get the tram.'

'In this weather?' Vernon looked up through the rain-streaked glass and then lowered his head and raised his eyebrows.

'Well, perhaps not.'

'Come then, we shall enjoy this together.'

Thea stared at the selection of food. There was a game pie, small bread rolls, dishes of pâté, butter and jam, and a plate of teacakes.

'We can toast the teacakes, look . . .' Vernon indicated a toasting fork hanging at the side of the fireplace, 'but now you must tell me whether you would like tea or coffee?'

'Tea, please, but—' Thea was about to tell him not to bother if it meant going all the way down to the kitchen again but he had already pulled aside a curtain to reveal an alcove in the corner of the room.

'I have a sink and a gas ring in here, sufficient for my needs while I'm working.'

While Vernon made the tea Thea supposed that that was where Adie must have made the coffee earlier. She wondered about Adie. Had she gone home? If so, where did she live? She wondered if she earned enough as a photographer's assistant to be able to afford comfortable lodgings.

And what of Vernon? This was a big house. Surely he didn't live here without staff? And yet he had gone to get the food himself rather than ring down for a maid.

'I don't keep a cook.' Thea was startled to find he seemed

156

to have read her mind – as he'd done before. 'Cooks can be temperamental about difficult hours, and they want to order your life for you. I make do with a skivvy and a couple of housemaids and I send out for most of my meals; the best restaurants will even send round someone to wait on table, if I require it. But this little repast we can manage ourselves!'

He smiled as if they were children arranging a secret feast. His manner was open and friendly. Throughout the day he had acted professionally. Although Thea had found it strange to be photographed by someone who evidently took his art so seriously, he had neither done nor said anything to make her feel apprehensive on a physical level.

She wondered whether she had previously judged Vernon too harshly. Perhaps she had only imagined the way he had looked at her in the green room that night. After all, she had been drinking wine for the very first time . . .

And now Thea found she had not enjoyed herself so much for a long time. In fact she wondered if she had ever enjoyed herself quite like this. Sitting here with Vernon, it did not feel wrong to indulge her appetite. Indeed, he kept pressing her to take more – to eat as much as she liked.

The game pie was rich, the bread rolls just crusty enough, and the pâté was satisfyingly coarse with a slight orangey flavour.

'We should really be drinking wine with this,' Vernon said, 'but I should hate to do anything of which your aunt would disapprove. I respect her too much.'

She watched as he cut the teacakes in half ready to toast them, and then he paused and said, 'It's getting darker. Shall I light the gaslamps or are you comfortable just sitting in the firelight?'

'Oh, just the firelight, please!' Thea exclaimed.

But as she watched him hold the toasting fork towards the

fire she wondered at that word 'comfortable'. Had he meant quite simply, did she like sitting in the firelight? Or was it something more than that? Had he really meant to enquire if she felt it was all right to be sitting alone with him in the firelight? Did he want to assure her that he respected her sensitivities?

She leaned back in her chair and observed the neatness of his movements as he turned the long metal fork round to toast the teacake evenly. She saw how the firelight glinted in his blond hair and realized once more what an attractive man he was.

'Don't just sit there!' He looked up at her and smiled. 'You must butter the teacakes as fast as I toast them, you know.'

'Oh, certainly.'

Thea found it easier to kneel on the rug beside the table and, as she dug the knife into the creamy butter and watched the butter melt and sink in to the crisp brown surface of the teacakes, releasing a pleasing yeasty aroma, she felt aware of her surroundings and her own actions as never before.

In leaving her father's house she had left behind her all those years of simply being alive from day to day. Since then she had been happy at her aunt's house but perhaps she had still been too shocked by the change in her circumstances to do anything more than sleepwalk hopefully.

Now, sitting in the circle of firelight, sharing food and drink and light-hearted conversation with this attractive and clever man, she felt as though she had at last begun to live.

158

Chapter Twelve

'Was Rosalie Parker as dreadful as I imagined she would be?'

Aunt Marjorie sat with her legs curled under her at the foot of Thea's bed, warming her hands round her mug of cocoa. A small fire burned in the hearth but, nevertheless, they were both bundled up in flannel dressing gowns, and her aunt also wore woolly bed socks. And with her hair braided into two plaits tied with ribbons, Thea thought she looked like a schoolgirl in a boarding school story.

'She was pretty dreadful,' Thea told her. 'Ellie was embarrassed, she hardly spoke, just did as she was told meekly. I think she was glad when it was all over.'

'You surprise me. I should have thought Ellie would have enjoyed the whole experience.'

'Yes, so should I . . .'

But Thea had an idea why her friend had been so subdued. However, she had promised to keep Ellie's secret for a while longer.

'I'm surprised Rosalie didn't ask to have her photograph taken along with her pretty daughter,' Aunt Marjorie said.

'She dropped enough hints.' Thea smiled as she

remembered how Ellie's mother had posed with them – supposedly demonstrating the correct stance – and her *moue* of disappointment when Vernon had thanked her and asked her to step out of the way. 'But Vernon – Mr Gray – was very tactful.'

'I don't mind if you call him Vernon. I do. Do you like him?'

Thea sipped her cocoa thoughtfully before she replied. 'Yes, I like him. Very much, in fact. But there's something about him . . . Oh, I'm not sure . . . something I don't understand.'

'What's that?'

'I don't know how to explain – I can't quite find the words.'

'You've had an expensive education – so try.'

Aunt Marjorie was enjoying herself. Thea suddenly realized how lonely her aunt's life must be. Of course, she had many friends; friends connected with the Church and her various charities, but there must have been no one to have cosy late-night conversations like this with. Not until now.

She wondered if Aunt Marjorie and her mother used to share confidences when they were girls. She imagined they did. Whenever her aunt had visited her father's house Thea had seen how easily the sisters talked together – providing her father wasn't there, of course. Sometimes she had been a little jealous to see them so close. Her own sister, Imogen, had never sought that kind of relationship.

'All right, I'll do my best,' Thea said. 'But, first, did you know that Vernon was one of the judges at the beauty contest?'

'I only found out when I read the report in the newspaper. But I'm not surprised. That sort of nonsense would appeal to him – to his sense of humour.'

'Well, that's partly it, you see . . .'

'You don't like his sense of humour?'

'Oh, I do! He's witty and clever and fun to be with – and I

160

think he's kind-hearted – yes, I'm sure he is – and I know I've only met him twice, but I should have been able to guess at that other side of him, shouldn't I?'

'Other side?'

'Well, you know, the photographs you showed me. The way he has helped you in your work with the poor children . . .'

'Did you expect him to talk about it?'

'No, but—'

'Whether it's money or their own time and skills that they give, the best kind of people don't flaunt their generosity, dear.'

'I know – and it's not that . . .'

Aunt Marjorie frowned. 'So what is it? Thea, I don't understand at all.'

'I feel ashamed of myself to admit this because, much as I enjoy his company, I must have judged Vernon to be shallow – at least not exactly shallow, but simply not the kind of person to show concern about those who are not an accepted part of society.'

'You're quite wrong.' Aunt Marjorie looked stern and Thea realized that she'd upset her.

'Then I'm glad to be.

'Vernon not only comes to photograph my unfortunates whenever he can,' her aunt continued, 'but he often takes a particular interest in one or other of the children – asks about them – goes to visit the family. And I'm pretty sure he helps some of them financially, although he would never tell me.'

'I'm glad you've told me this,' Thea said.

And she was glad, but the things her aunt had just told her had left her more puzzled than before. She had liked Vernon from the start and it had not mattered to her that there might not be anything more serious behind the light-hearted façade. Why should there be? After all, he wasn't harming anyone and

161

the work he did must give a lot of pleasure.

So to be told these things about him by her aunt meant that her own ability to judge people was at fault. And that worried her. And, of course, now there was something else to worry about. Something that she did not want to share with her aunt.

After Aunt Marjorie had tucked her in as if she were a small child, placed the cinder guard at the fire, turned out the gaslight and retired, yawning, to her own room, Thea sat up again and gazed at the comforting glow from the hearth.

She remembered the two of them, Vernon and herself, sitting in his studio earlier that day. The rain had settled into a steady drizzle and it streamed down the large areas of glass, making ever-changing patterns on the walls and floor. They had pushed aside the table and the remains of their meal and he had insisted on pulling the armchairs closer to the gas fire.

'It's very convenient, no cleaning out of grates, no having to deal with dirty ashes, just the turning of a tap, the application of a match, and you have a fire that starts and stays and finishes clean!' Vernon said.

'You sound like an advertisement in one of the home journals my mother reads.'

'Do I? Do you know, I can't resist a good salesman, so when the man from the gas company told me how cheap and efficient gas heating was, I believed him instantly. But I did have my way about one thing.'

'What was that?'

'He wanted me to have a stove; as they do in Germany or Russia, but I have this very English fondness for visible flames. I don't just want a source of heat; I want a focus of attention. Do you know what I mean?'

'I do.' Thea gazed contentedly at the fire.

'But, of course, a truly living flame would be better still,' Vernon said. 'Can you imagine sitting here before a hearthful

162

of blazing logs? The rain outside . . . perhaps the wind rising . . . the skies growing darker?'

Vernon's voice had taken on a dreamy quality and Thea glanced at him to see that he was sitting back in his chair so that his face was in shadow. She could not see the expression on his face.

'Yes, I can imagine it . . .' she said uncertainly.

'Just you and me, Thea, cocooned in a warm, comfortable world, alone together . . .'

Vernon's words trailed away and she did not know how to respond. She didn't know whether she was supposed to respond. She waited and the only sound inside was the hiss of the fire, while outside the rain continued and the wind did indeed begin to rise.

And then Vernon leaned forward. 'Thea,' he said, 'do you have any idea how beautiful you are?'

She was unprepared for the intensity of his gaze and it disturbed her. But she did not have to answer his impossible question because, at that moment, the sound of the front-door bell, far below, jangled through the house.

Vernon sighed. 'That will be your aunt.'

He rose from his chair and offered his hand to Thea to help her up. But, when she was standing, he did not let go immediately. His clasp was firm and yet his touch was warm and his skin soft. 'You must come again,' he said. 'I want to take some more photographs.'

She found it difficult to look into his eyes. 'But why?'

'For my own pleasure. I have rarely found such an inspiration for my work.'

'Inspiration?'

'Photography is an art, Thea. Don't you know that? Painters have watercolours, oils, a canvas. I paint with light and shade.'

Thea could hear voices growing louder as two people came

163

up the stairs. One was her aunt's and the other Adie's. So she had not gone home.

'Adie has been working in the dark room.' Vernon had read her mind again.

He moved away from her and went to ignite the overhead gasolier. The flames sputtered into life and the resultant glow chased the intimate shadows from the room just as the door opened to reveal Aunt Marjorie.

And so they had come home together. Aunt Marjorie had been soaked through but as uncomplaining as ever, and Vernon had insisted on getting them a cab – and paying for it. He would have come home with them but her aunt had refused his offer. Had Thea imagined it or had Adie looked pleased when it became obvious that Vernon was staying?

Once home Thea's first concern was to get her aunt to change out of her wet clothes while she warmed the pan of broth that Nancy had left for them. Her aunt had had much to tell her about her work of the day so she had not noticed that Thea might have been a little more subdued than usual. Thea had dismissed from her mind all the uncomfortable feelings aroused by Vernon's words and actions until now.

Now, lying in bed alone, with time to relive the scene, she knew what it was that was worrying her most. Vernon had told her that she was beautiful, that he enjoyed being alone with her, that he wanted to see her again. Of course, the reason for seeing her again was to take her photograph. And yet she feared it was more than that.

She feared it because of the intensity of feeling she had seen in his eyes. She believed he was falling in love with her. She knew that she could never feel that way about him. Oh, she liked him well enough, and, after what her aunt had told her about him, she must respect him too. But that was all. When Vernon had taken her hand there had been no leap of the senses there had been when Robert Hedley had simply looked at her.

And Robert Hedley had probably never given her a second thought. Or if he had, the thoughts wouldn't be complimentary.

In spite of the fire, the room was cold. Thea had kept her thick dressing gown on and the lumps and ridges it formed were uncomfortable. She moved restlessly, knowing that she was far from sleep.

Outside the rain continued to drench the suburban streets and the wind rattled the window panes. Just under a mile away, in the heart of the city, miserable figures huddled in any available doorway. There would be no sleep for them.

Robert Hedley stood at his kitchen window and watched as his late-night visitor hurried away along the quayside, then dived into one of the narrow streets that would lead him to the home where he still lived with his parents.

It was a wild night. The moon shone intermittently through the scudding clouds and revealed the anchored sailing ships dipping and swaying in the choppy water. Here, in his eyrie above the Tyne, Robert imagined he could hear the slap of the water against the side of the ships and the creaks and groans of the sea-weathered timbers.

In spite of the foul weather, the occasional sculler-boat pulled out from the quay, heading up- or downstream with its passengers or even, bravely, for the south bank.

Further along the quayside he could see the lights of several taverns spilling out on to the glistening cobbles, and each burst of wind brought the sound of drunken voices. Normally he enjoyed the sights and sounds of the riverside. He enjoyed the feeling of being a privileged observer, living here because he chose to, and making the best of a life that had not started well. But tonight he was too troubled to give himself to the scene below.

He turned back to the table where his supper lay half finished. He had better eat it, he supposed, or Lily Roper would take it as an insult. Luckily the mix of sliced potatoes and bacon tasted almost as good cold, especially if it was washed down with the remainder of a jug of ale.

Robert finished the meal that Billy Reid's visit had interrupted; delaying the moment when he would open the packet that Billy had brought him. But, eventually, he pushed his plate aside, took out the postcards and spread them out across the table. He stared at them with disgust and rage.

He wished he'd never seen them – wished he'd never been walking by earlier that day when the lads from the drawing office had been sitting outside with their bait. Cold as it was they'd been enjoying a short spell of freedom. Perched on a pile of old timbers in the yard, they'd laughed as they'd passed what looked like bits of paper around. As he'd got nearer Robert had seen that they were postcards.

He thought he knew what they might be: saucy pictures of chorus girls. That kind of thing was pretty common and fairly harmless.

But, intent on the cards, they didn't see him coming, and he had a chance to look at their expressions. The laughter turned to sniggers, then stopped altogether. One of the lads pushed the cards into his mate's hands and, murmuring something inaudible, he hurried across the yard and back up the steps into the offices.

That was when the others looked up and saw Robert coming. Shoving the postcards into their pockets and gathering up their bait boxes, they hurried after their pal. But one of the postcards had fallen into a gap in the timber. Robert picked it up and was staring at it when Billy Reid, one of the office boys, appeared from nowhere.

'Would you like a full pack, Mr Hedley?' he asked.

Startled, Robert looked up to find the lad watching him warily. When he didn't answer immediately, Billy reached inside his waistcoat and brought out an envelope. He flipped it open and shuffled through about a dozen postcards so quickly that Robert had only the briefest glimpse of the photograph on each one. It was enough.

'Can you get one for me?'

'Of course, man, or I wouldn't have offered. Shall I bring it to work tomorrow?'

'No!' Robert said quickly. 'You'd better bring it to my home. Do you know where I live?'

'Of course I do. Everyone does. You're getting to be famous. Tonight, then, after supper. Right?'

'Right.'

Billy grinned as he replaced the envelope inside his waistcoat but Robert imagined he had seen a quickly concealed flash of scorn in the lad's eyes. And, as well as scorn, surprise.

Robert knew that his work with the children at the Charity School, and with the homeless, gave him a certain standing with boys and men who had a hard enough background themselves. But he also knew that both the way he lived and his growing reputation as an artist were a source of speculation and gossip.

As Robert returned to his own work in the drawing office he wondered whether Billy would talk about this; tell the other men that Robert Hedley was one of his customers. No, he thought not. Discretion was a vital part of this business. He hoped he was right because he didn't want anyone else to know of his interest, not until he'd found out more about it.

Billy was as good as his word. His banging on the outside door a short while ago had been enough to waken the dead; no doubt he feared that he wouldn't be heard above the shrieking wind and the clattering of loose tiles on the roofs of the old buildings. But Robert had been waiting for him, listening out, and Billy didn't have to hammer on the door for long before it opened.

'Can I come in, then?' The rain had plastered his hair to his skull and his narrow face was wet and shiny.

Robert hesitated. No one from the shipyard had ever been invited to his home.

'Hawway, man,' Billy said. 'It's pissing doon. I'll droon if I stand here much longer!'

Reluctantly, Robert stepped back. But he barred the way to the stairs which led up to his living quarters.

'Leave the door open,' he said. 'You're not staying long.'

'Huh! That's all the thanks I get. Coming out on a night like this and giving you the pictures I promised to me da. You realize I'll hev to get some more for him, don't you? And that'll cost – and then, there's me trouble . . .'

The light from the gaslamp outside revealed enough of Billy's face to show the cupidity and the contempt. Robert handed over the sum of money Billy requested and watched as the lad shoved it quickly into some kind of money belt under his shirt.

'Can't be too careful doon here,' he said. 'All kinds of thieves and rogues – and lasses too – who'd be willing to part me from me hard-earned cash.'

He turned to go and Robert put a hand on his arm. 'Look, Billy, you're a fool to get involved like this.'

'What are you on about? I'm doing you all a favour, aren't I?'

'But at what cost? What if the bosses found out? You'd lose

your job. Then what would you do? Work as a general labourer? You're not built for it; it would finish you off. This job in the office could mean an easier life for you. Hang on to it.'

'I don't do it for nowt, you know. He pays me well enough.'

'Who pays you?'

'Give over, man. You know fine well I'm not going to tell you.'

'I could guess,' Robert said. 'For a start it's probably one of the printers – doing a bit of moonlighting – extra hours at some backstreet print shop. I can find out without your help, Billy. And I will.'

'Suit yourself.' The look was defiant but Robert sensed that Billy was afraid. His next words confirmed it. 'If you go making trouble and if they think I helped you it would be bad for me. I thought you wanted them pictures because you're just like any man. I didn't think you were some kind of governor's nark.'

Billy stared up at him and Robert saw that the lad was puzzled as well as scared. Why would Mr Hedley be talking like this, he was wondering, when he had been so keen to buy some of the postcards himself?

Robert had no intention of explaining himself. Not to Billy or anyone else in the drawing office who was involved. What was important was to find the source of this evil trade. Not just the printer but the photographer.

'Gan on, then, Billy.' Robert reverted to his former way of talking to try to cheer the lad up. 'Get yourself yem and get warm and dry.'

'So you won't say nowt? You won't report me then?'

'Not this time.'

'Ah, man! Divven't say that. What's that supposed to mean?'

'It means it's got to stop.'

'Oh, yeah. That's grand, isn't it? Mr Hedley's got what he wants and now it's got to stop.'

'Billy, I won't report you. But, believe me, I'm going to track down who's responsible. So I'm giving you a friendly warning to get yourself out of it now.'

The lad had stared up at him a moment longer and then he'd shrugged and attempted a grin. 'Tarra, then, Mr Hedley. I'll think about what you've said.'

Billy had stepped out into the rain and Robert had closed and bolted the door behind him. Half wishing that he hadn't involved himself, he'd sighed and climbed the stairs back up to his quarters.

Now he pushed the pictures back into the envelope and, reaching for his tankard, he drained his ale. The pictures he'd just bought were pornographic. Robert knew that this kind of thing existed and had started almost as soon as the invention of photography.

Pornography was not to his taste; especially as he knew that some of the girls who took part were driven to it by poverty. It was a sordid trade but he'd never believed he had the right to impose his opinions on others.

But these postcards were different. He had recognized some of the girls. Someone who lived locally was exploiting some of the very women that people like the Barretts, Marjorie Gibb and himself were trying to help – women who might deplore what they were doing but had been driven to it by the grinding poverty of their lives.

But worse than that, some of these girls were not just poor, they were young, very young. In fact they were still children. Someone had taken them off the streets and washed them and dressed them in revealing clothes, quite inappropriate for their years, and set them amongst backgrounds that gave the appearance of luxury, fine wall hangings, rugs and cushions, and then done the most unimaginable things to them.

The postcard that he'd picked up in the yard that morning had two girls on it, splayed out across the cushions, exposing their innocence to titillate depraved minds. One of the girls he knew to be no more than ten years old.

Chapter Thirteen

February

'Ellie, come in, the photographs have arrived!'

The photographs were spread across the dining-room table. As she walked towards it Ellie was distracted to see her mother folding the morning paper hurriedly and pushing it down between her ample curves and the arm of the chair she was sitting on.

'Well? Aren't you going to look at them?'

'Oh, of course.' What on earth could have been in the paper to make her mother look so flustered?

Ellie glanced at the photographs and tried to summon a smile. She failed.

'I'm really surprised at you,' her mother said. 'I should have thought you would be thrilled.'

'I am,' she said. 'They're lovely.'

'Lovely? They're superb!' Her mother rose from her seat and made a theatrical gesture as she swept her hand over the photographs spread out across the dark green chenille cloth. The newspaper fell to the floor. 'Mr Gray has caught just the right mood,' she said. 'You look appealing and yet not *too* flirtatious. Not *common*, if you know what I mean.'

Ellie picked up the paper and scanned it quickly. 'Who is responsible for this?' she asked.

'Responsible for what, dear?' Her mother looked uneasy.

'This item in the gossip column.'

'Oh, that . . . er . . . I'm not sure . . .'

'Oh, Mother, of course you're sure. It even quotes you . . . "Mrs Rosalie Parker, who once used to grace the boards herself, is confident that her daughter, Eleanor, who recently was one of the winners in the Blondes and Brunettes beauty contest, will shortly be leaving her home in Newcastle in order to join the world famous Gaiety Theatre in London." '

Her mother looked like a naughty child and her complexion reddened as she flustered, 'Well . . . er . . . the young man asked me what I thought the outcome of the contest would be and I . . . er . . . I told him—'

'When did you tell him?'

'What do you mean?'

'When did you talk to the young man – I presume you mean the reporter? Was it at the party after the contest?'

'Er . . . no.'

'I didn't think so, otherwise it would have been in the newspaper before now. You've been to the newspaper office, haven't you?'

Her mother subsided into her chair. She looked wounded. 'Well, yes, I have. But I don't know why you're so cross. If you had my experience in the theatre, you would know that publicity is important.'

'But you don't know if what you've told him is true. Now, if Mr Edwardes doesn't want me we shall feel foolish.'

Her mother's smile vanished, but only for a moment. 'Just look at these photographs!' she said. 'As soon as Mr Edwardes sees them I'm sure he'll send for you!' Her mother had recovered. 'And now we must choose the best ones to send

173

him. And do you know, I've already decided that we needn't send any of you and Thea together, only you.'

'Why?'

Her mother sighed. 'Ellie, are you trying to be difficult today? Thea doesn't want a career on the stage – she doesn't want to be taken on at the Gaiety. There's no point in sending pictures of her.'

Ellie wanted to confess that neither did she want a career on the stage. She was no longer interested and perhaps she never had been, but she really couldn't face her mother's undoubted fit of hysterics if she said so. 'But Mr Gray said that Thea, with her dark good looks, provided a good contrast to me, a foil.'

'Mebbe.' Her mother narrowed her eyes. 'If you want my opinion that was just an excuse to get her there.'

'Really?'

'I'm seldom wrong about these things and I think the photographer might be sweet on your friend. Look at the way he kept her back to take more pictures.'

'Yes . . . that's true . . . but that was for her aunt, wasn't it? It seems they know each other.'

'I can't imagine how or why. But, nevertheless, I noticed the way he looked at her and the way he talked to her so sweetly, even if you didn't.'

'Well . . . perhaps I did notice, but I thought he was simply being kind. Because she didn't really want to have her picture taken, did she? She only came to keep me company; you know that, don't you? We should be grateful to Thea.'

Her mother glanced at her uneasily and Ellie wondered if she really believed that the reason Thea had left home was because she could no longer get along with her father. Ellie herself had accepted that explanation readily because she didn't want to think about it too deeply. She didn't want to admit to herself that she and her mother might have been responsible for some kind of final argument between Thea and Mr Richardson by asking Thea to enter the beauty contest.

'Well, yes,' her mother said at last. 'You couldn't have entered the contest without her, so if anything comes of this, we won't forget her, will we? I mean, if you become rich and famous you will find ways to be kind to your childhood friend.'

Ellie didn't know whether to laugh or cry. Her mother's eyes were shining; her romantic imagination had obviously taken her to some wonderful golden future where Ellie was a star of the Gaiety, rich in her own right, and perhaps about to marry an earl or a duke. For didn't every Gaiety Girl have an ermine cloak in her bottom drawer?

Perhaps she was imagining herself being interviewed by the world's press . . . *'Ah, my daughter is still the same sweet-natured child,'* she would say, *'faithful to her friends and so good to her dear father and me . . .'*

The trouble was that Ellie didn't want that kind of future at all. Sometimes she wished that she had never entered the beauty contest. Except that, if she hadn't, she might not have met Lewis . . . no, she certainly wouldn't have met Lewis . . . and since she had, her dreams and ambitions had changed completely.

She knew that her mother would be disappointed. Marriage to an author, even an author who was rich and famous, did not compare with marriage to an aristocrat. But Ellie would be able to point out that the chances of the latter were extremely tenuous.

They didn't even know whether Mr Edwardes would want her to go to London and, if she did, she would probably end up in the chorus, no matter what her mother thought of her talents. And she was sure that there were more chorus girls who didn't marry dukes than those who did.

But Lewis was here now, and he loved her. He told her so every time they met. Her mother was sentimental. She would tell anyone who would listen that she had given up the prospects of a dazzling theatrical career in order to marry Henry Parker. Ellie knew that her parents loved each other; anyone who saw them together was in no doubt of that. So surely her mother would want the same kind of happiness, the same kind of marriage, for her daughter.

But the trouble was that Lewis hadn't actually proposed to her . . . not yet. Oh, if only he would, then she could risk her mother's anger and disappointment and tell her why she didn't want to go to London after all.

'Well, then, Ellie, I can see that I'm not going to get any help from you, so I'll ask your father to help me. He won't be long now, he's just going through the new music with the pianist.'

'Oh, yes, do ask Papa!' Ellie said. Her mother glanced at her suspiciously so she hurried on, 'After all, you and Father – after your years in the theatre – know much more about that kind of thing than I do, don't you?'

'Yes, but—'

'And it's such a lovely day. After all the wind and rain we've been having the sun is actually shining. I think I should call on Thea and persuade her to come with me to the coast. We will take the train to Whitley Bay . . . or Cullercoats, perhaps . . . and walk along the beach and I shall treat her to lunch at Watt's Café.'

'Well—'

'It must be miserable for her living with her dull old aunt. She deserves a treat, don't you think?'

'Well, yes, I suppose—'

'I mean, you said yourself that we should be grateful to her.'

'Did I?'

'Certainly. You said if anything comes of this, we should never forget her.' Her mother smiled and Ellie saw that she was entering her dream world again. She rose from the table and started to walk towards the door. 'So I'll go and get my coat on, shall I?'

'Wait, dear.' Ellie turned to find her mother rummaging in her handbag. 'Let this be my treat.' She held out a sovereign.

Ellie coloured. 'No, Mama, that's too much.'

Her mother smiled. 'What a sweet child you are. But I want it to be my treat – a real treat. And don't go to the beach café, nice as it was when you were a child. You don't want to sit at a trestle table with an oilskin cloth and sand blowing in every time someone opens the door. Go and have lunch at the Waverley – a proper hotel with nice white cloths and a silver service. You've got to start getting used to these little luxuries, you know.'

'All right, Mama.'

Ellie took the coin reluctantly and hugged her mother before hurrying from the room. She went up to her room and put on her outdoor clothes, then hurried down the two flights of stairs to the ground floor where she could hear Miss Bell, the accompanist, going through some new music.

She hurried out of the house before her father could emerge from the dance studio and ask her innocently where she was going. She didn't know whether she would be able to continue the pretence. For, although it was true that she was going to the coast, she had never had any intention of calling on Thea.

From the moment the delivery boy had brought the photographs to the house early that morning, Ellie had known that she had to see Lewis. Somehow she had to make him propose to her.

* * *

Aunt Marjorie sat at the table she used as a desk and unwrapped the parcel methodically. The string would be wound up neatly and the paper folded, then both placed in the box she kept especially for that purpose. Thea, sitting by the fire, glanced up from her book and smiled fondly. No matter how keen Aunt Marjorie was to discover the contents of the parcel, she could not break her prudent habits.

A moment later, Thea heard a slight gasp. 'Thea, come here,' her aunt said. She was looking down intently at the object still concealed from Thea by the wrappings in which it lay.

'Is something the matter?'

'No . . . just come and see.'

Thea stood behind her aunt and stared at the full-length photograph in the plain silver frame. Underneath the glass her sepia image was mounted under an oval cut-out. If you hadn't known the truth of it, she could have been standing on the balcony of a real ballroom, gazing dreamily across a real garden, instead of posing beside a prop balustrade in front of a painted backdrop.

Somehow Vernon had managed to instil the effect of moonlight falling on the girl – was it really her? – and on the garden behind her; a pale, ethereal light which gradually merged into the shadows of the trees in the distance. The folds of the creamy-white dress looked fluid; they shimmered as they fell.

She remembered Vernon telling her that, as a photographer, he 'painted with light'. She began to comprehend what he meant.

'Is there just one photograph?' she asked.

'Yes, just the one. Here's a note . . .' Her aunt unfolded the paper and read it quickly. 'Vernon explains that he didn't think it worth sending those taken earlier with Ellie. Pleasant

178

but not exceptional, he calls them. Whereas this . . .' Aunt Marjorie shook her head as if she could hardly believe what she saw.

But it had not been those earlier photographs that Thea had meant. It was the last one she was wondering about. The photograph for which she had let her hair down and gazed straight into the lens. Perhaps the pose had not been successful.

'Now I understand why my mother – your grandmother – was so captivated by the art of photography,' Aunt Marjorie said. 'If only she could have seen this portrait of you. But then your grandmother never saw you at all.'

Thea watched as her aunt pulled the frame support out and placed the photograph carefully towards the back of the table. Next she wound up the string and folded the paper. When she had done, she clasped her hands and rested them on top of the folded paper. All the time she was doing this she had avoided catching Thea's eyes. She looked troubled, and when Nancy knocked on the door and brought in a tray of coffee and biscuits, she seemed glad of the interruption.

When they were settled at either side of the fireplace, her aunt's continued unease prompted Thea to ask a question she had never asked before. 'Why did I never meet my grand-parents?'

'Well . . . you know they went to live abroad?'

'Yes, in France. But I seem to remember my parents going to visit them when I was small. They took Imogen but they left me at home.'

'With your nursemaid.'

'Yes, of course. But why didn't they take me?'

'I think you were suffering from some childhood illness . . . I can't remember what . . . but your grandmother was ill, dying, and she wanted to see us all.' Her aunt stared bleakly into the fire.

Thea frowned. She had been very small when it had happened – three or four, perhaps – so she couldn't remember the details. There had been piles of cases and boxes in the hall; her father had shouted instructions which her mother and the servants had scurried to obey. Nanny Douglas alone had sat quite still, impervious to the commotion and secure in her authority as she held baby Imogen, and waited until her employers were ready to set off.

And when they had gone at last, small though she was, Thea knew that the house was a happier place. Sarah, the nursery maid left in charge of her, had indulged her in ways that would never have been allowed when her parents were there. She had been carried about and petted, and given cake and sweetmeats, and allowed to wander as she pleased about the house, leaving a trail of toys and crumbs – with no one to scold her.

She remembered playing in the garden with Sarah and a young man Sarah said was her brother. They had run about and tumbled and laughed unrestrainedly. Could she really have been ill at the time?

'Why were my grandparents living abroad?'

'Your grandfather retired from the business – handed everything over to your father when he married your mother. Your grandmother was already quite poorly and he wanted an easier life for her – somewhere a little warmer.' Aunt Marjorie smiled a little sadly. 'My parents were fond of France, we had spent so many family holidays there.'

'So they retired there before I was born?'

'Yes.'

'And they never wanted to see me – their first grandchild?'

'Thea . . . it wasn't easy for them . . .'

'Why? Because of my grandmother's illness?'

'Yes.'

180

But her aunt had answered too quickly.

'So . . . my grandparents didn't particularly care to see me—'

'Thea—'

'And yet Grandfather obviously cared enough to make some sort of financial provision for me – a small sum of my own you called it.'

'Yes, he did.'

'A dutiful grandfather.'

Thea had never seen her aunt looking so uncomfortable and she had no wish to make her more so by questioning her further. And, in any case, she didn't know what questions to ask. She sensed there was a mystery but the implications were so frightening that she shrank from discovering more.

She watched as her aunt reached under the table to put the brown paper and string in the box she kept there and, suddenly, as Aunt Marjorie straightened up again, breathing heavily and a little red in the face, Thea asked, 'Who was my mother smiling at that day?'

Her aunt stared at her. 'What day? What are you talking about?'

'In the photograph – the last one in the album – you and she are on a promenade somewhere – in France, was it?'

'Yes, Biarritz.'

'Who took the photograph?'

'I've told you . . . your grandmother was the photographer in the family . . . She took most of the photographs of your mother and me together . . .'

'But not this one.'

Aunt Marjorie looked resigned. 'You're right. But why do you say that?'

'It's the way she's smiling.'

'Your mother used often to smile in those days. She was

181

happy, carefree . . . She was so young then, younger than you are now.'

'But there's something more . . . It's – oh, I don't know – it's as if she had a secret – a wonderful secret.'

Aunt Marjorie sighed. 'She had.'

Thea was surprised by her aunt's frank answer and encouraged to go on. 'She was in love, wasn't she? In love with the person who took the photograph?'

'Yes.'

Thea felt a sense of exhilaration. 'Was it my father? I mean, I know she was very young when she married, and whatever has become of their marriage, she must have loved him once—'

She stopped, appalled by what she had said. Her aunt seemed equally appalled. They stared at each other and the silence lasted for so long that Thea thought she had lost her chance of solving any mystery there might be.

Finally, when her aunt spoke, she seemed to be staring at a point beyond Thea, staring back down the years perhaps. 'No, it wasn't your . . . it wasn't.'

'But she loved him – whoever it was.'

'Oh, yes. She loved him. And he loved her – so very much, Thea. You must believe that.'

Thea frowned. She couldn't understand why it was so important for her to believe that this man had loved her mother so much, so long ago. 'So, why didn't they marry?'

'I don't know. They should have done.'

Her aunt shook her head. It was a signal that she wasn't going to say any more. Then she rose from her chair and gathered up their coffee cups, saying she would take them back to the kitchen herself. Thea watched her in silence.

When she was alone she stared out of the window as the first sunshine for days struggled through the clouds to reflect on the wet roofs of the houses opposite. She sat very still but her mind ranged restlessly through all the possible explanations for her aunt's words.

They should have done.

So why didn't they? Because he was promised to someone else? Then why had her mother responded to him in such a way? Unless she hadn't known until it was too late. That must be it. Her mother had fallen desperately in love with someone and then discovered that, for some reason, she couldn't have him. So, sad and disillusioned, she had agreed to marry one of her own father's employees, a man who had promised to take over the business and allow his master to retire and look after his sick wife.

Her poor mother . . . She had probably never smiled in that way again. All these years she had been married to a man she didn't love . . . No wonder the atmosphere in that house had been so oppressive.

And yet . . .

Her father had done well out of the transaction, so why couldn't he have been more pleasant to the beautiful girl who had brought him so much? Thea closed her eyes and tried to stop worrying about the vexed question of her parents' marriage. Now that she had left home she probably wouldn't ever know the answers to any of it . . . not even why her father seemed to hate her so.

Lily Roper stood with a mug of tea in her favourite place at the kitchen window of Robert Hedley's home. It was a fine day, bright but cold, and she watched as people hurried by on the quayside below. The crews of more than one of the sailing ships were busy on deck as they prepared to sail with the evening tide.

Lily wondered where they were going and what cargoes

they were carrying, and she wondered what it would be like to be one of the passengers who bought a passage to America or Canada and a whole new life.

She smiled as the idea came to her that she had a new life – of a sort. Now that she was working for Mr Hedley she had a bit money of her own. She could spend it on the bairns, on meat and milk, and even take a ticket from the tallyman to get them some new clothes.

She'd had to tell Patrick about the job. If he'd found out of his own accord, he'd have raised the roof. He was the master in his house and nobody dared do anything without his permission. That was why the older two lads had left home as soon as they could. So, she'd told him from the start and promised to give him a bit extra drinking money. That had kept him happy.

Lily's expression darkened. Thank the Lord Patrick had never found out about the other thing she used to do.

She almost burned with shame when she remembered how she used to go out at night – when she should have been home with the bairns – and hang about in the alleyways with the other poor women, waiting for some filthy, drunken brute to come along and relieve his base feelings on her for a bit small change. She'd been driven to it because she hadn't done her sums right and she'd got behind with the rent. With the threat of homelessness hanging over them she'd decided to earn a bit extra the only way that was open to her. Prostitution.

The first time she'd done it she'd been shaking so much that the man had almost felled her with one angry blow before he grabbed her with both hands and shoved her back against the slimy bricks of the wall behind her. He brought his face near to hers and, when he opened his mouth, she nearly gagged at the smell of spirits and stale tobacco.

'Keep still, bitch, or you'll get nowt for your pains,' he

snarled before pushing her clothes aside and shoving into her so hard that she thought he would tear her apart. She felt the rough bricks scraping at her back through her thin clothes as he moved inside her and she didn't know where she hurt the most.

When he'd done, he buttoned himself up, then tossed a handful of coppers on the cobbles and laughed as Lily kneeled to retrieve them. She waited in the shadows until he'd gone, then shoved the money into her pocket and hurried home.

Janey and Joe were asleep, thank the Lord. Lily didn't know how she could look into the eyes of her innocent bairns. She sat down and spread the coins out on the kitchen table. And then, as she looked at them, she started to laugh and cry. There, amongst the small change, lay a half-sovereign.

So she'd had the last laugh after all, for she was sure that her first customer hadn't meant to pay her that much. If it hadn't been for that half-sovereign Lily might never have gone out at night again.

Eventually she'd got hardened to it – but she'd never enjoyed it – and she didn't believe the women who told her that, with the right man, you could actually get pleasure from it.

Now, thanks to Robert Hedley, a living saint in Lily's eyes, she had put that kind of life behind her. She turned from the window and went to the table to sit and eat her bit of bread and dripping.

It was only when she had finished that she noticed the card lying on the floor beneath the table. She bent to pick it up. As she stared at the postcard she felt her guts heave and the bile rise in her throat. She was aware of the scalding tears running down her cheeks and she knew they were tears of rage. She was angry with herself for having believed, for one moment, that Robert Hedley was different from any other man.

Chapter Fourteen

'Well, I'm not sure . . .'

The woman – Lewis's housekeeper, no doubt – remained standing in the doorway; she observed Ellie with narrowed blue eyes.

She was tall and large-boned; the jet beads sewn on to the black silk of her dress ran down from the high ruffled neckline to the old-fashioned pointed waistline in shiny rows. Her fading auburn hair was swept back and up from her still-handsome face.

'Mr Sinclair does not like to be interrupted while he's working,' she said.

In spite of the bright sunshine, the wind slanting in across the North Sea was bitingly cold; Ellie began to shiver.

'Believe me,' she said, 'I'm not just a follower, someone who wants to bother Mr Sinclair for an autograph.'

The woman's expression remained doubtful.

Ellie fumbled in her purse. 'Here's my card,' she said. 'If you take this and show it to Mr Sinclair he will confirm that I am a friend of his.'

The housekeeper took the card and stepped back. 'Wait here,' she said.

Ellie blessed the moment when her mother had succumbed to the persuasions of the owner of the printer's shop on Shields Road and had ordered rather grand calling cards for each of them.

For a moment she thought that the woman was going to shut the door in her face and leave her standing on the top step but, almost as an afterthought, the housekeeper stepped back and ushered Ellie into the oak-panelled hallway.

She left the front door open but closed the half-glazed porch door and then hurried along the passage and up the richly carpeted stairs.

Ellie had never been inside one of these imposing houses overlooking the sea at Cullercoats, although one of the girls in her class at school lived in one of them and had invited her favoured friends home to tea now and then. Most of the houses were owned by ship owners or wealthy industrialists; business people who were not necessarily from the North East. In the past the little fishing village had been a fashionable resort, even for the aristocracy.

While she waited Ellie glanced round at her surroundings. The door of the front room was open and she peeped inside. Light streamed in through the tall bay windows to reveal solid mahogany furniture, a rich oriental carpet, more oak panelling – this time a rich golden colour, gilt-framed mirrors, and an abundance of fine art pottery and crystal ornaments. There was a black marble clock with gilt engravings on the mantelpiece and gold-framed paintings of sea scenes on the walls.

The room was supremely comfortable, but, more than that, there was an impression of effortless luxury. Ellie was impressed but she was also surprised. This was not what she would have expected to find in a house owned by Lewis Sinclair. The furnishings were rich but, somehow, dated; perhaps a touch provincial. Lewis was a fashionable author who, until very recently, had lived in London. Surely his taste would have been more *à la mode*?

But perhaps Lewis did not own this house – perhaps he was simply renting it. That was more likely. Ellie knew that some quite famous painters, including the American Winslow Homer, had taken houses in this area in the previous century.

'Will you come upstairs now?'

The housekeeper had returned and Ellie blushed when she realized that her curiosity had led her right into the front room. 'I'm sorry. . .' she began, but the woman smiled.

'I don't mind you looking at my fine things,' she said. 'Especially as I can see that you appreciate them.'

Ellie wondered at the woman's choice of words as she followed her up two flights of stairs. Was she not the house-keeper, then, but the owner of this house? Ellie considered this idea and wondered why she wanted to reject it. The woman was well-dressed and confident. Why should she not be the owner of the house? And yet . . . there was something about her . . . something about the way she spoke . . . just a hint of the local accent that suggested a more humble back-ground.

But then her husband could have been a self-made man – a local man made good – just like the fathers of some of the girls at Ellie's old school who, nevertheless, had turned up their noses at the idea of befriending the daughter of the dancing master.

'Here we are,' her guide said when they reached the landing of the second floor. 'Mr Sinclair has taken the top two floors from me, but not the attics. My live-in maids are in there.' The woman gave a hint of a smile.

She knows what I've been thinking, Ellie thought; she's making her position clear to me. Thankfully no answer seemed to be required and, at any rate, at that moment, Lewis opened the door that led to the room at the front of the house and hurried forward.

'Ellie, what a surprise! Come in. Mrs Fleming, could we have a tray of tea? But wait – Ellie, are you hungry? It must be nearly lunchtime . . .'

'Yes, I am.' Lewis looked flustered and Ellie caught his mood. She had blurted out the truth and then wished she hadn't for it just seemed to fluster Lewis even more.

'Oh . . . ah . . . Mrs Fleming . . .?' he said.

The woman smiled. 'Don't worry. I'll send up something tasty. In about half an hour.'

She hurried downstairs, black silk rustling, and Ellie marvelled how such a large woman seemed to move so gracefully.

'She's magnificent, isn't she?' Lewis stood with one hand on the stair rail as he too watched her fluid progress into the lower regions of the house. 'You can see why Cornelius Fleming fell in love with her.'

Ellie's eyes widened as she stared at him and he smiled. He took her hand. 'I can see you don't know the story,' he said as he led her into the front room. 'It's very romantic and I'm sure it will appeal to you, but first you must tell me why you have come here today.'

'Shouldn't I have done? I mean, you told me where you lived . . . you wouldn't have done that if you hadn't wanted me to visit, would you?'

'Sweetheart, don't look at me like that, as if you think I'm angry with you.'

'Are you angry?'

'Of course not. I'm just surprised. And as you can see . . .' he indicated a desk set in to the bay window recess. It was covered with sheets of paper, 'I'm working. Before Mrs Fleming knocked on my door I was with my detective, Hugh Martin, in a turret room in a Scottish castle trying to discover not only who has murdered the laird, but also how the culprit managed to leave the room when the door was locked from the inside!'

'And I've interrupted you.'

'And I welcome the interruption. My poor brain was going round in circles trying to solve the problem.'

'I'm not surprised.'

Lewis raised his eyebrows questioningly. 'Why's that?'

'Well, there's also the puzzle of how Mr Martin got into the locked room, in the first place, isn't there?'

Lewis's eyes widened even further and then he burst out laughing. 'Ellie, you're wonderful. I wonder how many people realize that there's such a sharp brain inside that sweet head of yours.'

Ellie flushed and dropped her head. She hid her embarrassment by pretending to concentrate on unbuttoning her coat. She had never done well at school, not like Thea, but she had never thought of herself as stupid. It was not because she was lazy, either – she knew she could have applied herself if she'd wanted to – it was simply that she had never thought a higher education was important.

She slipped out of her coat and gave it to Lewis. While he laid it over the back of an armchair she removed her hat and, walking over to him, laid it on top of her coat.

'So you're really not angry?'

'I told you. Perhaps I looked distracted when you arrived, but I'm not angry.'

'Then show me.'

'Show you what?'

'That you're not angry.'

'How shall I do that?' Lewis frowned as though he was puzzled but he had begun to smile as he moved closer and took her into his arms.

The kiss that followed left them both breathless and disorientated.

'There . . .' he said, and his voice was husky. 'Has that convinced you?'

'No.' Ellie placed her hands on his shoulders and slid them round to meet and clasp behind his neck.

'No? Then I'll have to try harder.'

This time Ellie followed the instinctive prompting of her body and pressed herself close to him. She heard his gasp of surprise and then he placed one hand low on her back and pressed her even closer. She hardly had time to acknowledge the leap of desire within her when his other hand moved between them and began to caress her breasts.

The touch of his fingers seemed to burn though the fine silk of her blouse, arousing her even further. She imagined what it would be like to have those fingers probe beneath the silk and brush across her skin. The excitement growing within her seemed almost unbearable. She began to lose all sense of time and place and even of identity.

It was Lewis who brought the moment to an end. He stepped away from her but he took hold of her hands.

'Ellie, we must stop,' he said. 'I'm sorry . . .'

'Sorry? Why?'

She was trembling. She was grateful when he put his arm around her and led her to a small sofa near to his writing desk. When she was seated he sat in his chair – putting the desk between them. His back was to the window and, with his face in shadow, Ellie couldn't see his expression. She felt at a disadvantage as she waited for him to explain.

'Because I shouldn't take advantage of you. You're so young—'

'I'm nineteen!'

Lewis smiled. 'So much younger than I am, then. And inexperienced.'

'Does that matter?'

'Don't look so worried. I'm glad you're inexperienced – but that's selfish of me.'

'Selfish?'

'What man wouldn't want to teach you the ways of love? But I shouldn't even be talking to you like this. Put it down to my lack of a proper upbringing.'

Ellie frowned. She didn't know what he meant by that, nor was she sure, even now, what his intentions might be. She was sure that he loved her. He had to, didn't he, after the way he had just kissed her? And the way his hands had moved over her body . . .?

She'd had some half-formed idea, prompted by schoolgirl lore, that if she allowed him to give way to his passions, he would be forced to ask her to marry him. That's what a gentleman would do, wasn't it? But now was he suggesting that he wasn't a gentleman?

She felt the hot tears well up and scald her cheeks as they began to flow freely. Before she could fumble in her skirt pocket for her handkerchief, Lewis left his seat and came round to kneel at her feet. He gave her a clean white handkerchief and, as she dabbed at her eyes, he said, 'Ellie, what am I going to do with you?'

'Marry me,' she said without thinking, and then covered her face with the handkerchief and held her breath while she waited for his answer.

It seemed the longest time she had ever waited for anything before she felt him pull the handkerchief away from her eyes. He held her hands and looked at her solemnly.

'Is that what you want?'

'Yes.'

'But what about your career? What about being a Gaiety Girl?'

'Mr Edwardes will not ask me to join the Gaiety, whatever my mother believes.'

'But if he did ask you?'

'I shouldn't go. Oh, Lewis, I don't want a career. All I want to do is to marry you! Don't you care for me at all?'

'Of course I care – and there's nothing I'd like better than to ask you to marry me.'

'Then for goodness' sake ask me!'

Lewis laughed but he looked troubled. 'Ellie, it's not straightforward—'

'Oh, no! You're not married already, are you?'

'No.'

'What then?'

'I'm older than you are – I'm thirty – and already too old to continue kneeling like this.'

'Eleven years! That's nothing!'

Lewis grinned lopsidedly as he rose to his feet and pulled the chair round so that he could sit facing her without the desk between them. 'Perhaps not,' he said. 'But . . . Ellie, have you read any of my books?'

The question caught her completely unawares. Could Lewis possibly be suggesting that if she hadn't read any, he wouldn't marry her?

'Yes I have,' she said, and hesitated, deciding to be honest. 'I've read one, *The Mystery of the Single Glove*. But I promise you I'll read more – I'll read all of them!'

'Sweetheart, it's not a test. I would still love you if you had not read any of them – if you had never heard of Lewis Sinclair. But as you have read one, I'm going to ask you a question.'

'I loved it – I couldn't put it down. Now I know why Thea gets so much pleasure from reading!'

'That wasn't the question – although, naturally, I'm very pleased with your answer. But what do you think of my detective hero, Hugh Martin?'

'What do I think of him?'

'Do you like him?'

'Yes I do.'

'Why?'

'Oh . . . because he's so clever – but not just clever, he's funny and kind and he's fair. He likes to know why people do the things they do.'

Lewis's eyes widened. 'That was the perfect answer,' he said. 'That is exactly how I want the reader to see him. But would you invite him into your home, Ellie?'

'How could I? He doesn't exist.'

'But if he did?'

'Yes . . . yes, I would.'

'In spite of his past?'

'His past? Oh, you mean because he had been to prison, poor man.'

'No, Ellie, don't feel sorry for him. Hugh Martin was a thief; he deserved to go to prison. But, fortunately for him, he learned the error of his ways and, when he had served his time, he decided to put his knowledge of the criminal fraternity to good use and work on the right side of the law.'

'Exactly. So why – if he existed – shouldn't I invite him to my home?'

'Because in the real world, my darling, he might not be allowed to put his past behind him. Real life isn't so straightforward.'

'Straightforward . . . real life . . . Do you mean . . .? Oh, Lewis, what are you saying?'

'I have based Hugh Martin on my own experience.'

'Your own . . .?'

'My publishers know, of course, and they would be prepared to stand by me if ever it became known that Lewis Sinclair – not my real name by the way – was once a thief.'

Ellie gasped.

Lewis continued, 'In fact the publicity – horrible though it would be – might help to sell books. You know the kind of thing that would be written – "Reformed criminal earns an honest living by writing about crime!" But, reformed as I surely am, how could I expect a sweet honest girl to marry me?'

Ellie stared at him in horror. At first she had been confused, not sure where fiction ended and fact began. She still half hoped that Lewis was making it up. That would be cruel of him, but perhaps it really was some kind of test to discover whether she truly loved him.

But the way he was looking at her now, so hopelessly, so despairingly, gradually convinced her that every word of it was the truth.

Strangely, she did not feel like crying. The more upset Lewis looked, the calmer she became.

'You should have told me,' she said at last. 'You knew that I . . . that I was attracted to you. You should have told me.'

'Ellie, you're so young – no, don't bridle like that. When I met you, you had just entered that ridiculous beauty contest—'

'Ridiculous! My mother—'

'No, listen to me. I thought the only reason that you had entered was to catch Mr Edwardes' eye, and I was right about that, wasn't I?'

'Yes, but it was my mother's idea—'

'I know that now. But at the time I thought you had your heart set on a theatrical career. I thought you were simply flirting with me.'

'How could you?'

'I know, I know, forgive me. But I found you so delightful, so lovely, that I simply couldn't resist you. I thought I would enjoy your company while I could and then you would go to London – leave me – forget about me – no harm done.'

'No harm done!' Ellie shook her head.

'Sweetheart, I'm sorry.'

'Sorry you may be but it's too late now. How am I supposed to stop loving you? If this was in a book you were writing, how would you solve that problem?'

Chapter Fifteen

Mrs Fleming came up to tell them that lunch was ready. Lewis led the way to his dining room next door, but he heard the two women murmur softly before Ellie disappeared in the direction of the bathroom.

One of the maids was to serve the meal but, before she went downstairs, Mrs Fleming paused on the top step and looked at him keenly. Lewis wondered if she'd noticed how subdued Ellie was now in contrast to her vivacity when she had arrived.

At the table Ellie was polite to the maidservant but otherwise silent. The meal of lemon sole fried in butter, potatoes and peas, followed by a milk jelly, was simple but delicious and Lewis couldn't help observing that, subdued or not, Ellie enjoyed every morsel of it.

The image of her mother came into his mind. Rosalie Parker was pretty and shapely but certainly overweight. Was that Ellie's destiny? Perhaps. But he didn't care. No doubt Ellie's father found great comfort in the arms of his buxom charmer and, in any case, Ellie had the advantage of having a sharp brain. A brain it seemed that she had never bothered to exercise before.

When coffee had been served and the maid left them alone, she broke her silence. 'Why did you come to live in Northumberland?'

'The countryside is so beautiful – the wide skies, the moors, the castles, the rugged coastline. A writer responds to the untamed elements – to nature . . .'

A spasm of irritation crossed her face. 'As far as I know you don't visit the country and you don't write about nature.'

'And I needed to get away from London, from the hustle and bustle of the city. There were too many distractions to keep me from my work.'

'But you seem to have found distractions in Newcastle – another city – where you visit the restaurants and theatres. Why don't you admit it, Lewis? You left London to avoid anyone who might expose your past, didn't you?'

'Ellie—'

'Didn't you?'

He sighed. He knew he would have to tell her. 'You're almost right. You must believe me when I tell you that I accepted long ago that my secret might be discovered some day. The more successful a person becomes the more people there are who would seem to take a delight in trying to pull you down. Envious people, Ellie, who cannot achieve much themselves, so they take comfort in spoiling the reputation of others.'

She remained silent and watchful.

'So, as I say, I had accepted that it could happen to me but I could not risk having someone else hurt—'

'Someone else?'

'Someone I might care for.'

'And there was someone you cared for?'

He reached across the table and took her hand. 'There was. I fell in love—' She tried to pull her hand away but he gripped it the tighter. 'I told her the truth about my past and she said she didn't care. I told her we'd leave London and I came ahead to find a home for us. She didn't follow me.'

He watched in amazement as Ellie's smile returned. She slipped out of her seat and came to stand over him. He looked up as she took his face in her hands and leaned forward to kiss him. He could smell her perfume; see the way the silk of her blouse moulded itself to her breasts. He wanted to bury his head in those breasts but she moved back.

'And do you still love her?' she asked.

'You know the answer to that.'

Ellie was weary after all the talking, after all the emotion, but pleasantly so. She stood at the window of Lewis's writing room and looked out across the bay. The fishermen's boats – cobles, they were called – had been hauled up on to the boat field opposite the row of grand houses. The wind had dropped and the sea lay flat and grey under the darkening sky. She could see the lights in the windows of the huddled cottages on the cliff tops overlooking the bay.

She knew she had stayed too long. She had kept Lewis from his work and she must never do that again. But, today, there had been things to be settled between them, things that had to be done, decisions that had to be made.

Lewis came up behind her and nuzzled her neck. 'I'd better come with you to the station. In fact I'll come up to town with you on the train, then put you in a cab to take you home.'

She half turned and smiled. 'Good. But before we go, do you know you haven't told me about Mrs Fleming. You said her story was romantic.'

'It is. Look . . .' With one arm round her waist, he used the other to point to the fishermen's cottages. 'Jess Rodgerson, as she was then, was born in one of those cottages. She grew up there with her mother and father and two older brothers. She was a beautiful girl – tall and lithe and flame-haired. She attracted the attention of more than one artist. She became a model for them.

'They painted her baiting the hooks for the men, or carrying her creel – her basket of fish – or standing on the cliff top with the wind in her hair as she looked out to sea, waiting for the menfolk to come home. You can find paintings of her in many an art gallery both in England and in Europe and even America. She was famous.'

'Was Cornelius Fleming an artist?'

'No, he was the son of an industrialist, the owner of an engineering works. They had a house in London but they kept one here, near their roots. This house.'

'So Cornelius fell in love with Jess and married her!'

'Yes. But it wasn't quite so straightforward. First of all he had to ask her brothers – her father was dead by then – for permission to court her. He found that his feelings were returned, so he paid for her to be tutored in speech and manners and deportment—'

'But why? Oh, of course . . . his family.'

'Exactly. By the time he introduced her to his parents, Jess was the perfect lady. They were married, Jess was carried off to London where she lived in style and produced a fine son to carry on the family business.'

'What a wonderful story! But Cornelius . . .?'

'Jess is a widow now. She has given up the London house to her son and daughter-in-law, and come back to live here, although she visits them often. Meanwhile it amuses her to rent rooms now and then to interesting people – artists, writers, theatricals, even.'

Ellie turned and put her arms round him. 'What a wonderful story. I'm glad you told me it. But, now, I'll have to think up a story of my own to explain to my mother why I've been out so long.'

No matter what part of the school building you were in, Robert mused, even here on the top floor, it seemed you could never escape from the smells of polish, disinfectant and boiled cabbage – the first two smells at least, quite alien to the home lives of the children who were now quietly working by the beams of the newly installed electric lights suspended from the high ceiling. All charity and board school buildings had rooms with high ceilings because it was believed – hoped – that the collected odours of the unwashed children would rise far above the heads of the teaching staff.

This room, at the very end of the brown-tiled corridor, had been set aside for the art class. To save the desk tops, old newspapers had been spread on each one. Robert had asked for tables and easels but, of course, there was no money for that. Some of the Board had even objected to the purchase of the paper and painting materials until Miss Gibb and her friends had offered to meet half the cost.

The children were quiet, their concentration intense. Robert moved from desk to desk, looking at the work in progress and murmuring advice and encouragement. He took a pencil from the hand of one of the boys and made a few adjustments to the drawing of a sailing ship.

'That's the way the sails look with the wind in them, isn't it?' he said.

The lad stared at his drawing for a moment; it was good but he was too careful a draughtsman, too precise; now a few strokes had given his composition life. He looked up and grinned. 'Ee, Mr Hedley,' he said, 'that's champion!'

It was late. When Robert gave the command the children began to clear up. They formed an orderly queue and moved one by one to place their drawings or paintings on the long bench under the windows. Then, without further instruction, they began to help Robert tidy away the art materials. They gathered up the jam jars of paint-clouded water, the brushes and the pots of paint and carried them over to the sink set into the bench which ran down one side of the room.

Jane Roper was scrambling under the desks for dropped pencils or brushes. She took them to Robert one by one. Each time he said 'Thank you, Janey', he was rewarded with a shy smile. Strictly speaking the youngest Roper child should not have been here. She was not one of the extra art pupils. She had no aptitude whatsoever and was happy to spend her time colouring in pictures of fruit and flowers in the book Robert had bought for her with his own money.

Janey had just turned up with her brother Joe one night. 'Me mam's out and I didn't want to miss me class,' Joe had said. He'd offered no further explanation.

Robert guessed that Joe had been left minding his little sister and he'd made no objection. He had simply sat Janey at one of the desks with paper and crayons and she'd been no bother. She'd enjoyed herself so much that Joe had brought her the next time, and continued to do so even when there was no further need.

Robert knew that he had displeased Grace by allowing Janey to come to the art classes. The headmaster's daughter disapproved of favouritism. She believed that all children should be treated equally. Robert knew that it irked her that not only did every other member of staff seem to have a soft spot for this child, but that the other children didn't seem to mind. The boys watched out for her just as her own brother did. And the older girls had made a special pet of her.

Grace, with her strict upbringing, no doubt thought that regardless of the child's sweet nature, it would be bad for

202

Janey to be cosseted so. Robert sometimes wondered if she were right. Perhaps the sooner the little girl learned what a hard place the world was, the better she would survive. He himself had survived an even harsher upbringing than Janey's.

And he probably wouldn't be where he was today if it hadn't been for the help of the Barretts, who had dedicated their lives to helping the poor. But how he wished sometimes that people like the Barretts could temper their high-minded Christian charity with ordinary human love and affection.

Robert sensed someone was watching him. He looked up to find that Grace was looking through the glass panelling that formed the upper half of the walls of the room. There in the dimly lit corridor she was very still, a ghostly figure with her pale face and her dark clothes.

How long had she been standing there?

He saw her start when she noticed that he was looking at her and then she moved towards the door. She opened it and walked into the room.

'Do you need any help, Mr Hedley?' she asked.

'No, thank you. It's all done.'

The children began to file out. Some of them would be met in the school yard by parents or older brothers and sisters; the older ones scorned such babying and went home alone. When the room was empty Robert switched off the lights and closed the door.

He and Grace walked along the corridor together and then began to descend the echoing stone stairway. Joe and Jane Roper had waited and were walking behind them. Grace glanced over her shoulder and quickened her step a little. At the bottom of the stairs, she turned and smiled at Robert.

'It's a cold night, Mr Hedley. Would you like some supper before you go?'

'That's kind of you, Miss Barrett, but I have to walk home with Janey and Joe.'

'You divven't hev to do that, Mr Hedley. I'm big enough to see myself and me sister home safe.'

Grace turned quickly to face the boy. It seemed to Robert that her smile was forced. 'Joe, you shouldn't have been listening to a private conversation,' she said. 'But, as a matter of fact, I agree with you, you are quite responsible enough to take your sister home.'

'It's not that Joe isn't capable,' Robert told her. 'It's just that I go home that way myself and we have got into the habit of walking together.'

'Well, if habit's all it is, I wouldn't miss the chance of a tuck-in,' Joe said. He grinned. 'Gan on, Mr Hedley, hev yerself a good supper!'

They had reached the outer door; the other children had all gone. Before Robert could reply to Grace, a shadow detached itself from the pillars at the gate and hurried across the school yard.

'Who's that?' Grace said, and instinctively moved closer to Robert.

Joe squinted into the darkness. 'Why, it's wor Luke,' he said as the figure stopped at the bottom of the steps and looked up at them. 'Luke, man, what are you doing here?'

'I've come to walk you home.'

'Is something the matter? Some kind of trouble?' Robert asked.

'No trouble. It's just that me ma asked me to come – save you the bother.'

'But it's no bother. Your mother knows that.'

'Aye, well, no doubt she has her reasons – and divven't ask me what they are. When I called by the night, she just said

204

that she'd been thinking and it wasn't right to expect you to look after the bairns the way you do.'

'I'm no bairn!' Joe exclaimed. 'Our mam could hev asked me to see Janey home on me own!'

'Well, she didn't, she asked me. So haad yer gob and let's get crackin'.'

The two children hurried down the steps and Luke Roper hoisted his little sister up on to his shoulders. 'Hawway, pet,' he said, 'let's gan yem. And on the way we'll stop at Nellie's and get some fish and chips for the lot of us. My treat.'

Robert frowned but he refrained from questioning Luke Roper further. He watched as Luke and the two children set out across the yard.

At the gate, Luke stopped and turned to say, 'By the way, me mam says it's been good of you to let Janey come to the drawing classes with Joe but she won't be coming again.'

'Why's that?' Robert asked.

'She didn't say. Perhaps she doesn't want to be a bother to you.'

'But she's no—'

Before Robert could finish the sentence Luke and the children vanished into the darkness. Grace laid a hand on his arm.

'It's no good trying to understand these people,' she said.

He turned to look at her. 'These people?'

She flushed. 'Oh, I know you consider yourself one of them—'

'I *am* one of them.'

'No, you're not! You've worked so hard. You've risen far above the – no, I'll say it – far above the feckless ne'er-do-wells like the Ropers' father.' She raised a hand. 'No – let me speak! You are a talented artist. You've gained respect. You are already being talked about here in Newcastle, and they say

205

you have the potential to become known well outside this region.'

'Fame indeed,' Robert murmured.

Grace's pale complexion mottled but she hurried on, 'You've risen above the circumstances of your birth—'

' "The circumstances of my birth"? Am I to be categorized as a worthy model for the deserving poor to emulate? You sound like one of the pamphlets handed out at public meetings.'

He smiled but Grace had caught the edge to his voice. 'I'm sorry,' she said. 'Perhaps sometimes I have to struggle to overcome the circumstances of *my* birth – the way I was brought up by people who consider it their life's work to care for the poor in any way they can and yet . . . and yet . . .'

'They still see them as a separate class – a different race almost. Your parents would give "these people", as you call them, the bread from their own plates – but not at their own table. Is that what you were trying to say?'

The cruel truth of his words was tempered by his smile. Grace placed a hand on his arm. 'I couldn't have put it so well. I love my parents, so I won't say a word against them—'

'Nor should you; they're good people.'

'But I'm different, Robert. Believe me.'

'I must.'

'Must?'

'You've just invited me to your table, haven't you?'

He laughed and was pleased to see Grace relax a little, become less intense.

'So will you join me for some supper?' she asked.

'You and your parents?'

She hesitated before she replied. 'They're out. They've gone to a concert in some dreary . . .' She faltered when she saw the way Robert smiled. 'In a church hall in Benwell,' she continued. Then she raised her chin and looked him in the eye. 'They will be late home.'

In the awkward silence that fell between them Robert became aware of distant sounds: the barking of a dog, a mother's voice calling her children in from playing in the dark; her angry voice scolding just before a door banged shut in the nearby street. Then all sounds were drowned out by the rumble and hiss of a train leaving the Central Station and steaming on to the bridge that would take it across the Tyne.

'Grace,' he said at last, and impulsively took hold of both her hands, 'Grace, I would like to have supper with you, but I don't wish to upset your parents.'

'Upset them?'

'Would you have invited me if they were at home?'

She sighed. 'I can't lie to you. No.'

'Then I can't accept.'

He let go of her hands but she grasped his and held them tightly. 'Why, Robert, why?' she said. 'Surely it wouldn't be so wrong to—'

'To deceive them?'

'All right, they don't know – not now,' she caught her breath, 'but I'll tell them as soon as they come home. Will that do?'

Robert shook his head. 'No, I'm sorry. I can't be underhand.' He raised their clasped hands between them and looked at her until she let go.

'Good night, Grace.' He turned to leave.

'No, don't go!' Grace stumbled down the steps after him. 'I've made the meal myself, I've set the table, I'll build up the fire. We can sit alone and talk and – listen to me, sometimes it isn't wrong to deceive your parents. Not when we—' She brought her hands up, clenching them convulsively at her breast as if she had realized what she had almost said.

'I mean—' she broke off, unable to control the sob in her voice.

Quickly he crossed the space between them and he saw hope flare in her eyes. She moaned softly and made to move even nearer but he took hold of her shoulders and turned her round so that she was facing away from him.

'It's cold out here,' he said. 'And you've had a long day. You work hard. I don't think your parents realize how much they ask of you.'

All the while he was talking to her, soothing her, he was guiding her back across the yard and up the steps into the entrance hall.

'I think you should go in and have your supper now,' he said.

'And you?' She turned to him hopefully. Perhaps thinking that now he had come this far he had changed his mind.

'I'm going to fetch Nivens from his cosy billet in the boiler room and get him to lock up. He can listen out for your parents coming home and let them in. Now, off you go.'

Robert opened the door that led to the Barretts' private quarters, and waited until she had gone through. She looked back one last time. Her lip was trembling. As she stood there hesitating, he pulled the door shut behind her.

Robert heard the anguished sobbing and walked over to the door. He reached out to open it but stopped himself just in time. He wanted to go and comfort Grace and yet, if he did, he knew it would make matters worse. He had seen the naked longing in her eyes so, no matter how cruel, he guessed it would be better to leave her alone.

For if he went to her now, she might read more into the action than he intended. She might convince herself that he felt the same way about her as she did about him and that he had only been holding back out of respect for her parents.

He moved back from the door and stood irresolutely in the entrance hall. Had he given her any reason to believe that he might care for her? He suppressed a groan for he acknowledged that he had. Grace Barrett was an intelligent and attractive woman and he had enjoyed the limited social contact they had when he visited the school.

He lived alone. He had no family. His life consisted of his work in the drawing office at the yards, and his own work, which was utterly consuming. He gave up his spare time to helping Marjorie Gibb in her attempts to save the orphaned and homeless children. He had no social life. Although he was respected by the men he worked with, he had no real friends.

So when Grace had made it obvious that she wished to be his friend, he had welcomed it. And, even when he had begun to suspect that she wanted more than friendship, he had not drawn back. He realized now how close he had come to considering marriage with the headmaster's daughter. If her parents' objections could have been overcome, she would have made him a good wife.

Except that he didn't love her. He knew that for sure now. Any feelings that he might have had, had been prompted by his own need for intelligent conversation and her obviously passionate nature. Marriage to Grace would have provided more than simple friendship.

But, if he had truly loved her, he would have carried her off and married her whether her parents approved or not, wouldn't he? He felt ashamed at the hypocritical excuse he had used for not having supper with her tonight.

But how could he have told her the truth? That ever since the day of the Christmas party there had been room in his thoughts – in his heart – for only one woman. Thea Richardson.

Chapter Sixteen

Robert drew his collar up against the wind and hurried towards the tram stop. He'd decided there was no time to go home for a bite to eat and supposed that was some kind of justice.

Tonight he'd promised to accompany Marjorie Gibb to the newly organized all-night soup kitchen at the old hospital. She needed an escort as she went about the streets rounding up the younger waifs and strays to make sure they got their fair share of whatever food was going.

Food. He thought regretfully about the pan of homemade broth that Lily Roper would have left for him and then frowned as he remembered what had happened earlier. Why had Lily sent Luke to collect his younger brother and sister? And why had she decided not to allow Janey to come with Joe to the art classes any more?

Perhaps there was some kind of trouble at home – she'd hinted that her husband could be awkward, more than awkward, when the mood took him. Robert decided that he would have to find out and see if he could do anything to help.

* * *

'I wish you weren't going out tonight.' Thea smiled at her aunt across the kitchen table.

'I must. We have a rota of volunteers and I can't let people down.'

'Well then, can I come with you?'

'That's out of the question.'

'Why?'

Her aunt shook her head and took a bite of cake. 'Lovely sandwich cake, this. Not bad for your first attempt.'

'The instructions in the magazine were foolproof.'

'And Nancy told me that you managed it without burning a single cake tin.'

Thea smiled. 'Nancy hovered over me every minute – there was no room for mistakes. But don't change the subject. Why is it out of the question for me to come with you? Because I'm young? Because I've had a so-called sheltered life?'

'Yes, for both of those reasons – no, don't say anything, listen to me – but more importantly because I love you and I don't want any harm to come to you.'

Thea felt the tears gathering as she gazed at her aunt's kind face. No one had ever said such a thing to her before. And there was no one that she would rather have heard it from.

'And I love you.' She reached across the table and took her aunt's hand. 'And I have never been so happy in my life.'

'What – living here? In this little house and learning to cook and look after yourself, after the way you were brought up?'

Thea's face darkened. 'And what way was that?'

Her aunt looked troubled. 'You know what I mean,' she said. 'Your father's . . . your parents' home has every comfort. There are servants to look after your every need—'

'Except the most basic need of all!'

'Thea . . .'

211

'And that I've found here with you.'

They stared solemnly at each other for a moment and then Aunt Marjorie picked up the teapot and filled both their cups, Thea's first. Her hand was shaking slightly and her own tea spilled into her saucer. 'Look, she said, '*my cup runneth over . . .*'

They both laughed.

'Dear child,' Aunt Marjorie continued, 'I have been happy too. It's like having a daughter of my own. Someone to come home to and chat to and share the concerns of the day with. I ask no more than this, you know. But as for you . . .'

'Me?'

'You have a good brain—'

'And what use is that if I'm not allowed to use it?'

'Don't be bitter. Your father wouldn't pay for further education and you feel cheated. I can understand that. But have you thought what other people do? People who have never had your advantages – no, listen to me. Have you ever thought of going to evening classes? If you're determined to learn there are still ways.'

'I suppose so.'

'I know so. And if you like we'll sort something out together.'

'Yes, I would like that.'

Marjorie was relieved to see the beginnings of a smile. 'And then, of course, one day you will marry. I hope you do and then – just think, Thea, then you might have children and for me it will be like having grandchildren of my own!'

Thea's smile vanished. 'My father says no decent man will want to marry me,' she exclaimed.

'Nonsense.'

'You think so?'

'Of course I do,' her aunt said. 'It's just that your father's idea of what constitutes a decent man and mine are very different.'

'I see.'

Her aunt smiled at her. 'I think you do.'

Thea cleared the kitchen table and, tonight, instead of leaving the dirty plates for Nancy as she used to do, she washed and dried them, and put them away on the dresser as her aunt enjoyed a few more minutes' relaxation.

'Shall we go through to the front parlour and sit by the fire until Mr McGrath comes?' Thea asked.

Her aunt got up and led the way along the narrow passage to the sitting room at the front of the house. 'Mr McGrath isn't coming,' she said as they settled at each side of the hearth. 'As I have nothing to take but myself tonight, it doesn't warrant the expense of a cab.'

'Then how—'

'I'll get the tram.'

Thea rose to her feet. 'I'm coming with you.'

'Thea, there's no need—'

'I can't let you go into town by yourself at this time of night.'

'Sit down, dear. Robert is coming for me.'

'Robert Hedley?' Thea sank back into her chair. 'The schoolmaster?'

Aunt Marjorie frowned. 'Schoolmaster? Oh, I see, you met him at the Christmas party so you think . . . No, dear, Robert Hedley is a gifted artist and he teaches drawing at the Charity School, but that is in his own time. Otherwise he works for a living in the shipyards.'

Thea stared at her aunt. 'The shipyards?'

'In the drawing office. Robert is a draughtsman, but before that he served his time as an apprentice in the yards. He was a joiner. Are you surprised?'

'Yes . . . I mean no . . . I don't know what to think . . .'

'Well, here's something more to ponder. Robert is a good man. He works hard and I've no doubt he will succeed; he'll be able to leave the shipyards far behind, although there's no shame in working for your living.'

'No, of course not.'

'But however high he rises he will never forget his beginnings. That's why he gives his time to the school and to help me even though it takes him away from his precious painting.'

'What are you saying?'

'Robert was a pupil at the Charity School himself. He feels he can never break free.'

'From what? You're talking as if he were ashamed of something. He was poor. There's no shame in that – you've told me so many times.'

Aunt Marjorie sighed. 'Yes, he was poor. But more than that, his— Ah, that will be Robert now. Don't get up, dear. I'll go.'

Robert noticed the difference as soon as Marjorie Gibb opened the door.

'Come in before you're blown in!'

Marjorie smiled up at him and put her hand to her forehead as a gust of wind dodged round his shoulders and caught at her hair. She was welcoming, as she always was, so the difference wasn't in her. Or perhaps it was . . . There was a more contented air about her. But that wasn't all of it.

Robert looked around as she led the way along the narrow passage. The walls, brown below the dado rail and cream above, still needed a fresh coat of paint, the carpet runner stretching away to the steeply rising stairs and then beyond to the kitchen area was still worn, the lino it covered cracked and

214

risen in places, but, even so, the very house seemed to be as contented as its owner was.

Then Robert realized what it was. It was the smell. The comforting smell of home baking permeated the air, banishing the old, slightly musty damp smell – the smell of loneliness.

Robert could appreciate the difference all the more keenly because it was only since Lily Roper had started leaving meals and a bit of baking for him that his own home had taken on a more welcoming air.

As Marjorie walked ahead of him into the front parlour Robert was pleased to think that this good-hearted spinster had started to look after herself at last and he wondered why. He wasn't prepared for the shock of discovering the answer.

'You've met my niece, haven't you?'

Marjorie moved aside to reveal Thea Richardson standing by the fire. She looked as though she had just risen from her seat and she seemed to be as shocked as he was.

Robert tried to define his feelings. No mystery, really. He wanted her so badly that he'd had to retreat behind a wall of indifference – an indifference that was wholly false. In truth he couldn't get her out of his mind. But it was more than that. Thea had entered that other dimension, that mysterious well of thought and emotion that was the source of his inspiration.

He thought of the drawings he had already done and those he knew he would be compelled to do in future. But he could never tell her.

Thea was the daughter of a respectable middle-class family and her father had no doubt made proper plans for her. Plans that didn't include marriage to the son of a poor, raddled, drunken whore who hadn't the faintest idea who his father was.

So, although he must be polite to Marjorie's niece, he could not allow himself to be too friendly in case she misinterpreted his intentions. He hoped it wasn't too late. He'd seen the hurt in her eyes that day in the tunnel underneath the railway line. He knew that just a short while earlier, and taken unawares, he had not been able to disguise the way he had responded to her. He had seen the answering flame blaze in her eyes. Young and inexperienced as she was, she wouldn't be able to understand why he seemed to have changed so suddenly.

And now, meeting him once more in her aunt's front parlour, her beautiful eyes were wide and vulnerable as they regarded him. She seemed to be waiting for his reaction. He hated himself for the way he must act if they were both to be saved hurt.

'My niece is living with me now,' Marjorie said without further explanation.

'I see,' Robert replied, but he didn't see at all. Why would a young woman, brought up in a prosperous household and whose main concern seemed to be to enjoy herself gadding about with her pretty, frivolous friend, want to live with her impoverished relative who devoted herself to good works?

'And we're having such fun, Thea and I,' Marjorie continued, 'reading our favourite books, gossiping like giddy girls and eating together late at night when I come home, just like boarding school pupils having a midnight feast! And, do you know, Thea is learning to cook!'

Robert saw the two women smile at each other. He was pleased for Marjorie but he still didn't understand. Perhaps the Richardsons had realized, at last, that Marjorie had been neglecting herself. Perhaps Mrs Richardson had decided to send Thea along to look after her aunt. He felt in his heart that that was unlikely, but at the moment he could think of no other explanation.

'Sit here by the fire for a moment, Robert.' Marjorie indicated the chair at the opposite side of the hearth to Thea.

'I shall make you a cup of tea. No, dear—' Her niece had started to get up but Marjorie gestured for her to sit again. 'I shall do it. And I'm going to cut you a slice of the cake that Thea has baked.'

She hurried away to the kitchen, leaving them alone.

They sat just a few feet away from each other and didn't say a word. Thea, taking her cue from him, had relapsed into silence. She had turned her head to stare into the fire and Robert, after studying her profile and observing how the warm light made her skin glow, making her all the more desirable, had to look away in case his body betrayed him.

He looked around the room, at the faded wallpaper and the heavy curtains with huge hems suggesting they had been taken down from some much larger window and adapted to fit their new setting. Then his eye fell on the photograph in the silver frame that was standing on the table at the back of the room. Wordlessly he rose and went to look at it more closely.

She had left the door ajar so when Marjorie Gibb returned with the tray she half turned and pushed it open with her shoulder. When she entered the room the first thing she saw was her niece staring into the fireplace intently, almost as if she were looking for pictures in the burning coals.

Marjorie and Amy used to do that as children when they were sitting by the nursery fire, surrounded by all the childhood toys and trappings of their privileged life. They had been so happy then. Certainly she, Marjorie, had never been so happy since. Until now when fate had sent her Amy's daughter to love and care for.

Thea, who had arrived here at odds with the world. At war with a father who had treated her harshly, and in pain because she felt her mother had never cared for her. Had Amy loved her daughter?

Marjorie would probably never know. It was a subject they never discussed, taboo, a forbidden area as so much of her sister's life had become ever since that last holiday . . .

Marjorie pushed the door shut behind her the same way she had opened it. The other occupant of the room was standing near her desk and he had picked up Thea's photograph. He was staring at it raptly. Reluctantly, it seemed, he tore his gaze away from it and turned to look at her but she didn't think that he could really see her. His eyes were still focusing on another image.

Thea had risen to fetch the occasional table from the window bay. Marjorie set the tray down and turned to see Robert putting the photograph back, on her desk.

'Lovely, isn't it?' she said.

'Yes, lovely,' he said quietly.

'Vernon took it, Vernon Gray. I can't remember whether you've ever met him on one of our expeditions.'

'No, I haven't.'

'Of course not. You're usually at work when we go. But now, turn that chair round, would you? Thank you. I'll sit here and pour your tea and you must sit by the fire again and get thoroughly warm before we leave the house.'

Robert took his seat obediently and Marjorie poured his tea and cut him a slice of cake. 'Here you are. But you know Vernon's work?'

'I know he's popular – fashionable – and that he considers himself an artist.'

Marjorie smiled. 'And you? Do you consider photography an art?'

'I'm not sure.'

'Then I shall have to convince you. But not now – I can see by your doubtful expression that it might take too long!'

Marjorie watched him as he sipped his tea. It was strange,

she thought, that two of the men she admired most, Robert Hedley and Vernon Gray, should be on opposite sides of the ongoing debate about whether photography could truly be art.

They were both good men, willing to give up their own time to help her in her work and yet, it had just occurred to her, they might not agree with each other. She glanced at Thea. Marjorie would be interested to hear what she thought about the subject but her niece was strangely subdued.

Perhaps she's sulking because I won't let her come with me, Marjorie thought. It's unlike the child to sulk, she's usually so straightforward – but then she can't very well say much with Robert here, can she?

Suddenly she had an idea. She turned and, opening the drawer of her desk, she took out the large photograph album and opened it, holding it up so that Robert could see the page.

'Vernon took these, you know. And they're definitely not fashionable! It's very good of him. Apart from providing valuable records, I treasure them as personal mementoes.'

Robert studied the photograph she was displaying intently. Thea, half interested, had glanced over.

Marjorie suppressed a moment of irritation. Whatever was the matter with these two?

'May I see the album?' Robert asked.

'Certainly.' Marjorie handed it to him and turned to Thea. 'And that has reminded me that Vernon has promised to come with us on our next trip to the seaside. My friends Mrs Shaw and Miss Moffat – you met them at the Christmas party, remember? – well, my friends and I are going to organize a trip to Whitley Bay as soon as the weather allows. I'll be very grateful for your help then, Thea. I hope I can count on you.'

'Of course.'

What on earth was the matter with the girl? Why was she so subdued? And what was wrong with Robert? His tea had grown cold and his cake was only half eaten. But at least he was taking an interest in the album.

She watched as he turned the pages and stared intently at each photograph. 'Good, aren't they?' she asked him.

'Yes. I'm glad you showed them to me.' And that was all he said as he closed the album and handed it back to her without even a smile.

As he did so a sudden gust of wind rattled the roof slates and sent a fall of soot down the chimney to land in the hearth. Marjorie remembered the gust of wind that had greeted her as she opened the door to Robert earlier and she tried not to give way to a shiver of superstition.

What was the old proverb? *When the wind is in the east 'tis neither good for man nor beast.* Was it an east wind, she wondered. Or was it an ill wind? *'Tis an ill wind that blows nobody any good.*

What am I doing? she thought in exasperation. Sitting here like a foolish old maid, afraid of portents. Nonexistent portents! She tried to laugh at herself and couldn't. She suppressed a sigh.

Less than an hour ago she had been so happy, so content with her life and so hopeful that she would be able to help Thea towards a better future. But now she felt uneasy and anxious and she hadn't the faintest idea why.

'Well, Robert,' she said as she returned the album to the drawer, 'I suppose it's time to go.'

'Yes.' He rose to his feet.

'I'll get my coat,' she said, but she lingered for a moment and glanced around the room softly illumined by the lamps and the flickering fire. So warm, so comforting. She was passionate about her work with the homeless – it had always been more to her than a duty – and yet tonight she felt that her own hearth and home – here with Thea – were more important.

Selfish, she told herself as she went out into the hall to collect her coat and hat from the stand. I mustn't become selfish because I am so happy. In fact, that's all the more reason to try to help other people.

When she returned to the front parlour Robert Hedley and Thea were standing looking at each other. She could have no idea what had been said but she couldn't help noticing how large Thea's eyes seemed to be as they stared up into his.

He was the first to realize that Marjorie had come back into the room and he stepped back a little and tried to smile. 'Don't worry,' he said, 'I'll see that your aunt gets home safely.'

As they walked towards the tram stop, last year's shrivelled leaves swirled out from under the garden hedges and danced around their feet. Marjorie realized that for the first time ever she had no wish to go out into the night. The bitterly cold wind was knife sharp, and it was only the thought of the poor souls who had nowhere else to go but the streets that stopped her from turning round and going back home.

Chapter Seventeen

'So you actually plan to marry the girl?' Vernon asked.

They had dined together at Alvini's and now they were sitting by the fire in the photographer's comfortable first-floor drawing room, nursing glasses of brandy.

'It seems so,' Lewis said. 'At least so she tells me.'

'*She* tells *you*?' Vernon raised his eyebrows. 'But what about her theatrical ambitions? I thought she wanted to be a Gaiety Girl?'

'Not any more. In fact, I don't think it was ever her own idea.'

'Of course it wasn't. It was that ridiculous mother of hers.'

'Ridiculous?' Lewis was surprised. Not by Vernon's words, but by the tone of his voice. 'It's not like you to be cruel.'

Vernon laughed and his smile affected his words, turning them into gentle banter. 'Am I being cruel? I don't mean to be. The lady is wonderfully preposterous. She's like a *nouveau riche* society hostess trying to impress – a character that you might put into one of your books for light relief.'

Lewis smiled. Perhaps he had imagined the sarcasm. He must have done for, intelligent and sophisticated as Vernon undoubtedly was, Lewis had never known him to be unkind. In fact, he mused, Vernon seemed to sail through life on a very even keel, devoted to his work but never seemingly stirred by passion.

That was why – and this was selfish – he enjoyed his company so much. Vernon was a pleasant companion with whom he could relax when he wasn't working.

The two men had met only a few months before at a dinner in the Liberal Club. The club occupied an old building that had formerly been the Pilgrim's Inn in Pilgrim Street. Inspired by tales of travellers of old on their way to worship the relics of St Francis at the Grey Friars Monastery, the chef had given the dinner a medieval flavour. In fact the menu declared it a 'Traditional Olde Worlde Banquet'.

Barley broth, soused mackerel, venison pasties and honey-crusted pork were followed by apple tansy pudding and marzipan sweetmeats. The wine waiter served spiced ale to the gentlemen and something he called 'posset' to their wives and daughters. This proved to be a concoction of spiced milk and wine. Lewis thought it looked disgustingly curdled but it must have tasted good judging by the number of times the ladies' drinking goblets were filled as the meal progressed.

But whoever had brewed the posset could have had no idea of its potency. Just as the dessert dishes were being cleared away Lewis watched in astonishment as, without a word, one of the lady guests fell face forward on to the table. A second later, as if it had been planned, the lady sitting opposite to her fell over backwards, chair and all.

As other guests rushed to help, they too began to succumb, both ladies and gentleman reeling about and sliding to the floor helplessly. The scene became surreal, with guests going down like ninepins and the horrified staff not knowing whom to assist first. Lewis realized that the ale as well as the posset must contain some desperately strong ingredient. Not fatal he was pleased to see, for even those felled were simply smiling and giggling foolishly. But, nevertheless, he was glad that he had refused both drinks in favour of a wine that he actually recognized.

And then he'd glanced across the table to find that one other guest was staring around in amused amazement, Vernon Gray. At that moment the photographer caught his eye and raised his own glass in salutation – an ordinary wine glass containing what looked like ordinary red wine. Vernon, too, had refused the 'medieval' concoctions.

Lewis and Vernon put down their glasses and rose from the table as one, then they fled from the dining room, collected their hats and coats from the surprised cloakroom attendant and burst out into the street, at last giving way to laughter. When he had caught his breath Vernon suggested that they should end the evening at Alvini's where he regaled Lewis with near scandalous but amusing anecdotes about some of the city worthies.

Lewis cradled his brandy glass and glanced at Vernon as he recalled the way their friendship had begun. There had been much shared laughter since then and, yes, there had been moments when Vernon's wit had been more than sharp. The fact that it had struck home now must be because the target was so close to home.

'Nevertheless,' Lewis said, 'the preposterous woman will probably become my mother-in-law. So, tempting as it might be, I had better not put her in a book.'

'But you've told me yourself, people never recognize themselves.'

'Mrs Parker might not, but her daughter would. Ellie is very sharp.'

'And you wouldn't want to do anything to hurt her?'

224

'Never.'

Vernon rose from his seat and went to fetch the brandy from a small table behind them. The firelight glinted on the cut-glass decanter. He filled up their glasses. 'Have you told her?'

'Of course.'

Lewis knew what he meant. Vernon was the only person outside London who knew his secret. Once they had become friends, he had asked Lewis outright why a successful author had chosen to leave the metropolis and live in a provincial city.

Lewis had not been able – would not have wanted – to lie. Anyone who became his friend must take him for what he was: a former thief who had served his time and who had changed his ways.

'And it makes no difference to her?'

'Apparently not.'

'But what about her parents?'

'That might be a problem.'

'You don't look too worried.'

'Ellie told me not to be.'

'Ellie told you not to worry? I don't believe what I'm hearing. Ellie Parker is lovely. I'm not surprised that you've fallen in love with her. But how old is she? Eighteen? Nineteen? And, forgive me, Lewis, lovely though she is – how can I put this? This is not going to be a "marriage of true minds", is it?'

Lewis shook his head. 'Don't underestimate her as, I admit, I did before I got to know her. Ellie is very wise. She'll find a way.'

'The little minx is not planning an elopement to Gretna, is she?'

Lewis laughed. 'It was mentioned – if all else fails.'

'Well, whatever happens, I wish you luck. And you know you can count on me if you need help.'

'I know and I'm grateful. But now it's late. I should go.'

'Don't bother.' Vernon withdrew his watch from his fob pocket and glanced at it. 'It's nearly midnight; you've missed the last train to the coast. You can stay here with me.'

Lewis watched as his host tidied the glasses on to the table and then swept the hearth before putting up a cinder guard. He was the other sort of bachelor to Lewis himself. Vernon lived alone in this big house relying on a minimum number of staff to cook and clean, and he did not think it beneath him to keep the house tidy.

Whereas Lewis, even though his background was probably much more humble than that of the middle-class photographer, would have sunk into squalor if he could not have afforded to pay to be properly looked after.

Ellie would be perfect for him. Not only would she make the most enchanting bedfellow, he knew instinctively that she would order his life, keep all distractions at bay, and allow him to write uninterrupted. She had said as much. In return she would demand his wholehearted devotion. That he would give her willingly.

'Come,' Vernon opened the door and led the way out on to the landing. 'I'll loan you some nightclothes.'

Lewis followed him up the stairs that led to the second floor where he knew from previous experience the bedrooms were situated. He wondered if Vernon ever felt lonely rattling around in this big house. Apparently none of the staff lived in. The attic rooms they would have occupied no longer existed, the top floor having been converted into the studio.

The darkroom, where Vernon developed and printed the photographs, was in the basement. The kitchen had been

226

moved to the back of the ground floor where there was also a grand reception room and a library. But, when he wasn't working, Vernon occupied only the first floor where he had his sitting and dining rooms, and the third with the bedrooms and a bathroom.

Such a large house for one man to live in all alone, Lewis thought. But then Vernon, always a good companion, seemed also to be happy with his own company. His offer of a bed tonight had been for Lewis's benefit, not his own.

Something made Lewis glance over the banister rail and down the stairwell. He could see right down to the basement. There was nothing moving so what was it that had caught his attention?

The house was silent. The cavity below him was dim and shadowy – but not as dark as it should have been. When they had come upstairs to the sitting room, earlier, Lewis remembered that Vernon had switched off the electric lamps as they ascended. But now there was a faint glow on the ground floor, or perhaps in the basement, as though someone had switched one on again.

Impossible. Vernon must have left a light burning in the hall, perhaps in anticipation of Lewis's departure. Or perhaps he was in the habit of leaving it on all night? He was about to draw his friend's attention to it but, at that moment, they reached the landing and Vernon strode towards one of the bedroom doors.

'You can sleep in here,' he said. 'The linen's fresh since the last time you stayed and you know where the bathroom is. But, before you settle, I want to show you something.'

Lewis followed Vernon to his own bedroom. At a flick of a switch the light revealed a room so lacking in personal touches that it could have been a hotel room. Lewis had glanced in here once before and he had wondered how Vernon had left so

227

little imprint of his own character on the solidly comfortable sleeping quarters.

But this time there was a difference. His host had preceded him to the fireplace. A fire burned low in the hearth, proving that the man did, at least, require creature comforts, but when he saw what Vernon was looking at he was stunned.

'Well, what do you think of her?' Vernon asked.

Lewis gazed up at the large framed photograph hanging on the wall above the mantelpiece. It was a head and shoulders portrait of a girl. No . . . a woman. And yet in spite of the way her lips were parted so suggestively, and the way her eyes, with a slightly unfocused gaze, seemed to smoulder with hidden passion, there was still an air of innocence about her. Or perhaps vulnerability was a better word.

The luxuriant dark hair framed a face of striking beauty, the flowers, one in her hair and one tucked in the neckline of her dress were white . . . for purity? But a purity that was in imminent danger of being sullied.

'Well?' Vernon prompted.

'That's . . . that's . . .'

'Thea Richardson. The portrait that her aunt will never see.' His lips curled in the faintest of smiles.

Lewis let that go by and said, 'But . . . she looks so . . .'

'Seductive?'

'No!'

His response was sharper than he intended and he wasn't sure why. Perhaps because he had sensed an innate decency in the girl and didn't want to cheapen her.

'Desirable, then?'

Lewis glanced at his friend. Vernon's eyes were bright; he had never seen those pleasant features so animated, so expressive of emotion.

'Yes, certainly,' Lewis said. 'And you desire her.'

Vernon relaxed a little. 'I don't deny it. But what do you think of the portrait – aesthetically, I mean?'

'A masterpiece. I don't know how you did it – to get her to look like that.'

Vernon frowned. 'I meant technically, but why should a mere wordsmith be able to appreciate the photographer's art? But, as for getting her to look like that, it was surprisingly easy.' He saw Lewis raise his eyebrows. 'No, really, I'm not saying anybody else could have done it – and I'm certain that Thea herself doesn't know what lies within her. But it's all there, Lewis, waiting . . . waiting for someone . . .'

He let his sentence trail away and Lewis saw that his friend was already trying to fit himself back into his unruffled, urbane persona. He wondered whether Vernon knew that he had revealed so much of himself.

Lewis recognized now, something that he should have known all along. That the photographer was a much more complex character than he had given him credit for.

Hidden depths . . . still waters . . . The writer in Lewis smiled at the clichés that sprang to mind. But in this case they were correct. Vernon who was tall, good-looking and undoubtedly talented, would be a much more interesting character to put in one of his books than Rosalie Parker.

But what part would Vernon play? Hero or villain? Lewis realized with a *frisson* of unease that the answer to that question was no longer straightforward.

As they hurried through the lamp-lit city streets Robert Hedley and Marjorie Gibb heard a strange tearing sound above their heads and they stopped to look up and discover what it was.

'There, look!' Marjorie exclaimed, and she pointed to a theatrical billboard on the side of a building. The wind was worrying away at a loose corner of a poster, gradually tearing it down, and then, as they watched, the poster tore completely in two and half of it was whipped up and away across the rooftops.

Marjorie laughed like a child and Robert thought what a good woman she was and how much he liked her. And then the wind changed direction and the poster came hurtling back down and towards them. Robert took her arm and pulled her out of the way.

The poster wrapped itself around a startled young woman who tore it off and hurled it to the ground before hurrying away and vanishing into the narrow canyon that was Pink Lane.

'What is it?' Robert asked. Marjorie was staring after the retreating figure.

'Nothing ... I thought I recognized her, but she promised ... Oh, well we'd better get on.'

Robert took Marjorie's arm and guided her towards their destination, the Central Station.

It was past midnight and the last train had gone; the figures huddled in the shelter of the grand portico were not late travellers. Robert hated Marjorie to come here. It was a known pick-up place for prostitutes of both sexes, and they or their pimps could get nasty if they thought their business was being interfered with. That's why he wouldn't leave her side for one minute.

But although Miss Gibb did try to save some of the women from this kind of life, that was not her intention tonight.

It was the children she was concerned with. Boys and girls, orphaned and homeless, who, somehow, had ended up here, seeking a warm dry place to sleep and having no idea of the kind of life they could be drawn into.

There was only a small group of children there tonight. Marjorie, with Robert close behind her, rounded them up and told them about the hot food on offer at the soup kitchen.

As soon as she was satisfied that they knew the way to the old Holy Jesus Hospital, she turned to Robert and said, 'Almost done.'

'Almost? Don't you think you've done enough tonight? I promised your niece I would see you home in good time. When you were getting your coat she told me that she worries about you.'

'Did she?' He had never seen her look so pleased. 'She's a good girl, and sensible too. So you needn't worry.'

'Which means?'

'Which means she'll have gone to bed.'

Robert sighed good-humouredly. 'Which also means that I won't be able to persuade you to go home and try to get a decent night's sleep.'

Marjorie's smile faded. 'Robert, forgive me.'

'Forgive you?'

'You have to get up early for work. You need your sleep more than I do – no, really, as I get older I seem to need less.'

'You're hardly an old woman.'

'Thank you for saying so, but now, just one more errand, and we'll both go home.' She smiled up at him and began to cross the road towards the entrance to Pink Lane.

'Marjorie . . .' Robert found he had to hurry to catch up with her. 'Stop – you can't go there. Not at this time.'

'I'll be all right if you come with me.'

'But why? Why now?'

'That girl, the one the poster blew against. I'd just like to make sure. If it's who I think it is, I've been trying to persuade her to give up this kind of life. But, quite rightly, she asked me how on earth else would she feed her baby. But she promised to wait a while and give me a chance to find her a job. Well, I've found a place for her. A friend of mine is willing to take

231

her on as a domestic. Only as a scullery maid and she won't earn much but she'll get her meals.'

'And her baby?'

'She has a married sister who'll help out.'

'You think of everything, don't you?'

'Someone has to.'

Even at this time several of the drinking places were open. Raised voices and laughter echoed from side to side of the narrow lane, and unsteady figures stumbled across the cobbles, some of them making for the women who stood on the corners of darkened alleyways.

The women, seemingly casual, and often in deep conversation with each other, all stood with one foot tucked behind the other so that the sole of one shoe was showing. That was where their price was marked.

Robert held Marjorie's arm tightly and, as they passed one pair of gossiping women, two youths came towards them. They were a little unsteady on their feet. One of the youths bent down to read the price on the sole of the nearest woman's shoe, and his friend took the opportunity to raise a foot and push him over.

The first youth rolled around on the ground, laughing helplessly, and his mate offered a hand to pull him up again. But whether it was accidental or deliberate they both ended up on the ground.

Only then did the women deem to notice them. One of them went to stand over them, arms akimbo.

'Piss off, you great pair of boobies,' she said. 'You'll scare proper customers away with your daft behaviour.'

She extended a toe and pushed at one of them. He immediately half sat and grabbed at her skirt, trying to lift it, until he lost his balance and fell back again.

The youths laughed even louder and the women sniffed

disdainfully and walked away from them to take up pretty much the same position as before a little further up the lane.

No one paid Marjorie and Robert much attention, thank God, but he wondered what on earth the denizens of Pink Lane made of the plainly dressed, middle-aged woman and her companion.

Perhaps they think she's come here to find a gigolo, he thought, and I'm going to oblige her. Wickedly, the thought made him smile, although he knew, liberal-minded New Woman though she was, he could never tell Marjorie about his musings.

'There she is,' Marjorie said. 'It is the girl I thought it was.' She gripped Robert's arm. She was frowning.

Robert saw why. The girl in question was arguing with a man. She was small and slight – she looked no more than sixteen – the man wasn't tall, but he was brawny. They could hear his angry words and her protests.

'Listen, bitch, you should have been here hours ago!'

'The bairn – I had to find someone to mind the bairn—'

'What about your sister? She'd be glad enough of a bit extra cash.'

'That's true – but not if I've earned it this way.'

'Stuck up little madam. I'm sick to death of her and her righteous ways. She only talks like that because she's got a husband, poor bugger, to take care of her. But how else is a slut like you going to earn enough to feed her bastard brat?'

The girl began to cry.

'Stop that! Stop snivelling, you little slut, or I'll clout you one!'

Robert was appalled at her next words.

'No, Da, no,' she said. 'I'll do anything you say. Divven't hit us!'

She was sobbing loudly now and this infuriated the man – her father – even more. He took her roughly by her arms and brought his face close to hers. 'Will you stop that! Who's going to fancy you the state you're in? How can a man enjoy hisself if you divven't stop snivelling long enough to let him have his way?'

The girl stopped making any noise but her sobs escaped as gulps of air.

'Now,' her father said, 'I've got the first one lined up for you. He's in there.' He nodded towards one of the drinking houses.

'No!'

The protest had come from Marjorie. Robert took her arm and held it but she shook him off and strode forward.

'Let her go!'

The man turned his head, distracted by her voice, but he held on to his daughter.

Robert caught up with her and whispered urgently, 'For God's sake, let me deal with this!'

But Marjorie was in fighting mood, too indignant to hear him. 'I said, let her go!' she repeated.

The girl's eyes were huge as she looked over her father's shoulders. 'Miss Gibb,' she breathed. 'It's all right . . . divven't cross 'im.'

Her father's attention snapped back to the girl. 'Do you know this woman?' he asked.

'Yes.'

'And how's that?'

'She . . . she tries to help. She finds jobs . . .'

Her father gripped her shoulders all the more tightly and pulled her towards him so that she had to turn her face away as he hissed into her ear, 'Finds jobs? Finds jobs! I know all about women like her. They think it's better for lasses to work their fingers to the bone as a skivvy in the houses of their fine friends. Work themselves to death for a few shillings a week instead of making a bit real money for a good night's work.'

'And what use is that to her if she never sees that money?' Marjorie Gibb challenged.

'What did you say?'

'You heard me. I know very well that you take every penny that the poor girl earns— Oh . . .'

Too late Marjorie realized her mistake, but she stared at the man steadily, and Robert began to ease himself in front of her.

The girl's father let go of her and she slumped against the wall. Slowly he turned to face Robert and Marjorie. His eyes glittered in the lamplight.

'And how do you know that?' he asked.

'I'm guessing.'

'No you're not. You know because the ungrateful little bitch told you.' He turned to his daughter and raised his arm. 'I'll teach you!' His arm began to descend towards the terrified girl.

'Robert – stop him!' Marjorie said.

And what Robert did next would haunt him for ever. In the split second he had to make up his mind, he decided that rather than try to stop the enraged father, he would first pull the girl out of harm's way and then turn to face the consequences.

He moved swiftly, took hold of one of her arms and pulled and pushed her into the nearest doorway. Then he turned to face her father just in time to see the blow that was intended for his daughter land on Marjorie Gibb.

Marjorie must have been moving towards the girl also, probably intending to keep her safe. But Robert would never know if that was what was in her mind for she never spoke again.

Even though her attacker was caught off balance, the blow was sufficient to send her flying across the narrow lane to fetch up against the wall opposite. Robert heard the sickening crack of her head as it hit the bricks, and then saw her fall to the ground, where her poor head received another blow from the corner of a doorstep.

He was aware of the girl sobbing in the doorway behind him and of the man who had caused this vanishing into the shadows. But they were not his concern. Not now.

As he crossed the lane towards his friend, he saw her roll over slowly until she was lying on her back. Her eyes were wide open in an expression of surprise as she stared up and beyond the crooked rooftops, beyond the smoking chimneys, to the stars.

But, even as he kneeled to cradle her in his arms, Robert knew that she couldn't see them. In fact she would never see the stars again.

Chapter Eighteen

'But you said you'd see she got home safely. You promised!'

Robert had never known so much anguish as at this moment. They sat at the kitchen table. There was still some warmth from the range so he had thought it the best place. Thea bundled up in an oversize dressing gown ignored the cup of tea he'd made her and stared at him as if she still could not believe what he had told her.

'I know. I'm sorry.' He could barely speak.

'But how did it happen? Why did the man attack her?'

Robert took a deep breath and tried to steady his voice. 'He didn't – at least I don't think he meant to. She just got in the way. I think she was trying to protect the girl.'

'She would . . . of course . . . She wouldn't think of her own danger.'

Robert wondered how much Thea knew about Marjorie's work. He hadn't told her all the details of what had happened tonight; only that her aunt had tried to save a girl from being harmed.

'But why didn't you stop him? Why didn't you stop him hitting my aunt?'

'I would have done – I told you, I pulled the girl out of the way and when I turned round it was too late.'

'Too late.'

She breathed those words so quietly; there was no accusation in her voice, but Robert had to turn away from the look in her eyes.

He had failed her. He had failed Marjorie and he had failed himself. One wrong decision on his part had caused all this grief. And yet the decision had been made in the heat of the moment – and he couldn't have known that Marjorie would step forward into the line of danger.

'No!' he protested aloud. It was madness to think like this. It had happened – and he would have to live with the consequences for the rest of his life.

He looked back to find Thea gazing at him. She was frowning, puzzled at his outburst. He knew he could not explain it to her. That would be treading on dangerous ground.

'But why didn't you bring her home?'

For a moment he thought she had lost her mind – had forgotten what he had told her – but then he realized what she meant.

'I thought it better to leave her in the infirmary – in the mortuary.' There was nothing he could add to make the words less bleak.

He knew that he would never be able to tell her the full story. He must have seemed like a madman, wild and staring, as he strode towards the cab rank carrying Marjorie in his arms.

The cab driver had been wary about taking him, probably thinking them both drunk, but Robert had climbed in awkwardly, not wanting to let go of his precious burden for one moment, and barked out hoarse orders to take them to the infirmary.

Then the nightmare ride, the sound of horse's hoofs echoing

through city streets, and all the while knowing it was hopeless – knowing that there was nothing they could do – but he had to try.

'I see,' Thea said, and for a moment he thought he had spoken out loud. But then he realized that she was simply acknowledging the last thing that he'd said to her.

'Would you like me to take you home?'

'Home?'

She drew her brows together in puzzlement. She was tired, in shock; he could see that she was having difficulty concentrating.

'To your father's house.'

Thea gave him the strangest of looks. For a moment he thought a different sadness had touched her, some other hurt that he could have no notion of. But then she straightened her shoulders and looked at him levelly.

'This is my home.'

'But I'm sure they wouldn't want you to be alone here – not now.'

Again, that tightening of her lips, that spasm of pain. 'I won't be alone,' she said. 'Nancy will come in the morning. I'll have to tell her what has happened.'

She looked worn out with grief and fatigue. Perhaps it was better to leave her be. Encourage her to go back to a warm bed for a few hours rather than drag her out into the chill pre-dawn air.

Robert glanced towards the window. The sky was still pitch-dark but it would soon be time for him to go to work.

'Well,' he rose from his chair, 'I should go . . .'

She had clasped her hands on the scrubbed wooden table top and was staring down at them. She sighed.

'Miss Richardson . . . Thea . . . would you like me to stay, at least until Nancy comes?'

'No.'

Still she didn't look at him so he began to walk towards the door. 'Don't bother to see me out,' he said. 'I'll make sure the door shuts securely behind me.'

It was as if she hadn't heard him. Still without speaking, she rose and followed him along the narrow passage. It smelled cold and damp again. The comforting aroma of home baking had gone. The letter box was rattling in the wind. Would it never die down?

He opened the door and, after he had stepped out on to the path, he turned to find her standing watching him gravely.

'Go in. It's cold,' he said.

'You should have brought her home,' she said, and closed the door.

He fought down the urge to fling himself against the door and hammer on it until she opened it again, to take her in his arms and beg her forgiveness again and again. But that would probably cause her even more pain and he could never do that, no matter what it cost him.

If there had been little hope before of ever making Thea his, there was none at all now. As Robert began his long walk home, he knew that the woman he loved would never want to set eyes on him again.

The walls of the white-tiled corridor curved up into an arch overhead. It was like entering a tunnel that led to the underworld. Every now and then wooden plaques attached to the wall pointed the way to the enquiry desk with gold-painted fingers.

Eventually Thea came to a booth something like a ticket office at a station. She peered through the glass into a neat, seemingly empty office. There was a bell set into the narrow protruding counter on her side of the glass and a printed card inviting her to ring for attention. She did so.

The man appeared so suddenly that she would have been shocked had her senses been working normally, but she was living a kind of half-life, hemmed in by her sorrow, not noticing or caring too much about the world around her.

He was wearing a dark jacket and a high, uncomfortable-looking collar. His greying hair was thinning and his complexion pale. He looked as if he never saw the light of day.

Charon . . . waiting to ferry the spirits of the dead across the river Styx . . . but I have no gold coin to place in her mouth . . . or her hand . . .

The man raised the glass window that separated them. 'Can I help you?' he asked. He smiled although, used to grief, he had a detached air, as though he could not allow himself to become involved.

When Thea explained who she was and why she had come, he opened the ledger on the wooden surface between them. After studying it carefully, he frowned and looked up.

'I'm sorry, Miss Richardson, but Miss Gibb is no longer here.'

'No longer here?'

For a wild moment hope surged within her. Aunt Marjorie was no longer in the mortuary. Of course she wasn't. Robert had made a mistake. Her aunt wasn't dead. She was still alive but gravely wounded and in the infirmary – or perhaps she had already been released and was on her way home. And she, Thea, wouldn't be there to greet her!

The world shifted and she leaned weakly against the wall in front of her, clinging on to the wooden counter for support. The man in the office looked concerned and he turned from her to pour water from a carafe into a clean glass.

He pushed the glass towards her, an infinitely sad look in his watery eyes. She knew that her hopes had been foolish.

She took the glass and drank, then closed her eyes.

'Are you all right?' She opened her eyes to find the man looking worried. 'Do you want me to fetch a female attendant?'

'No.' She sighed. 'But please explain. Where is my aunt – Miss Gibb – where is she now?'

'At Hall's.'

He said this as though it was sufficient explanation and Thea raised her eyebrows.

'The undertakers,' he added.

'But why? I mean, who arranged this?'

The man consulted the ledger again. He glanced at her in surprise. 'A Mr Richardson, the deceased's brother-in-law.'

Thea flinched, both at the mention of her father's name and at the description of her aunt – accurate though it might be.

'So this Mr Richardson will be . . .?'

'My father,' Thea confirmed.

'Then how is it that you didn't know he'd been to make arrangements?'

'I've been living with my aunt. I haven't been to my father's house since – since it happened.'

'Ah, I see.'

But he couldn't possibly see, Thea thought, and there was certainly no need to tell him any more.

'Then if you go home now, your father will be able to explain everything.' He began to close the ledger.

'No, wait!' Thea thought quickly. Rather than reveal her complicated family situation she resorted to half-lies. 'My mother will be grieving – Miss Gibb was her sister – I'd rather learn the facts from you now than cause any further upset at home.'

'Of course.' He had accepted her explanation. 'But, to satisfy my curiosity, how did you know what had happened?'

'A friend of my aunt's, Mr Hedley, came to tell me.'

'Ah, yes.' The man looked pleased to find that name written in his ledger. 'It was Mr Hedley who brought your aunt to the infirmary, and, as the police had to be informed—'

'The police?'

'Of course. Your aunt was attacked in the street. This is a criminal offence – murder, in fact. Not that I hold out much hope of the villain ever being found and brought to justice even though the witness got a good look at him. The police will do their best but he'll stowaway or sign up with a deep-sea skipper leaving on the next tide, then he'll jump ship when they reach foreign parts like many a criminal before him. Valparaíso, San Francisco – who knows? He'll never come back to Newcastle, you can count on that. Oh – forgive me!'

Thea knew she had paled. The poor man looked disconcerted and he reached for the carafe again. She allowed him to fill her glass and she managed a smile as she thanked him.

'But you haven't explained,' she said. 'How was my father involved?'

'The police, I imagine. Mr Hedley will have told them all he knew about Miss Gibb's family background.'

'Of course.'

And Thea could see the logic of it. Her father was the head of the household and also an influential citizen. Naturally, he would be the one to be informed rather than a nineteen-year-old girl.

'Will you go home now?'

Thea realized that his question was prompted by concern so she simply nodded assent. He was not to know that to her 'home' did not mean her father's house.

Walking back along the corridor she noticed that the floor sloped upwards as the corridor curved round. The slope was so slight that she had not been aware of it on the way in.

243

Now, retracing her steps to the outside world, she found it was important not to look back.

'Lissen, hinny, you've got to eat something,' Nancy said.

'No – really, I couldn't.'

'Well, you've got to try. This broth is just what you need to keep your strength up.'

Thea looked at her. It was hard to make out any sign of emotion in the woman's plain face but perhaps this was Nancy's way of dealing with her grief – by keeping busy.

'All right then,' Thea said. 'But just a little.'

'Take your coat off then; you've sat like that for hours.'

Thea got up from her chair at the kitchen table and took her coat off. Nancy's daughter, Ellen, who had been sitting by the range, got up and came to take it from her.

'That's a good lass,' her mother said. 'Go and hang it up in the hall.'

The child did as she was told without a word and Thea suddenly felt sorry for her. 'Nancy, I'm sorry—' she began.

'Why's that?' Nancy set a plate of broth on the table and began to slice some bread.

'Poor Ellen has had to listen to – to all this.'

'Divven't fret. Our Ellen's upset about your aunt, don't mistake, but she's wise beyond her years. She'll get over it. And so will you. Life goes on. Now eat that up – you know very well your aunt wouldn't want you to sit moping.'

Thea began to sup the broth, subdued into obedience by the woman's reproving tone. When Ellen came back into the kitchen, Nancy ladled out bowls of broth for both of them and they joined her at the table.

And sitting there with her aunt's maid and her daughter, sharing a meal in the house her aunt would never return to, for the first time Thea wondered what would become of her – whether she would be allowed to stay here, and if not, where on earth was she to go.

'So when's the funeral?' Nancy asked.

Thea looked up, startled. 'I don't know.'

'Then we'll have to find out.'

'But how?'

'Can't you ask your father?'

'I . . . don't . . .'

'Never mind. Hall's, you said? I'll call by. And now, after you've had a cup of tea and a slice of bread and jam, you'd better write notes to those two friends of hers, telling them what's happened. You know, Mrs Shaw and Miss Moffat. Their addresses will be in your aunt's book in her desk in the front room. Do you think you can manage that?'

'Yes.'

Thea mused how unreal this was. Not just because she was taking her meal in the kitchen – she had got used to that over the last few weeks – but to be taking orders from a servant, someone her mother and her sister would consider one of the lower orders.

But there was no offence meant in the way Nancy spoke to her. On the contrary, she was trying to help in the only way she knew how: by encouraging Thea to deal with the practicalities. Nancy's own life had probably allowed no time for the luxury of sensibility, only plain common sense.

She refused the bread and jam so Nancy carried her tea through to the desk in the front room. She built up the fire, then came to stand beside Thea.

'Tell them you'll let them know about the funeral as soon as you know yourself. Ask them to tell whoever else should be told,' she said as Thea got the writing paper and envelopes from the drawer. 'And when you've finished, our Ellen'll deliver them by hand. I don't think they live far away and it'll give the lass something to do.'

Thea nodded and Nancy left the room, closing the door behind her.

Chapter Nineteen

Inside the dimly lit church she had been protected, surrounded by her aunt's friends; she doubted whether her father even knew she was there. After the service, following the coffin, he had led the procession from the church, staring straight ahead, her mother and sister, heavily veiled, behind him, and then a small group of their friends.

Thea had kept her head bowed as though in prayer. She and her party had waited until they had all gone before joining on behind.

But now, as the clergyman led the way up the broad central path of the cemetery towards the waiting grave, Thea felt exposed. Exposed both to the keen wind that did not seem to have stopped blowing for days, and also to the curious glances of the well-dressed party which attended her mother and father.

Neither of her parents nor her sister looked back towards the less well-dressed but larger group which followed on behind them. But others did, and if any of her mother's friends recognized Thea, they must have thought it odd that she was there at her aunt's funeral and yet apart from the immediate family.

Instead she walked with Mrs Shaw and Miss Moffat, and a host of people whose names she did not know, apart from Mrs Barrett, representing the Charity School. These people had known and loved her aunt and wanted to pay their last respects.

Robert Hedley had not come.

The grave diggers waited at a respectful distance and the party gathered round the grave. Without having planned it, Thea found herself directly facing her parents and her sister across her aunt's coffin.

She was shocked to see how small her mother seemed to have become. All in black and with a veil so dense that Thea could not see her expression, her mother nevertheless gave off an aura of great sadness. And, more than that, of defeat.

Neither her husband nor her other daughter supported her. She stood alone. No matter what had passed between them previously – or rather what had not passed between them – Thea ached to go and comfort her. To offer her the simple warmth and kindness that she had experienced herself during her short time with Aunt Marjorie.

But she couldn't. She knew in her heart that her mother would reject her, as she had always done.

And what of her sister? Imogen should have been standing close to their mother at a time like this, but instead she clung on to their father's arm as if it were he that needed comforting.

But when Thea, at last, dared look straight at her father she was startled to discover that it might not be comfort that Imogen was offering but support. Her father, when she had last seen him, had been an upright, vigorous man who gave every appearance of being in rude health.

Now she saw that he was clutching a silver-headed walking stick on which he leaned heavily, and his usual high-coloured complexion was a sickly grey. The broken veins, which had once traced blue patterns across red cheeks, now looked almost

248

purple on the parchment skin. He kept dabbing at his eyes with a large white handkerchief. Thea knew that whatever was making his eyes water, it would not be grief.

Thea could not imagine what ailed her father to have wrought so drastic a change. She could only guess that he had some form of cancer. She tried to stand back and examine her feelings; she discovered that she was more shocked than grief-stricken.

Then as the clergyman recited the age-old words of committal and the coffin was lowered, Thea was glad to be amongst those who had truly loved her aunt.

She watched as one of the grave diggers approached her mother and offered her the token handful of earth. Her mother seemed to shrink for a moment and then she took it and dropped it into the grave. It landed with a soft thud on the coffin and those standing beside Thea seemed to sigh in unison.

The two groups of mourners slowly went their separate ways through the churchyard and the grave diggers began to shovel earth into the grave. Then one man whom Thea had never seen before detached himself from her father's party and made his way to her side.

'Miss Richardson, may I have a word?'

Mrs Shaw and Miss Moffat stepped back and waited as Thea asked, 'And you are . . .'

'Charles Blackwell, your father's solicitor.'

'Well, Mr Blackwell?'

Mr Blackwell was very tall and thin. His hat didn't seem to fit properly on to his narrow head and he was having difficulty hanging on to it in the wind. In spite of the circumstances Thea wanted to laugh. Or perhaps it was *because* of the circumstances, perhaps her grief and lack of sleep had made her susceptible to hysteria.

Mr Blackwell held the brim of his hat with his right hand and turned his face sideways against the blast as he said, 'Your father did not expect to see you here, today.'

'I'm sure he didn't. He certainly didn't inform me – or any of my aunt's friends – that the funeral was taking place.'

'Yes, well, as you are here, I will take advantage of the fact to tell you that I am coming to see you tomorrow.'

'*Tell* me?'

'Er – yes, tomorrow – if I may.'

'You may.'

Gravely Thea offered her hand and Mr Blackwell let go of his hat in order to shake it. She watched with calm detachment as the wind snatched his hat and tossed it first up into the branches of the trees to startle the rooks into cawing flight, and then down again to spin across the churchyard.

She kept herself in control while she watched the lanky figure of Mr Blackwell dodge and hop around graves until, inevitably, he stumbled and fell on to an elaborate arrangement of memorial wreaths. The rooks shrieked with laughter.

Thea dropped her head into her hands and her shoulders shook. Mrs Shaw and Miss Moffat were at her side instantly, murmuring words of comfort as they took an arm each and led her towards the lich-gate.

It was just as well, Thea reflected, they had no idea that the strange sound she was making was suppressed laughter.

When everyone had gone, Robert stepped out from his vantage point under the shelter of the trees. He had slipped into the church just before the service started and sat at the back. Then he was first out, making his way to a place where he could see without being seen.

The grave diggers took no notice of him as he approached the grave and stood silently with bowed head, paying his respects. It didn't take the men long to complete their task and Robert watched as they placed the floral wreaths on the mound of freshly turned earth.

The sharp smell of damp earth mingling with the flowers was not unpleasant. The rooks, startled by that ridiculous man's hat, had still not settled and were circling high on currents of wind and cawing loudly. It's like a scene from a gothic novel, Robert mused, a burial on a cold day, the branches of the trees soughing in the wind, the mourners dividing into two sharply defined groups.

How Marjorie would have appreciated this, Robert thought. She'd had a keen sense of humour and if she'd been watching, a ghostly presence at her own funeral, she would have laughed out loud as the lanky scarecrow of a man dodged round the graves in pursuit of his hat and finally fell on to one of them.

Robert turned to leave and went over that incident in his mind. He'd been some distance from them but he'd seen Thea stop to talk to the man and he'd caught her antipathy towards him from the tense way she'd held herself. And he was also pretty sure that she had deliberately caused the poor fellow to let go of his hat.

He gave way to a surge of pure joy as he recalled the way Thea, brave, straight-limbed and defiant, had faced the man she obviously perceived to be her enemy across the gravestones. He would have given anything to have been able to stand by her side, to be her champion, instead of lurking like a thief under the dropping elms.

Then Robert frowned as he remembered her bowed head and shoulders when the two women, friends of Marjorie's, had led her away. Had she been sobbing? Maybe. But more than likely she'd given way to laughter. And he didn't blame her for that. In fact he mourned all the more the loss of a chance of friendship with a young woman of such spirit.

His anguish was the keener because, when he'd allowed himself to think of Thea, he had soon realized that she was more Marjorie's niece than Samuel Richardson's daughter. Rich and well-educated she may be, but he'd seen at the very start that her character was entirely different from that of her pretty, frivolous little friend Ellie Parker. But, foolishly, he'd allowed his vision to be obscured by a lingering sense of inferiority and shame.

Shame . . . He had nothing to be ashamed of. No child can help the circumstances of his birth. And as for being of an inferior class, surely his growing reputation as an artist would have made him an acceptable suitor for Thea's hand?

But even as he thought this he realized that he was doing Thea a further injustice, for he sensed that however her parents might allow their judgement to be swayed by his material success, Thea herself would have accepted him even if he were truly the poor schoolmaster she had first imagined him to be.

A sudden violent gust of wind shook the branches of the trees, sending a spray of icy raindrops across the churchyard. Robert took out a handkerchief to dry his face. The cold was making his eyes water. Leaving the grave diggers to their business, he began to walk away.

Why had Thea not been part of the family party, he wondered. It was clear now that there must have been some estrangement, and if Marjorie had been helping Thea in her time of need then her loss might have grave implications. This thought brought a fresh wave of guilt and despair. His failure to save Marjorie had not only resulted in the loss of a dear friend but had probably blighted any chance there might have been of him and Thea coming together.

Nancy had not been to the funeral. Thea had told her she was welcome but her aunt's maid had preferred to stay behind and prepare a table for any of Miss Gibb's friends who might want to come home with Thea from the church. She didn't think they'd be made welcome in Samuel Richardson's grand home.

Thea was glad that some of them accepted the invitation and, for a while, the house did not seem quite so bleak as it had in the last few days. Everyone was shocked at the manner of Aunt Marjorie's death but no one, it seemed, held out much hope of the man who had attacked her ever being caught.

He had vanished it seemed, either into the maze of slum backstreets by the river, or, more likely, he had fled Newcastle altogether. Perhaps he'd stowed away or signed up as crew on a ship to America, as the mortuary attendant had suggested.

Apart from the fact that everyone was dressed in black, the scene was so normal that Thea was taken aback when Miss Moffat offered to pack up her aunt's clothes.

'I'm not sure what you mean,' she said.

Miss Moffat's round face took on the expression of an anxious child. 'Oh, my dear,' she said, 'I assumed you would know. It's just that we all agreed some time ago that, when the time comes, our earthly belongings should not be wasted. They should go—'

'I understand,' Thea interrupted her. 'And of course you must take whatever is useful.'

'I'll leave all the personal things, and of course you can look at all the bundles before they leave the house.' Miss Moffat still looked anxious.

'Don't worry. I trust you completely.'

'But you still must look – it's the way we do things.'

'Then I will.'

'I'll come along tomorrow, dear. It's best to do these things quickly.'

Thea agreed but she felt a surge of panic when she thought of her aunt's clothes being so quickly removed from her home, though she was sure that this kind little woman was right. Miss Moffat pressed her arm and moved away.

Thea was suddenly weary and she was glad when her guests began to take their leave. When they had all gone Ellen helped her mother clear up, and the three of them sat at the kitchen table drinking hot sweet tea and nibbling at the sandwiches that were left.

'Went well, didn't it?' Nancy said. 'It was as good a send-off as we could afford. The tin's empty now, like.'

Thea sipped her tea and puzzled over what Nancy had said. *Send-off?* She supposed that meant the funeral tea but she didn't know what the last sentence meant.

'Tin?' she asked.

Nancy got up and took an old tin down from the dresser. The faded yellow colouring suggested that it might once have contained mustard powder. Nancy took the lid off and held it upside down. Nothing fell out.

Thea frowned.

'It's me housekeeping tin,' Nancy explained. And when Thea still didn't respond, she continued, 'Miss Gibb trusted me to do the shopping and pay the bills. She gave me the money every month and she was happy to let me manage it. Well, it's all gone.'

'I see.'

Thea began to feel uneasy. Her own allowance had been paid into her aunt's bank account and Thea had only a little left of the last sum she'd been given.

'And then there's me wages,' Nancy said. 'I got them weekly.'

'You must be due a payment, then?'

'Aye.'

'I have some money – I'll put it in the tin – but I don't think it's sufficient.'

The two women stared at each other across the table. Ellen, sensing that something was the matter, looked up from her plate. Her sharp gaze went from one grown-up face to the other but she didn't say anything.

Nancy sighed. 'So I'll have to look for another place, then. But what will you do, gan back yem? Back to your father's?'

Thea shook her head miserably. She couldn't go home, she didn't know whether she was going to be allowed to stay here – and, even if she was, she wasn't sure that her allowance would be sufficient to live on.

And what of Nancy? Would the other working women she shared a house with be able to see her through until she found another position? And even if they did, Thea couldn't imagine another employer being as tolerant of Nancy's ways as her aunt had been.

'Cheer up,' Nancy said. 'Like as not Miss Gibb will have remembered you.'

'Remembered me?'

'In her will.'

'Oh . . . I hadn't thought of that.'

'You never know,' Nancy said as she rose to gather up the dirty dishes, 'she might have left you the house and a nice little bit money to go with it. So, don't worry, I'll see you through until you know what's happening. Then you can settle with me one way or another.'

The next morning Miss Moffat surprised Thea by arriving straight after breakfast. She took a cup of tea with her and then went up to Aunt Marjorie's bedroom. Nancy had not been told of the arrangement and didn't look too pleased. She was mollified slightly when Miss Moffat asked her politely if she had time to help.

So it was Ellen who answered the door to Mr Blackwell.

Thea waited while the child, in an over-sized pinafore, opened the door and said, 'Miss Richardson is waiting in the sitting room.'

Mr Blackwell sat awkwardly on the chair Thea had indicated with his document case on his knee and, as no one had offered to take his hat, he placed it on the floor beside him. He seemed to be marshalling his thoughts before he decided on a line of action.

Thea gave him no help. She looked at him as calmly as she could, although it was hard to keep her eyes from straying to the hat which had caused her father's solicitor so much trouble the day before.

When he finally began to speak he was brisk and to the point.

'You will be allowed to stay in this house,' he began.

'Allowed?'

'Yes.' He cleared his throat and made a show of taking a sheaf of papers from his case and glancing at them. 'You see, this property was made over to Miss Gibb for her lifetime, but it was stipulated that it return to the family after her death.'

'The family?'

'Her sister, your mother, that is. Or had she predeceased Miss Gibb then it would have passed to you and your sister.'

'I see.'

So far, Thea had managed to make sense of what he was saying although she had a suspicion, borne out by the deliberately patient tone of his voice, that Mr Blackwell was patronizing her.

'But your mother, naturally, doesn't wish to make you homeless.'

'Oh, naturally.'

Mr Blackwell shot her a startled look; he was obviously unsure whether she was being sarcastic. When he couldn't make up his mind he returned his attention to the sheaf of documents that Thea suspected he was simply using as a prop.

'So, you may stay here until you marry, or until you come in to your inheritance at the age of twenty-one.' He looked up again. 'You know about your inheritance?'

'Yes, my aunt told me.'

Mr Blackwell paused, perhaps expecting some expression of gratitude or pleasure but, when none came, he continued, 'Another thing you should know is that whatever money your aunt once had, she poured it all into her charities. Some might say she was imprudent, because for many years now, she has been living on an allowance generously provided by your father.'

The solicitor caught Thea's look of disbelief and added, 'It was a condition of the business passing to your father that Miss Gibb should always be provided for.'

'I see.'

'But the allowance . . .' Mr Blackwell hesitated and with awful certainty, Thea knew what he was going to say next. 'The allowance ceases with her death.'

'Of course,' Thea said.

'I tell you that in case –' Mr Blackwell rustled the papers; was it too fanciful to assume that his hands were trembling? – 'in case you had any hopes of an inheritance.'

When Thea didn't respond he adopted a cheerier tone. 'But your father, you will no doubt be pleased to hear, is willing to continue to pay you an allowance. I will open a bank account for you immediately – tomorrow, in fact.' He smiled at her.

'Will the allowance be the same amount as before?'

'Of course. It remains constant until your twenty-first birthday in –' he glanced at his papers again and, to do him justice, looked dismayed at what he found there – 'in just under two years' time. Ah, now, Miss Richardson, have you any questions?'

'No, I don't think so. You've explained everything very well.'

'Good. Now if I may be allowed to put these documents on this table,' he rose and went to the desk at the back of the room, 'I would like you to sign them. But we'll need a witness. Is there anyone in the house other than that child?'

'Yes, the child's mother, and also a friend of my aunt's.'

'Good, you may call either of them, but first let me tell you what you are agreeing to.'

Thea had already risen from her chair but the tone of his voice made her hesitate to join him at the table.

'In order to gain the right to stay in this house, you must agree to stay away from the family home.'

In spite of everything that had gone before, Thea's tone was bitter. 'So my father is willing to pay to keep me away.'

'Ah . . . as a matter of fact your mother has endorsed . . . She also requests—'

'My mother!'

The anguish in Thea's voice embarrassed him and he looked down for a moment but when he raised his eyes to meet hers again his manner softened. 'I'm sorry, but your father is ill. Did you know?'

'I didn't know, but I saw him at my aunt's funeral. I was shocked. Is it . . .?'

'Cancer.'

'I'm sorry.' And Thea had spoken the truth. She could not wish it upon anyone to suffer such obvious pain. She was subdued when she said, 'And my presence in the house would upset him? You don't have to answer, I understand.'

'Miss Richardson, I don't know what to say. I have not been informed of the full circumstances – the reason why you are estranged from your family – but I must follow instructions . . .'

He looked so genuinely uncomfortable that Thea felt sorry for him. 'I know,' she said. 'And I don't want to make your job more difficult. I'll go and fetch a witness.'

Thea found Miss Moffat and Nancy in the kitchen, taking a rest from the task of clearing out Aunt Marjorie's bedroom and drinking tea. When she explained that she wanted one of them to witness a legal document, Nancy shook her head and grinned, explaining that she couldn't write very well.

Miss Moffat obliged and returned to the kitchen straight afterwards. And Mr Blackwell put the papers back in his case and prepared to leave. But at the door he paused.

'Ah . . . one more thing . . .'

'Yes?'

'I'm instructed to tell you that should you wish to marry before the age of consent – before you are twenty-one – you are to ask for your parents' permission through me – not directly.'

'Oh.'

Thea could think of nothing more to say and Mr Blackwell left.

She wondered whether he would go straight to her father's house and report that everything had gone as planned; that the daughter who had brought shame upon the family had signed the document willingly and agreed never to darken their doorstep again.

Thea knew she was thinking in the language of a cheap novel and she smiled. She was pleased that she had at least managed to retain her sense of humour.

Nancy managed to provide a meal of bread and cheese, and Miss Moffat spent most of the rest of the day sorting Aunt

Marjorie's clothes. Eventually she asked Thea to go upstairs and inspect her work.

Thea had prepared herself for the sight that greeted her: dresses, coats, hats, gloves, even underwear all in their separate piles on the bed and on the top of the chest of drawers, but the reality was unnerving.

'There are people who'll be glad of these, dear,' Miss Moffat said. She looked at Thea anxiously. 'You can take comfort from the fact that your aunt will still be helping people.'

'I will. Thank you for doing this.'

'Do you want to go through each bundle – there might be something you want to keep.'

'No, I don't think so. Although you might ask Nancy the same question.'

Miss Moffat smiled. 'Good girl – your aunt would have liked that. I'll tell Nancy to put aside anything she thinks might suit. By the way, Nancy and Ellen have agreed to come with me now, and carry some of these things to my house; she's sorting out some brown paper and string.'

'Brown paper and string . . .'

Thea thought sadly how her aunt had opened any parcel she received so carefully, saving the wrappings to be used again. She sat down on the edge of the bed and stared straight ahead of her.

'Oh, my dear!' Miss Moffat came to stand beside her and put an arm round Thea's shoulders. 'Perhaps I should have waited, but you've been so brave that I forgot how young you are.'

Thea looked up in surprise. 'Brave?'

'Yes, dear. Marjorie would be so proud of you.'

At that moment Nancy came into the room with the box of paper and string. Ellen crept in behind her and Thea, in a flash of insight, saw that the child was frightened to be in the dead woman's room.

'We can't take everything tonight,' Miss Moffat said, 'so it won't take us long to wrap what we can carry. But we can leave it, if you like, and I could stay here a little longer with you.'

'No, that's all right, but I'll go downstairs now,' Thea said. 'And, if Nancy doesn't mind, I'd like Ellen to come with me and make me a cup of tea. Could you manage that, Ellen?'

'Oh yes, miss.'

Thea saw the child's face lighten and she took her hand as they went downstairs together.

Before she and Miss Moffat left, Nancy insisted on building up the fire and bringing Thea a cup of cocoa. 'Will you be all right on your own?' she asked.

Thea was surprised. 'I've been on my own since . . . since . . .'

'It's different the night of the funeral,' Nancy said. 'To tell the truth, I don't like leaving you.'

'No, honestly, I'm fine.'

Thea was all the more moved by Nancy's concern because she remembered the uncertain start of their relationship.

'Well, then. Ellen and me had best be off and help Miss Moffat.' The lady in question could be heard coming down the stairs. 'Run along and put your hat and coat on,' Nancy told her daughter.

When Ellen had left the room, Nancy drew closer to Thea and asked, 'Is everything going to be all right, then? You know . . . your position here? Did Mr Blackwell have good news for you?'

Thea couldn't face telling Nancy the conclusions she was rapidly coming to so she said simply, 'Well, not entirely good but I can stay here.'

Nancy's answering smile made Thea bite her lip. Since coming to live here she had begun to learn the fundamentals of housekeeping, but not nearly enough. When the others had gone she would sit down with paper and pencil and try to work out how much money she would need, not only for food but also for the essentials of living such as coal and gas, and oil for the lamps, not to mention cleaning materials and any clothes she might need.

'Ready, then, our Ellen?' the maid asked as her daughter and Miss Moffat entered the room.

Miss Moffat was already dressed for the street, as was Nancy. She was carrying a largish box covered in maroon leather and embellished with lacquered gilt brass-work.

'This was on top of the chest of drawers,' she said. 'I think it must contain your aunt's jewellery or whatever. You should deal with this yourself, Thea – as soon as you feel able.'

Thea had seen the box each time she had entered her aunt's room and, like Miss Moffat, she'd always imagined that Aunt Marjorie kept any trinkets that she owned in there. It was a place for her aunt's most personal belongings and just now she shrank from even looking inside.

Miss Moffat sensed her distaste for the task and smiled gently as she placed the box on the desk. 'I'll put it here,' she said, 'near your photograph. Now,' she became brisk once more, 'I'll come back for the rest of the parcels tomorrow evening. Nancy has agreed to help me again.'

'Don't get up,' Nancy said. 'Stay there by the fire.'

The grown-ups were already out of the room when Ellen suddenly ran back to stand beside Thea. 'Good night, Miss Richardson,' she said. And then she leaned forward to kiss Thea's cheek.

'Good night, Ellen,' Thea murmured with a break in her voice.

She knew that she had already decided, however the sums added up, that she couldn't afford the luxury of a servant. She would have to say goodbye to Nancy and Ellen. So now, the child's simple act of affection was enough to release the tears that she had been holding back all day. But she waited until she heard the front door slam before she gave in to her grief.

Even as she sobbed, she acknowledged that her emotion was selfish. She wasn't just crying for the loss of a dear good woman – she was also crying for herself now having to face the fact that she was truly alone in the world and she didn't have the first idea how she was going to manage.

Chapter Twenty

March

'Shall we have some pastries with our morning coffee, Mama? I could easily run along to the baker's.'

Ellie smiled as sweetly as she could. Her mother was warming her slipper-less feet by the fire in the first-floor sitting room; the morning paper lay unopened on a small table beside her.

As ever, the beat of the piano and the thump of dancing feet echoed up from the studio below, and Rosalie Parker unconsciously moved her plump silk-stockinged toes to the rhythm of the music as she wiggled them up and down as near to the flames as was comfortable.

She looked round and smiled at her daughter. 'Oh, would you, sweetheart? Such a cold start to the year this has been – we need to spoil ourselves a little, don't we?'

'What would you like? An éclair? A vanilla slice?'

'You choose. Take some money from my purse – over there on the writing desk – that's right. Now, surprise me!'

Her mother smiled in anticipation of the treat and reached for the newspaper. Ellie hurried from the room.

Instead of bothering to button herself up into a coat, Ellie snatched an evening cloak of midnight-blue velvet from the cloakroom and, as she sped along the street towards the baker's shop on the corner, the cape swirled dramatically and several passers-by turned to look and smile.

With the cake box to carry, she had to return more sedately and she found her feet dragging as she turned into her own driveway.

Susan was waiting for her in the entrance hall. Ellie untied the ribbons of the cape with her free hand and Susan lifted it from her shoulders and hung it in the cloakroom.

'You know what to do?' Ellie asked.

'Yes. But I still don't like it.'

'Oh, Susan – it's not so dreadful. I mean, you want me to be happy, don't you?'

'That's blackmail!' But the dancing school's maid of all work was laughing when she said it. Then suddenly she frowned. 'Are you sure your mother won't put two and two together?'

'I'm sure. I've always been able to convince her when . . . when—'

'When you've been telling her downright lies!'

Susan's tone was level but there was a hint of disapproval in her expression and Ellie felt uncomfortable. She wasn't used to being criticized.

'Oh, go on with you,' Susan said. 'I'm as bad as you are to encourage you.'

Ellie smiled brilliantly. 'Right then. Remember, give me ten minutes – and you know what to say?'

'I do,' Susan laughed. 'I've been rehearsing!'

'Then "give it your best!", as my mother would say.'

Ellie sped up the stairs. She was already halfway up when Susan called out, 'But how do you know that—'

Ellie turned and, raising her free hand, put one finger to her

265

lips and shook her head. She knew what Susan was about to ask and had no intention of answering her.

She found herself holding her breath as she opened the door to the sitting room and looked in. Her mother was so intent on reading the *Daily Journal* that she appeared not to have heard her. Ellie entered the room and closed the door quietly behind her.

The tray had been sent up from the kitchen and placed on a table. Two cups and saucers waited beside the coffee pot. There were also plates and cake forks in anticipation of the treat Ellie had just brought home.

She placed the cake box on the table and began to untie the red paper ribbon.

'Well, miss,' her mother said without raising her eyes from the paper. She sounded angrier than Ellie had ever known her to be before, 'how are you going to explain this?'

Rosalie Parker lowered the newspaper slowly on to her ample knee and turned to glare at her daughter. Ellie, who had always previously managed to get her own way by a combination of sweet artfulness and downright manipulation, had a moment of misgiving.

But then she noticed that, no matter how angry her mother might be, the effect was spoilt by the round indignant eyes, like that of a cross baby, and the trembling, impossibly blonde curls. She sensed her mother's vulnerability and it gave her strength.

But for perhaps the first and last time ever, Ellie felt guilty about the way she had behaved. She knew that her mother loved her and wanted only the best for her, and she regretted that their idea of 'best' was so different. And now it was too late to act any differently from the way she had planned.

'Explain what, Mama?' she asked.

'This item in the *Daily Journal*!'

'I don't know what you're talking about. I haven't read the paper this morning.'

Her mother's glare became even fiercer but she didn't say anything. She simply handed the paper to Ellie. As she did so a couple of sheets fell to the floor and, even at this moment, Ellie smiled, remembering how her long-suffering father would complain mildly that by the time he got the paper it resembled rumpled bed linen.

'What am I supposed to be looking at?' she asked her mother.

'That column – the gossip – you know, matters of interest to society.'

Ellie knew very well where to look but she had to keep up the pretence of innocence. In order to help her to do so she retreated slightly and went to sit by the table, bending her head low over the paper and half hiding herself behind the coffee pot.

She skimmed through the items quickly, finding the one that had so perturbed her mother and read it with satisfaction. The young reporter had done a good job – and why shouldn't he? The facts were all true – well, most of them – and it was indeed an item to interest local ladies. It hadn't been too difficult to persuade him to adopt a few small subterfuges.

When she thought she'd taken long enough she lowered the paper and said, 'Oh dear.'

'*Oh dear!*' her mother exclaimed. 'Is that all you can say? "*Oh dear!*" '

'What else should I say?'

'You can tell me whether it's true or not! Come here, miss. Stand here where I can look at you and tell me whether it's true that you've been sneaking off to meet this man behind our backs!'

Ellie went to stand beside her mother, who snatched the paper so violently that it tore.

'It doesn't say that!' Ellie said quickly. 'There's nothing about "sneaking off"'!'

Rosalie Parker sat up straighter in her chair and stared at Ellie witheringly before she lowered her gaze to the paper.

'Remember Miss Eleanor Parker?' *she read aloud*. 'The lovely young woman who seemed poised on the brink of a career in the theatre? Well, Mr George Edwardes, the general manager of the world famous Gaiety Theatre in London, may have difficulty in persuading her to leave her home town of Newcastle after all.

'Miss Parker, it seems, has caught the eye of the famous detective novelist Mr Lewis Sinclair, now resident in the North East. They first met at the party which followed the Blondes and Brunettes beauty contest at the Olympia Theatre. The contest was won by Miss Parker and her partner, Miss Dorothea Richardson: Miss Parker being the "Blonde".

'Mr Lewis and Miss Parker have since been seen about town, taking coffee together, and perhaps discussing their future.'

By the time her mother had finished Ellie was having difficulty in hiding her smile. The piece was exactly what she had hoped for when she had slipped into the newspaper office and asked for the reporter who had covered the beauty contest.

She was careful to keep her head down as she waited for her mother's next words.

'*Seen about town!*' she gasped. 'People have seen you together otherwise it wouldn't be in the newspaper!'

One of Ellie's worries dissolved away. So at least her mother believed that part of it.

'So that means we haven't been sneaking about,' Ellie said. And then wished she hadn't.

Her mother's face became dangerously red, almost purple, and her refined accent slipped disastrously when she bellowed, 'Yer didn't tell yer pa and me that you were off to meet this fellow when yer left the house. You said you were going window-shopping or off to see Thea. That kind of behaviour is sneaky!' Rosalie Parker suddenly thought of something else. 'Is she in on this?'

'What do you mean?'

'Thea Richardson. Has she been encouraging you to lie to your parents? I wouldn't be surprised. Look at the way she deceived her own father about the beauty contest!'

'That's not fair! You and I persuaded her to behave like that – she did it for me!'

Ellie was stung to genuine emotion; all the more because she felt guilty about the way she had treated her old friend. Why, she hadn't been to see her for weeks and weeks, even though she knew her aunt had died – her mother had seen the announcement in the paper. And she still felt uneasy about the reason that Thea had left home . . .

'Yes . . . well,' her mother said, 'but tell me whether she knew about you and Mr Sinclair.'

'Yes, she did. But before you say anything, she wanted me to tell you and Father straight away.'

Her mother was shaking her head. 'You've made a fool of me, Eleanor.'

Her mother hardly ever called her by her given name. Ellie realized this was serious. 'Oh, no, Mother. I wouldn't do that.'

'But you have. I've told all my friends that you are going off to the Gaiety. I even told the— I mean, there was even that

269

piece that somehow got into the newspaper.'

Her mother had forgotten that she had admitted to telling the newspaper herself, and that suited Ellie very well. She didn't want her 'putting two and two together' as Susan had said. And where *was* Susan? Surely ten minutes was up?

'Well, you know . . .' Ellie hesitated and then took the plunge. 'You know, you might have made a fool of me by doing that.'

'What do you mean?' her mother asked petulantly.

'If Mr Edwardes doesn't want me to go to London, we will look very foolish. People might even . . . might even laugh at you.'

'What!'

'I mean, they will say that you are foolishly fond – that you have made empty boasts – out of love, of course. Because you love me and are proud of me, but still foolish . . .'

Come on, Susan!

Her mother stared at her for a long moment and then she pulled herself together. 'If that happens – and I'm sure it won't – I'll blame the newspapers!'

At last there was a tap on the door.

Thank goodness.

Ellie's mother pushed a stray curl back from her forehead, sighed and called, 'Enter.'

Susan came into the room and Ellie didn't dare look at her.

'What is it?' her mother asked.

'This letter, Mrs Parker. It's just been delivered.'

'A second post?'

'No, a maidservant brought it to the door. She said it had gone to their house by mistake.' Ellie risked a meaningful glance and Susan added, 'Some days ago.'

Rosalie Parker held her hand out for the envelope. 'Some days ago? But why has it taken so long for them to send it on?'

270

'Apparently the – er – mistress told someone to run along here after breakfast, but it – er – slipped down behind the coat stand and was forgotten about until the hall was swept out today.'

Her mother raised her eyebrows and Ellie couldn't tell whether she was surprised that servants were allowed to be so forgetful of an order, or that a household was so lackadaisical that the hall was not swept out every day. Probably both.

'And which house was this?'

'She didn't say.'

'I'm not surprised. Embarrassed, no doubt. But didn't you think to ask?'

'No, I'm sorry.' Susan looked suitably contrite.

'Never mind. Run along. Now let me see . . . Ellie, come here!'

'What is, Mama?' Ellie risked a grateful smile at Susan before the door closed behind her, and went to sit on a footstool by her mother who was staring at the unopened envelope.

'The postmark – look – it's from London. It will be from Mr Edwardes. Oh, I hardly dare open it!'

But she did open it, of course, tearing at it so clumsily that the letter fell out and nearly fluttered into the fire. Ellie reached out quickly to save it, her own heart pounding. She couldn't have all that effort wasted now!

She handed it to her mother and leaned back a little to watch her read it. When she saw her mother's expression change from eager anticipation and hope to one of disbelief and then utter dismay, Ellie felt truly sorry – but not in the least guilty.

Her mother didn't say a word but she continued staring at the words on the paper as if waiting for them to rearrange themselves into something that she wanted to see.

'Is it from Mr Edwardes?' Ellie asked at last.

Her mother nodded mutely.

'And what does he say?'

Her mother could only shake her head, although a small sob escaped her as she handed the letter to Ellie. Ellie read it quickly. Bless the man, he couldn't have put it better. It read:

Dear Mrs Parker,

Thank you for sending me the photographs of your delightful daughter Eleanor. I did enjoy looking at them. However, although she is truly beautiful, I am sorry to say that I cannot offer her a place at the Gaiety.

I'm sure that you, with your own theatrical experience, would know that the only opportunity for your daughter in a London theatre, as an unknown young woman from the provinces, would be as a chorus girl. And as I have a long waiting list of girls eager to fill any vacancies, it would be unkind of me to offer any hope of a place in the near future.

Yours sincerely,

George Edwardes

Ellie folded the letter neatly and looked at her mother, who was gently shaking her head in bewilderment.

'What was the point of it all?' she murmured. 'What was the point of raising our hopes when he obviously never intended to offer you a place?'

'Perhaps he was just being kind.'

'Kind? How on earth was such behaviour kind?'

'Well . . . you know . . . at the party after the beauty contest you did rather attach yourself to him and—'

'Are you suggesting it was my fault? I distinctly remember Mr Edwardes asking me to send him your photographs. Why would he do that if he didn't mean to consider you seriously?'

272

Ellie would have liked to have said, *Because he wanted to get rid of you!* But she couldn't be so cruel. And, besides, although she might have thought that once, she'd since learned that wasn't strictly true.

So she told her mother, 'I'm sure he did consider me seriously and we will just have to accept the fact that I'm not good enough.'

'Oh, don't say that!'

'Very well. We must believe that Mr Edwardes means what he says. That I'm just another pretty girl from the provinces – one of many – and the waiting list is too long.'

'But how will I be able to face my friends? And all the parents of your father's pupils? I said— I mean, they believe that it is only a matter of time before you will be going off to London.'

Her mother had started to cry. Ellie leaned forward on the footstool and offered her a clean handkerchief. She watched as her mother dabbed her eyes, leaving her to her misery for a while.

Then, judging that the moment was right, she picked up the crumpled newspaper and pretended to study it. Keeping her eyes on the newsprint she said, 'How fortunate that this item appeared in the paper...'

Her mother, still sniffling, looked up sharply. 'Fortunate?'

'Yes. Don't you see what it means? We needn't ever say that Mr Edwardes didn't want me.'

'Needn't we?' She stopped crying.

'Well, if I am to marry Lewis—'

'What!'

'As I said, if I am to marry Lewis, you can say that I have given up a chance of a career for love. That's so romantic, isn't it?'

'We-ell...'

273

'And he's famous, you know. And rich. That would be quite a feather in your cap, wouldn't it, to have your daughter marry such an important man?'

Her mother stared at her without speaking for such a long time, and with such a frown of concentration, that Ellie began to be afraid that she would work out what had really happened. She forced herself not to lower her gaze – and hoped that her mother couldn't read the truth in her eyes.

At last her mother reached for her hand and she sounded almost eager when she asked, 'And does he really want to marry you?'

'Yes, he does.'

'And you do love him, Ellie?'

'Yes, I do.'

'I mean, I want you to be happy. I don't want you to marry the man just to . . .' she stared crying again, 'just to save me embarrassment.'

'Oh, don't!' Ellie was surprised to find herself crying too and she reached for her mother's hands and held them tightly.

'Well,' her mother said between her sobs, 'I suppose Mr Sinclair had better come to see your father.'

'I'm not sure what I was expecting,' Lewis told Vernon one morning a few days later, 'but Mr Parker turned out to be quite delightful. So well-spoken, so gentlemanly and, above all, so dapper. A complete contrast to his wife. But it was quite obvious that they speak as one, and that their daughter's welfare comes first for both of them.'

They sat by the fire at one end of Vernon's studio while Adie Hall moved about quietly at the other end, preparing the scenery and props for a photographic session. She worked without instruction and she had only stopped once in order to bring them a tray of tea and biscuits when Vernon asked for it.

Adie took her own refreshment away to the other end of the room and sat quietly by herself. Lewis had often observed that the relationship between Vernon and Adie was probably more easy-going than that between other masters and their employees. Vernon gave instructions which Adie was happy to obey, sometimes without question, but sometimes not without making intelligent suggestions of her own – and Vernon was happy to accept her judgement.

Lewis suspected that there might be an element of hero-worship in the way the strange-looking girl treated her master. But Vernon didn't seem to take advantage of her devotion – indeed, he didn't seem to be aware of it – so perhaps his only fault was to take the young woman for granted.

'So, from the smile on your face,' Vernon said, 'I take it that Mr Parker gave permission for you to marry his daughter?'

'Yes he did.' Lewis suddenly looked more serious. 'Even though I told him the truth.'

'The truth? You mean you told him about your past?'

'Ellie didn't want me to at first, but I persuaded her that it was the only honourable thing to do.'

'And if he had said no?'

'It doesn't bear thinking about.'

'You really love the girl, don't you?'

'I do. Heart and mind, body and soul. Can you understand that?'

'Yes. I can.'

Vernon spoke so quietly that he was hardly audible; he didn't elaborate but Lewis knew very well who his friend was thinking about. Thea Richardson.

'So,' Vernon seemed to come back from some distant place, 'did you tell them the whole sorry story?'

'I did. I made no excuses. I told him I came from a fairly humble background. My father was a senior clerk in a shipping office earning barely enough to keep my mother and me comfortably. They sacrificed much to send me to school. It wasn't much of a school but I did well there, and, who knows, I might have gone on to better things except that my father died and I had to leave.

'I ended up with a job in the very same shipping office. And a huge burden of resentment. I had glimpsed a way to a better life and it was denied me.'

'So you turned to a life of crime. Do you know you've never told me exactly what sort of thief you were?'

Lewis laughed drily. 'A petty one. Adjusting the clerks' annual outing fund, going on to some imaginative ordering of and paying for nonexistent stationery.'

'Ah – your imagination! Your creative imagination.'

'I'm ashamed to say I was good at it. But it was only when I fell in with a greedier thief than I was and tried to profit from an entirely imaginary cargo of oriental carpets that I came to grief. We were found out and I went to prison.'

'Where you learned your lesson and changed your ways.'

'I learned that I never wanted to go to prison again. I also never wanted to cause my mother such grief again. It was her horror at what I had done and yet her total support and love for me that made me utterly ashamed.'

'And . . . and what became of your mother?' Vernon looked embarrassed to ask the question and Lewis smiled.

'She's living in Bournemouth with her sister, and the two of them have every comfort that I can provide. I told Ellie's parents everything.'

'And what was their reaction?'

'Mrs Parker was horrified, especially when I told her the effect my imprisonment had on my mother. But Mr Parker listened quietly, and at the end of my tale he asked one or two questions. I answered them and I told him – God help me –

that I would understand if he never wanted Ellie to see me again.'

'That was risky.'

'He said he wanted time to think about it and I prepared to take my leave, but he suddenly stood up and shook my hand. He said he knew very well that I needn't have told him and that was one of the reasons he was happy to give his consent – at which Ellie and her mother started to cry – and, do you know, I felt like crying too!'

'So,' Vernon said, 'a happy ending, then. But, tell me, Lewis, there's something I don't quite understand. How could Ellie have known what the contents of the letter would be? Had she spirited it away and steamed it open before she went to the newspaper with her bit of "society gossip"?'

'No, there was no need for that.'

'She was so sure that Mr Edwardes would not want her for the Gaiety.'

'She was sure, and that was the irony of it.'

'Explain.'

'You see, Mr Edwardes did want her. There were two letters, and her mother will never know about the first one. It took Ellie completely by surprise. I'm not sure what she wrote in her reply to Mr Edwardes – I've asked but she won't tell me. Perhaps she invoked the spirit of romance. In any case, his second letter said exactly what she wanted it to say.'

'She must really love you, then, to give up the prospect of a glittering career.'

'I suppose she does. Why are you frowning?'

'It must have occurred to you that, charming though she is, she's shown herself to be capable of – how shall I put it? – devious behaviour?'

'I'm hardly the one to complain.'

'No, I suppose you aren't.'

'Don't worry, Vernon, I'm aware of her faults but I love her as she is. But I've been selfish, what about you?'

His friend stared into the mid-distance. 'I suppose you mean what am I going to do about Thea?'

'I do.'

'I shall have to wait. You know her aunt died?'

Lewis nodded.

'Well, I'm told that Thea is still living at her aunt's house in Jesmond. I wrote her a letter of condolence and I said I would call – if she wanted me to. Her reply was polite but noncommittal. I shall wait a little longer and then call anyway.' Vernon smiled and rose from his chair.

Lewis looked round and saw that Adie had vanished but the door that led to the dressing room was open and he could hear a low murmur of voices – amongst them, children's voices.

'A family portrait,' Vernon said without being asked. 'And, now . . .'

'Of course. You want to start work.'

Vernon insisted on seeing Lewis all the way down to the front door but as they descended, Lewis wondered how long the family whose portrait was to be taken had been waiting in the dressing room. He hadn't heard them arrive, usually the doorbell rang through the house loud enough to wake the dead.

His novelist's imagination began to ponder on the possibilities. There must be another entrance somewhere and Adie, who had been going about her duties so quietly that she could have come and gone without him noticing, went down at a prearranged time to let them in, then she would lead them up the back stairs.

That would be it. But there was something else that he couldn't easily explain. Vernon was a fashionable photographer, he didn't come cheap, and yet the voices Lewis had

278

heard, both the children's and the adults', had been undeniably coarse.

They had not sounded like the sort of people who could afford to have their portrait taken by Vernon Gray.

Chapter Twenty-one

April

Thea stood at the sink in the kitchen, her hands red and sore from immersion in the cold dishwater and tried to pretend that she couldn't hear the front doorbell. It was only just past noon but the room was dark.

A few feet from the kitchen window was a high brick wall; Thea looked out and upwards and saw that the grey sky was heavy with rain clouds. If it started to rain then whoever it was would stop ringing the bell and go away.

She hadn't answered the door for some time now; days – or it could be weeks, she was beginning to lose track of time – because she was ashamed of the state of the house.

Nancy had gone. Miss Moffat had found her a job as a school cleaner. At first, Thea had imagined it would be easy enough to look after a house with one person living in it, but she soon realized that she'd had no idea of the amount of sheer physical effort required to keep the place clean. And how difficult everyday tasks became without heat and hot water. And both heat and hot water depended on being able to light the kitchen range and keep it going.

It had looked easy enough. Aunt Marjorie's copy of the

Book of Household Management even had diagrams, along with the straightforward instructions. It looked so simple. The correct arrangement of cinders, paper, sticks and coal laid in a clean grate should have required no more than one match to light the fire, and usually Thea was successful in this, but keeping the fire going was another matter. Particularly the fire in the range.

And without the range, she had neither heat for cooking nor hot water for washing. Most days she ended up huddled miserably over the fire in the sitting room, boiling up a kettle on the tiny hob for a hot drink or for a basin of water to wash herself. She couldn't remember when she had last washed her hair.

She emptied the bowl of water and turned to face the enemy, the kitchen range. She already knew from the cold air creeping out from the corners to reclaim the room that she had lost the battle again. She sighed. At least the fire in the sitting room was still going – or at least it had been a few minutes ago. She would huddle in there and try to lose herself in a book until it was time to go to bed.

She looked up at the row of bells above the door that led into the hallway. The bell marked Front Door remained silent. Whoever it was must have gone away. Nevertheless, Thea crept silently along the narrow passage, keeping to the wall as if the uninvited guest might be peeping through the letter box. She knew this was fanciful but she couldn't help herself.

She opened the half-glassed door and saw the usual note on the doormat. She opened it and read it. This time it was from Mrs Shaw. Her aunt's old friends had not neglected her. Either Miss Moffat or Mrs Shaw had called regularly, sometimes together, to see how she was but, after their very first visit, when the house was cold but still reasonably free from dust and grime, Thea had not answered the door and they had started leaving little notes enquiring after her.

Thea had taken care to reply to each one, slipping out after dark and delivering her answer by hand. She thanked them for their concern and made up some pretext of having been out visiting.

Sometimes she really had been out; walking across the Town Moor, wrapped up warmly against the chill spring weather. But even though she could feel the damp creeping into her bones, she would stay out as long as possible – anything rather than be cooped up in the house alone with her thoughts.

But she had not made any visits – any social calls. After all, who was there who would want to see her? Certainly not her family and, as for the person she'd considered to be her friend, Ellie Parker, she'd had no word or welcoming sign from her at all.

Thea thought that Ellie might have written a note of condolence when Aunt Marjorie had died – the funeral notice had been in the local paper – but there had been no note then or since. Thea found that she was too proud to make the first move.

The fire in the sitting room was still alight but it was spluttering feebly for attention. Thea picked up the coal scuttle; it was empty. Wearily she made her way back through the house to the kitchen and then into the scullery where the door opened into the back yard.

Once out Thea could smell the acrid smoke issuing from the maze of surrounding chimneys. The rain that had been threatening had started, cold, driving rain that seemed to cut through her on the short dash across the yard to the coalhouse. She should have stopped long enough to put a coat on – an old mackintosh hung on the back of the door just for occasions like this – but it was too late now and Thea was wet through by the time she had wrestled with the rusty old sneck on the coalhouse door.

'Oh no . . .' Thea murmured aloud in dismay as she glanced at the remaining lumps of coal scattered amongst the dust on the coalhouse floor.

She had meant to order more but wasn't sure which day the coalman called. She had the vaguest notion that you had to catch him when he came down the back lane with his horse and cart, or at least leave the hatch open for him, but she had forgotten to do either.

She was reluctant to leave the hatch open permanently, so she would have to open it each morning and close it each night starting tomorrow. Now, as she filled the scuttle, she saw that there was probably enough coal left to light one fire for a few more days.

It gave her some satisfaction that she could forget about the range until she had more coal. As for the dining room, she didn't even go in there these days, and her bedroom would have to remain like an ice box.

She managed to save the fire by holding an opened double sheet of newspaper across the hearth's opening after she had added some coals, a tip from the same *Book of Household Management*, although it was suggested that a proper blazer would be more suitable. Thea had not been able to find anything that resembled the drawing of a blazer so she used an old newspaper instead.

Holding the paper across the gap made the air rush in through the grate, encouraging the flames to blaze away.

Thea listened to the crackling sound and watched as a satisfactory yellow glow shone through the paper. Then a brown singe mark appeared in the centre. The brown mark spread rapidly, then, without warning, erupted into flames.

Thea pushed the paper away from her and let go. She sat back on her heels and watched with childish delight as the burning paper whooshed up the chimney and out of sight.

She had enjoyed the bright moment of fierce warmth but she realized that she had been careless and that she must take more care in future or she might start a fire that would consume her home.

She pushed a wisp of hair back from her brow and saw that her hands were black with coal dust. In the light of what had just happened, she placed the cinder guard before the fire before returning to the kitchen to wash her hands and face in cold water. Then she filled the small kettle to take through and make some tea.

She hadn't been out to buy fresh provisions for days so she made do with cracker biscuits spread with fish paste. By now the rain was beating against the windows and the sky was darker than ever. But Thea didn't draw the curtains; neither did she light the reading lamp.

She sat by the fire quite enjoying the feeling of being alone, sheltered from the elements in a room that was warm for the moment and sufficient food to satisfy her dwindling appetite.

It was probably the flaky cracker crumbs that brought on the fit of coughing.

Robert never ceased to wonder at the middle-class women who were content to spend hours preparing the huge coppers full of soup for distribution to the poor, when very few of them had ever cooked a meal for their own families and some had never been inside the kitchens in their own houses.

Wrapped up in clean white pinafores, and with cooks' caps covering their fashionably styled hair, and with their sleeves rolled up, they cut the meat into small pieces, broke up the bones and put everything into the coppers with at least ten gallons of water.

Then they washed and sliced the vegetables – onions, carrots, turnips, leeks, anything that was available, including the green tops of celery – and added it all to the meat liquor along with brown sugar and salt and half a pint of beer. Everything was left to boil for about four hours, but two hours before the soup was wanted, rice or barley would be added along with some herbs and seasonings.

It wasn't just because soup was cheap to make that the local benefactresses considered it the best form of food for charitable purposes. Many of the people who came to the soup kitchens were ill and weak and the soups and broths provided were easy to digest.

These women were easy to mock and, indeed, they were even accused by some who they tried to help of being patronizing. But Robert would never criticize them. Whether they were genuinely moved by the plight of those they helped or they were playing at being 'Lady Bountiful' in order to attract approval, the service they gave to the poor was desperately needed and provided the only hope of survival for all too many until society at large recognized its responsibilities.

Marjorie Gibb had known that the world must change – and she had had every hope that it would – but, until that day, she had been prepared to give everything she had, and that had ultimately included her life, to feed and clothe the starving souls she found on the streets of Newcastle, one of the richest cities in Europe.

As yet no one had been designated to take Marjorie's place so Robert agreed to go alone on the nights that she would have been on duty. He glanced at the trestle tables already set out and waiting, and sniffed the aroma of meat broth as it spread out from the kitchen to fill the draughty corners of the dining hall with comfort.

Marjorie used to love this moment, when everything was almost ready and they were just about to set out, knowing that they could bring a few brief hours of warmth and security to those who might have given up hope.

'Come along, my friend!' she would say to him, and off they would go together.

Tonight Robert wept unashamedly as he set off through the rain-drenched streets without her.

Rather than go backwards and forwards, Robert would round up a group of children at a time and put the oldest one in charge, giving the child directions to the old hospital and tickets for admittance. The tickets didn't really mean anything, for most of the ladies in charge would never have turned away anyone they deemed worthy of help.

'Worthy of help.' That was the vexing question. For there were those who believed that the poor divided up into the deserving and the undeserving, and Robert was supposed to send only the deserving to the soup kitchen.

The rain had grown heavier all day and the streets were deserted. Robert knew it wasn't because the homeless had suddenly found somewhere to live. It was simply that they would be hiding in arcades and doorways, hoping not to be moved on until the rain stopped.

He had just sent a ragged little group away, clutching their tickets and running across the wet pavements with cold bare feet, when he saw a face he recognized. The girl was about twelve years old. She was standing under a lamp so he got a good look at her as she spoke to two other youngsters.

She was better dressed than the others. Instead of a ragged skirt and a shawl she wore a three-quarter-length coat over what looked like a warm dress and she also wore shoes. Robert couldn't hear what she was saying but the tone of her voice was persuasive.

Suddenly she saw him looking at her and drew back into the shadows. The other two girls looked around uncertainly and then, seemingly at a command from the other girl, they ran away.

Robert was unsure what he should do. He didn't want to frighten the child but he did want to speak to her. He could call out her name, he supposed, but he didn't think she would answer, not if what he suspected was true.

Mary Watson belonged to a large family that Marjorie had helped one way and another over the years, taking them food and clothing, and arranging treats for the children such as picnics and river trips.

Mary was personable and good-natured and Marjorie had hoped that she would be able to find her a job in domestic service when she left school. So his old friend would have been appalled if he had told her that Mary Watson was one of the girls he'd identified in the pornographic photographs sold by Billy Reid.

And now, it seemed, she might be soliciting other unfortunate children to join her. It would make sense for whoever was responsible for the photographs to send out someone that the children knew and trusted.

Robert withdrew as far as the entrance to the arcade and waited. Because of the rain the streets remained quiet. And perhaps because of the rain Mary would be more successful in persuading other children to leave the streets in favour of a warm dry place where perhaps they would be given a bath, some supper and a bed for the night. He wondered at what point the following morning they would realize what they would have to do.

Eventually he heard the sound of footsteps. He frowned; it

sounded as if there were more than one person coming towards him. Mary had not been alone. He wondered if he were going to discover, at last, who was responsible for the photographs – and what he should do – but as they approached him, Robert saw that the other person was another child.

Or was she? As they drew closer he could see that the second figure was a little taller than Mary and her build slightly more substantial. She was not a child but a young woman, who wore an old-fashioned cloak with a hood pulled up to cover her head and throw her face into shadow.

He was still wondering whether he should step out and confront them when the young woman sensed his presence and gripped Mary's arm. They both stopped and peered into the entrance to the arcade. He moved forward slowly, not sure what he was going to say but they didn't give him a chance to say anything. As soon as they saw him, they took flight.

He stared after them, knowing he'd missed his chance. He also knew that he would not forget that face. If he ever saw her again, he would know her. The woman's expression revealed by the lamplight had been one of alarm, but also hostility. Her face framed by the dark hood was unnaturally pale and her staring eyes had been round and slightly protuberant. And if eyes were the mirror of the soul, Robert did not like what he saw there.

By midnight all the good ladies had gone home and left the running of the soup kitchen to equally dedicated men. The men, most of them elderly and retired from work and business, would feed the stragglers, wash the pots and clean up the kitchen. Strictly speaking their customers were not allowed to sleep there but those in charge waited as long as possible before turning them out into the cold morning.

Robert had to leave. He had already done his bit and he had

to get up for work in a few hours' time. Miss Moffat was hovering near the doorway. Her brother, a doctor in general practice, always came to collect her in his motorcar. She smiled as Robert approached her.

'Hugh was called out to a confinement just before I left home tonight. It must have proved more complicated than he imagined. Poor woman,' she added feelingly.

'Would you like me to walk you home?' Robert asked.

'And then walk all the way back to your studio? I couldn't ask it of you. And, in any case, Hugh will definitely be coming for me, and if I wasn't here, he'd be cross.'

Miss Moffat smiled and tried to make light of it but Robert, just like all her friends, knew that Alice Moffat lived in awe of her clever brother and his stern academic wife. It was a pity that she had no other option but to live with them.

Robert was about to bid her good night when something made him ask, 'Have you seen Miss Richardson lately?'

'Thea?' She looked troubled. 'No. In fact Mrs Shaw and I have only seen her once since Marjorie's funeral. We've just about given up calling, for she's never at home. We write notes and she always answers them politely, saying she's sorry she missed us, but . . .' She stopped and looked unhappy.

'What is it?'

'But she never suggests a more convenient time or hints that she would like to see us at all. And you know Cissie Shaw and I were Marjorie's closest friends. It's very strange.'

'No, not strange,' Robert said, and Miss Moffat looked at him questioningly. 'I think I know why she's behaving like that. I think it's *because* you were Marjorie's closest friends.'

'I don't understand.'

'Don't you see, I believe Thea – Miss Richardson – is grieving so deeply that she would find it too painful to see you.'

'Perhaps.'

But Miss Moffat didn't look convinced and she still looked troubled a moment later when her brother's motorcar drew up and she hurried towards it. Tyrant or not, Dr Moffat got out of the car and helped his sister in. He even turned and waved cheerily at Robert. The confinement must have gone well, after all.

Robert watched them go and then set off to walk home. He remained thoughtful. The reason he had given Miss Moffat only half explained Thea's behaviour, he believed. But he couldn't have told her the rest of it.

Miss Moffat, Mrs Shaw and all their associates were still engaged in the activities which had brought about Marjorie's death. He believed that Thea wanted to distance herself completely from a world where such tragedies could happen.

But, all the same, it was worrying . . .

Perhaps he should go and see her himself one night after work. And if she wasn't at home he would keep trying until he satisfied himself that she was all right. Then he smiled at his own duplicity. He knew he was deceiving himself if he believed that the only reason he wanted to visit Thea was to check on her welfare.

He didn't just *want* to see Thea, he *needed* to see her even though it would cause him pain to face the hurt in her eyes – the hate even – when she was confronted by the man who had allowed her aunt to die. Whatever her feelings, Thea Richardson had become as necessary to him as living and breathing and painting. And, because he believed nothing could ever come of it, the frustration was tearing him apart.

It didn't help to know that the very intensity of his wretchedness had probably inspired him to do some of his best work. He knew that he would trade all his talent and his growing fame just to be allowed to spend the rest of his days with Thea. In fact he hardly knew how he was going to go on without her.

He was nearly home. Another turn and he would be able to glimpse the river at the bottom of this steep winding street. The rain had stopped and wispy clouds scudded across the night sky. The moon shone brightly on the glistening cobbles. Robert stopped and stared at the old buildings outlined with silver.

He caught his breath at the beauty of it – the terrible beauty of this city.

Chapter Twenty-two

Thea opened the door of the scullery and flinched at the cold air. The movement brought on a coughing fit and she cried with exasperation as the spasms racked her body. She pressed both her palms flat and hard against her chest and the coughing stopped. But it had left her throat feeling as if it were lined with sandpaper. Just like her eyes.

She kneeled to pull the cardboard box out from under the wooden bench and blinked to try to clear her vision. What she saw through the rheumy blur made her groan with despair. She'd stopped the delivery of the morning paper as an economy, and now Aunt Marjorie's hoard had dwindled to three or four yellowing double pages. The box next to it was equally short of firewood. Bundles of sticks could be bought at the nearest corner shop but she hadn't been out for days.

She stared from box to box gloomily. She couldn't light the range after all. Yesterday, she had gone out to the coalhouse to find it full of coal. Just looking at the shining mountain of black diamonds had given her spirits a lift. It was like a fairy story, she thought, only instead of a heap of gold the little people had left her something much more magical: coal, the source of warmth and comfort.

Obviously she would have to pay for the coal and she still wasn't sure how. Perhaps the coalman, like Rumpelstiltskin, would appear tonight and set her three tasks. Thea found herself laughing weakly as she filled the scuttle and carried it through to the sitting room, ready for the morning fire.

She had gone to bed dreaming of a tank full of hot water – just think, a bath! – and the pan of soup she would make with the half-packet of lentils and the shrivelled onions and wrinkled carrots left in the vegetable rack. Then, clean enough to face the world, and with warm food inside her, she would have gone to the shops for provisions – and cleaning materials.

First she must feed and look after herself and then start on the house. She was ashamed that she'd given in so easily.

But her new plan of action wasn't going to be so straightforward after all. Looking at the paper and the firewood, she realized she would have to settle for a meagre fire in the sitting room. Well, she would boil enough water at least to wash herself and she could cover up her hair with a scarf before she went to the bank in the High Street to draw some of her allowance.

She knew it was her own fault for having waited so long, and it was ironical that now she was beginning to deal with her grief, her body seemed to be letting her down. She felt more than tired, she was exhausted, and couldn't understand why when she'd done nothing but mope around for so long.

Something else she couldn't understand was why Robert Hedley hadn't called. She knew that he probably didn't regard her highly. The first time they'd met he'd dismissed her as a social butterfly who had no real interest in her aunt's work. He'd made that only too clear by the way he'd hardly spoken to her that night he'd called here.

That night . . .

But surely after what had happened simple human kindness should have prompted him to call again and see if she was all right, not because he cared personally for her welfare, but out of respect for Aunt Marjorie.

Thea stared at her reflection in the flyblown mirror Nancy had placed over the sink. She hadn't put her hair up that morning – it took too much effort – and it was hanging down over her face. She pushed it back with one hand and hated how lank it felt. She noticed that there were beads of moisture on her brow, but how could she be perspiring when the house was so cold?

Thea tipped the remaining few sticks into the box containing the paper and carried it through to the sitting room. She kneeled in front of the grate and gazed at the cold ashes.

She reflected how for most of her life she had woken up to a warm bedroom because someone had been in there while she was still sleeping and had raked out the hearth, laid the fire and lit it. In the coldest months the fires burned all night because someone banked them up carefully. Her sister's and her parents' bedrooms would be equally warm and aired. And when they all went down for breakfast, they would find fires burning in every room of the house.

She reached for the rake and began to rattle the cinders until the dust fell through into the tray below. She would have to empty the tray into the bin in the yard otherwise the fire wouldn't draw properly.

A short while later she sat back on her heels and gazed with satisfaction at the economical arrangement of cinders, paper and sticks. She was definitely getting better at this and it shouldn't take more than one match to get it going.

In her mind's eye she could already see the flames crackling and feel the heat. She put a hand to her brow and frowned, she really was hot, burning in fact, and her hands were shaking.

She reached for the match box and had to concentrate on holding it steady. There were three matches left – Rumpelstiltskin's three tasks? She took one from the box but she was laughing so much that she had to wait before she struck it. The match flared and Thea leaned forward to touch the paper but, just before she did, the flame fizzled out.

She stared at the burned wood in disbelief. 'How could you?' she asked it. 'Never mind, there're two more where you came from!' Am I really talking to a box of matches? she thought as she struck the second match and leaned forward quickly before it dared go out.

The protruding paper began to smoke and she held the match as long as she could. Luckily, by the time she had to drop it, the paper was burning and she sat back and almost wept with relief as she heard the welcoming crackle. Just to make sure, she used the other match to light another protruding bit of paper.

After a few minutes, she wasn't sure exactly how many, the sticks had caught and were burning satisfactorily. Thea got up and hurried through to the kitchen for a kettle of water. While she was there she half-filled a bowl with cold water and set it on the kitchen table. She would add hot water to it and wash in here. Her limbs were aching and somehow even the thought of going upstairs was daunting.

When she got back to the sitting room she stared at the fireplace in disbelief. Instead of the cheerful glow she had been expecting there were only a few wisps of blue smoke. For some reason the coal hadn't taken. Hurriedly she put the kettle down and sank to her knees before the hearth and started to blow between the bars of the grate.

Each time she blew the grate sent out small puffs of soot. Her lungs hurt but she had to go on. She couldn't give up if there was any chance of encouraging any remaining spark to take hold.

She blew and blew until the tears were streaming down her soot-stained face but to no avail. The coals collapsed to reveal a few charred sticks; the paper had burned away entirely. She would have to start again.

But what with? There might just be enough sticks left, she supposed, and there was still Aunt Marjorie's box of brown paper to raid, but she had no matches. Thea frowned. She wasn't sure about that. It would be worth searching along all the shelves in the kitchen. Nancy might just have left a box of matches somewhere . . . yes, she would go and look.

But not right now.

Thea hauled herself into the nearest armchair and took her handkerchief out of her pocket. The perspiration was running down into her eyes. She wiped her brow and smiled wryly to see the handkerchief streaked with soot. What a Guy I must look, she thought . . . Guy Fawkes, who certainly wouldn't want me to find the matches! She started laughing again.

Suddenly she realized that she didn't need the fire. She was hot enough. She would just rest here for a moment . . . perhaps put her feet up on the little stool . . . she groaned as she lifted her legs. They felt heavy as lead. How heavy is lead, she wondered, and why do people say that?

Yes, anyway, she would rest for a while, close her poor prickly, sticky, scalding eyes, and wait until her head was clear of smoke. Smoke? Then she would go through to the kitchen and strip off and wash in clear cold water. Then . . . Then what was it she had to do?

She frowned and even that small movement of her brows caused her pain. She couldn't remember what it was she was going to do next. Perhaps if she could sleep for a while . . .

She leaned back in the chair and found that even the back

of her head hurt as it touched the soft velvet. But she didn't have the strength to move forward again – nor to close her eyes. She stared blearily towards the window where the pattern of the lace curtains seemed to move and dance against the cold grey light . . .

'And will you ask Thea to be a bridesmaid?'

Lewis and Ellie had managed to escape from Mrs Parker's energetic wedding preparations to Alvini's, where they faced each other over cups of hot chocolate.

'No.'

Ellie had replied a little too emphatically and Lewis raised his brows. 'But she's your best friend, isn't she?'

Ellie coloured a little and Lewis knew that whatever she said next might not be exactly accurate. How quickly I've come to read her, he thought, and how little I care that she isn't quite perfect.

'Well, yes, of course, she's my friend. But it might not be proper.'

'Why not? Oh, because she will still be in mourning for her aunt?'

'Yes.' Ellie couldn't meet his eyes.

'You did write to her, didn't you?'

'No, and I feel dreadful about that – I really do. But so much has been happening.'

Lewis reached for her hand. 'It's my fault too. We've been so taken up with each other that we've been selfish. So why don't you ask her anyway? You might find that, in spite of convention, Thea might like to be your bridesmaid.'

'I'd like to – really I would – but I can't.'

'Whyever not?'

'Thea and I are so different. I mean, I'm small and fair—'

'And absolutely exquisite,' Lewis interjected.

297

She smiled and continued, 'And Thea is tall and dark. So it would upset everything.'

'I know I'm a mere man, but I'm not sure what you mean.'

'Oh, Lewis, of course you do. It would upset my mother's plans for the bridesmaids and the dresses and the flowers – oh, and everything.'

'I begin to see. Your mother has a picture of how everything should look and Thea wouldn't fit in.'

'Exactly.'

'Poor Thea.'

Ellie pouted. 'Don't look at me like that. All the brides-maids are going to be children – girls from the dancing school. They'll be dressed like flower fairies—'

'And you will be Titania!'

Ellie frowned and then she said, 'Oh, Shakespeare. Well, yes, something like that. And you can see that Thea just wouldn't fit in. I mean, she'd hate it.'

'How wise you are, my darling. From what I know of your clever friend, she might indeed hate it. But you are at least going to invite her to your wedding. I hope?'

Ellie sipped her chocolate and put her cup down with something of a clatter. She pursed her lips. 'Why this sudden concern for Thea Richardson?'

'Because I know what great friends you were, and I don't want the break-up of that friendship on my conscience.'

Lewis meant every word he said. He had liked Thea Richardson and saw no reason to hurt her. Ellie had been thoughtless rather than cruel and he wanted to put things right.

Ellie looked thoughtful. 'You're right of course. And now I feel dreadful that I haven't even told her we are going to be married. I'll write—'

'Write?'

'Oh, all right, I'll go and visit her as soon as I find the time.'

'I knew you would.' Lewis beckoned the waiter and asked for the bill. 'And as I must go home and get some work done, I'd be happy to think that you'd go along right now.'

'Right now?'

'Unless you want to go home and help your mother, of course?'

Ellie smiled. 'You know I don't.'

They were both laughing as they made their way out into the Haymarket.

Thea, too weary to move from her chair near the cold hearth, was nevertheless fascinated by the passing show as people walked by the window. There was barely any garden at the front of the house and Aunt Marjorie had kept the privet hedge trimmed low so as not to obstruct the light.

The lace curtains, which prevented anyone looking in, did not obscure the view from inside. Men and women walked by sometimes singly, sometimes together, and if Thea sat still and concentrated she could hear snatches of conversation that gave her a fevered glimpse of other people's lives.

'No, the tram didn't stop,' a bowler-hatted young man said to another. 'I don't know why . . .'

A little later two women gossiped, 'And hasn't the missus paid you yet?'

'Not for three weeks now. The talk is they're in Carey Street . . .'

And more mysteriously another woman said to her companion, 'Well, I hardly like to tell you, Bella, but when she walked in the room she found . . .'

Thea tried to imagine what on earth the woman had found.

All sorts of possibilities sprang to mind. Some of them made her blush.

Then she laughed out loud when she saw a young woman, all on her own, stop and complain loudly, seemingly to thin air. But when the woman bent down and then popped up again with a small child in her arms, Thea realized that she was not mad.

Or at least she was – but only in the sense that she was furiously angry. The child was carried off grizzling loudly. Thea listened to its howls of rage diminish as its mother walked further away. She waited for the next piece of entertainment.

It came when a group of schoolgirls hurried by laughing and chattering. Their pleasant young voices reminded her of her own schooldays. She had been happy at school. She'd got on well enough with most of the girls even though she was aware that they thought her a little eccentric because she'd actually enjoyed the work.

Work had been her escape, she supposed. She'd gone to school eagerly each day, happier there than at home. What was it about home that had been so dreadful? Thea frowned. Was it something to do with her sister? No, Imogen had been their father's favourite but that was hardly her fault.

Her father . . . that was it . . . He'd made his dislike of her plain, brutally so – and her mother . . . her mother's indifference had been even more wounding.

But I'm here now, Thea thought, seeking comfort. I've never been so happy and it's all because of that silly beauty contest. I'm here with Aunt Marjorie . . . No!

Confused as she was, Thea found tears welling up as she remembered her true situation. The tears were hot and, as she rubbed at her face, she found that her skin was hot too. Strange that it should be so when the room should be cold without a fire.

She began to cough and as the cough subsided she felt her head pounding, a dull, heavy pounding that seemed to echo round the room in time to the beat of her heart. She closed her eyes and willed the noise to stop. In time it did but strangely it seemed to leave an echo somewhere outside her head. But then that too stopped.

When she looked at the window again she found to her shock that someone was standing there looking in, bending towards the glass, peering close. She shrank back in her chair and the image wavered and backed away. Perhaps she had imagined it.

The light began to fade and she realized that she had lost all track of time. She had intended to go to the bank and get some money out, but when she screwed up her eyes and peered at the clock on the mantelpiece she found she had left it too late. Without money she couldn't go to the shops. She would have to wait until tomorrow.

There was sufficient lamp oil left to light the reading light, she supposed, and then remembered that she didn't have any matches. She might as well go to bed; there was nothing else to do.

And then the pounding started again but this time she recognized it as someone knocking at the front door. It would be one of Aunt Marjorie's friends, she supposed and, as before, she decided not to answer it. The knocking didn't last long, thank goodness.

A few minutes later – no, it must have been an hour or two because the streetlamps had been lit – she saw that menacing shape again looking in through the window.

This couldn't be allowed. This was some thief thinking the house must be empty because there was no smoke from the chimney, the lamps weren't lit and the curtains weren't closed after dusk. Those were the telltale clues for burglars, weren't they? She must show her presence – and that she wasn't afraid.

At last she summoned up enough energy to rise from the chair and walk across the room. Within a foot of the window she stopped. As she suspected, the shape revealed itself to be a man, his outline big and powerful. She was glad that her eyes were bleary and that she couldn't see him properly, for then she might have shown her fear.

'Go away!' she mouthed, staring straight at him, and she reached up to draw first one curtain and then the other.

She stood there shaking until she heard the front gate clang shut and then with the adrenalin still flowing to keep her moving, she walked slowly from the room and into the draughty passage. She checked the front porch and found not one note, as she'd expected, but two.

She kneeled down to pick them up and had to steady herself with a hand on the cold tiles. The light from the nearby streetlamp streamed in through the fanlight above the door and it was easier simply to crouch there and read them rather than stand up again.

Thea opened one of the notes and, in her feverish state, she laughed to find it came from Rumpelstiltskin, or rather from an indignant coalman, who had scribbled across the top of the bill that he had seen her sitting there and would appreciate prompt settlement. So that was who had been peering in at her – at least on one occasion.

The other note was from Ellie.

Thea – called to tell you about my wedding. The house looked empty. Please get in touch, love, Ellie.

Ellie was getting married. Her friend had called to see her after all this time with such important news and she hadn't even answered the door. But would she have wanted to? Did

302

she want to see Ellie – her old school friend whose feather-brained escapade had caused Thea so much trouble and who hadn't bothered to get in touch since Aunt Marjorie died? Now at last she had called but only to tell Thea about her own wedding.

Yes, she would have answered the door, Thea decided, if only to tell Miss Eleanor Parker what she thought of her!

But as her surge of rage subsided Thea groaned. Would she really have wanted Ellie to see the state she was in? Ellie who always looked as though she had walked out of an advertisement for floral soaps or scented shampoos? And the house was such a mess too.

Thea was deeply ashamed.

I was furious with my father for not allowing me to go to university – I thought I would be wasting my days – I thought myself so clever and yet I can't even look after myself or keep one little house clean.

Well, tomorrow everything will change, she thought. I don't feel well but a good night's sleep should put that right. Clutching both notes Thea stood up again. But to her alarm, the walls of the small porch wavered and started to spin around her.

I must have stood up too quickly, she thought, as first the ceiling seemed to come down and then the floor came up to meet her. She was aware of being thankful that her head landed on the doormat, rough though it was, and then she blacked out completely.

Robert Hedley took a tram as far as the Central Station and then began to walk the rest of the way home.

He was angry with himself for going to see Thea Richardson tonight but he was also angry with Thea because she obviously wouldn't even consider talking to him about what had happened the night when Marjorie died.

He supposed her youth excused her. She was young and vulnerable and wounded enough to be cruel. And how could she even guess how much she meant to him? And if she could guess, he wondered, would she still have acted in the same way?

He could still see her standing there like an angry child, telling him to go away. He'd felt like smashing the window and taking her in his arms and covering her cross, hurt young face with kisses until she agreed to listen to him.

But she'd drawn the curtains, shutting even the sight of him out, and he'd gone meekly as she'd told him. Now was not the time.

But he wouldn't give up. No matter how many obstacles there were, no matter how hopeless it seemed. Now that he'd seen her again, alone and defiant in the darkened room, he wanted her more than ever. And he wouldn't let anything stand in his way.

The streets glistened after the recent rainfall and the neat gardens smelled of fresh-washed vegetation. As the sun strengthened, steam began to rise from the pavements, although the air was still damp enough to trap the ever-present pall made by the thousands of coal fires.

Vernon gazed at the row of neat terraced houses: chimneys gently smoking, doorsteps newly soap-stoned, and fancy lace curtains hanging at sparkling windows, in all except one house. The house where Thea was living.

No smoke rose from the chimney and when he opened the gate he saw that the doorstep was scuffed and grimy. He glanced at the window: the heavy curtains were still closed in spite of the fact that it was mid-morning. Was it foolish to imagine that the house had an uncared-for air about it?

Had Thea abandoned her aunt's house and returned to her father's more luxurious villa? Vernon didn't think so. The talk amongst the business gentlemen who dined at Alvini's was that old man Richardson was still furiously angry with his elder daughter and, even though he knew himself to be at death's door, he did not want to see her; had forbidden his wife to have her in the house.

So where had she gone? And if she had gone anywhere why hadn't Lewis told him? He presumed that as Thea and Ellie were friends, Ellie would know what had happened to her.

As he stood hesitating with one hand on the gate, a thin woman with a tight, mean mouth stopped on the pavement beside him. 'Do you live here?' she asked.

Taken aback by her abrupt manner Vernon hesitated before he shook his head. She stared at him suspiciously before she pushed past him and marched up the short front path. She glanced at the window balefully and shook her head.

'Hawway, you divven't fool me,' she said out loud. 'I know you're in there, hiding behind the curtains this very minute and waiting for me to gan away.'

Then she turned to the door, took hold of the brass door knocker and began to bang away.

'Wait a minute,' Vernon said at last. 'Who exactly are you?'

She stopped the infernal banging, thank goodness, and turned to glare at him. 'What's it to you?'

'I . . . I was about to call here myself.'

'Friend, are you?'

He walked towards her. 'Yes.'

'Then perhaps you can get her to answer the door and settle this bill.'

She took a piece of paper from the leather bag that Vernon just noticed was hanging across her shoulders. A bill collector's bag. She handed the paper to him. It was a bill for coal.

305

'My man put ten bags of Shilbottle best in the coalhouse yesterday and he wants paying for it.'

'Yesterday?' Vernon asked. 'But surely there is no need to be so aggressive if the coal was only delivered yesterday?'

'Aggressive, am I? If that means we don't want to be cheated then that's what I am.'

'Cheated? I can't believe Miss Richardson would want to cheat you.'

'Miss Richardson, is it? I knew the lass stayed on when the old woman died. But Miss Gibb always paid promptly. Coal delivered during the day, money collected that night.'

'And what you're saying is that you weren't paid last night.'

'That's right.'

'Perhaps Miss Richardson was out?'

'No she wasn't. My man saw her sitting there, just sitting staring at him bold as brass even though he'd been banging on the door just like I am now.'

The woman took hold of the knocker again and Vernon raised a hand to stop her. 'Don't do that. Just explain.'

'Explain what?'

'You said your man – husband – saw Miss Richardson sitting there. Where?'

'In there.' She gestured towards the closed curtains. 'In the front room. He looked in the window when she didn't answer the door.'

'Yes, you told me. Look, I'll pay the bill.'

Vernon reached into his pocket then dropped two sovereigns into the woman's outstretched hand. The bright coins lay on her pale palm; the lines were ingrained with coal dust. Vernon wondered if this scrawny stick of a woman helped her man to fill the sacks. It must be a hard life.

'Keep the change,' he said, and her attitude changed miraculously.

306

'Why, there's no need for that, mister,' she said. 'I just want the bill settled.'

'No, it's for your trouble. But, please, I want you to tell me, if you can, exactly what happened when your husband called yesterday.'

She did better than that. She said that normally the coal should have been delivered a week before, but when her husband had driven his cart down the back lane the coal hatch was closed. That happened sometimes if the last delivery had been eked out a little bit further.

So, yesterday, finding the hatch open, he'd delivered the usual order and called that night to collect the payment. Just as usual. After banging at the door, he'd glanced through the window—

Vernon noticed that she hesitated while telling him this, and he could picture the coalman peering through to see whether anyone was at home rather than simply 'glancing' in.

—and had been surprised to see the young woman sitting staring at him as large as life. Oh, she could see him, all right, his wife stated, she simply ignored him. And it wasn't good enough. They had enough folk trying to dodge payment without someone in a respectable neighbourhood starting these tricks.

She flushed when she said this and then she suddenly seemed to remember that she had been paid, and more than was owing.

'Thank you for telling me,' Vernon said. 'But one more question. The curtains were definitely open?'

'Are you calling me a liar?' She bristled again.

'No, of course not, but—'

'Of course they were open. How else would me man hev seen her?'

307

'How else.' It wasn't a question. Vernon had heard enough and now he wanted her to go.

'And will she be wanting any more coal?' the woman asked.

'I'm not sure. You'll have to find that out for yourself.'

She pursed her thin lips and looked as if she wanted to tell him that this was most unsatisfactory but, in the face of his silence, she eventually turned and left him, taking care to clang the gate shut loudly behind her.

Vernon raised his hand to seize the knocker, then he paused. The coalman's wife had knocked loudly enough already. But had Thea been hiding somewhere, peeping through a crack in the curtains, waiting for the woman to go away?

No, he couldn't believe that. She must be out. And yet . . . what was he to make of what the woman had told him? Thea sitting without moving and simply staring at the coalman the night before?

He stared thoughtfully at the window where the curtains now remained resolutely closed. Perhaps she wasn't up yet?

He made up his mind, knocked vigorously and waited. Nothing happened. There were no signs of movement in the house, no inner doors opening, no footsteps coming towards the door. And yet there was something . . . the faintest of sounds . . . a sigh? A groan?

'Thea!' he called and, thoroughly alarmed, he bent down to peer through the letter box.

As his eyes became accustomed to the dimness inside the house he saw her lying less than a foot away from him.

'Thea!' he called again. 'For God's sake answer me. Get up, please, get up!'

There was no response at all. Had he imagined the groan before? What could he do? The front door was far too solid for him to break down and he didn't relish breaking the window of the front room.

Wait a minute . . . the coalman's wife had mentioned the back lane. Of course, these rows of terraced house had back lanes. Taking a note of the house number on the door, Vernon raced down the street, round the corner and along to the entrance to the lane.

The back door was bolted, and although the opening to the coal house was ajar, Vernon didn't relish landing on top of the pile of Shilbottle best. It was easy enough to reach up and pull himself on to the wall. And hoping that no one was looking out of a back window and would mistake him for a burglar, he dropped quickly into the yard.

He tried the house door. It wasn't locked, thank God, and soon he was racing through the house and along the passage to where Thea lay half in and half out of the entrance porch.

'Thea—'

He dropped to his knees and eased her head and shoulders up to rest against his body. She should have been cold from lying on the cold floor with a draught coming under the front door, but she was hot, feverishly hot. Her cheeks were flushed and her hair, her beautiful hair, was lank and lifeless-looking. But nothing, it seemed, could mar her beauty.

Her eyes remained closed and her breathing was laboured. He rose to his feet carefully, taking care not to knock her head against the wall, and carried her into the front room. There was nowhere to lie her except one of the easy chairs so he lowered her gently into it and pulled up a footstool for her feet.

Then, not wanting to leave her for a moment longer than necessary, he ran out into the front street, knocked furiously at the house next door and ordered the startled housemaid to fetch the nearest doctor.

He had desired her for too long, and would not lose her now.

Chapter Twenty-three

July

'I can't understand you, Thea. You ought to look more pleased with life, considering that you're to be married tomorrow.' Ellie shook her head, her expression a mixture of perplexity and exasperation. Thea smiled.

'That's better,' her friend said, 'but only just. I mean, I know you've been ill – dreadfully ill – but for Vernon's sake you must make an effort. He loves you so much, you know.'

'I know.'

They were sitting at a table set by the window in Thea's room, the room in Vernon's house which had been her bedroom, sitting room – and prison – for so many weeks now. But she shouldn't think of it as a prison. It was large and light, airy and comfortable, and it was always full of flowers; flowers that Vernon brought her almost every day.

Today the window was open and the lace curtains moved gently in the breeze. It was warm, and the friends were sipping iced Russian tea, having just taken a light lunch of scrambled eggs and ham followed by a lemon sorbet. Thea had watched Ellie eat her share, and more, with amusement. Her friend seemed to have blossomed in every way since her recent marriage to Lewis. If she wasn't careful she would soon be as generously proportioned as her mother.

'You do love Vernon, don't you?' Ellie asked suddenly.

'I suppose I do.'

'*Suppose?*' Ellie's eyes widened. 'You only *suppose*? But you've agreed to marry him. I mean, the only reason one should get married is for love, isn't it? Like the song says – "For love alone!" '

Thea wanted to ask her friend what exactly she meant by love, but she knew this would only irritate her. In spite of her practical and sometimes devious nature, Ellie was a romantic, and she had been lucky to find a man who not only seemed to fit all the notions she had of true love and happy ever after, but who also attracted her physically.

Thea knew this because Ellie had told her – not in so many words, but all her hints of married love leading to rapture and a previously undreamed of ecstasy could only mean that 'tug' she had felt when she had first met Lewis, the 'delicious shiver' she had described, had developed into something more.

Thea had never felt this way about Vernon. He had probably saved her life, and for that she would be forever grateful. He had brought her to his home and nursed her back to health as a mother would. As her own mother should have done. He had seen to it that she had the best of care and the most loving attention and, once she had started getting better, he had spent hours with her, reading her favourite books to her, talking to her about things serious and things inconsequential. It was easy to respond to a man like Vernon and she had truly enjoyed his company.

But all the time she had been aware that his feelings for her were of a different nature than hers for him. There was no excitement, no thrill when she looked into his eyes. She believed that love should also mean passion, that the person you married should be someone you wouldn't want to live without.

This was not the way she felt about Vernon – and yet, when they were together, he had the ability to make her happy, to spoil her and make her forget all the things that were grieving her. They got along well together. She would never forget that day in his studio . . . sitting by the fire as the day darkened and the rain poured down. She had felt so alive . . . so aware . . . so truly grown up for the first time.

They already shared so much – perhaps the other kind of love, Ellie and Lewis's kind of love, would come with time . . .

'You're not just marrying Vernon to avoid scandal, are you?' Ellie asked suddenly.

'Scandal?'

'Well, you know . . . living here in his house. I mean, I know he took on that fierce dragon Mrs Collins to be cook-housekeeper, but as a servant she isn't a completely satisfactory chaperone, is she?'

'I suppose not.'

Thea didn't tell Ellie that, in any case, Mrs Collins did not live in the house. She arrived early in the morning in time to chivvy the daily help, and left after supper each night. Sometimes, if Vernon was out, she would leave earlier than she should have done, confident in the knowledge that Thea didn't seem either to notice or to care.

Ellie was frowning at her so she said, 'Don't worry, I'm not marrying Vernon only to safeguard my reputation.'

'Well . . . if you say so . . .'

Thea didn't tell her friend that she didn't care about her reputation. Why should she? Nobody else did, it seemed, and if the truth about her was known, they would care even less.

She knew that Vernon had gone to see her mother to ask if he should bring her home to the villa in Jesmond and her

mother had said no. And now that Thea had read the letter
that Aunt Marjorie had left for her she could understand why
her mother wouldn't want her in the house – a constant
reminder . . .

Vernon had told Thea some story about her mother probably
not wanting to make her condition worse by moving her, but,
if that was what her mother had said, Thea could see that
Vernon did not believe it. She wondered if he too had read the
letter. If he had, it seemed to have made no difference to his
love for her, and how could she refuse a man like that?

'Thea, you have that look again,' Ellie said.

'What look?' Thea sighed.

'There, you see! You even sound despondent. But just now
you looked distracted – far away – as if you were brooding
about something. Oh, no!' she exclaimed suddenly. 'You're
not still thinking of Robert Hedley, are you?'

Thea was shocked. 'Why on earth should I think of him?'

'Well, I could see the effect he had on you . . . you know . . .
at the Charity School party.'

'Nonsense! That was months ago. Of course I don't think
of him.'

But Thea picked up her glass of tea and took her time
drinking it. Ellie was much more intelligent than many gave
her credit for and she also seemed to have an intuitive sense of
people's inner thoughts and emotions. For, of course, it was
true that she still thought of Robert Hedley – often – and she
couldn't get over the hurt that, after her aunt had died, he had
never tried to see her again.

Sometimes Thea dreamed that it was Robert who had found
her instead of Vernon. That Robert had carried her back to his
artist's studio and then declared his love for her . . .

But that hadn't happened. The dreams faded with the night,
and morning brought the reality that Vernon was the only one

who cared. The only one who hadn't abandoned her.

She put her glass back on the table and smiled as cheerfully and as convincingly as she could; she was about to tell a lie. 'You mustn't worry about me, Ellie. If I seem a little down it's because neither my mother nor my sister will be coming to my wedding tomorrow.'

'Oh, of course! I should have guessed. But you know, you should try to understand. Your father is extremely ill. Perhaps they think they shouldn't leave him.'

'I'm sure you're right.' Thea tried to make her smile express gratitude for her friend's thoughtfulness.

'And that's why the occasion is to be so modest, isn't it? I mean, your father being so ill, you could hardly have a grand affair.'

'That's right. You and Lewis will be our witnesses and our only guests. But Vernon has promised that Mrs Collins will provide a wedding breakfast like no other.'

'Was Vernon disappointed?'

'Why should he be?'

'Well, he may have wanted more of a show on your wedding day.'

'Oh, no. He quite understood.'

In fact the suggestion that their wedding should be a quiet affair had come from Vernon. He had mentioned her father's illness as the reason but Thea had imagined that he had been pleased to keep the occasion quiet. And, God forgive her, she hadn't been able to care sufficiently to be curious about his motives.

'So – do you know you haven't shown me your wedding dress?'

'Do you want to see it?'

'Thea! Of course I do!'

'In the wardrobe. You can get it out if you wish.'

314

Ellie shot her a curious glance. Thea knew that any other bride would have hurried to get the dress herself, would have been only too keen to show it to her friend, but she couldn't pretend and she remained sitting while Ellie hurried over to open the wardrobe and lift out the wedding dress.

She heard her gasp and there was a moment of silence before Ellie said, 'Thea . . . I don't know what to say . . . it's so beautiful. So plain, severe even, but nevertheless you will look stunning in it. Oh, do come and hold it for me, I'm too short and the train will get crumpled.'

Thea held up the gown so that Ellie could step back and look at it properly. The dress was made of lustrous ivory satin, high-necked and fitted in to the waist as modern fashion decreed, and the long sleeves ended in tiny points which would almost cover the back of her hands. The train was not too long – there would be no bevy of little bridesmaids to manage it – and the cream lace veil would fall only halfway down her back.

'And your hair?' Ellie asked.

'Up, of course, with a coronet of dark green leaves, and cream and white flowers to match the bouquet.'

'What a waste!'

'What do you mean?'

'No one will see you – except Vernon and Lewis and me, of course.'

'But you are the most important people, aren't you? My bridegroom, my best friend and her husband. Ellie – are you crying?'

Thea put the dress and veil back into the wardrobe and turned to lead her friend back to the chairs by the window. Ellie was still sniffing as she sat down. She took a handkerchief from her pocket and dabbed at her eyes.

'I'm sorry, it's just that my wedding was so different – so

happy – and I feel dreadful that you weren't there—'

'I was ill.'

'Yes, I know, it couldn't be helped. But, Thea, I called at the house, you know, the day before Vernon found you.'

'I know, I found your note.'

Ellie scrunched her handkerchief into a ball. 'I feel so guilty.'

'Why?'

'You know why. If I had taken more time – looked in the window . . .'

'Why should you?'

'Stop it, Thea! It only makes it worse that you haven't reproached me. I should have been more concerned to find out why you weren't answering the door. I should have known you were there.'

'Yes you should – you should have been concerned enough to find out what had happened to me. But at least your conscience seems to have been troubling you.'

Ellie dropped her head. 'It has. In fact I'm surprised you still want anything to do with me.'

'So am I. Oh, for goodness sake' stop torturing that handkerchief and listen to me. Strange though it seems, I still want us to be friends. We all need friends and what you and I have had – perhaps still have – shouldn't be wasted. That's all I'm going to say. Except please stop sniffing and cheer up. Remember – tomorrow is my wedding day.'

Ellie looked up to see Thea smiling at her and she began to laugh. Soon they were both laughing and if there was an edge of hysteria to Thea's mood Ellie didn't notice it.

After putting her ruined handkerchief away Ellie said, 'But explain – you haven't been out – did Vernon order the gown? Was it made specially for you?'

'Yes, Vernon designed it and Adie Hall brought the dressmaker.'

'Adie Hall? That strange little woman who hovers in the shadows of the house? Vernon's assistant, isn't she?'

'Yes, she is.'

Thea thought how accurate Ellie's description of Adie was. Adie did seem to have the ability to vanish into the background and, sadly, with her bloodless complexion and round protruding eyes, she could be described as strange.

'Thea – does Adie live here?'

'What makes you ask?'

'Well, Lewis and I have discussed this. He's stayed here now and then, you know, and once he thought he saw lights and movement in the lower part of the house.'

Thea frowned. 'I'm not sure. It's never been mentioned.'

'Why don't you ask her? Or ask Vernon?'

'I might. But does it matter?'

'I should imagine you will want to know who lives in your own house.'

Ellie sounded exasperated again and Thea smiled. 'All right, I'll ask him.'

'You're a funny girl, Thea. I would be very keen to know if Lewis had a single young woman living under his roof.'

'I'm sure you would – and I'm sure he wouldn't dare. Oh, come on, Ellie don't be cross with me, today of all days. And my wedding gown won't be worn once and then forgotten, you know.'

'What do you mean?'

'Vernon is going to take some photographs – we shall keep them for ever, he said – and the best one will be just like a portrait – a painting.'

'Oh, I see. Yes, he is good, isn't he?' Ellie suddenly looked faintly coy. 'In fact, Lewis says that he will commission Vernon to take photographs of all our children, although he doubts if they will look as adorable as those angelic creatures downstairs.'

'Angelic creatures?'

'Don't say you haven't seen them? The pictures on the wall of the main reception room? Haven't you been down there?'

'No, I haven't. I've barely left this room.'

'You make it sound as though Vernon is keeping you prisoner here – like some princess in a fairy tale!' Ellie laughed as she gathered up her lace shawl and her parasol. 'Come along then, you must walk down the stairs with me – we'll peep in at them.'

The main reception room on the ground floor was used as a waiting room for Vernon's fashionable clients. Since she had been living here, Thea had seen and heard people come and go but she had never looked into this room. It was empty now. Vernon was busy in the studio and it seemed that no one else would be coming today.

The room was furnished like a sitting room in a grand house, with comfortable sofas and richly patterned oriental rugs. But it was the framed photographs hanging round the walls which drew the attention. There were one or two family portraits but the majority of them were of children, beautiful children.

Mostly girls, they were dressed in white, with soft, shining ringlets framing innocent faces. They gazed out of the photographs with huge wondering eyes, or in small groups they looked at each other with shy smiles. The girls held flowers or porcelain dolls; one portrait showed two children – brother and sister? – engrossed in a large open book.

Thea could see why Vernon claimed that he was an artist, just as much as a painter was, but somehow, no matter how attractive he had made the children look, they remained unreal. She could not imagine them putting down the flowers and the dolls and playing as real children did.

'I suppose that's how their parents want to see them . . .' she mused out loud.

'But of course. Wouldn't you?' Ellie asked.

'No, I don't think so. But they are lovely.'

Thea stood on the top step and waved as her friend walked away. The sun was warm and the city air was dusty from the continuous traffic of hansom cabs and delivery carts. The odour of food cooking in a nearby restaurant mingled unpleasantly with the ever-present smell of horse manure.

Thea wondered if she would ever get used to living in the middle of town like this; even the large garden at the back of the house and the tall stone walls were not enough to keep the sounds and the smells of the city at bay.

But once the massive front door was closed, she acknowledged that the house was cool and pleasant. And so large that with Vernon busy in his studio and Mrs Collins and the rest of the staff busy somewhere in the domestic offices she felt that she was completely alone.

She climbed the stairs slowly, pausing now and then to rest. At times she still found herself out of breath. Vernon had told her that he'd been frightened that she was going to die. The influenza that had laid her low had been bad enough, and lying in the cold passage all night had brought on complications.

She remembered very little of the first few days in Vernon's house except that he had hardly seemed to leave her side. Every time she opened her eyes he'd been there, sometimes looking at her anxiously, sometimes giving instructions to the nurse he had hired.

Once, in the very early morning, she had wakened to find him sleeping in his shirtsleeves in an armchair by her bed. He'd looked so tired that she found herself crying. No one had ever cared so much about her before – or rather no one but

Aunt Marjorie, and she had died just as Thea had begun to enjoy their life together.

The window was slightly open and, outside, the birds had started their morning chorus. Vernon sighed and moved his head but his eyes remained closed. The stubble on his cheeks was golden. Even unshaven he was an attractive man. Thea felt her lids grow heavy but she watched him sleeping until the moment she fell asleep again herself. As she drifted off she knew that, at that moment, she had come as close to loving him as she ever would.

The doctor had called almost daily and eventually the nurse had been dismissed and Mrs Collins had taken over. Vernon had spent less time in her room but he'd visited morning and evening, sometimes taking his meal with her.

He'd brought her books to read, piling them precariously on the bedside table and then, one day, the letter . . .

'I've brought this for you, Thea,' Vernon said.

He was holding a largish box covered in maroon leather. Thea recognized it as her aunt's trinket box. She had never got round to opening it.

'When I brought your things from your aunt's house I thought it might be important.' He placed it on the bed and watched as Thea stared at it. 'I looked inside,' he said after a while. 'I hope you don't mind. There's a letter there – addressed to you.'

She was unable to speak. Vernon leaned over and kissed her brow. It was the first time he had ever done that. Then he left the room without saying another word.

Thea took the box in her hands and stared at it for a long while. She knew it would be painful to look at her aunt's personal belongings, and yet sufficient time had passed, surely, to lessen the feeling of intrusion. The lacquered brass-work was dull; it needed cleaning. Thea found herself weeping gently at the thought that she had somehow neglected her aunt's memory.

She opened the lid carefully – the box wasn't locked – and looked inside. The letter lay on top of the other contents: a fat cream envelope with Thea's name on. She lifted it out and laid it aside, postponing the moment when she would read her aunt's words.

Underneath the envelope there was a jumble of shiny objects, like the contents of a pirate's chest in a pantomime, but Thea imagined they would hardly be made of gold and silver or real gems. The brass key lay there, probably never used, beside a chainlink coin purse, a small cut-glass scent bottle studded with coloured glass, and a corsage watch and its brooch.

Thea took them all out and laid them on the counterpane. She examined each one. The purse was oval with a chain attachment and a ring for carrying it on a finger. Inside were a few foreign coins; she thought they might be French – or were some of them Spanish? The lining was silk, the chain links were delicate and light. Thea realized that it was made of silver and not of steel.

Next she picked up the cut-glass bottle. It was decorated with a delicate filigree of silver, studded here and there with green glass stones. She opened the hinged lid and sniffed. The bottle was empty now but there was a lingering scent that she could not identify.

The silver case of the corsage watch was covered with sparkling paste jewels, as was the brooch that went with it. Thea examined the brooch and saw that it was shaped in the form of a spray of tiny bell-like flowers . . . of course . . . lily of the valley. She picked up the scent bottle and identified the scent this time. Muguet . . . Muguet de Bois, Aunt Marjorie's favourite. Her mother liked Parma Violet . . .

And then she remembered something else. The scent bottle that stood on her mother's dressing table and the watch she wore sometimes on special occasions. Her mother's scent bottle was similar but it was decorated with amethysts. Her corsage watch was studded with diamonds and the flowers on the brooch were shaped like tiny violets – amethysts again. They had been given to her by her father, Thea's grandfather, and the gems were real.

Not paste, but diamonds on her aunt's watch and the brooch then; not green glass but emeralds set into the filigree of the scent bottle. Her aunt, who was the least vain of women, had kept these precious items only because her father had given them to her. There must have been many a time when she could have done with more money to support one of her causes – or to have a few more little luxuries in her own life – but she had obviously never dreamed of selling them.

And Thea knew that she would never sell them either – supposing she was allowed to keep them – supposing that Mr Blackwell didn't descend on her and demand that they be returned to the family 'estate'.

She returned them to the box and picked up the letter. The envelope was open, it had never been sealed and when Thea glanced quickly through the pages she saw why. The letter was unfinished. Her aunt must have intended to write more but had not been allowed the time to do it.

She wondered, briefly, whether Vernon had read it and decided that she didn't mind if he had. He had proved himself her friend and deserved her confidence. She sat back amongst the pillows and began to read.

My dear Thea,

I hope that you never have to read this letter. If you are

322

reading it, and if what it contains is news to you, then I apologize. I apologize because it means I have not had the courage to tell you myself.

I mean to tell you, I will tell you, the only thing that holds me back is the fact that your mother never wanted you to know and I don't want to betray her – my own sister. But you are my niece, and I love you, and you deserve to know the truth. I have seen what your life has been and I am deeply ashamed that I stood back and never tried to help you.

He promised to take care of you, Samuel Richardson. In return for inheriting the family business, he promised that you and your mother would want for nothing, and I suppose he has kept his side of the bargain. You have been fed and clothed and educated to a point, but nothing was said of love.

We thought he loved your mother. I'm sure he did. I don't want to believe that he was so cold-hearted and calculating as to offer to marry her only to become your grandfather's heir.

You are an intelligent young woman and by now you must have guessed what I am trying to tell you. Samuel Richardson is not your father and, no matter how much – or little – he may have loved my sister, I believe it was too much for him to watch another man's child growing within her.

Did love turn to hate? Who knows? He's certainly capable of love. He adores his own child, Imogen. That is plain for all to see, and I believe, whatever he may have said, that he was glad to have an excuse to turn you out – cut you off without a penny so to speak. Imogen will inherit when he dies and I believe that's what he wanted all along.

I know he's been strict, harsh even, but I find the person I can hardly bring myself to forgive is your mother. I cannot understand why she has stood by and let you go without comfort. Was she frightened to give affection? To show her love for you?

No!

Thea found she was gripping the neatly written pages and she laid them aside.

Yes, my mother was frightened, she wanted to be able to tell her aunt, as frightened of him as I was, but, no, there was no love for me. She kept me at a distance; she never sought my company or tried to comfort me when ... when ...

Thea moaned softly and sank down into the soft feather mattress. As the memories returned she found herself curling up and trying to pull the bedclothes over her head to block out the light.

But the dark was worse. The warm dimness beneath the blankets gave no comfort. She remembered the times she had stayed locked in her room, sobbing with distress. It wasn't just the beatings; it was the way he looked at her when he told her to raise her skirts and lie face down on the bed. The indignity of lying there and feeling him pull down her underwear. The horrible silent pause when her bare flesh was exposed.

She had thought he hated her – and perhaps he did – but, even then, some inner knowledge had told her that this was not the way a father should look at his daughter.

At least now she had the satisfaction of knowing that she had been partly right – she was not his daughter. But she had still been a child and as such she should have been protected by his own decency. And, thank God, he had found enough restraint to hold back. Apart from the beatings he had not touched her, and as she had grown to womanhood even the beatings had stopped.

Her aunt was right: he had probably been glad of an excuse to send her away. But it wasn't just a matter of the inheritance, Thea was sure of that.

No matter how disturbing, Thea found the knowledge had brought a certain kind of relief. After a while she sat up in bed again and wiped the tears from her face with her hands. Then she picked up the letter. The pages were crumpled and she had to straighten them. She continued reading.

But at least your mother doesn't seem to favour Imogen. She seems to keep herself apart from both of you. She has become a pale shadow of the girl she used to be. Oh, Thea, if you could have known my younger sister as a girl – so lovely, so carefree, so affectionate and so ready to trust – to love. Poor Amy, that was her undoing.

And yet I can't blame her. I was deceived too. I thought he truly loved your mother, I thought he would keep his word. Forgive me, I'm rushing ahead of myself but you realize that I'm talking about your real father, don't you? And I don't want you to think badly of him for I believe there must have been circumstances beyond his control that made it impossible for him to return and marry her as he had promised.

So how did she meet him? We were holidaying in Biarritz. Your grandmother loved the place but that year the spring weather was uncertain, and it was so cold we might as well have been in Whitley Bay. The waves were crashing on to the Grande Plage with the wind blowing the spray all over the promenade.

One morning Mother and Father chose to stay in the hotel and read the newspapers while Amy and I went for

a constitutional. Your mother wanted to see the waves –
someone in the hotel had told us they were spectacular,
and they were!

Oh, Thea, can you imagine the two silly girls that we
were, laughing and screaming with mock terror when
the wind got into our skirts and blew us along the
promenade? Blew your mother straight into his arms!

He was so handsome. Tall and dark and handsome
just like a hero in a romantic novel, and your mother – I
can see her now – she looked up into his eyes and almost
fainted. Whether it was with terror or delight I'll never
know. But she certainly fell in love with him at that very
moment.

Well, unconventional as it seems, that served as an
introduction, and we were soon walking through the
narrow streets of the old town as if we'd known each
other for years.

He was on holiday too, but he was so knowledgeable.
He told us about Napoleon III being nagged to take
holidays in Biarritz by his Spanish wife, Eugénie, and
that's how the place became fashionable. He took us to
the church of St Martin – so quaint and somehow cosy –
and he promised to escort us on a visit to the harbour of
Port Pêcheurs as soon as the weather was better.

For, of course, from the start, we assumed that we
would meet again. In fact we arranged to meet in our
favourite café the very next day. And you can blame me
for this, Thea – we didn't tell your grandparents. He was
foreign and we thought your grandfather might not
approve. I was older and supposed to be wiser so I
suppose the responsibility was mine – but how can I be
sorry when the result of all this was you, my dear?

He was kind to me but it was plain to see that he had

fallen in love with your mother. Sometimes I couldn't bear to watch them – the way they looked at each other. And that was why, when the weather improved – you wouldn't believe how warm it can be there at that time of the year – I would sit over coffee and pastries for an hour or longer while they went for walks together to the Miramar beach where the scenery is so craggy and so beautiful.

I can't excuse what happened but, again, I'm glad it did. I don't know what he told her of himself but she seemed confident that he would approach our father and one day he did.

We were walking on the promenade and we stopped so that Mother could take our photograph. Up he popped, out of nowhere, and offered to take us all together – and then Mother and Father together and then just us two girls. He was so charming that my father invited him to dine with us that night at our hotel.

I'd never seen Amy look so happy. I'm sure Mother guessed that we had already met and that was just as well in view of what happened later.

He never came to join us for dinner.

What a nightmare that night was, with your mother waiting and hope draining from her lovely face as the hours passed. For the rest of our holiday we never saw him. Amy and I walked about the town for hours every day but he was nowhere to be found. But even after we returned to Newcastle your mother went on hoping.

'He knows,' she kept telling me, although I didn't know what it was he knew at first. 'He knows and he's thrilled about it. He'll come, I'm sure of it.'

Thea, my darling child, he never did, and I don't know why. I knew him too, remember, and I will never believe that he would have deserted your mother – and you – willingly.

You can guess the rest. Our parents were shocked but they wanted to do the best for your mother and by arranging the marriage to Samuel Richardson they thought they had. He was hard-working and intelligent; they were honest with him. He had always admired your mother from afar, as they say, and although it wasn't quite what he had hoped for, he seemed happy to marry her.

Perhaps his nature overcame his good intentions. I don't know. Perhaps seeing you grow into something strange and beautiful soured his love. Who can tell?

I think when I summon up enough courage to tell you this sorry tale in person I will give you this letter anyway. It's easier to write things down, isn't it? But you will want to ask questions, and I will answer them as best I can

The letter ended there, seemingly in the middle of a sentence. As Thea looked back over the pages she thought she could see that it had been written over several days. Who knows what her aunt would have written next?

And Aunt Marjorie was right – there were many questions that she would have liked to ask and now she never could. She scanned through the pages feverishly and realized that Aunt Marjorie had not once mentioned her father's name.

Thea stared ahead gloomily. Would she ever be able to ask her mother about him? Not while Samuel Richardson lived, and maybe never.

But now, no matter what Aunt Marjorie had believed, Thea could not help feeling that the man her mother had trusted had had no intention of coming back for her – of marrying her.

Did she feel sympathy for her mother? She supposed she did. Deserted by her lover and married to a man who'd made her life a misery.

As she'd folded the pages of the letter and put them back in the envelope she came to a decision. She had realized that she, at least, had the chance of marrying a man who cared for her.

Chapter Twenty-four

The sun did not shine for Thea's wedding. The skies had been overcast all day and the wind cold, but at least the rain had held off. Until now. It was almost ten o'clock at night and Thea stood at the front door with Ellie while the men walked to the Haymarket to fetch a cab to take her friend and her husband to the Central Station.

Ellie was wearing a midnight-blue Russian blouse coat, pouched at the waist and with a wide collar of white satin decorated with a pattern of smoky sequins and pearls. She had worn it to the wedding along with a blue hat trimmed with silk flowers, pinned on top of her upswept hair. Her gown of cream delaine was relatively plain apart from the large fussy bow at the neck caught with a diamond starburst pin.

'Do step back, Thea,' Ellie said. 'Don't get that lovely dress spotted with rain. It's so filthy here in town with all the soot.'

Thea, with Ellie's help, had changed from her wedding gown as soon as they'd returned from the church. Covered with a clean sheet, it now hung in the wardrobe waiting for the photographic session that Vernon had planned.

The dress Thea wore now had been made by the same dressmaker who had made the wedding gown. It was one of many that Vernon had insisted on having made for her. He'd designed them himself and Thea couldn't fault them. He seemed to know perfectly what would suit her tall, slim frame and also that she preferred uncluttered lines and subdued colours.

Her new dresses were almost as plain as those worn by pupils in a convent school except that the choice of fabrics, soft and clinging, gave them a sensuous air. Thea was puzzled by the paradox.

She stepped back to stand beside her friend and Ellie reached out and touched Thea's softly puffed sleeve wonderingly. 'Nun's veiling,' she said, as she stroked the lightweight woollen fabric. 'You wouldn't think nuns would wear anything so transparent, would you? But then they probably wear many more clothes underneath than you do.'

Ellie giggled. She had enjoyed several glasses of champagne and her cheeks were flushed. 'I hate to think what nuns' underwear might be like, don't you?'

Two top-hatted men passing by in the street looked up. Their faces, illuminated by the light from the open doorway, showed surprise.

'Hush!' Thea said. 'Those people heard you.'

Ellie brought a hand to her mouth and widened her eyes. 'Whoops-a-daisy!' she said. 'I'm sorry. But, anyway, you look lovely; that pale grey with your dark colouring shouldn't work – and yet it does, ravishingly so – and,' she lowered her voice to a whisper, 'I'm sure your underwear is gorgeous!'

And Ellie was right – her underwear was gorgeous. Adie had brought boxfuls of luxurious silk, lace and nainsook camisoles, basques, knickers, underskirts and chemises for her to choose from. Thea had never been confronted with so many pretty things in her life and she found herself seduced by the luxury of it all. She had eased her conscience by accepting only half of what she could have had, but she had an uneasy feeling that Aunt Marjorie would not have approved at all.

Thea thought it best not to respond to Ellie's banter. Her friend obviously needed to go home to bed and she felt guilty that she had encouraged her and Lewis to stay longer than they had intended. After all these weeks of living in Vernon's house a certain easy intimacy had grown between them, but tonight would bring a different kind of intimacy and she had wanted to delay the moment.

She had seen Vernon raise his eyebrows and smile every time she'd urged Ellie to take another morsel from the cold table. Of course he knew what she was doing but he didn't seem to mind.

But then he had started to fill up Ellie's glass, almost certainly knowing the effect it would have on her until, at last, Lewis had realized that he must take his wife home.

'Look – is that the cab?' Ellie leaned forward and peered out through the fine drizzle.

Thea looked too and saw the twin beams of coach lamps approaching. 'Yes, I think it is. Here, you must take this,' Thea took an umbrella from the stand. 'We don't want your hat spoiled.'

'Thank you. Thea! For goodness' sake don't open it – not in the house. Here, give it to me.'

Ellie held her arms out so that the umbrella opened up outside. 'Aren't you at all superstitious?' she asked, not looking at Thea.

'I try not to be.'

Ellie turned her head and smiled over her shoulder. 'I forgot – you were always the sensible one at school, weren't you?

Sensible and serious. If only the other girls could see you now!'

The hansom cab drew nearer. Thea could see the horse's breath mingling with the misty air. The driver huddled on his seat in waterproofs.

'Well, then, what can I say?' Ellie asked. 'I've hardly been married long enough to offer you advice.'

'Advice?'

'For your wedding night, goose!'

'Oh, that sort of advice.'

Ellie turned her body to face Thea but kept the arm holding the umbrella stretched out of the house. The umbrella moved slightly in the wind. 'Your mother should have had a talk with you. Mine did,' she began to giggle, 'I hardly liked to tell her that it was not necessary.'

'What are you saying?'

'Can't you guess?'

'I suppose I can. You're a shameless hussy.' They both laughed.

'But, tell me the truth,' Ellie said, 'haven't you and Vernon been tempted to . . . well . . . you know . . . all this time as good as alone in this house together . . . haven't you . . .?'

'No we haven't.'

'Don't sound so stern! But in that case, all I can say is that if you love him everything will be all right. And if he is as considerate as Lewis is, it will be more than all right.'

The cab had stopped at the door and as Lewis and Vernon got out and hurried up the steps towards them Thea was able to hide her expression of doubt.

'Watch out, sweetheart!'

Lewis laughed as he took the umbrella from his wife before she did him damage. He raised it to hold over both of them and Vernon stepped inside and took his place beside Thea. He put his arm around her waist. She knew they must look like an established couple.

'Good night, Thea,' Lewis said. 'I hope we gave you time enough to say your fond farewells.'

'Farewells? You make it sound permanent,' Thea said.

'Well, not permanent, of course, but we shall have to restrict our social life for a month or two. I have a deadline,' Lewis explained. 'And I am going to be completely selfish and ask my wife to both see to the orderly running of our household and to keep the world at bay until the manuscript is delivered to the publisher.'

'And I am to be your secretary,' Ellie said.

'That, too.'

Ellie took Thea's hands in her own. 'You don't mind, do you? I mean you've just been married. You will have better things to do than sit and gossip with your old friend.'

Ellie's smile was knowing and Thea felt uncomfortable. She removed her hands gently. 'Don't worry. I understand.'

'I knew you would,' Lewis said. 'You know, since we married I've discovered that I need Ellie to look after me. I wouldn't be able to work at all if I didn't know she was somewhere in our apartment, waiting for me, ready to talk to me at the end of the day.' Lewis glanced up at Vernon, and Thea thought he looked embarrassed to have revealed so much. 'Anyway,' he continued, 'we mustn't outstay our welcome, Ellie. These two will want to be alone.'

'Of course.' Ellie darted forward again to kiss Thea on the cheek and then she and Lewis hurried down the steps and got into the cab. Thea saw Lewis lean out, shake the umbrella, fold it and withdraw it into the darkness of the cab. She and Vernon stayed to watch for a moment.

A cab that had been standing at the other side of the square set off in the same direction. Both drivers urged their horses at a dangerous speed considering the driving rain and the wet cobbles.

Vernon smiled. 'That fellow's aiming to catch the last train to the coast, no doubt, just like our friends. They should manage it – it's not too far to the station.'

Thea felt sorry for Ellie, who loved warmth and comfort. Now she faced the train ride home in a draughty ill-lit carriage, and a cold, wet walk along the promenade to their home.

'We shall be in bed long before they are,' Vernon murmured as he closed the door.

He kept his arm around her as they climbed the stairs. She could feel his body heat through the fine fabric of her dress and it emphasized how cold she felt. Vernon switched off the electric wall lights as they ascended and when they reached the floor where the bedrooms were situated Thea remembered something Ellie had told her, something about Lewis staying here one night . . .

She glanced down over the stair rail and sure enough she saw a light glowing far below. Had Vernon left the hall light on? She couldn't remember. She became aware of Vernon's arm tightening around her waist and felt his mouth nuzzle into the back of her neck. His breath was warm and yet she felt icy tremors shiver down through her body. She felt unease begin to coil and knot within her.

'Don't take too long,' he said.

Thea pulled away and looked at him questioningly.

'In the bathroom. I know you'll want to prepare yourself.'

'Oh, yes.'

'I'll wash in my room.'

Vernon left her on the landing and closed his door behind him. Thea wondered whether she was supposed to follow him there when she'd had her bath. She realized that she didn't

335

even know what the sleeping arrangements were to be now that they were married.

In her own room she undressed and put on her dressing gown. It was ivory cashmere trimmed with white lace, another of Vernon's gifts and very different from the flannel dressing gowns that she and Aunt Marjorie used to wear.

When she looked under her pillow for her cotton nightdress she found it had been replaced with one of white satin, high-necked and virginal but, nevertheless, luxurious. Furthermore the bed linen had been changed to sheets of fine white silk. So they must be going to sleep in here.

In the bathroom there was an array of bath salts and toilet waters on the glass shelf that hadn't been there before and several thick white towels hung on the heated towel rail.

Thea turned on the taps and picked up a glass jar labelled 'Fragrant Bath Salts' with no mention of what fragrance it might be. She took the stopper out and scattered some in the water. The salts, like tiny chips of glass, were a mixture of pastel colours, and as they dissolved the scent that curled upwards in the steam was floral.

She made sure her hair was pinned up securely and lowered herself into the water. She hoped that she would be able to relax, to ease the tension that was gripping her, but she couldn't. She was too anxious about what was to come.

Vernon had told her not to be too long and when she returned to her room he was standing by the night table with his back to her. He wore a red silk dressing gown. The water jug and basin had been placed on the floor. In their place was a tray and on it two glasses and an ice bucket containing a bottle of champagne.

On hearing the door open, Vernon took the bottle from its bed of ice and opened it. He turned round smiling. 'Get into bed. I'll pour our drinks.'

When she removed her robe she realized how exposed she felt in her new nightdress. Although it covered her from neck to ankles, the fabric was so fine that it clung to her body, revealing every curve. She climbed into bed quickly and pulled the bedclothes up over her breasts. She heard Vernon laugh softly and looked up to find him walking towards the bed with her glass of champagne.

'Here you are. Wait, we'll drink together.'

He returned to the night table for his own glass and the bottle and placed them on the bedside table at his side of the bed. Was this always to be 'his' side from now on, Thea wondered.

Then Vernon took off his dressing gown and Thea averted her eyes hastily. He was naked. He laughed as he slipped into bed and reached for his glass.

'Shall we drink to the two of us?' he asked.

'Yes.'

Thea sipped her champagne and found it delicious. Her surprise must have shown, for Vernon said, 'Yes, I saved this one. It's special. And as you had very little to drink earlier you can allow yourself to have some more. Drink up.'

No sooner had she finished her glass than Vernon filled it and soon she found that she was on to her third glass. Surprisingly it seemed to have had no effect on her. She certainly wasn't giggling foolishly as Ellie had done.

But she did find that she was relaxing. The tension that had knotted itself inside her was loosening. And as it loosened another feeling took over, one of pleasurable anticipation. She caught her breath as Vernon leaned nearer to fill her glass, the sharp tang of his hair dressing filled her nostrils; she noticed how the golden hairs on the back of his wrist glistened in the lamplight.

How many glasses had she drunk now? She'd lost count.

She knew only that her head was clear – no not clear – it seemed somehow to have expanded. And so had her senses. Everything was sharper, more distinct.

Vernon pulled the pins from her hair one by one and she felt the strands lift from her scalp, uncoil and snake down on to her shoulders. She shook her head slightly and dark wings fell forward to frame her face.

She was aware of everything: the small fire crackling in the hearth, the soft glow of the lamplight, the lavender perfume rising from the bed linen. The delicate engraving on the crystal glass she was holding made sharp points against the skin of her fingers; the taste of the champagne was like . . . was like . . . honey . . . except she had never known honey to explode in tiny bubbles on her tongue before.

And then when the bubbles had burst she discovered there was a lingering slight bitterness that did not blend with the other tastes.

Nevertheless she was disappointed when Vernon took the glass from her. 'That's enough, I think.'

He leaned across and put the glass down on the table at her side of the bed and, as he did so, his arm brushed against her breasts. The feelings this aroused in her took her by surprise. She looked down and was puzzled to see that her nipples were pushing against her nightdress. And as she gazed at this phenomenon Vernon cupped one breast with his hand.

'No . . .' she murmured, without meaning it.

He began to caress her with his fingers and the sensations she experienced were so exquisite that she could only sink back into the pillows and give herself up to whatever he wanted to do to her. Not just her breasts but every part of her seemed to have become extra sensitive. The drag of the satin against her skin as Vernon's hand roamed across her body was delicious.

He undid the bow at her neck and fumbled with the row of tiny buttons that went down to her waist, then raised himself up on one elbow to part her nightgown and gaze at her. She felt a twinge of discomfort, lying there with her body exposed like that, and she raised her hands to try to cover herself, but he raised himself, caught both her hands and pushed them back down on to the bed and held them there.

'Beautiful,' he murmured, 'so beautiful,' and Thea heard the breath catch in his throat.

Then he lowered his head towards her and what she glimpsed in his face made her widen her eyes with alarm. Instead of the gentle expression she was used to, the lines of his face were taut. His eyes were hard; his fair skin was blotched with angry colour and there were beads of perspiration along his brow.

'Vernon . . .?' she whispered urgently.

He didn't reply. Instead he kissed her so fiercely that she could almost feel her lips bruising. She tried to sink back into the pillows and turn her head but he brought one hand up and grasped her face. He turned it back savagely and began to kiss her again, thrusting his tongue between her lips to fill her mouth. She gagged and felt as if she was choking on the stale taste of tobacco.

All the delicious feelings of excitement and anticipation vanished. Instead she experienced terror and disgust as he moved his body down on to hers. He brought one hand up between them and pushed her nightdress up. Then without pausing he forced her legs apart with one hard knee and thrust into her.

The pain was so intense that she screamed. Surely that would make him stop, but instead it only seemed to excite him the more. She felt hot tears stream down her cheeks as he moved within her. She heard his grunts of exertion and her own sobs. She knew that she wasn't simply crying with the pain but with the sheer humiliation of what was happening to her.

She had no idea of how long the torment lasted, or how the man who had been so kind and gentle, so courteous and thoughtful for all these weeks could have turned into this savage beast.

This was not what Ellie had led her to expect. '*If you love him it will be all right,*' her friend had told her. So was this her punishment for marrying Vernon without loving him? And if she had truly loved him would he have acted any differently? Would he have been as considerate as Lewis supposedly was, and then, in Ellie's words, would it have been, '*more than all right*'?

By the time he gasped his completion, withdrew and rolled off to lie exhausted by her side, Thea had descended into a deep pit of despair – so deep that she was almost beyond caring what happened to her. She lay staring up at the ceiling and the dancing shadows cast there by the dying fire.

And then, to her horror, she felt him take her in his arms again. She flinched and tried to move away but her caught her fast and pulled her into his embrace.

'Thea . . . so beautiful . . .' he murmured, and she braced herself for a further onslaught. But instead he brushed strands of her hair back from her brow and started kissing her face tenderly with kisses like butterflies. 'My sweet girl,' he whispered, 'my angel, you can have no idea how much I adore you.'

Vernon eased himself back on the pillows and pulled her into the crook of his arm; he settled her face against his breast. His skin felt clammy. Her sweat mingled with his to form pools of discomfort. For a while he stroked her head tenderly, as if she were a child to be soothed, then his movements slowed and stopped. His regular breathing told her that he had fallen asleep.

She tried to edge away but he stiffened and pulled her close. She lay there for what seemed hours before he sighed and loosened his grip. By then she was too exhausted to do anything but pull her nightdress round her body and turn her back to him. She wanted to lose herself in sleep but was too distraught.

As the fire died and the room darkened Thea heard the clock of a city church chime twelve. Not hours then, but less than two since she had come to her marriage bed. If this was what it meant to be a wife, she wondered how long she would be able to endure it.

Less than a mile away in the villa in Jesmond, Amy Richardson lay and listened to another church clock strike midnight. Her husband was dying. He had been mortally ill for months but now she had been told he would not last the night.

Dr Swanson had ordered her to rest, there was nothing anybody could do, and the nurse would come for her when she judged his last moments had come. How can you tell when a person's last moments have come? Amy wondered. But the nurse, a fresh-faced, cheerful woman, was qualified and experienced so she supposed she could trust her.

Imogen had been almost hysterical. The doctor had given her a sleeping draught and Nurse Robson had dealt with her swiftly and efficiently, undressing her and leaving her in bed in her own room with Mrs Bostock to watch over her before returning to her patient.

And Samuel? Amy wondered how conscious he had been of the things that were happening around him for the last few days. Dr Swanson had assured her that the draughts he gave him would dull his pain – but would they also dull his mind?

Did he know that Thea had been married that morning? When Mr Blackwell had brought the papers for him to sign, giving his permission for Thea to marry Mr Gray, Samuel had barely commented, showing no curiosity, it seemed. But was it significant that he had hung on to life until now – until the day he was no longer responsible for his wife's mistake?

Everything would go to Imogen. Amy wondered what her loving parents would have thought of that. Well, Imogen was their granddaughter too; it was just that she had a different father.

'*No . . .*'

She realized that she'd cried aloud and she turned her face into the pillow. She must not think about him. Why subject herself to pain, pain that had hardly diminished after all these years? How could it when, as Thea grew, she looked more and more like her real father?

There were days when she could hardly bear to look at her own daughter in case a smile, a laugh, a sudden movement of her head or a glance from those huge dark eyes brought the only man she had ever loved back so vividly that her heart would break all over again.

Why had he abandoned her?

He had known that she thought she might be with child. Had he not believed her? Had he imagined that a young inexperienced girl did not know the facts of life? But, in any case, he loved her – or so he'd told her over and over again – and he'd asked her to marry him, whether or not she was pregnant, so why had he not come to the hotel that night?

He'd told her that there was no impediment to their marriage – he was promised to no one, and as an orphan had been in control of his own fortune since his twenty-first birthday. So why hadn't he come to ask her father for her hand?

So, instead of marrying the man she loved she'd been given to Samuel Richardson. Her parents were not uncaring but they wouldn't have been able to stand the shame of an illegitimate birth – and, to be honest, neither would she.

Samuel had convinced them that he'd loved her, and perhaps he had. At first, throughout her pregnancy he'd been thoughtful and attentive; he hadn't come to her bedroom. For that she'd been grateful.

But once Thea was born, the beautiful dark-eyed, black-haired child, Samuel had changed. At first he had avoided all contact with the baby but then, as she grew, he had watched her with cold eyes, resenting any childish smile, forbidding any childish pleasure, until at last confrontation and warfare developed between her intelligent headstrong daughter and her cold-hearted husband.

Was Samuel always cold-hearted or had circumstance made him so? She would never know. But she would carry with her to the grave the memories of what had happened in the marriage bed. He had come to her room when she had barely got over the birth and taken her so savagely that she'd wanted to die.

And it had gone on like that: cold brutal physical intimacy that was all the worse for her to bear because she had experienced lovemaking of a completely different kind with her lover. And she was reminded of the ecstasy she had experienced so briefly every time she looked at Thea.

'Mrs Richardson, he wants you, to tell you something. I think you should hurry.'

Nurse Robson stood over the bed. Amy hadn't heard her knock and enter. She tried to concentrate on what the nurse was saying and she looked up, dazed.

'I'm sorry, were you sleeping? But I think the time has come.'

343

'Don't apologize.' Amy got out of bed and pulled on her robe. 'Have you told Imogen?'

For once the woman looked indecisive. 'If you want me to, I will, but . . .'

'What's the matter?'

'Will she be able to control herself? It wouldn't be kind to the man to subject him to deathbed drama.'

'She loves her father. Can you convince her that she must not make his last moments more difficult?'

'I'll try. But I'll give you a while to yourselves. I'm sorry, Mrs Richardson, but it won't be very long.'

It was the genuine concern in the good woman's eyes, the caring note in her soft voice, that brought the tears to Amy's eyes rather than the knowledge that her husband was about to die. But Nurse Robson mistook it for genuine grief and drew her to her comfortable bosom in a swift, wordless embrace before setting off to waken Imogen.

Amy wasn't prepared for the fact that his eyes would be open. Open and staring at her, following every movement as she entered the room and walked towards him. She felt like turning and running out again, his expression was so fierce.

Was he going to take hold of her and pull her into bed with him? Submit her to one last terrible embrace before the breath left his body?

She saw that he was raising his hand, slowly, feebly, the fingers skeletal, the skin yellow. What was he doing? Pointing at her? Did he want her to go? To leave him be? No, his hand turned over and those dreadful fingers beckoned her. He wanted her to come nearer.

'Amy . . .' he breathed and the sound was dreadful. It was as if death was already rattling in his throat. 'Come closer . . . take this . . .'

He fumbled under the bedclothes and brought out a piece

of folded paper. Even in the dim glow of the bedside lamp she could see the paper was old and yellowed, the writing faded. She took it gingerly from his hand.

'Read it,' he commanded with a hint of his old authority. 'I want to see you read it.'

Amy moved nearer to the lamp and opened the paper. She lowered it so that the light fell on it and in doing so she caught a glimpse of her husband's eyes as he watched her. She tried to ignore his greedy gaze and concentrated on the letter, for that's what it was. It was addressed to her.

She had never seen his handwriting but after only a few words she knew who it was from. She thought she might faint but she had to go on – she had to know . . .

'Amy, my darling,' the letter began, 'what must you think of me?'

By the time she had finished the tears were streaming down her face. He had not abandoned her, not intentionally; it had been an accident, pure and simple. On the way to their hotel that night he had been knocked down by a young man on an unruly horse and taken to hospital, where he had lain semiconscious for more than a week.

It was even longer before he could talk sense and, by then, Amy's father had taken them home to England. Frantically, her lover had set out to find their address and then he'd written to her, begging her forgiveness for his seeming desertion and asking if he could come to her. He said he would wait at his hotel in Biarritz for her reply.

'Please write soon, my darling,' the letter ended. But of course she hadn't because she had never received it.

She was filled with a terrible anger. She raised her head and stared at her husband. He was shaking his head.

'Not my fault,' he whispered. 'I found it with your father's papers after he died.'

'But—'

He knew what her question would be. 'I don't know, Amy. I don't know whether it arrived before or after our wedding, and I don't know why your father kept it. Guilt perhaps? Guilt because he didn't tell you . . .'

Amy wondered how long the man she had loved – still loved – had waited in Biarritz before returning to his home in San Sebastián. Surely if he had no reply and if loved her he would have come to England to find out why?

Unless he had received a reply . . . from her father . . . saying that it was too late!

Amy felt the sobs rack her body. She clasped the letter to her heart as she wept and the slack-jawed lines of Samuel's face hardened into disgust. His lips moved and he looked towards the door as he breathed, 'Imogen . . .?'

There was an expression of anxiety in his eyes, anguish even, but then they ceased to focus and his jaw dropped. With one last sigh of disappointment he was gone.

'No!'

Imogen ran across the room, her robe and her pale hair billowing behind her, and sank down on her knees by the bed. She took one of her father's hands and brought it to her face. Nurse Robson followed and stood behind her. She made as if she was going to take hold of the girl and raise her to her feet but Amy shook her head.

'Let her be,' she said quietly. 'Someone should mourn him.'

The nurse shot her a puzzled look at her words, but seemed satisfied by the tears still streaming down Amy's face.

'Why didn't you tell me?' Imogen accused. She glanced wildly first at her mother and then at the nurse. Tears streamed down her cheeks too. 'Why didn't you tell me in time so that I could say goodbye? He must have thought that I don't care!'

Nurse Robson looked guilty. She had promised the wife

346

more time with the husband and in doing so had denied the daughter. Amy did not want the poor woman to be troubled so she tried to mend the situation. She stuffed the letter in the pocket of her robe and went forward to comfort her daughter.

She kneeled down beside Imogen and put an arm around her shoulders. 'Your father saw you as you entered the room,' she said even though that was probably not true. 'He saw you coming and he spoke your name.'

'Did he?' Imogen turned her ravaged face towards her.

'Yes, didn't you hear? The very last word your father spoke was your name.'

And that at least was true, although Amy alone knew that Samuel had been asking for his beloved daughter rather than saying goodbye.

Nurse Robson came to stand at the other side of the bed. 'We can't leave him like this,' she said. 'There're things to be done – and it's better if you leave everything to me.'

'You want us to leave the room?' Imogen's tone was challenging.

'It would be better.'

Imogen got to her feet and glared at the nurse across her father's body. But Nurse Robson stood firm.

'Very well,' Imogen said. 'But when you have . . .' there was a catch in her voice, 'when you have done whatever you have to do, I want you to come for me. I will sit with my father until morning.'

She'd made no mention of her mother, and Amy, rising wearily to her feet, saw Nurse Robson's eyes widen in surprise. Then she said, 'Yes, Miss Richardson.' She didn't even glance at Amy; she had accepted the young girl's authority.

Samuel Richardson was dead but, even before his eyes had been closed, another tyrant had taken control of the household.

Chapter Twenty-five

August

Ellie stood in the middle of the ground-floor sitting room and looked around her. Lewis was up in their own apartment working, and she had come in to see if the housemaids had been dusting and polishing properly while Mrs Fleming was visiting her family in London. Ellie liked to imagine how she would completely reorder everything in here if the house was hers.

Mrs Fleming had told them she was reluctant to leave Cullercoats, where she had been born and brought up in one of the fishermen's cottages, but she was beginning to feel that, as she got older, she ought to live nearer to her children and grandchildren. She had thought of buying a smaller house, just somewhere to bring the little ones for holidays, and selling this imposing mansion overlooking the bay.

Lewis had half joked that if she ever decided to carry out her plans he would like to buy this house from her. It was only half a joke because, in the short time since their marriage, he and Ellie had been deliriously happy here. So, although originally he had left London in order to protect his new identity, he had come to feel that he would like to make his home here permanently.

Ellie stared musingly at the solid old-fashioned furniture, the paintings in their heavy frames and the profusion of ornaments, and mentally cleared everything out in order to start again. She walked over to the window and gazed up at the dark red silk brocade curtains. They could stay, she supposed, although, in spite of the linings and the lace curtains that covered the whole window, they had caught the sun and faded a little at the edges.

Before turning away, her eye was caught by a movement on the promenade opposite. A man had stopped to light his cigar. Secure in the knowledge that the lace curtains that covered the whole window meant she could see but not be seen, she stayed to watch. Ellie frowned. It was him again. She had known it would be.

The same smartly dressed man had passed by the house several times lately. He always seemed to have some pretext for stopping and glancing over. He would light a cigar as he was doing now, tie a shoe lace or even take a handkerchief from his pocket and mop his brow – although Ellie didn't think the summer sun was as hot as that.

She had mentioned it to Lewis and he had suggested that the man was one of the summer visitors; the little fishing village was a popular resort. But Ellie didn't think so. His habit of always stopping exactly opposite the house was beginning to worry her, especially as she had only noticed him the day of Thea's wedding, when she had imagined that she and Lewis had been followed home from the station.

'Is it wise to have left the shipyard?' Grace asked Robert. 'I mean, you were doing well there – a senior draughtsman.'

'Do you doubt that I shall be able to make a living? Are you worried that I shall starve in a garret?' He smiled at her.

'Of course not.'

Grace looked around at the paintings displayed on the walls of the art gallery. Just about every one of them bore the small label denoting that it had been reserved. Robert saw her frown as she regarded the ragged children, the street vendors, and the squalid tenements.

'You don't like them? Robert asked.

'Oh, they're good – very good. It's just that I don't understand why people who could afford to fill their homes with beautiful and attractive images such as your other paintings – I mean of the sea and the river and the sailing ships – should want to be reminded of such – such squalor.'

'I don't know the answer to that, Grace, but I know I shall always want to paint such scenes.'

'Well,' she said, 'whatever you choose to portray, you are a tremendous success. Even the London papers have carried favourable reviews. But . . . but . . .'

Robert, who knew that he would do very well financially out of this, his first exhibition, said, 'Will it last? Is that what you're trying to say?'

'I suppose I am.'

'Who knows? But would you excuse me for a moment? I have some arrangements to make.'

Grace nodded, and Robert left her to go to talk to the owner of the gallery about a client who was to come for a private viewing. Grace began to walk towards the door to the street, looking at the paintings as she went.

When Robert joined her once more she didn't even notice him. He stood behind her as she stared up at the full-length portrait of the dark-haired girl in the red dress. The girl was tall and graceful, and her face was half hidden as she lifted a filmy black lace veil to drape it across the Spanish comb in her piled-up hair.

Robert touched Grace's shoulder gently and, startled, she

turned to face him before she'd had time to hide the anguish in her eyes.

'It's – that's Thea Richardson, isn't it?' He didn't answer. 'Did she pose for you?'

'No.'

'But it is her – it looks so like her. But why paint her like a Spanish lady?'

'I'm not sure,' he said. And then he smiled as he shook his head. 'It just came to me – call it inspiration.'

He saw her flinch and wished he'd chosen his words more carefully.

'But she's married now, isn't she? She's Mrs Vernon Gray.'

Robert knew that it was Grace's own unhappiness that gave the cruel edge to her voice. She hadn't liked his answer, hinting as it did that the very thought of Thea inspired him. But his own misery prompted him to be kind.

'I'm glad you came – and I'm glad that I was here when you did.'

Grace's eyes widened in surprise. 'Are you?'

'I – I always enjoyed our talks at the school, Grace.' He hoped she couldn't sense how forced he sounded.

'Did you?' She was disconcerted. She searched his face for a moment and then said uncertainly, 'So did I.'

He wished he had more to offer her. 'Well, then,' he said, 'the gallery will be closing soon. Shall we go?'

They walked to the door together and out on to the narrow pavement of The Side. 'Which way?' Robert asked. 'Are you going straight home?'

'I'm not sure. It's such a pleasant day; I thought I might walk for a while. Up the hill to the city, perhaps, or down to the quayside. I haven't decided,' she said.

'Why not walk just a few yards to the coffee shop? Let me treat you to coffee and pastries.'

351

Grace looked so pleased that Robert felt guilty.

'I'd love to come,' she said. 'But you know I can't.'

'Why? Because of your parents' objections?'

'Partly. Although I don't see how they could object to my socializing with such a famous artist!' She laughed and Robert noted how pretty her fleeting happiness made her appear. 'No, it's not my parents,' she said. 'It's the terms of my employment. I must not "frequent coffee shops or ice-cream parlours with any gentleman who is not a member of my family"!'

'And what would happen if you disobeyed the rules?'

'I should be dismissed. That is,' she paused and added significance to her next words, 'if anybody actually saw me in such a place.'

He knew immediately what she meant and he leaned towards her and whispered as if they were conspirators, 'We shall have to make sure that nobody does!'

They were still smiling when the full-bodied aroma of coffee drew them into a narrow doorway a little way down The Side. The tables near the window were occupied because the people sitting there wanted to look out on the passing scene and the glimpse of the river the view afforded. But Robert guided Grace towards the back of the room where partitioned booths were set along the wall.

'This will do,' he said, and they laughed self-consciously as they slid into the seats in one of the booths.

Robert watched Grace as she studied the menu. She looked both pleased and excited, like a child being taken for a treat. She was doing something she shouldn't – breaking the rules, risking her job – and she was obviously exhilarated. Her pleasure made him feel guilty.

While they sipped their coffee Grace talked about his paintings for a while, and then she asked, 'Do you intend to stay in that place by the river?'

'Why not? The rent is cheap and I've worked hard to make the accommodation just what I want.'

'But there are some very grand – I mean spacious – houses in other parts of the city.'

'Respectable parts of the city, you mean?'

'Well, yes, I do. And you could find a house quite large enough to accommodate a studio.'

'Grace, wherever I lived wouldn't make *me* any more respectable in your father's eyes, you know.'

Grace didn't answer. She picked up the coffee pot and seemed to concentrate on filling their cups. After a while she said, 'Nevertheless I shall bring my parents to the gallery. I know they will be impressed by your achievements.'

Not much later Robert said that he had to go back to the gallery where he was to meet an important client who wished to discuss a commission with him. He offered to get her a cab but Grace said that she would walk. She said she couldn't allow him to pay for it and neither could she afford such a luxury on a teacher's pay.

Robert watched her hurry away through the crowds with mixed feelings. He had intended to be kind but perhaps he should not have invited Grace to come to the coffee shop with him. In the past, without intending to, he had encouraged her to entertain hopes of something more than friendship. To be honest, he had half flirted with the idea of having such an attractive and intelligent wife. At the time he had been safeguarded by the fact that he had known that her parents would never approve of such a match.

But now? The fact that Thea was married had obviously revived Grace's hopes. And she had hinted that her parents might come round to the idea now that he was achieving success – and perhaps riches. Would they?

How famous would he have to be before the Reverend

William Barrett would forget that Robert's mother had been a prostitute who had no idea who the fathers of her two children were?

And was there any amount of fame that would make the good headmaster forget that that same mother had fallen asleep in a drunken stupor and suffocated her baby, Robert's little sister?

It was only the actions of William Barrett and his wife that had saved his mother from the gallows. They had taken Robert and placed him in the orphanage and sent his poor mother off to an asylum where she had indeed given way to madness as she grieved for her two lost children and what she had done to one of them. She was still there.

So, supposing that Grace's parents could ever forget such horrors, and that was unlikely, what of Grace herself? He could never ask her to marry him without telling her of his history. And how would she react? It would be unfair to put her to the test – especially as he knew, instinctively, that she would fail it.

By the time he had lost sight of her amongst the crowds, he knew it was idle to even speculate on such matters for he could not marry without love and he would never love Grace.

In fact he would never be able to love anyone but Thea.

'I'm sorry, Mrs Sinclair, he wouldn't go. He stood and argued on the step until Mr Sinclair came down to see what the commotion was.'

'Stop, Betsy, what are you saying?' Ellie had come back from a shopping expedition to be met at the door by a worried housemaid. 'Anyway, will you at least let me in?'

'Ee, I'm sorry.' The girl stood aside until Ellie entered, then closed the door behind her.

Ellie could hear voices from upstairs. Angry voices. 'Who's here?' she asked the maid.

'That's what I was trying to tell you, madam. He made a fuss until Mr Sinclair let him in. I know you said the master must never be disturbed when he's working, but the minute you'd left the house this chap appeared and – well, he's up there, now.'

'I see. Take this shopping basket through to the kitchen, will you, and remember to put the chops in the ice box. I'm going upstairs.'

Betsy hurried away. She looked upset, Ellie thought, and so she should. Why hadn't the girl had the gumption simply to slam the door in the man's face? She stopped outside the door of their first-floor sitting room. She could guess who the visitor would be, of course. It was interesting that he should have waited to call until she had gone out.

And he was lucky that she had, she thought. She didn't usually do her own daily shopping, but Lewis had been more than usually intense about his work today and she'd needed to get out of the house for a while. And look what had happened.

Both men stopped whatever they were saying and turned to look at her in surprise. They hadn't heard her coming. They were standing facing each other across the hearth rug. Ellie noticed that the arrangement of summer flowers that she'd placed in the hearth had been knocked over.

For a moment she couldn't think what else to do so she hurried over and, kneeling down, righted the vase and replaced one or two of the flowers that had fallen out. She stared helplessly at the spilled water.

'Get up, Ellie, my dear. Betsy will see to this later.' Lewis came up behind her and helped her to her feet.

'But what happened? Have you been fighting?'

'No, sweetheart. I just got rather agitated for a moment.'

She looked into his face and saw that he was smiling. It was all right then. Or was it?

'Aren't you going to introduce me to the lady . . . *Lewis*? That's your name now, isn't it?'

As Ellie had thought, it was the man who'd been watching the house. He was about the same age as Lewis and smartly if a little flashily dressed. She didn't like the sly way he was smiling.

'You know very well that this is my wife. She doesn't wish to know you, and I think you'd better go now.'

'Very well. But think very carefully about my offer.'

'There's no need to think about it. I won't be accepting it.'

'Then you must take the consequences.'

Her husband merely nodded and Ellie exploded. 'Lewis, will you please tell me who this is and what is going on here!'

'I think you should,' the man said. 'I'd like to hear what you're going to say.'

Ellie looked from one to the other. Their visitor was smirking unpleasantly but Lewis merely looked bored. She felt like shaking him, but then he said, 'I don't mind your hearing. Ellie, this gentleman is trying to blackmail me.'

'Blackmail?'

'As you've probably guessed he knows that I haven't always been Lewis Sinclair. He knows that I was once in prison.'

Ellie heard their visitor give a slight gasp of surprise. 'How does he know that?' she asked.

'Because he was there too. I'd already started writing stories when I was in prison. Foolishly, like any new author who wants to be praised, I used to copy them out and circulate them amongst my fellow inmates. Apparently, when I began to be famous, it didn't take this blackguard long to put two and two together. He thinks I will pay handsomely for him to keep my secret.'

'But now you see that I already knew the truth,' Ellie told the man. 'Lewis held no secrets from me. So your threats mean nothing.'

'Don't count on it,' he said.

'And Lewis's publisher knows too,' she continued. 'So will you please leave at once, and don't bother us again.'

He had the nerve to laugh at her. 'I'll go. But my offer stands. Don't worry, I'll see myself out.'

Ellie waited until she heard the front door close before she turned to Lewis and asked, 'What does he mean, the offer still stands? I know the truth, your publisher knows the truth . . .' She stopped and looked aghast as the truth dawned on her one moment before Lewis said it out loud.

'He means he'll tell the newspapers. And if he does then the general public will know.'

'How much does he want?'

Lewis stared at her in astonishment. 'Not too much, as a matter of fact. Just a nice little percentage of my royalties. He doesn't want to kill the golden goose, he had the nerve to say.'

'Then you must pay him.'

'Ellie, why?'

Lewis took hold of her arms and tried to look into her face but she twisted away and went to stand by the window. She didn't answer him.

Lewis didn't come after her. He said, 'Listen, sweetheart, we talked about this a long time ago. I didn't pretend that it could never happen.'

'But you left London!'

'I should have made it clear that it could happen anywhere. I thought I had. But, as I told you, if my reading public knows the truth it might even be good for the sale of my books—'

'Your books! What about me?'

'I know, my darling. It will be unpleasant for you.'

'Unpleasant? It would be hideous!'

'I agree, and you don't know how sorry I am that this has happened. But to give in to blackmail, to be beholden to that odious fellow for the rest of our lives – wouldn't that be much, much more hideous?'

'But everyone thinks I've married a famous author!'

'And you have!'

'Don't smile! Don't try to baby me. Our wedding was reported in the newspapers, all the girls – all the little snobs I used to be at school with – they'll have read it, and they'll have been jealous . . .'

'Is that why you married me? To make your friends jealous?'

'Don't tease. You know very well why I married you.'

'No, Ellie, sweetheart, I no longer think that I do.'

'So you're working for a real toff now, I hear.'

Luke grasped his mug of tea and faced his mother across Robert Hedley's kitchen table. He dropped in from time to time to see her, always without warning, but when he came he knocked at the door like a proper visitor and otherwise behaved himself, and she'd got used to it, although she remained on edge. Luke didn't think it was because of his presence. He was convinced there was something else bothering her.

'What do you mean?' she asked. 'I'm still working for Mr Hedley. I hevn't got another job.'

Luke grinned. 'It's Hedley I mean. He's left the yards, he's doing well with his paintings – I hear he's famous.'

'Is he?'

'Don't you read the papers, Mam?' He saw her scowl and realized what he'd said. 'I mean – I know you don't bother with the newspapers – I mean, not until they're wrapped round a bundle of fish and chips, but hasn't anybody told you?'

'It's all right, Luke. Don't go on. You know I can't read very well, especially if the print's small. I was never a scholar . . .'

She paused and stared bleakly beyond him towards the window. With the light on her face Luke could see how the hard lines drawn by poverty had softened a little. He could almost see how bonny she must have been as a young lass; this job with Robert Hedley had made her life so much easier. So why was there such a look of misery in her eyes?

'Yes, I know he's famous now,' she said. 'And I'm pleased for him.'

'So why aren't you smiling?'

'I've got used to heving the place to meself . . . just to get on with me work and nobody to bother me – except you!' There was a flash of humour. 'But now that he's left the yards, he's around a lot more.'

'And he gets in your way. Is that it?'

'No. Whenever he's at home he works in his studio. I hardly see him. He telt me just to get on and leave his dinner as if he wasn't here. That I wasn't to bother him.'

Luke put his mug down on the scrubbed table top more forcefully than he'd intended. 'He hasn't bothered *you*, has he, Mam? That's not what you're trying to tell me, is it?'

'What do you mean? Oh . . .' Lily blushed. 'No, he's never touched me.'

'So what is it? For a while now I've watched you getting more and more het up about something and it's driving me crazy. Mam, you've got to tell me what's wrong!'

Lily didn't say anything for a while. She seemed to hold her breath, and then she let it go with one long sigh. 'I hevn't telt you before because I need this job, and I was worried you'd think I should leave, but I found a postcard . . . a photograph . . . you know . . .'

'No, I divven't. Where did you find it?'

'Here, in the kitchen.'

'So? What was it? Alnwick Castle in all its glory? A view of the lighthouse at Whitley Bay?'

'Not that kind of photograph.'

'What kind of photograph, then?' But he thought he knew and he stared at his mother, hoping that he was wrong.

'You know . . .' Lily could no longer meet his eyes.

'A saucy photograph? A pretty chorus girl showing more than a lady should? Was that what it was? That's not so bad, Mam. A lot of men like to look at things like that.'

'It wasn't saucy – it was disgusting!' Lily's face was white with fury. 'And the pain of it is, Luke, that I just about worshipped the man!'

'Disgusting? No – you must be wrong.'

'No I'm not. Look, I'll show you.' His mother got to her feet. 'I found it on the floor – there – right under the table. I got such a shock that I put it back right there – where I found it – face down! I didn't want to let him know I'd seen it.' Suddenly she had found her tongue and Luke could only sit and wait for her to finish. 'And the next time I came it had gone and he's never mentioned it.'

'Wait a minute!' Luke held up his hand. 'If it had gone, how can you show me?'

'Because he put it with the others.'

'Others?'

'Yes. Next time I cleaned his bedroom I – I looked – I mean . . . I'm ashamed to admit – no I'm not – I looked around. There was an envelope stuffed between some books.'

'All right, Mam. Get them.'

Lily wasn't long. When she came back she almost threw the envelope down on to the table as if it was burning her hand. Luke took the postcards out of the envelope and stared at them unbelievingly. When he had done he looked up to find his mother crying.

'Luke – some of those bairns – I know them – by sight, I mean.'

'So do I.'

Luke had lived on the streets since he was a bairn himself. He knew this kind of thing went on, but seeing these pictures made him feel sick. He slipped the postcards back in the envelope. If they'd been in any particular order then too bad.

'Now I know why you didn't want Janey going to the art classes. But, anyways, put them back where you found them. I'll put the kettle on and make another brew. We'd better talk about this.'

He made the tea for his mother and made her sit down and drink it.

'What upsets me most,' she said after a while, 'is that I thought he was a good man.'

'And you don't think so now?'

'How can he be?'

'Hev you ever been into his studio?'

'You know I'm not supposed to – but, yes, I hev. Once with you and once with a visitor.'

'And hev you looked at the pictures in there?'

'No – I mean, I did that day with you.'

'But the other pictures?'

'Never. You're not saying that they're like – like those postcards, are you?'

'No, I'm not. Couldn't be more unlike.'

Luke remembered the drawing of the dark-haired girl. That might have shocked his mother if she'd seen it but he knew there was a world of difference between that picture and what they had just looked at.

'Mam, there's a puzzle here.'

'Puzzle?'

'Some men like looking at that sort of thing – God knows

why – but I don't think Robert Hedley is one of them.'

'So why does he hev them in the house?'

'I'm not sure, but I hev an idea.'

His mother didn't speak but she looked at him hopefully. He realized that she wanted desperately to hear anything that might restore her former good opinion of the man.

'Robert Hedley works with poor children, doesn't he?'

'You mean the classes – the art classes at the school?'

'Aye, I do, but it's not just that. He walks the streets at night with the other good folk, rounding up the bairns that hev nowhere to sleep, taking them to the soup kitchens, arranging for the sick uns to go to the sanatorium – you know the kind of thing. He was with that poor woman who got felled that night, remember that?'

'Yes, but what does all that mean?'

'It means that he might hev come across those pictures in an innocent way. He might hev recognized some of those bairns the way we did. Suppose he's trying to do something about it?'

'What do you mean?'

'Suppose he wants to put an end to it? That would be like him, wouldn't it?'

'Yes, but why doesn't he?'

'Because the men responsible for this kind of thing are making a canny bit of money, so they play very clever. They're breaking the law and they don't want to be found out.'

'So what can anyone do?'

'I'm not sure.'

'Luke – what are you thinking?'

'Mm? Nivver mind – but divven't fret. And I don't think you hev to worry about your Mr Hedley. You can work here with an easy mind. He's not a bad un, I'm sure on it.'

'But . . .'

Luke rose from his seat and went to put an arm round his mother's shoulder. 'I'd better gan now. And you'd better watch that pot.' He nodded towards the stew pan gently steaming on the stove. 'You divven't want to spoil his meat and tatties, do you?'

Luke grinned encouragingly and was pleased to see his mother's answering smile. Suddenly she surprised him by standing up and hugging him as if he were a bairn. When her scrawny arms went round him and she pulled him close until her head was resting against his chest, he felt tears spring to his eyes. It had been a long, long time since his mam had shown him any such obvious sign of affection.

It hadn't been her fault. Life with his father had brutalized them all. He remembered once falling down in the street when he was a very small child. He'd begun to cry and his mam had picked him up and hugged him, trying to soothe away his tears.

'Divven't make him soft, woman!' his father had shouted before seizing him and throwing him roughly to the ground, kicking him for good measure before dragging his mam into the house and slamming the door.

'You're a good lad, Luke,' Lily said to him now, and he felt emotion choke his throat.

'One day, Mam,' he murmured, unwilling to break away, 'one day I'll hev a home of me own and you and the bairns will come to live with me.'

'Aye, that's right, son.'

Luke didn't know whether she really believed it – she knew what kind of life he led – but at that moment he was determined to make it come true one way or another.

Meanwhile he had a mystery to solve. None of his business, some might say, but they'd be wrong. He might be a criminal but he knew what real evil was and Robert Hedley wasn't the only one who wanted to put an end to it.

Thea sat in the new armchair and looked around the small sitting room wonderingly. Her aunt's good but shabby furniture had gone. Everything was up to date and surprisingly stylish. The heavy lace curtains had given way to hangings so delicate that they allowed the sun to flood in and reveal that even the wallpaper and carpets were new.

Her mother, smaller than ever, it seemed, and fragile in mourning black, sat at the other side of the hearth, which was filled with an arrangement of summer flowers.

'I'm sure Marjorie wouldn't have minded,' she said interpreting Thea's expression correctly.

'Do you mean she wouldn't have minded your moving in here?'

'Well, that, too, but I meant the . . . the rearrangement.'

'You've put all her things out.'

'Thea, there was nothing valuable – and I sent it all along to the Salvation Army.' Her mother looked at her anxiously and Thea relented.

She tried to make her expression more amenable when she asked, 'Why did you come here?'

'Imogen . . .' she began, and hesitated.

'My sister didn't put you out, did she, like you discarded Aunt Marjorie's redundant belongings?'

'No, of course not – oh, you're joking. But Imogen likes things her own way and, as the house belongs to her now, I thought it best to – to let her enjoy her inheritance.'

'I see.' Thea couldn't help smiling. Her younger sister had always got what she wanted one way or another when her father was alive, and now that he was dead there would be no one to control her at all. 'She's very young to be left in charge of a household, don't you think?'

'Imogen has always been old for her years. And she knows

that I'm here if she needs me – but I don't think she will. And, as for the business, she will have the board of directors to advise her, and she'll have to listen to them until she comes of age.'

'And then there'll be no stopping her – now the North East and tomorrow the entire British Empire will be buying their groceries from Richardson's!' Thea laughed, and was pleased that her mother did too.

'But you?' Thea asked reluctantly – after all, why should she care? 'Are you provided for?'

'Well enough. I shall be able to live here comfortably and perhaps to travel a little.' Her mother looked anxious suddenly, as if she wished she hadn't added that last bit.

'So why did you write to invite me here?'

'I wanted to see you. I mean, you're my daughter . . .'

'I've always been your daughter.'

'I know,' she whispered, accepting the rebuke.

'Why do you want to see me now?'

'I didn't come to your wedding – I couldn't – you know why.'

'Yes, I do.' Thea softened her tone. 'You couldn't leave him.'

'It wouldn't have been seemly.'

Thea knew in that moment that her mother had never loved her husband. Not at all. Not the tiniest bit of her heart had been given to the man who had married her and saved her reputation – and given her daughter his name. If she had done it would have been more than seemly behaviour that kept her at his side while he lay dying.

'And you care what people think, don't you?'

Her mother looked puzzled. 'Yes, of course.'

'Did you invite me here to apologize?'

'Apologize?'

365

'For not coming to the wedding.' But there was so much more Thea wanted to say. Apologize for never once over the years trying to intervene when Samuel Richardson – she could no longer think of him as her father – had treated her so cruelly; never once shown her the slightest sign of affection.

All this must have shown in her face for her mother suddenly said, 'I haven't been a good mother, have I?'

'Don't.'

'But, Thea—'

'Don't talk like that; I won't be able to bear it. Just tell me why you wanted to see me.'

'Just to see you . . . to try to talk, to find out if— Oh, can't you understand?'

'I'm trying to.'

At that moment they were interrupted by a knock on the door and, when her mother called, 'Enter,' Thea was surprised to see Nancy come into the room.

Her mother smiled. 'I thought you would be pleased. I went to a deal of trouble to find Marjorie's old staff.'

'What do you mean, *staff*?' Nancy said as she placed the tray she was carrying on a small table top of Benares brass. 'There was only me and me bairn – and our Ellen was never paid nowt. But I'm not on me own now,' she said directly to Thea. 'There's a cook and the lass that answered the door besides. Our Ellen sends you her love, Miss Thea,' she said just before she left the room, 'and I hope we'll be seeing you here more often.'

Thea was amazed by the exchange that had just taken place. She thought of the stiff and formal atmosphere in her former home. Not one of the staff there, not even Mrs Bostock, the housekeeper, would have spoken without being asked to.

'I like Nancy,' her mother said, surprising her further as she poured the tea. 'She talks to me about Marjorie – and you when you were staying here.'

Thea remembered her aunt's words when she had described her mother in the letter: . . . *so lovely, so carefree, so affectionate and so ready to trust – to love* . . .

Looking at her now, even with the severe black of her mourning clothes draining all the colour from her skin, Thea thought she could glimpse the girl she'd been long ago when she'd fallen in love with the man who was to become Thea's father.

'You are surprised at the change in me?' her mother asked.

'Yes.'

'Are you shocked?'

Thea frowned. 'Why should I be shocked?'

'After all, I am in mourning.'

Her mother glanced down at her own black dress and then seemed to stare pointedly at Thea's cream muslin afternoon dress trimmed with gold satin ribbon. Thea had not even considered going into black, although she knew it would shock people. She wondered if this was an opening for her mother to reproach her.

But her mother smiled at her. 'My life has changed now,' she said. 'I am on my own and I can please myself how I live. Your father was very authoritarian.'

'My father?' Thea asked. 'Oh, you mean Samuel Richardson.'

Her mother's blue eyes widened. She put her cup down carefully. 'So, Marjorie did tell you.'

'And that's why you invited me here. To discover whether I knew that your husband was not my father.'

Her mother seemed to shrink back as if from a blow. 'I thought she might. I know I made her promise once to keep

367

my secret, but Marjorie was always one for the truth – no matter how inconvenient.'

'Was that what I was – am? Inconvenient!'

'No, Thea, no. That's unfair. I simply meant that Marjorie was incapable of prevarication and, furthermore, she always loved you.'

'Just as well.'

Her mother ignored the interruption but she looked unhappy as she continued, 'I knew that she would want you to know the truth. I just don't know how much she told you.'

'She died before she could tell me,' Thea said.

'Then how—'

'She left a letter.'

'I should like to see it.'

'No. It was written to me.'

Everything her aunt had told her was surely the truth and perhaps her mother had a right to see it. But the facts revealed belonged to Thea – she had read them over and over, thought about them, made them part of herself, and she didn't want anyone – even the person with the most right to do so, to intrude or change anything now.

'Then at least tell me how much you know.'

'I know that you were on holiday when you met, that you fell in love, that Aunt Marjorie liked him—'

'Did she?'

She hardly dared look at her mother before she said, 'And that you became lovers. And then . . . then he let you down . . .'

She heard her mother catch her breath. 'You know so much,' she said.

'So *much*? But I don't even know his name. I don't know my father's name.'

'Carlos,' her mother breathed. 'His name was Carlos.'

Chapter Twenty-six

'Have you not been happy at all? All these years . . . did you think of him all the time? Did you take no comfort from the birth of your daughters?'

After the first awkward moments they had begun to talk freely and Thea found that there were so many questions she wanted to ask. She could see that it was difficult but she could also see that her mother was trying her best to answer her. Perhaps trying to make amends for the long years of silence.

'At first I thought it might be bearable,' her mother said. 'Samuel seemed to love me. But as the baby – you – grew within me he changed. Perhaps he should have thought more deeply about the responsibility he was accepting.'

'Your father's business!'

Her mother sighed. 'Oh, yes, that. He fulfilled that part of the bargain. The business prospered.'

'But not your marriage.'

'No. And the more unhappy I became, the more I thought of Carlos – my lover.' Her mother whispered the last two words and Thea thought she seemed to relish them. 'You are a married woman, now,' she continued, 'so I can tell you this. My life with Samuel – my intimate life—'

'You mean what takes place in bed?'

Her mother's pale face coloured, 'Yes. It was brutal. And it was made all the worse because he never spoke, never murmured my name. There were no endearments, no words of tenderness or of love.'

They stared at each other, lost in their own thoughts; Amy no doubt remembering all her years of submission to a cruelly cold husband, and Thea reflecting that Vernon at least would always tell her how beautiful she was. Always take her in his arms afterwards and hold her, whispering how much he adored her.

Could that be what Ellie had meant? Was the act of love simply to be endured by women in order to be granted the grateful tenderness that came after?

'And it was made worse because I had known something so much better with Carlos,' her mother continued at last, 'something truly wonderful. Forgive me, I shouldn't be talking like this, but it's such a release after all these years to be able to say that I loved – still love – him. And who better to tell than his daughter?'

For a moment her mother's eyes had shone as Ellie's had when she'd told Thea of her love for Lewis, then Amy closed her eyes and leaned back in her chair. Thea realized that she was weeping. Instead of feeling sympathy all the hostility returned.

'But your daughters . . . Women are supposed to love their children, aren't they? Didn't having Imogen and me bring you any happiness?'

Her mother opened her eyes and looked at her. 'I should have found comfort in your birth, shouldn't I? Especially yours – the daughter of the man I loved so much. But instead I found torment. Every day of your life you reminded me of him – and the life I could have had. I found it easier to keep my distance. Forgive me.'

'I don't know if I can.'

'Cruel Thea.'

'I've had good teachers.'

'Thea, we mustn't fight.'

'But surely I still remind you of him? Isn't it just as painful now?'

'Not quite. Samuel is dead. I'm free, and—'

'You're not hoping to find him, are you? You said you were going to travel – are you going to try and find my – find Carlos?'

Her mother laughed softly. 'That would be foolish, wouldn't it? In all likelihood he is married; the last thing he would want to know now is that he has a grown daughter.'

'How inconvenient that would be!'

'Don't – I'm sorry – but, no, I'm not going to look for him. But I may try to find out what became of him. Do you see the difference? Just to know if he's happy.'

'And that would make you feel better.' Thea was seething. 'I think I'll go now.'

'Thea – no – don't let's part like this. Look, I'll ring for Nancy. We'll have more tea – and cake, perhaps? Please don't go.'

Thea agreed but she didn't stay much longer. Her mother asked her if she was happy with Vernon and Thea told her that she was. What else could she say? How could she complain about a man who showered her with clothes and gifts, who never said an unkind or cruel word?

The only time they had come close to quarrelling was when she'd tried to hint that what happened in bed was distasteful to her. He truly didn't understand. He'd told her that most women felt the same as she did but, because they loved their husbands, they submitted cheerfully.

And there it was. She didn't love him. She knew, too late, that she should never have married him.

When Thea left her mother that day, she didn't promise that she would see her again. She hinted that she had a very busy life, a diary full of engagements, and that she would have to wait a little and see what could be done.

They neither kissed nor embraced when they parted.

Rosalie Parker looked up from her fashion magazine and pursed her lips. 'Still here, Ellie?'

'You can see I am, Mama.'

'And still not talking?'

'I don't know what to say.'

Her mother sighed. 'Ellie, you're married now. You should be at home with your husband.' Ellie remained silent and, after a moment, her mother continued, 'You arrived here last night with your bags and baggage and a face as long as a fiddle, you wouldn't eat, and you went straight up to bed. And from the state of your eyes this morning you've been crying all night. Your dear father thinks you might be – I don't want to be indelicate – but that you might be expecting, and that you're suffering a little female trouble, but as far as I'm concerned it's perfectly obvious that you've quarrelled with Lewis. And yet you won't let me help you.'

'There is no help.'

'For goodness' sake, child, don't be so dramatic. I don't know who you get it from! Just make your mind up to go home and put things right.'

'I don't know how to.'

'Well, you won't mend things by staying here.'

'I don't think things can be mended.'

'What is it?' Rosalie looked frightened. 'It's not . . . not another woman, is it? He hasn't let you down, has he?'

'No. It's nothing like that.'

'Thank goodness.' Her mother tried to make a joke of it. 'We won't have to face a scandal, then!'

But if Lewis persists in defying that odious man, Ellie thought, we *will* have to face a scandal, and I don't know if I can bear it. And what of my parents? How will they cope if Lewis's past becomes general knowledge?

She knew instinctively that her good, kind father would weather the storm. But her mother . . . she would never be able to face any of her friends again. Her life would be ruined.

Lewis, how could you do this! she thought angrily.

She wondered if it would be any good to go back and plead with him to do as the man said for her mother's sake. But it might already be too late, she thought gloomily. Maybe that fellow has already been back and Lewis has sent him packing. Her lip trembled.

'Ellie, sweetheart, don't cry,' her mother said. 'You know Lewis is probably as miserable as you are.'

Is he? Ellie wondered, and frowned when she remembered the hurt in his eyes. He thought that she didn't love him – that she'd married him simply because he was rich and famous. How could he believe that! The truth was he couldn't love her. If he did he would be prepared to do anything to save her from scandal!

In spite of what she had told her mother, Thea's social diary, a large grand affair bound in French morocco, was completely empty. In the cab on the way home from the visit to her aunt's old house she reflected that not only did she have nothing to do in the house, she had nowhere to go. Ellie was playing the part of Lewis's amanuensis, a willing slave with secretarial as

373

well as domestic duties, and, of course, Thea had no other real friends.

Those girls she knew from her schooldays, who were already married and might have included her in their social circle, were wary of her reputation. They had always been slightly in awe of her and now there was the added complication of deciding whether she was quite respectable.

After all, she had lived in the photographer's house for some weeks before she'd married him, and what was all that business about her father having put her out of the house? It was something to do with her and that silly little goose Ellie Parker entering a beauty contest wasn't it? How common!

Thea could guess what they were saying about her and she didn't care. The only person whose good opinion she valued had been Aunt Marjorie. Visiting her house today had brought back not only the painfully fond memories of her aunt but also the half-formed ideas and plans about doing something valuable with her life.

She had been angry with her father – Samuel Richardson – for not allowing her to go to university. Now she understood why he had been reluctant to spend another penny on her education. Why should he? He probably thought he had done his duty by raising her until she was old enough to marry.

'No decent man will want to marry you now . . .'

She remembered his angry words the last time he had spoken to her. He was angry because he considered what she had done would spoil his chances of marrying her off – getting her off his hands – and yet he had also been strangely excited, almost relishing the idea of Thea dressed provocatively, as he put it.

What else had he said? That she had *'flaunted herself'*? And that she'd *'offered her body for men to ogle'*?

Even now she felt hot with shame when she remembered

his words and yet the shame was all his. She realized now that the feelings he had for her were far removed from those of a parent. He had desired her – and, what was worse, he had desired her when she was far too young, her childish body still undeveloped, for his feelings to be in any way acceptable.

Aunt Marjorie had observed that he had been strict and even cruel but she could never have guessed the full horror of it.

But what now? Her aunt had more or less told her that what she did with her life was up to her. As for education, there were always evening classes. Thea wondered what Vernon would say if she told him that she wished to study ancient history or the classics? She imagined he would be amused and he would raise no great objection.

But did she want such a course of study? She wasn't sure. She remembered that Aunt Marjorie had promised her that she could become more involved in her work with the homeless. She still had her aunt's address book . . . she could get in touch with Miss Moffat or Mrs Shaw. They would tell her what was needed, how to be useful. By the time she got home she'd decided that's what she would do.

To her surprise Vernon was delighted.

'That's marvellous,' he said. 'As a matter of fact I've been asked to photograph the annual picnic of the Poor Children's Holiday Association on the beach at Whitley Bay. Why don't you come with me – help me to organize the children? Poor old Miss Moffat gets them so flustered that they won't stand still and Mrs Shaw makes them so nervous that they won't smile – just solemn rows of children looking apprehensively at the camera! I have a feeling that you will have a way with them. You'll be able to make them look as though they are actually enjoying the day out.'

'Do you think so? Then I'd love to come.'

Thea couldn't say why she was so pleased that Vernon thought she would be good with children. She had never thought about it before but she hoped he was right and, after the disturbing visit to her mother, her spirits lifted considerably.

Vernon had bought a motorcar, the new Daimler Tonneau, and on the day of the picnic the three of them travelled in style to the coast. Vernon looked like a character in one of Jules Verne's stories, in his new water- and windproof motoring coat, his cap and his goggles, and Thea and Adie were snug in the back seat with a rug of grey wolfskin over their knees.

They needed the rug, for the car was open-topped and, even though it was a bright sunny day, the breeze was keen. Thea wore a fawn silk and alpaca dustcoat, 'recommended for lady passengers', and her straw hat was secured with a long, wide chiffon veil which could be adjusted to protect her face. The veil was emerald green because that colour was considered the most effective protection for the complexion. Or so Adie had assured her.

Adie had chosen and ordered their motoring clothes from the Army and Navy Stores catalogue, and Thea would have felt mean if she had not encouraged Vernon's assistant to order the same outfit for herself. Vernon was pleased that she had.

'Keep the funny little thing happy,' he'd murmured, and Thea had wondered whether he'd noticed that Adie had been more subdued than usual lately, and certainly not as friendly towards Thea as her former behaviour had suggested she might be.

So now she and Adie sat, in the back of the car, in identical outfits, with their veils pulled up over their faces like yashmaks; they could have been the wives of a Turkish pasha being taken for a day's outing.

As they motored down the coast road, a journey of about ten miles, the chug-chugging of the car and the wind in their faces made conversation difficult, so Thea was content to sit back and enjoy the new experience.

She had telephoned Miss Moffat and told her she was coming. Dr Moffat's wife had answered the telephone and made it quite plain that she didn't approve of her husband's sister receiving personal calls.

'The lines must be kept open for my husband's patients,' she snapped. 'But just this once . . .'

Thea heard her calling, 'Alice! This call is for *you*!'

When Miss Moffat answered she sounded so subdued that Thea started by apologizing. 'I'm sorry to have annoyed Mrs Moffat,' she said, 'but I didn't know that you mustn't telephone a doctor's house if you weren't a patient.'

'Don't take any notice of Julia,' Miss Moffat said quietly. 'She spends hours on the telephone herself talking to her grand friends. It's just that . . . well . . . I'm a guest here.'

Thea suddenly had a clear picture of what life must be like for good-natured Miss Moffat living in her brother's house at the mercy of her sister-in-law. No wonder she was always out and about. It was just as well that she had her 'good works' to fill her days.

She was delighted when Thea told her that she would be coming to the picnic and she promised to introduce her, gradually, to Marjorie Gibb's other good causes.

'Although I'm not sure if your husband will allow you to mingle with some of the poor souls we deal with,' she added.

Thea didn't respond to this but she wondered if her short time living with Aunt Marjorie had been her only taste of independence. Before that she had been bound by Samuel Richardson's rules and now it seemed she must ask permission of a husband. But as for Vernon 'allowing' her to do anything,

377

she would have to discover how much he was prepared to indulge her.

When they reached Whitley Bay, they parked the car on the promenade, and Thea and Adie carried the picnic hamper down Watt's slope while Vernon followed with his camera and equipment.

The wind had blown the sand into ridges where it met the bottom of the concrete slope and Adie stumbled. Her side of the hamper nearly hit the ground. Thea seized both handles and righted it.

'Sorry,' Adie murmured. 'I wasn't looking where I was going.'

Thea gazed at her. They had both adjusted their veils before they left the car and now Adie's pale face, framed by the emerald green material, looked paler than ever. In fact she looked unwell.

'Are you all right?' Thea asked.

'Just a little tired. I'm not sleeping well.'

Thea recalled the occasions she had looked down the stairwell and seen lights in the lower floors of the house. It had happened more than once since her wedding night and, finally, she had asked Vernon if Adie lived in the house.

'Of course,' he'd said. 'I thought I'd told you. Often she works late and rather than send her back to some lonely lodging house in a cab, I allowed her to turn a couple of the basement rooms into a little apartment for herself.'

He'd been so matter-of-fact when he'd explained it that Thea had not wanted to say that he certainly hadn't told her and that perhaps he should have.

That explained the mystery, Thea supposed. But it hadn't explained why Vernon's assistant so often wandered about at night instead of getting the good night's sleep she so obviously needed.

378

The children were already on the beach; it was hard to miss them. In spite of the bright sun, the worrisome wind had driven away all but the regular dog walkers, and the picnic party sat in an obedient circle in grand isolation.

Their dark shabby clothes thrown into high relief against the white sparkling sand made them look like a flock of timid but obedient baby birds waiting for some order to take off and enjoy themselves.

Miss Moffat, Mrs Shaw and a stocky cheerful young man Thea didn't recognize sat in the middle of the circle, taking sandwiches from a huge hamper and reaching across to hand them to the children. The young man, whom Thea later discovered to be Mrs Shaw's son down from Cambridge, occasionally filled up enamel mugs from stone bottles of lemonade.

'Ah!' Mrs Shaw saw them coming and stood up, scattering crumbs and sand from her skirt. 'Thea, my dear, and your husband, Mr Gray!'

Thea glanced sideways at Adie to see if she minded not having been included in the welcome but the girl's eyes were cast firmly downwards as she concentrated on holding up her end of the hamper once more.

'I've kept them as neat and tidy as possible for you, Mr Gray. I haven't allowed them to run around and get flustered although it would have been too cruel not to allow them to eat!'

'Of course – and thank you,' Vernon said, and he turned to wink at Thea.

His secret smile, which had once seemed so special and should have made her happy, now only confused her. She wanted to be able to respond to him, to love him as he told her he loved her. But this Vernon, the easy-going, good-natured man, was not the only Vernon.

Was she the only person who knew that passion made him seem cold and ruthless? And even worse, he didn't seem to be aware of the change that came over him. She was ashamed to admit to herself that she welcomed, longed for, the nights that he didn't come to her room but stayed in his own instead.

'Right, children,' Mrs Shaw commanded, 'stand up and make sure there are no crumbs on your clothes or on your faces.' The children stood obediently. 'Rupert dear,' she said to the young man, 'would you help Miss Moffat pack up the hamper? We can eat the rest of the food later.'

In no time at all Mrs Shaw had the children – there were about thirty of them – standing in three formal rows. 'Will that do, Mr Gray?'

Vernon scanned the subdued rows of children. Their faces were a mixture of fright and resignation. 'They look as if they've been lined up for the firing squad,' he murmured to Thea before he turned to Mrs Shaw and said, 'Splendid. Don't you think so, Thea? And you, Miss Hall, don't you think they look grand?'

Adie Hall seemed to have a coughing fit and she sat down quickly on top of their own picnic hamper.

Thea was baffled; the children clearly did not look like a good advertisement for the Poor Children's Holiday Association. But then she heard Vernon say to Mrs Shaw, 'Now it may take a while to set up my equipment and you and Miss Moffat have already endured several hours on duty. I suggest that Rupert takes you both to the tearooms and orders a pot of tea and perhaps some toasted teacakes. My treat,' Vernon handed some coins to young Rupert, 'I insist. And don't worry, I'll send Miss Hall to tell you when I'm ready to take the photographs.'

Mrs Shaw hesitated but a grateful Miss Moffat came over and kissed Thea on the cheek before linking arms with her friend and leading her away. Rupert looked pleased to escape.

The children remained standing exactly as they'd been told although Thea noticed one boy in the middle row start to fidget. She realized with pleasure that it was Joe Roper, the lad she'd first met at the Christmas party, and, standing in front of him was his sister, Janey.

'Beautiful, isn't she?' Adie asked. She too was staring at Janey, whose ribbons had come loose to allow her red-gold curls to hang halfway down her back.

At that moment Janey became aware that she was being stared at and she looked at them with widening eyes. Then she must have recognized Thea for she smiled and waved. So did her brother.

'Do you know those two children?' Adie asked.

'I've met them once before.'

'Are they brother and sister? They look as if they might be.'

'Yes, they are.'

Thea wondered why Adie was so interested but decided it must be natural curiosity. Vernon had begun to set up his camera.

'He must take great care here on the beach,' Adie told her. 'If any sand got into the mechanism the camera could be ruined.'

Without looking up from his task Vernon called out, 'Thea, have you forgotten? I want you to try and make the children look as though they're enjoying themselves.'

'Oh . . . Right oh.'

She stared at the children, perplexed. The wind was sharper and now, as well as subdued, they looked cold. In fact one or two of them were beginning to shiver. What should she do? Pull funny faces? Tell jokes? Then she had an idea. It was really quite simple. They had been brought here to enjoy themselves and so far they had been confined to sitting in an orderly circle to eat their sandwiches. They were children, they needed to play.

'Is this where you want them to stand?' she asked Vernon.

'Not quite, but Adie will see to that. She knows what sort of background I like.'

'Right then,' Thea said. 'Adie, if I take the children away for a moment will you draw three lines in the sand marking out exactly where you want each row of children to stand?'

'Yes. But what are you going to do?'

Thea eased the pin from her hat and, putting the chiffon scarf inside it, laid it gently on the sand by the hamper. 'Just watch.'

First she told them to remember whether they were in the front, the middle or the back row. Then to turn to the child at each side of them and take a good look, to ask his or her name if they didn't already know it, so that they would know exactly who they should be next to when they returned. And then, taking them as far away from Vernon and his camera as possible, she started a game of Chain.

She chose Joe Roper to be 'he' and told the other children to run away from him. As soon as he caught someone they had to link arms and run together to catch the next, and so on. It wasn't long before an unsteady line of children was running and stumbling across the sand.

At first they were quiet, intent on the game, concentration catching their lips between their teeth. But as the line of children grew it swerved out of control and they began to cry out. Then the breathless laughter started and soon they were shrieking with enjoyment. Overhead the circling gulls swooped and shrieked in appreciation. As the line grew longer, it became more and more unsteady, and the children's faces grew flushed and finally red with exertion and enjoyment.

Thea took off her coat and tossed it over the picnic hamper.

She ran with the children, directing the line – but at the same time encouraging the 'prey' to dodge and weave. Soon she was laughing as loud as any of them.

When the last player was caught they all flopped as one on to the sand where they rolled and exclaimed and giggled just as they should have been doing from the start.

Thea sat down beside them; she looked at their shining eyes and their carefree gestures and she thought that if you ignored their clothes, they looked like any children anywhere, not just those poor enough to qualify for a ticket to the Poor Children's Picnic.

'I'm ready now,' Vernon called, and he sent Adie to the beach café to fetch the others. By the time Miss Moffat, Mrs Shaw and Rupert returned, Thea had the children standing in their preordained rows. Now they faced the camera confidently and smiled as though this was the most marvellous day out they'd ever had.

Fortunately, by the time Vernon took his pictures, the wind had died down sufficiently so that no little face was obscured by a stray lock of hair and no lines were broken as a child took off in pursuit of an errant cap or ribbon.

When he was satisfied that he had the best exposures he could hope for, Vernon packed up his equipment. The children were told to sit again and the remaining food was shared out.

Thea, Vernon and Adie sat a little apart, enjoying the contents of their own hamper. Rupert Shaw came to join them.

'I say, Mrs Gray,' he said, 'I was watching you from the café window – playing with the children, you know – jolly good.'

'Thank you.'

Thea looked at him. Mrs Shaw's son was not much older than she was. He was the type of 'suitable' young man who would be invited to her old school's Christmas dance. The girls would sit at one side of the hall, freed from school uniform but still identical in flounced white silk evening gowns and elbow-length gloves, and the boys, fearfully smart and self-conscious in formal evening wear at the other.

Both sets of young people had been taught the latest dance steps by Ellie Parker's father. The dancing would begin when the small orchestra hired for the occasion struck up daringly with the latest popular dance tune. First one hesitant youth and then another crossed the intimidating expanse of shining floorboards and asked the girl of his choice to dance with him. Many lifelong partnerships had been formed after one of these dances.

Thea was pleased by Rupert's awkward compliment but could think of nothing to say to him so she reached into the hamper and offered him a selection of the goodies Vernon had had delivered from Alvini's. Rupert was delighted and quickly filled a plate with cold jellied chicken, small ham loaves, and pigeon pie, all much more appetizing than the meat and fish paste sandwiches in the other hamper.

When Vernon produced a bottle of light ale, Rupert glanced hastily at his mother and, seeing her occupied with the children, he grinned and accepted a glass. Soon he and Vernon were engaged in talking about photography and the latest cameras, and Thea was left to enjoy her own choice of food.

Adie ate hardly anything. She picked at some lobster and mayonnaise packed into a shell on a bed of salad and abandoned it hardly half eaten, but she took a long drink of ale straight from one of the bottles.

'Thirsty work!' she said and smiled self-consciously when she saw Thea's surprised glance. Then, without another word she got up and walked down to the shoreline where she stood looking out to sea; a small figure forlorn against the expanse of the ocean.

Thea wondered if she should go after her. It was hard to tell because Adie's complexion was always pale. Thea suspected it was lack of sleep. She worked long hours; often Vernon did not leave the darkroom and come upstairs until long past midnight. But today she had looked even more bloodless than usual. Perhaps she should mention it to Vernon, tell him he was being selfish and the girl was working too hard.

'It's been interesting talking to you,' she heard Rupert say, 'but I'd better report back to the commanding officer. My mother wants me to do something to keep the little beggars occupied until it's time for the train home. Must admit, haven't a clue what to do.'

'What about sandcastles?' Thea asked. 'I'll help organize them if you like?'

'Would you? That would be marvellous!'

'Thea, I don't want to spoil your fun, but I'd like to take these slides back to the studio. I've got some work to do in the darkroom,' Vernon said. Then seeing her disappointment, he smiled at her. 'But you can stay if you like – come home on the train, then take a cab from the Central Station if you're tired.'

Adie must have sensed that he was leaving for she began to walk back up the beach. Thea couldn't help noticing how her footsteps dragged. But when she came to the group of children she stopped and leaned over to have a word with one of them. It was Joe Roper.

Thea wondered what she was saying but was distracted when Vernon took her arms and kissed her brow. 'I didn't realize what a child you were,' he said. 'When I saw you running about on the sand like a harum-scarum schoolgirl I think I loved you more than ever.'

Rupert helped Vernon and Adie carry everything back to the car and, as she watched them trudge across the sand, Thea couldn't help feeling just like Vernon's description of her: a high-spirited schoolgirl who had been let out to play for a few hours.

'Oh dear, we've no buckets and spades,' Miss Moffat said, 'they'll need them if they're going to build sandcastles.'

But that problem was solved by Mrs Shaw, who claimed that there was 'a little money to spare in the kitty' and sent Rupert and two of the older lads off to the little shop on the promenade to buy as many buckets and spades as were needed.

Thea was down on her knees digging a tunnel through a sandcastle which towered above her, when she became aware of someone, Rupert Shaw, she thought, digging through from the other side.

'I hope we're both on the same line!' she said, but there was no reply.

'Gan on, miss,' Joe Roper encouraged her, 'you must be about through to the middle by now.'

Now she was lying flat, she could feel the cool sand through the layers of muslin, her right arm was stretched out as far as possible when suddenly the back of the tunnel crumbled away and her fingers were scrabbling against other fingers.

'Done it!' she said and then gasped with surprise when the other hand gripped hers firmly.

She pulled her hand free, withdrew it from the tunnel and scrambled breathlessly to her feet. The man at the other side of the sandcastle rose, smiling. It was Robert Hedley.

Chapter Twenty-seven

'I didn't know you were here.'

Low clouds raced in from the sea. The wind had strengthened again and it tugged at Thea's hair, loosening it from the pins. She was conscious of wet grains of sand clinging to the pale green muslin of her dress.

'I've not been here long,' he replied.

They stared at each other with the width of the sandcastle between them, ignoring the children playing round their feet. Then each stepped back to allow the young tunnellers to turn their attention to digging a moat.

'You've been sketching?' Thea indicated the small notepad lying by his feet.

He picked it up and slipped it into a pocket. 'A little. Just impressions – lightning sketches,' he smiled; 'none of them stays still for very long.'

Some unspoken message passed between them and at the same moment they turned and started to walk towards the water's edge. Thea self-consciously brushed the sand from her dress and then tried to catch at the strands of hair blowing across her face. She glanced sideways and saw that Robert was gazing straight ahead. He looked troubled.

They stopped just short of where the waves frothed in the shingle. 'It's coming in,' Robert said, 'the tide. Some of those sandcastles will soon be washed away.'

'Oh dear.' Thea turned to watch the happy scene behind them. 'I should have thought of that and kept them all further up the beach.'

'But dry sand isn't so easy to work with.' He said this so seriously that Thea smiled.

'I've so enjoyed myself today,' she said.

'I didn't know you would be here,' Robert said.

'And I wasn't expecting you would be. But I'm glad you came. There's something I've wanted to say to you.' Her smile faded.

'What's that?'

He turned at last to look at her and, as their eyes met, the shock was so great that she had to stop herself from backing away. There it was again, that same feeling, that same tug at her senses that she'd felt all those months ago the first time she'd met him. She dropped her head.

'It's about my aunt,' she said, and even without looking at him she felt a different kind of tension spring between them. 'I – afterwards – I wondered if you thought I'd blamed you for what happened.'

He didn't respond and she looked up. The pain in his eyes was almost too much to bear. 'You did think that!' she said. 'Oh, no, please forgive me!'

'Forgive you?' he said. 'What have I to forgive? It was I who didn't take proper care of my dearest friend. As you said, I should have brought her home to you.'

Thea's eyes widened. 'But I meant— Oh, no, I wasn't reproaching you, blaming you in any way for what happened. I simply meant that I wanted her – her body brought home –

388

'not left in some cold infirmary ward.'

'And don't you think that is reproach enough? I couldn't even find the man responsible, bring him to justice. The police told me he'd probably stowed away, gone to—'

'Stop! I know. There's no need for you to say more.'

They stared at each other, emotion enclosing them so that the cries of the playing children receded as did the shriek of the gulls. They heard the fierce drag of the retreating water on the nearby shingle but not the gentle swoosh of the incoming waves until, without warning, one surged around their feet.

They both looked down as if they didn't understand at first what had happened, then Robert took her hand and they ran back up the beach a little way. They were laughing. Robert kneeled down to pull a frond of seaweed from Thea's skirt and when he stood up again they smiled at each other.

'It's all right now, isn't it?' Thea asked. 'Between us, I mean? I know my aunt wouldn't want us to go on being unhappy, would she?'

'No, she wouldn't.'

'She would want us to be friends.'

He agreed to that too, but he looked away quickly.

'Is it rain or is it spray from the waves?' Thea asked as she turned her face into the wind and felt the drops of moisture.

'Both, I think.'

Behind them Mrs Shaw had started marshalling the children into a group. Most of them had shed their shoes, and socks too if they had any, and they were scrabbling amongst the pile to find those that belonged to them. Rupert whistled cheerfully as he collected the buckets and spades, and Miss Moffat looked as if she would topple into the hamper each time she bent over it to put in the cups, plates and empty lemonade bottles.

'I should help,' Thea said.

'No – wait a little longer.'

So they stood a while, halfway between the children and the sea, talking quietly about that dreadful night and the fact that it looked as though the man who had effectively murdered Marjorie Gibb might never be caught. They moved only when the tide, sweeping in more swiftly now, threatened to soak them once more.

'Your shoes will have a salt mark,' Thea said.

'And yours. Is your skirt dry?'

'Almost.'

The fine drizzle was becoming heavier. Soon it would turn into proper rain. Joe Roper came running towards Thea with her coat and hat. Janey followed with the chiffon scarf, laughing as she streamed it behind her like a knight's pennant. By the time she had put on her coat and hat, Robert was caught up in the preparations to leave the beach.

The children walked up the slope and through the town to the station in an orderly crocodile, getting quicker as the rain got heavier. Mrs Shaw and Miss Moffat led the way and Robert and Thea offered to walk behind. Two of the older lads carried the hamper between them and made quite a show of it, constantly asking the little ones to clear the way. Rupert, like a friendly family dog who did not quite know who to walk with, hurried backwards and forwards, making real conversation between Thea and Robert impossible.

On the train they somehow got separated and Robert looked longingly over the heads of the children to where Thea sat with one small girl resting against her shoulder and another sitting on her knee. She didn't seem to mind that the warmth inside the railway carriage had released unpleasantly musty odours from the children's damp clothes.

Robert smiled when he saw that her hat had tipped sideways at a crazy angle and that her beautiful veil was tied as clumsily as a fishwife's shawl. How different Thea was from her little blonde friend. As Robert remembered her, Ellie Parker would no doubt have played with the children just as enthusiastically, but she would probably have emerged even from inside the tunnel of the sandcastle looking as neat and dainty as a picture book beauty on a box of chocolates.

Thea was different, and the difference made her infinitely more desirable.

He tried to suppress the image of Thea lying prone on the sand as she tunnelled into the sandcastle, the soft fabric of her dress clinging to her long limbs, defining the shape of her body.

And then Thea standing at the tide line, the pale green dress blending both with the streaks of greeny blue in the late afternoon sky and the reflected colours of the waves; her dark hair escaping all restraint and lifting round her perfect face, making her look like a Nereid – a sea nymph of Greek mythology.

He thought of all the drawings he had done of her, the picture in the gallery. Those were from memory, but what if he could see her, watch her, every day?

Wake up next to her every morning . . .

He knew he would never tire of her, nor of painting her.

'Goodness, Thea, what have you been doing? You look like a scarecrow!'

Stung for once, Thea replied, 'You don't look so wonderful yourself. But why are you lurking on my doorstep?'

'I'm not lurking. I've been ringing the bell but no one has bothered to answer. Try for yourself. And no wonder I look a mess, having to stand here in the rain!'

'For goodness' sake, Ellie, come on in.'

Thea used her key. Vernon and Adie would be working in the darkroom and it was late enough for the domestic staff to have gone home. 'I've been to the beach for a picnic with some children,' Thea said, hating herself for bothering to explain her dishevelled appearance.

Ellie followed her into the house and upstairs to the morning room. A small fire burned in the hearth and, after divesting herself of her damp outer garments, Thea kneeled down, removed the cinder guard, and put the kettle that she kept there on the hob. She made a pot of tea.

The steady rainfall had darkened the skies but Thea didn't light the lamps. She preferred to sit in the firelight. She had much to think about . . . disturbing thoughts . . . Perhaps it was as well that Ellie had arrived to distract her.

'Cosy, this,' Ellie said as she took her cup from Thea, 'everything to hand.'

She's trying to be nice, Thea thought, and regretted the way she had snapped at her friend when she'd arrived home; especially when she sat back in her own chair and looked at Ellie properly.

'Ellie, is something the matter?'

'Yes.' Ellie looked anguished. 'Oh, Thea, I can't tell my mother. I think it would kill her!'

'For goodness' sake—' Thea had been going to tell her friend not to be a drama queen but she had caught sight of the tears welling up in Ellie's eyes. 'Well, can you tell me?'

'That's why I came. I must tell someone and you're my best friend.'

'Am I?'

Thea's dry response surprised Ellie. 'Of course you are. How can you ask such a thing?'

'Never mind. Just tell me what the problem is.'

Ellie sighed. 'First I must tell you something about Lewis. I know that you of all people won't betray my confidence . . .'

When Ellie had finished her story of the threat of blackmail and exposure, Thea said, 'I'm sorry. This must be truly dreadful for you, but Lewis is quite right not to give in to blackmail.'

'Thea! I thought you would be on my side!'

'You're talking like a schoolgirl,' Thea said crossly, and she saw Ellie's eyes widen. 'Tell me, why did you really marry Lewis?'

'That's just what he said before I walked out!'

'Walked out? You mean you've left him?'

'I . . . well . . . not finally. I mean, I need time to think. And so does he. So I went home to my mother.'

'Home to your mother. Have you any idea how pathetic that sounds?'

'Why are you being so cruel?'

'Ellie, you shouldn't have to think about it. I'm sorry I asked you why you married him. I know you love him. I know it's not just because he's rich and famous. You could have been rich and famous in your own right if you'd become a Gaiety Girl.'

'Well, to tell the truth, that was my mother's idea.'

'I know that. But if Lewis hadn't come along you would have allowed her to push you into the limelight. No, the moment you set eyes on him you forgot all about that ambition. And about me,' Thea added.

'What do you mean by that?'

'You know that it was because of the beauty contest that my father threw me out?'

'I guessed. I'm sorry.'

'There's no need to be. I'm glad that I had that time with my aunt. But you might have come along to visit – to see if I was all right.'

'I don't know what to say.'

'But I understand why you treated me like that. It was because you were head over heels in love.'

393

'I was . . .'

'You said he was completely honest about his past?'

'Completely.'

'And you still loved him?'

'Of course.'

'So what's the problem?'

'You *know* what it is. It's the thought of everyone else knowing that my husband's been in prison. Don't you understand?'

'I do. But I have to tell you, Ellie, that it shouldn't matter to you.'

'But what about my parents?'

'Well, of course your mother will be upset—'

'Upset! That's hardly the right word!'

They looked at each other and smiled as they thought of Rosalie Parker's reaction – and, strangely, the mood lightened.

Thea said, 'Your father is wise and kind. If he agreed to your marriage he must have considered the risk and accepted it.'

'Do you think so?'

'I do. And if the worst does happen you can be sure he will look after your mother.'

The coals shifted and settled in the grate. Ellie stared into the flames for a while and then she said, 'I've been selfish and cruel – to you, I mean.'

'Yes you have.'

'So why do you still bother with me?'

'Because you can be joyful and happy and fun to be with. And warm and generous—'

'Generous?'

'When it suits you!'

They both laughed.

'So what are you going to do?' Thea asked eventually.

Ellie shook her head. 'I just don't know.'

'Where is he?' Luke had opened the door of his parents' home just an inch or two and he peered around cautiously.

His mother was sitting by the fire with some mending. She looked up and smiled at him. 'Where do you think?'

Luke grinned. 'At the Keelman.'

'Or lying in some gutter, drunk as a boiled owl.' Lily shook her head. She had long since given up hope of her husband ever changing his ways. She put her mending down on the crackett, reached forward and, taking a fire iron, she used it to push the hob nearer to the flames. The kettle began to steam gently. 'Fancy a brew?'

Luke closed the door behind him and placed a newspaper-wrapped bundle on the table. 'A cooked chicken,' he said. 'Caught it trying to escape from Donkins' – gave it a helping hand.'

He noticed that the table top was scrubbed clean, as was the floor, and Lily herself looked fresh and bonny. Amazing what a difference it made when you could afford a bar of soap.

His mother was staring at him. 'What is it?' he asked.

'It's what you do,' she said. 'It worries me.'

'I know, Mam. But what else is there? Breaking me back digging tramlines like me brother Matt?'

'At least I divven't hev to worry meself sick over him.'

'Do you worry about me, then?'

'You know I do.' She smiled at him as she placed the old brown teapot on the table and spooned in the tea leaves. 'But whisht, will you? The bairns are sleeping.'

Luke looked at his brother and sister lying on their mattresses at the sides of the room. The blankets were clean and their rosy-cheeked faces looked happy in repose.

'They've been on the beach all day,' his mam told him. 'The picnic – you know – came home full of it. And their bellies were full too, so you can put that chicken in the scullery. It'll do for tomorrow's dinner.'

Luke did as he was told and came back to find his mother pouring the tea. 'I didn't pinch that chicken, Mam.'

She looked up at him as she took her seat. 'Didn't you?'

'No.' He sat opposite her and reached for his cup. 'Donkin gave it to me.'

'Give over!'

'Honest. And he asked me if I wanted a job.'

'He what? But—'

'Oh, aye, he knows all about me. But I've always got on with him, I've been nice and polite, like, when I gan along to see if he's giving owt away at closing time. We usually hev a bit crack – a laugh. I think I amuse him.'

'But you – a butcher!'

'No, Mam, not that. Just someone to help out in the back shop. Help with the books – gan roond getting orders from the big houses. He thinks I'd look good dressed smart – I'd impress the lady customers. Or so his daughter telt him.'

'So that's the way of it.'

'Aye, and she's a bonny lass,' Luke laughed.

'Are you going to do it?'

'I said I'd think about it. You know, if I could get a home together, you and the bairns could—'

'And what would Miss Donkin think of that?'

'What's Lucy got to do with it?'

'Lucy, is it? Well, everything, if matters are going the way it looks. No, Luke, you needn't worry about me.'

'But me father—'

Luke's voice had risen and Lily raised her hand and nodded towards the bairns. 'I'm not sure what's happened to your da

396

but he's not the same. Oh, he can still get into a right paddy, but the last time he raised his hand to me – whisht and lissen – he fell over before he could strike me.'

'Drunken bastard!'

'No, Luke, no. That's the puzzle of it. He wasn't drunk. But he was unsteady and he was even shaking a bit. I'll never forget the look in his eyes as he lay staring up at me from the floor. Frightened, that's what he was, frightened. Anyways, I helped him up and sat him in the chair – right there by the fire – and he just sat for the rest of the night with his feet up on the crackett. He didn't gan out drinking. I went to bed and he was still sitting there the next morning, snoring like an old porker.'

'So what are you telling me?'

'When he gets angry now, it's more as if he's in a rage with himself. He barely speaks to me and the bairns. It's as if he's off somewhere in a world of his own. And it's not a happy one.'

'Serve the bastard right.'

'Aye, but anyways, he doesn't bother me, I can do what I like these days.'

They sat and drank their tea in companionable silence, and after a while Lily got up and shovelled a little more coal on the fire.

'I've something to show you,' she said as she sat down again. She reached into her apron pocket and drew out a white envelope. She passed it across the table.

'What's this?' Luke asked as he opened the envelope. 'More postcards?'

'Aye, just a couple, but divven't fret – just look at them.' Luke put them on the table and looked, his eyes widening. His mother came round to stand next to him. She rested a hand on his shoulder. 'Aren't they bonny?' she asked.

Luke stared at the cards. Each one showed a pretty little

lass, dressed in beautiful clothes. One girl sat on a step nursing a baby doll; the other, who had the most angelic expression, held an open prayer book in her hands and stared heavenwards with huge expressive eyes.

'Proper little mazers,' he said. 'Where did you get them?'

'Our Joe brought them back from the picnic. Some wife gave them to him. She telt him our Janey could be in one of those pictures.'

'Janey?'

Luke turned and, resting his arm along the back of the chair, he stared down at his little sister. Her eyes were closed but as she breathed softly her dark lashes seemed to tremble on her cheeks; her hair, spread out on the pillow, was a mass of shining curls.

'The woman telt our Joe to bring her to the studio, that's what she called it, she said she'd get paid— What's the matter?'

'I don't know. I'm not sure if I like the sound of it, little bairns getting paid for having their photographs taken. Think on them other photographs.'

Lily's features sharpened into an expression of distaste. But then she said, 'I know, I hev, but I'm sure this is above board.'

'Why's that?'

'Well, the woman telt Joe that I could go too, to look after Janey. They wouldn't do anything wrong if I was there, would they?'

'I suppose not. But why would they pay anyone just to hev their picture taken?'

'Joe asked her that. She said because it could be sold on – pretty postcards – or even to advertise something. You know, bath soap, custard powder and the like.'

'Custard! I can just imagine it. Janey tucking in to a dishful of goo and a little bubble coming out of her mouth saying

"Mmm!" Posters all over town. Everywhere you look there's our Janey and her custard. That's a thought!'

'They might give us some custard!'

Both of them laughed and then Luke asked, 'So, are you gan to gan?'

'I thought I'd ask you what I should do.'

Luke looked hard at the postcards. He turned them over and looked at the back but he learned nothing. There was a line drawn down the middle and a little box to tell you where to put the stamp but nothing more.

Lily, sensing that something was puzzling him but not quite knowing what it was, said, 'The woman telt Joe they were only samples.'

Luke made a decision. 'So where is it you hev to gan? Where is this photographer's?'

'There's another slip of paper in the envelope – that's right.'

Luke read what was on the paper and then put it back in the envelope along with the two postcards. He slipped the envelope into his inside pocket. 'If everything's above board I don't see why the bairn shouldn't make a few coppers. But leave this with me. I'll see what I can find out.'

Luke slipped out into the night. His mother hadn't asked him what he'd managed to find out about the other postcards. He'd promised to look into that too, just to set her mind at rest that Robert Hedley didn't have anything to do with them.

Luke was still convinced that Hedley was playing the same game that he was; trying to find out who was behind them. But his nosing around and careful questions hadn't got him very far. Someone was making money out of this – probably a great deal of money – and they were keeping very quiet about it.

Luke had managed to turn up one name: Billy Reid. A shifty little sod, he was, who had a good job in the yards and

399

yet was greedy enough to want to make more by selling this filth to the punters.

Luke knew it was no use confronting him. He'd be too scared of his masters to give anything away. And probably even he wouldn't know who took the pictures. Besides, the little runt covered his tracks well. Very well. And even if he could be followed, the trail would in all likelihood stop at some backstreet print shop. Although that would be one step nearer . . .

But there was something else. There was talk, whispers rather, of a funny little woman who went around the streets at night talking to the homeless bairns. She always chose the bonny ones . . . and then no one saw them again. Or that's what the gossip was.

That knowledge sat uneasily with his mother's story of some woman offering Janey money just to have her photograph taken. Although it seemed to be above board if Janey could take her mother along with her. No . . . it still needed investigating, he decided.

It was late, and although it was still August there was a nip in the air, a touch of autumn. Luke turned his collar up against the light rain. He was glad that his mother's job with Robert Hedley made it possible for her to keep a good supply of coal. The slum building she lived in was damp and draughty. This winter Joe and little Janey might stay free from coughs and colds.

And the person who had made this possible was Robert Hedley. That's why Luke was uneasy about what he had to do. But if his instinct was right – and he was usually right about people, that's how he'd survived on the streets for so long – Robert would prove an ally.

He reached the bottom of the street. He had to decide now which way he would go. Should he turn left to the deserted tavern where Luke and one or two of his trusted street pals had set up home behind the boarded up windows, or turn right and walk along the quayside to the old warehouse where the artist lived?

He turned right.

Chapter Twenty-eight

Long after Luke Roper had gone, Robert stood at the window of his studio and looked out across the river. He was too troubled to sleep. He watched the scene below. The tide was on the turn and several ships had slipped their moorings and were making their way downriver.

Even with his windows closed he could hear the throbbing engines of the steamships and the rhythmic churning of their propellers as they cut through the water. He could see the neat rows of lights in portholes, and the lonely masthead lanterns of the sailing ships.

The wet cobbles on the quayside glistened in the pools of light beneath each streetlamp and huddled figures hurried through the rain. Some were crew, returning unsteadily to their ships from the many taverns, and some were workers on nightshift in the docks or the shipping offices.

Other, more sinister figures, moved more cautiously: the pickpocket jostling a drunk, then vanishing into the shadows, and the street women, half hidden in alleyways, waiting to relieve the sailors of their money in ways that could be called more honest.

Newcastle was a great seaport. Every tide brought ships into the river from all over the world. And on every tide manufactured goods – and coal – went out. Fortunes had been made, the citizens had prospered, and yet, on the streets at night, seeking any shelter they could, there were poor souls who had reaped no benefit whatsoever.

Luke Roper was one of those street people, Robert supposed, earning what he could when he could, and not being too fussy about breaking the law, although Luke was more intelligent than most and he had half hinted that he might be going to settle for a more regular way of life.

Luke's visit tonight had surprised him – but it had also solved an old mystery. Now Robert knew why Lily Roper had suddenly become distant and barely civil towards him, although she continued to clean and cook for him in an exemplary manner.

Lily had become wary of him because she had found the postcards that he'd bought from Billy Reid. And Luke, prompted by concern for his mother, had determined to investigate the matter.

Luke, it seemed, had given Robert the benefit of the doubt and was prepared to share information with him. He'd found Billy Reid, and he'd been scornful when Robert said that he'd warned the lad off.

'Did you really expect him to give up something so profitable?' he'd asked.

Robert had had to admit that at first he had hoped so, but then he'd realized that Billy had simply become more careful – more cunning. Luke had confirmed this and they'd both agreed that to follow him back to the print shop might be possible but in the long run might not prove useful.

Robert knew that if one unscrupulous printer was prosecuted and put out of business it might not be the end of the problem. The printer, just like Billy, might have no idea who the photographer was – he would use an accomplice as the go-between and cover his tracks – or, even if the printer did know anything, he might be too frightened to reveal it.

Luke had told him that he'd heard about a 'funny little wife' who went about the streets at night soliciting the bonniest bairns. And also that the rumour was those bairns were hard to find afterwards. Luke believed the worst: that once used they were disposed of – murdered. It was easy enough to get rid of someone whom no one would come looking for. Easy enough to throw a little body or two into the Tyne.

That would be evil indeed but Robert didn't believe it. He'd seen Mary Watson alive and well, procuring other children on the streets, and that was after she had posed for the photographs. Why waste a valuable commodity?

Robert knew only too well because of the work he had done with Marjorie, that the child models, their innocence violated as it had been, would simply vanish into the sort of brothel that specialized in the very young – in 'virgins'. There were men who would pay a considerable sum for an unspoiled eight-year-old.

Robert hadn't told Luke that he'd seen the woman in question. He hadn't told him of the night he had watched Mary Watson and another girl approach children near the Central Station. If Marjorie had lived, Mary might have left the streets but now it seemed she had taken a step further and was procuring other girls even younger than herself.

When he'd looked closer he'd seen that the 'girl' with her was probably a young woman. Could she be the same woman who'd given Joe Roper the pretty postcards? Luke had told him that he intended going to the studio himself to follow it up. He'd shown him the address. The name of the photographer was Vernon Gray. But Robert had already known that it would be.

By the time he'd arrived at the beach earlier that day to join the picnic, the photographer had already left. Thea had told him that Vernon and Adie had gone, but she had wanted to stay.

'Adie?' he'd asked.

'His devoted assistant!'

Thea had laughed but he'd thought the laugh sounded strained.

So it must have been Adie who'd given Joe the postcards. But was Adie also the woman who roamed the streets of Newcastle at night looking for likely children? Robert thought that she was. And that meant that Vernon was the photographer that both he and Luke Roper were looking for.

If he were honest with himself, Robert had suspected this for some time. But he hadn't told Luke. So now he must wait while Luke 'looked into things'. He couldn't stop him and he knew he shouldn't.

But why had he done nothing himself? Robert groaned and leaned his head against the cold window. He watched his breath obscure the view and then he closed his eyes. The reason for his failure to act was obvious. Vernon was now married to Thea. How could he pursue a course of action that would hurt the woman he loved?

'Are you hungry? Would you like a bite of supper before you go up?' Adie asked.

'All right, but don't bother to set the table,' Vernon said. 'We'll eat here by the fire.'

They had been working in the darkroom and now she and Vernon were relaxing and talking over the events of the day in Adie's bedsitting room in the semi-basement. She had drawn the red plush curtains but they could still hear the rain beating against the window.

Adie pulled forward a large leather ottoman to serve as a low table and went into her tiny kitchen to set the tray. Bread rolls, cold chicken and cheese savouries – she'd salvaged them from the picnic hamper – but the bottle of red wine was from her own supply.

Just as she was about to pick up the tray she felt the retching begin and she leaned against the sink, clasping the cold glazed rim with both hands. When it was over she drew a glass of water and sipped it. She'd learned her lesson the first time when she'd gulped the whole glassful down and immediately begun to retch again.

Putting the glass down on the wooden draining board, she took a sip of wine straight from the bottle to sweeten her breath, then she put a smile on her face before she carried the tray into the room.

Vernon was sitting back in his chair with his long legs stretched out across the hearth rug. He had taken off his jacket and tie and unloosened his top shirt buttons. He turned to smile lazily.

'You've made it cosy down here,' he said.

Adie set the tray down. She bent her head so that he could not see her momentary displeasure. If it had been Thea he would have got up and taken the tray from her, made her sit down, filled her plate for her. Instead he was content to let her wait on him even though she had been working all day instead of romping on the beach with those dreadful ragamuffin children.

'Will Thea mind your having supper with me?' she asked as she poured him a glass of wine.

'Thea will be sleeping by now. She came home so tired that she could barely eat the meal Mrs Collins had prepared. Old

Collins went home in high dudgeon – ridiculous phrase that, isn't it?' he asked as he held up his glass of wine and stared at the starbursts of reflected light from the fire on the curved glass. 'I don't even know what it means. What is a dudgeon, for goodness' sake?'

'It's a state of indignation. Resentment.'

Vernon lowered his glass and looked at her, suddenly serious. 'You're a clever little thing, aren't you, Adie? I don't know what I'd do without you. But are you indignant? Do you resent what I – what has happened?'

Adie didn't answer at once and in the silence she became aware of the coals shifting in the grate and the steady pattering of the rain on the window panes. Vernon couldn't even admit openly that he'd had a choice; evidently in his mind it was something that had 'happened', not something that he'd done.

She knew that for all his brilliance and his education, he had no moral sentience, or rather if he was aware of the difference between right and wrong, he did not think the rules applied to him. And she had been happy to go along with this – more than happy if it meant that she could make herself useful to him, make it impossible for him to carry on without her help, make him grateful enough to indulge her.

The truth was that the thought of Vernon making love to Thea excited her. He'd always indulged himself, and his jaded palate now craved innocence. Adie's too. Thea had been like a virgin sacrifice to her own desires. Helping to choose the trousseau – the camisoles trimmed with broderie anglaise, the nainsook knickers with lace inserts, the moirette underskirts and the silk nightgowns – had fed Adie's fantasies.

On the nights she had lain down here alone, her imagination had carried her further. She knew what Vernon was like when he was overcome with passion and she relished the idea of

Thea's shock and distress. Thea would have no idea how to coax and tame him as she herself had.

When he came to her from Thea's bed her own enjoyment was intensified.

Vernon continued to look at her gravely. His fair hair had fallen forward, softening the line of his brow and making him look vulnerable.

'No, I don't resent it,' she said, and was relieved to see him smile.

Vernon didn't like being criticized. He would never defend himself, he would simply go. And tonight she wanted – needed – him to stay.

'You know it makes no difference?' he said. 'I promised you that.'

'I know. Now eat your supper. I don't know about you but all that sea air has made me hungry.'

It was the truth. Once the nausea had passed, her appetite had returned. She was relieved to see him relax and as they ate their supper they talked about the day's work and work they still had to do.

She was surprised when Vernon offered to make them cups of cocoa. 'Like Darby and Joan,' he said. 'We'll sup our cocoa by the fire together.'

By the time he came back from the kitchen Adie had undressed and put on her nightgown and robe. The robe was new, bought at the same time as Thea's trousseau; it was made from pink cashmere trimmed with white lace and it was full enough to completely obscure the line of her body.

Vernon raised an eyebrow. 'You like pretty things, don't you?'

'Why shouldn't I?'

She hadn't meant to snap and she held her breath but Vernon simply laughed.

408

'No reason. And that baby pink is most appealing. That's right, take the pins out of your hair and let it down. Do you know, that's what I like so much about you, Adie. At times you look just like a fetching little schoolgirl. Now sit by the fire with me and drink your cocoa like a good child.'

Thea wasn't sleeping. She had lain at her side of the bed as she always did, her limbs straight, her muscles tense, unable and unwilling to relax until she was sure that Vernon was not coming to join her.

Tonight she had been more overwrought than ever. She felt guilty for having been so happy for a few hours. Not because she had enjoyed playing with the children. If it were only that. No, she felt guilty because she had asked Robert if they could be friends when she had known that her feelings for him went far beyond friendship.

Long after midnight, when she was certain that Vernon was not coming, Thea allowed herself to relax and she spread her limbs across the bed, enjoying the feel of cool silk against her hot skin.

Images of the day filled her mind: the clouds racing across the sky; the gulls calling as they wheeled higher and higher; the sharp tang of the fresh salt air; the waves breaking on the shingle, one wave catching them out and making them run up the beach laughing.

She flattened her palm on the silk sheet as she recalled the moment when Robert had taken her hand in his. The *frisson* as their palms touched. The firm grip of his long fingers. She remembered that they'd held on to each other for just a little too long and then they had dropped their hands self-consciously, neither wanting to acknowledge the intimacy of the moment.

Desire . . . that's what it had been, she realized . . . and it was something she had never felt for Vernon.

More guilt. Vernon loved her, he desired her, and yet his lovemaking repulsed her. It must be her fault – she had married without love. And yet . . .

She felt herself begin to tense up as she thought of the change that came over Vernon as his passion mounted. The sudden hard fury when he entered her, the savagery of those terrifying moments it took him to reach his climax. Perhaps even he did not realize what he became.

And what of her own feelings? Those feelings Vernon had begun to rouse in her the very first time they had made love? They had vanished the moment he took her so forcefully, and fright and loathing had made sure that they never returned.

Until now.

Suddenly Thea seized her pillow and hugged it close, trying to quench the longing that raged within her. She felt hot with shame. Shocked at herself that she could be lying here alone in her marriage bed, and imagining not her husband's hands on her body, but those of another man.

Luke had washed and shaved at the pump in the yard behind Donkins' early that morning while Lucy produced some decent clothes that her father had done with. Now, in the back shop, they were finishing a breakfast of fried eggs, bacon and black pudding.

'Are you going to take the job, then?' Lucy asked. It was early; her father was not yet back from the abattoir. 'You'd fill your belly like that every morning, if you do.'

Luke cleared his plate from the table and put it in the sink while Lucy poured a mug of strong tea.

'That's blackmail,' he said. 'But if you throw in a kiss and a cuddle, I'm your man.'

'Hawway now, give over,' Lucy said, but her cheeks were pink. 'Sit down and sup that tea.'

Luke did as he was told. He knew that he'd been lucky that Lucy Donkin had taken a fancy to him, especially as she was a right bonny lass. It would be no hardship to wed Lucy if that's what she wanted, nor to work for her father and mebbes even learn a bit about butchering if he wasn't too old at nearly eighteen to start.

'So shall I tell me da?' Lucy asked.

'Aye, pet, do that. But I won't be starting today.'

'But the clothes . . . you asked . . . I thought . . .'

'There's somewhere I've got to go first. Divven't worry,' he took her in his arms, 'it's nothing underhand. It's just something I promised to do for me mam.'

He took his time walking up through the town. The rain overnight had washed the pavements clean and Earl Grey, looking down from his monument, must have thought what a bonny fine town this was, with its broad streets and grand buildings. As good as London if not better, some would say.

But, as the town came to life and the shops and offices opened up for another day's business, the wide roads soon became clogged with traffic and the smell of horse droppings filled the nostrils.

At the bottom of Northumberland Street Luke dodged one of the new electric trams and ignored the shouted curses of the driver. In Ellison Place the only traffic was the milk and ice carts going from house to house. Taking a piece of paper from his pocket he checked the house number and walked up the front steps of the photographer's house.

She answered the door herself. He was sure it was her – the 'funny little wife' who had approached his brother Joe on the beach. Could she also be the woman who went round the streets at night luring children into the dirtiest of trades?

He saw her thin lips tighten and her strange pop eyes widen as he continued to stare.

411

'Well?' she said. 'I asked you what your business was.'

Luke smiled. He didn't want to antagonize her, not until he'd been inside and had a good look round. 'I'm sorry,' he said. 'I didn't mean to be rude. It's just I didn't quite know how to introduce myself.'

'And who are you, then?' she asked. She had responded to his smile, women usually did, and was waiting patiently enough for him to continue.

'Luke Roper, the brother of a little lad you spoke to on the beach yesterday. You said that you wanted to take me sister Janey's photograph.'

'Oh, I see. But I was expecting your mother to come.'

'Yes, I know. But me mam asked me to come and find out what it was all about. What kind of pictures you'd be taking. I hope you don't mind.'

'Of course not. Why don't you come in.' She was all sweetness and light now, and she stood back to allow him to enter. 'I'm Adeline Hall, Mr Gray's assistant. I'll be able to answer all your questions.'

She opened one half of a large double door and showed him into a grand room. 'These are the kind of pictures we'll be taking,' she said. 'Aren't they beautiful?'

And they were. Luke stared at the framed photographs hanging on the walls and displayed on tables. Beautiful children, clean and shining children, all dressed in the kind of clothes that only the rich could afford.

'Who are they?' he asked.

'Some of them are brought to Mr Gray by their parents who want a portrait – just like a portrait an artist would paint. Others are children we find, just like your little sister.'

'Why?' he asked.

'Because it isn't only the rich who are beautiful. Children of the poor can be just as lovely before the grim life they lead shows in their faces. Mr Gray is an artist – he wants to capture that loveliness before it fades, and if he can ease their lives a little by paying them for the privilege of taking their pictures, that's even better, don't you think?'

Luke stared at her to see if she were serious. Her words were highfalutin and she spoke as if she'd learned them by heart. She stared back unwaveringly. She was nodding her head gently as if she knew he would agree.

'But what do you do with them?'

'The pictures? Sometimes we simply display them here for Mr Gray's clients to choose a pose. Sometimes we make postcards of them and sometimes, if the child is lucky, we can sell the picture to a manufacturer to be used in advertising.'

'Oh, yes, custard!'

'I beg your pardon?'

'Nothing – just a joke between me mam and me. And the children?'

'The children?'

'What do you do with the children – when you've done with them?'

Perhaps she sensed a hardening of his attitude because that funny light in her little pop eyes came on again. 'Ah, yes,' she said. 'We always feel sad when we can no longer give them any work—'

'Work?'

'As models. But we pay them well as long as we can and, sometimes, we allow them to keep the clothes.'

Luke wondered if that were true or whether the crafty little body had appraised his own smart gear, which had obviously been made for a more portly man, and judged it second-hand.

'Like a proper charity, aren't you?'

She glanced at him sharply, alerted by his words and yet still half taken in by his apparently friendly smile. 'You could

413

say that,' she said after a pause. 'But, of course, this is a business venture – and your sister is an extremely beautiful child. She would be well paid for work that isn't too onerous.'

'Not too hard you mean? The problem is our Janey's a mite timid.'

'As I explained to your brother, her mother could come with her – look after her until she gets used to it all. Then I'm sure after she'd seen what we do, she'd be happy to leave Janey with me.'

Luke was silent for a while, as if thinking it over, and then he said, 'Seems all right – but could I see where you take the photographs?'

She seemed taken aback. 'But why?'

'So's I can tell me mam.' He grinned as if taking her into his confidence. 'You know what mothers are like. She'll want to know all about the place – what it looks like and all.'

'We-ell, I suppose so. Would you wait a moment while I make sure Mr Gray isn't working in the studio?'

'Of course.'

She left the room and closed the door behind her. Gone to ask the gaffer, Luke supposed. He didn't know about these things but he didn't think the photographer would be taking pictures at this time of the morning. That's why he'd come so early, before the day's work would have started.

She came back quicker than he thought she would. She was out of breath but smiling. 'It's all right, come up. Mr Gray is working in the darkroom.'

'Darkroom?'

'That's where he turns the magic of what happens in the camera into the finished pictures.'

Sales talk again, Luke thought, but he made himself look suitably impressed. 'And is that difficult work?' he asked.

'Not to someone like Mr Gray. But, of course, it's

414

complicated and it involves the use of specialist equipment and chemicals.'

'Chemicals? Isn't that risky? And smelly?'

She smiled as if he were a curious child whose questioning had gone on too long and who was just about to try her patience. 'A little, but with proper ventilation that's no problem and anyway, the darkroom is down in the semi-basement, well away from Mr Gray's living quarters. Now, would you like to see the studio?'

Luke looked around as they went upstairs. Turkey carpet, gilt-framed mirrors, gold-embossed wallpaper, new electric lamps fitted on the walls. There was money here. Photography must be a good business – whatever kind of pictures Vernon Gray took.

As they reached the first landing a door opened and a tall young woman appeared. She was dressed to go out. She and the photographer's assistant half smiled at each other but the young woman didn't stop to speak. She hurried past them and headed towards the stairs. Luke turned to watch her go down; the image that remained was the straw hat, with its ridiculous confection of feathers and flowers, perched on her piled-up hair.

He turned in time to see that his escort was also watching the young woman. The blood had drained from her already pallid face and her round eyes were glittering with . . . with what – displeasure? Dislike? Rage?

For a moment even Luke was shaken by what he imagined he saw there and then she realized he was watching her, and dragged up a smile. It was painful to watch. Embarrassed, Luke almost couldn't look her in the eyes.

'That was Mrs Gray,' she said.

And how she hated saying that, Luke thought, but immediately she turned and gestured for him to follow.

415

In spite of himself Luke was impressed by the room Adeline Hall introduced as 'the studio'.

The huge expanse of glass – a bit like the painter's setup – the cosy little sitting area and the other end of the room a bit like a stage, with different backdrops, the little woman explained, to show make-believe gardens or grand sitting rooms and the like. Then the props: chairs, sofas, tables with plants on them, footstools, a few nice-looking rugs and embroidered cushions.

Suddenly Luke became very still as he focused on a certain arrangement of soft furnishings. 'And is there where you take all the pictures?' he asked.

'Yes.'

'And this is where you'd want my sister to come?'

She frowned. 'Yes. Where else?'

'All right. I'll go now.' Luke turned and headed for the door.

'Wait – there's a little dressing room there – through that door. That's where your sister would get ready. Wouldn't you like to see it? Tell your mother about it?'

'No thanks. I've seen enough.'

Luke left her standing in the middle of the studio and he hurried down the stairs. After a moment, in which he imagined her surprise, he heard her hurrying down behind him.

She called out but he didn't answer her, and he didn't stop until he reached the street. He stood for a moment, disorientated by the light and the sounds of the outside world, breathing heavily and clenching his fists as he tried to control his rage.

Chapter Twenty-nine

The day was warm and bright, and most of the customers of the coffee shop preferred to sit at the tables which had been set out under the canopy on the pavement. But Ellie and Lewis sat inside, at the very back near to the swing door that led into the kitchen, just like the first time. She felt just as nervous.

'I'm pleased to see you, of course, but why did you ask me to meet you here?' Lewis asked.

There were all kinds of reasons. She hoped it would remind him of their first assignation; she hoped that would make him feel sentimental. But also it would save the humiliation of being turned away if she had simply gone home.

She took a sip of her hot chocolate before she asked, 'Are you still angry with me?'

'Is that why we're here? Because you're frightened of me?'

'I could never be frightened of you.'

'I should hope not. And I could never remain angry with you. So tell me, why did you write and ask me to meet you at Alvini's instead of coming home to talk to me? Unless . . .' he faltered, 'unless you've brought me here to tell me that you are not coming home at all.'

'No!' Ellie cried out, and she reached across the table with both her hands. He took them and grasped them firmly, pulling them in towards his body. 'I *want* to come home,' she said. 'I just didn't know if you'd have me.'

'Of course I'll have you, sweetheart.' He frowned. 'But let me tell you—'

'No, let me speak first. I know you will not change your mind about the blackmail and it doesn't matter. But whatever that dreadful man has in store for us, I still want to come home and be with you.'

She saw her husband's eyes fill with tears. She began to weep herself. 'Here, take my handkerchief,' he said. 'I'll have to use this napkin.' He smiled disarmingly and she felt that old familiar tug at her senses.

Ellie lifted her half-veil and dabbed at her eyes. When she handed him back his handkerchief he said, 'I'm glad you spoke first, for now I can tell you that it's over.'

She felt her insides turn to ice. 'He's going to tell the newspapers? Well,' she sighed, 'we'll face the consequences together.'

Lewis smiled. 'Darling girl, I've never loved you as much as I do right now, but there aren't going to be any consequences.'

'What do you mean?'

He was looking pleased with himself. 'I'm a writer of detective stories, aren't I?'

'Yes, but . . .'

'Well, I decided to emulate my own hero, Hugh Martin, and do some investigating of my own. It was too easy. Knowing what I did about my former fellow prisoner, I knew of certain trails I could follow. Of course I wouldn't have known if I hadn't once been a criminal myself.' He looked grave for a moment. 'However,' Lewis continued, 'I discovered that he's far from a reformed character.'

'That much is obvious!' Ellie exclaimed.

Lewis smiled. 'There are a number of unsolved crimes – fraud cases, mostly – that look suspiciously like his handiwork.'

'So what did you do?'

'I gathered a little evidence. It wouldn't stand up in court as it is but it could provide further leads.'

'I think I understand,' Ellie said.

'So then I told him that I wouldn't be blackmailed and that if he went to the newspapers there was certain information that I would give straight to the police.'

Ellie stared at him. 'But, Lewis, that's a sort of blackmail too, isn't it?'

Lewis looked at her in astonishment and then he burst out laughing. 'You're wonderful, Ellie, do you know that? I don't think I shall ever tire of you.'

'I should hope not!' Ellie drained her chocolate and spooned up the froth from the bottom of the cup. 'Shall we go home now?'

'You do understand that this kind of thing could happen again?'

'I do.'

'And I'll never change my mind about blackmail?'

'I know that, Lewis, and I think that may be one of the reasons I married you.'

The children in Robert's paintings were real; they were like the children at the beach yesterday once they had started to enjoy themselves.

Thea took her time, looking from one painting to the other: there were girls playing hopscotch on cracked pavements, boys running and dodging across cobbled roads, and both boys and girls playing leapfrog on a patch of litter-strewn waste ground. Her favourite was the one of three small girls

419

playing shops with broken bits of crockery while two older lads looked on.

The children's faces were often dirty, their hair tangled, their clothes ragged, but they were vibrantly alive, whereas the children in Vernon's photographs might be truly beautiful but they lacked something; their eyes were empty of that vital spark, Thea realized. They were idealized, picture-book beings who had nothing to do with real life.

She felt guilty for acknowledging this truth about the difference between Vernon and Robert's work just as she felt guilty for even being here at the gallery. But she had not been able to help herself. After meeting up with him again yesterday she had decided during the sleepless hours that followed that even though she must try to avoid seeing Robert Hedley again there was no harm in going to see his work . . . was there?

Not all the paintings of children were happy. There was a match girl with a pinched face, standing barefoot on the corner of a city street on a snowy day as well-fed warmly clothed citizens hurried by. Then a newspaper boy managing his stack of papers, even though he was on crutches. And a small child howling with terror in an alley doorway as two policemen with grave faces examined the lifeless form of its mother.

Suddenly, looking at Robert's powerful depictions of life on the streets of Newcastle, Thea knew what her work must be. Just like her Aunt Marjorie she must devote her life not just to helping these children now, but she must also endeavour to make sure that conditions would never be so harsh again for all the children that came after.

She moved on to admire the paintings of the river at all times of the day and in all seasons, with the tall, graceful sailing ships and the businesslike steam ships. There were paintings of the bustling life on the docks with the variety of people. There were also paintings of the city streets, both the elegant and the squalid. Robert had captured the city in all its moods.

Just as she was about to move on again she became aware that two young men seemed to be discussing her. They looked at her keenly, glanced up at a painting on the wall behind them, looked back, saw that she was observing them, looked embarrassed as they raised their hats politely, then moved on.

Intrigued, she waited until they had left the gallery and then went to look at the picture where they had been standing. She was stunned. Even though the face was half-obscured by a veil, she knew that the girl in the red dress was supposed to be her. She felt the colour rush to her cheeks as she wondered if anyone who knew her had seen the painting and recognized the likeness.

She felt her heart racing. Robert had painted this . . . but she had never posed for him . . . he must have painted her from memory. But why?

She was aware that someone, a man, had come to stand behind her. She must go; she had much to think about. She turned to find that the man was Robert.

'Why?' she whispered. 'Why me?'

He spoke almost as quietly as she did. 'You know why.'

They looked at each other without speaking, and the emotion he couldn't hide matched her own feelings. She closed her eyes and turned towards the painting before she opened them again.

She tried to smile. 'But the dress?' she asked. 'So red . . . and so Spanish. Why?'

He smiled. 'It just seemed right.'

'It is,' she said. 'My father is Spanish.'

They sat in the same booth of the coffee house where he'd sat with Grace Barrett. Grace had wanted his friendship, and she'd hinted at more, but he'd known in his heart that it was impossible.

He could never talk to Grace the way he was talking to Thea now. Over the tall glasses of Russian tea she had told him why she had been forced to leave home and what she'd recently discovered about her own parentage. And, amazingly, he'd told her about his own poor mother, what she had done and where she was now.

They had shared confidences with complete trust, somehow knowing that neither would think less of the other because of anything their parents had done. They marvelled at what they had in common. Their backgrounds and upbringing couldn't have been more different and yet neither of them knew who their father was – though at least Thea had a name for hers – and both had a half-sister, although Robert's had died so tragically.

'Do you ever see your mother?' Thea asked suddenly.

'Sometimes.'

'Does she . . . does she know you?'

'Is she completely insane, do you mean?'

'I'm sorry, I shouldn't have asked.'

'No, it's all right, you can ask anything. There's no one else I can talk to about her. Her poor mind is weak – sometimes she can't remember who she is or why she's there.' Thea reached across the table and rested her hand on his clenched fist. 'Although I believe that to be a blessing,' he said, and he unclenched his fingers and took her hand in his. Her skin was like cool silk. 'But, yes, sometimes she knows me.' He sighed.

'And does she love you?'

Nobody else would have asked him that question. Robert was sure that even the good and compassionate William Barrett and his wife would find it hard to conjecture the love of a prostitute for a bastard son. But Thea was looking at him with those dark disturbing eyes as if the answer was important to her.

'Yes, she loves me,' he said.

'Ah.'

Thea withdrew her hand; he was loath to let it go but he couldn't stop her although he dearly wanted to. She was married to someone else. Robert grasped his glass of tea with both hands. Thea was married to a man that Robert suspected of being involved in the filthiest of trades, child pornography. She could not know, not Thea, for if she did she would never stay under the same roof for one moment longer.

What would happen when she did find out? If he and Luke Roper found the proof they needed Robert would have to tell the police; have Vernon prosecuted. What then? Would Thea's heart be broken? Did she love her husband?

'What is it, Robert?' she asked. 'Why do you look so troubled?'

'Thea – are you happy?'

She was obviously taken aback by the abruptness of his manner. She shrank back so that her face was in shadow. The silk flowers on her hat trembled. 'Why do you ask?'

'I . . . you're married now . . . your aunt would want to know . . .'

He was hiding his own concern behind his old friend's name, he knew – and so did Thea. She smiled. 'Aunt Marjorie liked Vernon. She was grateful for the photographs he took of the children's outings. He never asked for payment.'

'No, I don't suppose he did,' Robert said quietly. Now he knew that Vernon probably used those occasions to look out for likely children for his other photographic sessions.

'And, besides,' Thea continued, 'Vernon saved my life.'

'What?'

Robert listened appalled as Thea told him of her descent

into illness and squalor after her aunt had died. How she had avoided Marjorie's kind friends out of shame for the state of the house and how, finally, without food or coal, she had collapsed and lain all night in the cold passage.

If Vernon had not been concerned – and concerned enough to break into the house and find her – she would have died.

To make it worse Robert realized that he must have been there himself. He'd looked through the window and watched as she'd risen from the chair, walked towards the window and stared at him before gesturing for him to go away.

He'd thought she was angry with him because of Marjorie's death. But he shouldn't have gone. He remembered with shame that *he* had been angry. Angry because he'd thought Thea too young and immature even to discuss things with him.

He'd been so taken up with his own feelings – his pride – that he'd been blinded to the signs that something was wrong. The dark, neglected appearance of the house, no smoke coming from the chimney – these facts should have alerted him but they hadn't, and he'd walked away. He'd left it to Vernon to find her and take her away and save her life.

And now, if his suspicions were correct, this was the man he had to destroy.

Luke was waiting for him. A new Luke, Robert noticed even from a distance, and it wasn't just the respectable clothes. Instead of standing in a doorway, merging into the shadows as he observed the passing scene through watchful eyes, Luke now stood boldly on the cobbled road, turning his head now and then to look above the crowd, not afraid to be seen by anyone.

When he saw Robert coming he waved and gestured impatiently. He didn't smile or speak as Robert opened the door; he simply followed him up the stairs and into the kitchen.

'We were right,' he said as he took his seat opposite to Robert at the table. 'It's him.'

'Are you sure?'

'Of course I'm sure. The woman who answered the door – funny little goggle-eyed thing with a face like turned milk – she answers the description of the wife who gans round the street at nights.'

With Luke's description of the woman and her pale face and round staring eyes Robert was sure. But he still had to ask, 'Is there anything else?'

'Why, aye, man. Get them cards. The ones that made me mother's stomach turn.'

Robert brought the cards and gave them to Luke. He watched him flick through them until he chose a couple. He nodded to himself and then pushed them across the table. 'See them cushions? The ones the poor bairns are lying on? I've seen them – in his studio.'

Robert stared down at the cushions. 'It's not proof. I imagine that you could find cushions like that in other studios.'

Luke clenched his fist and banged it on the table. 'You don't want to believe me, do you?'

'Why do you say that?'

'Because of her. The dark-haired lass.'

'Who—'

Luke sat back in his chair and appraised him. 'The flush on yer face is enough to tell me it's the truth.'

'But how—'

'I seen yer drawing of her. Don't blame me mam. I made her let me into yer work place – yer studio – and I seen the drawing you made of her, and right bonny she is too, with just her hair to cover her modesty.'

'I've never—'

'Seen her naked?' Luke laughed. 'I'll believe yer. You've

425

got a fine imagination, then, I'll give yer that. But, anyways, I seen the drawing and today I seen the woman in the flesh. Oh, divven't worry, she had all her clothes on and a bonny fine bit of nonsense on her head – atop of that lovely black hair. She passed by quick on her way out of the house – the photographer's house – but I recognized her straight away. And, Robert man, I divven't know what the two of you mean to each other but I'm not daft. I can work out that you wouldn't want to do owt to harm her.'

Robert stared at Luke. He saw the challenge in the lad's eyes. 'I might have to,' he said at last.

Luke's eyes narrowed. 'So you still want to put an end to his dirty business?'

'I do.'

After a long, cool appraisal, Luke nodded. 'I believe you. So what do we do next?'

'We need some proof – no,' he held up his hand, 'the cushions won't be enough. We need to find cards like this in his house or, if not the prints, at least find the plates in the darkroom.'

'Darkroom? She telt me about that. It's where he gets the pictures out of the camera, isn't it?'

'Something like that. Did she show you the darkroom?'

'No, but she telt me where it was.'

'He probably stores the plates there.'

'Plates?'

'Pieces of glass that come out of the camera – they have the image – the picture – on them.'

'I think I know what you're on about. Just tell me what I'm looking for.'

'Looking for?'

'Hawway, man, you know very well I'm going to get in there.'

426

'But that's—'

'Breaking the law?' He laughed. 'How else are we going to nail him?'

'All right. They're pieces of glass about six inches square. If you hold them up to the light you'll see the pictures. Wrap them up in something, don't break them, bring them to me. Just bring what you can carry.'

'And what will you do?'

'I'll take them to the authorities. I have a certain standing, now – it'll be enough to get a search warrant.'

Luke didn't stay long after that. When he stepped out on to the quayside he saw the shadows were lengthening. It was quiet. There were quite a few folk about but they seemed subdued. Even the air was still – and close.

He looked up at the sky and saw gulls flying upriver – in from the sea – and even they were silent, their white plumage stark against the black clouds. The clouds were heavy – storm clouds? Still, he didn't have far to go to the old tavern that was still his home.

Not for much longer he hoped, and he knew he must be crazy to be planning to do something that might put paid to his hopes of a proper job and feet under the table with Lucy Donkin. But this morning he had experienced anger like he'd never known it before.

I must get it from me da, he thought, as he remembered the moment his heart had surged in his chest until he'd thought he was going to choke right there in the photographer's studio. It had happened when he'd seen the rugs and the cushions, the patterns the same as those on the cushions in those pictures.

The images of those poor little bairns, their faces blank, their eyes empty as if they were drugged, their bodies arranged for dirty old men to take pleasure over, had leaped into his mind. And they had asked his little sister Janey to come here!

Oh, that funny-looking woman had said it was going to be all proper and lovely, like, with bonny frocks to keep and money to be made. But Luke wondered how many other poor bairns had been drawn in like that. Starting off posing for one of the sugar-sweet pictures in that room downstairs and then ending up on a postcard that was sold underhand to perverts!

He didn't know how he'd managed to control himself in front of that little woman but he'd known he had to. His resolve had hardened. He was determined to put a stop to it for Janey's sake and for all the other bairns. Robert Hedley had told him what to do and he would do it.

And if that spoiled a sweet little romance for the painter and the photographer's dark-haired wife then that was just too bad.

Thea moved restlessly in her bed and pushed at the bedclothes. She felt hot and clammy; her nightdress was sticking to her limbs uncomfortably. She knew she would feel better if she went to the bathroom, sponged herself down and changed her nightdress, but she just couldn't summon up enough energy.

And besides, she did not want to encounter Vernon. She had not heard him come up yet and there was still time. She knew he had been working downstairs as he did on many nights, but if he hadn't come by midnight she had learned that it was safe to go to sleep. So when she heard the church clock strike the hour, she decided to get up and make herself comfortable.

Then, as she began to get out of bed, the curtains billowed in a sudden gust of wind and the room filled with light. The flash was momentary and Thea was puzzled only for a few seconds before there was a crash of thunder. The storm which had been threatening all day had started.

She remembered that the window was open and she hurried across the room. By the time she reached the window the floor beneath it was already pooled with rain. She pushed the lower casement down but before she could step back and draw the curtains, the lightning flashed again, illuminating the whole sky, making it as bright as daylight.

The houses, the trees, the gardens with their tall stone walls appeared for a moment, looking just like a photograph with the natural colours drained and all the lines in sharp contrast. And in the few seconds before it went dark again Thea saw a terrified white cat leap down from the roof of an outbuilding and also the violent movement of the back gate blowing backwards and forwards in the wind.

She closed the curtains quickly as the lightning flashed again and the thunder rumbled. She decided to forget about changing her nightdress and get back into bed and dive under the bedclothes like a frightened child. But in the silence between the bursts of thunder she heard something else . . . a noise from inside the house.

Instead of getting into bed she opened the door reluctantly and stepped out on to the landing. She could hear voices – raised in anger. Disorientated only for a moment she walked forward to lean on the banister. The voices were echoing up from somewhere below – probably the basement.

Someone was shouting. Was it Vernon? Then some-one else . . . a high-pitched squealing . . . Adie? Their words were indistinct above the howling of the wind but there was no mistaking the tone. As well as the noise of the storm Thea imagined she could hear echoing crashes and bangs from below as if objects were being thrown about in fury.

Thea frowned. Ought she to go down and see what was happening? No . . . Vernon would be embarrassed if his wife suddenly appeared to witness a confrontation between him and the assistant who patently adored him.

As she closed the door behind her and went back to bed Thea wondered if the moment had come when Adie had not been able to control her feelings for Vernon any longer; if what she had overheard was the final eruption of her long-suppressed emotion.

The storm seemed to move over the city without abating, and Thea lay and listened to the sound of the thunder recede into the distance. She remembered that once when she was a little girl and frightened by a storm one night, Sarah, the nurserymaid, had told her that the thunder was the sound of God moving his furniture about. Sarah had got into bed with her and they'd cuddled up until the storm passed over. That must have been when her parents and Imogen were away visiting her grandparents.

Thea realized that she had pulled the bedclothes right over her head and, smiling at herself, she emerged from her cocoon to listen. She could hear the wind howling round the house and the rain beating on the windows but the rumbles of thunder were very faint now. Until, suddenly, there was an almighty crash directly overhead.

She sat up startled, her heart pounding. She knew almost immediately that it hadn't been thunder. Had a chimney pot, loosened by the wind, crashed into the roof? Had a window blown in?

Thea got up and pulled on her robe. She opened her door and moved quickly across the landing to knock on Vernon's. There was no answer – of course, he must still be downstairs. But she opened the door anyway and saw that his bed was empty – had not been slept in.

She hurried upstairs to the top floor. Perhaps Vernon had heard the crash too and was on his way up, or was already there – although she doubted it.

She halted briefly when she saw that the door to the studio was wide open. Vernon always closed it after him because the huge area of glass meant that for most of the year the room was cold, and the cold air would spill down through the house.

Even before she entered the studio she could feel the wind – and the rain it carried – and when she stepped inside her eyes were drawn immediately to the glass wall opposite.

The only light was provided by the moon, which shone intermittently through gaps in the scudding clouds. Thea edged forward cautiously. What could have caused the gaping jagged-edged hole in the glass?

Had something – some heavy object – been blown against the window? There was nothing on the floor. Yes there was. The black cloth that Vernon pulled over his head when he took the pictures was lying there. But where were the camera and tripod it had been covering? Vernon always left them standing here. There was no sign of them.

She edged nearer, looking at the floor all the time, careful not to tread on broken glass. But there was hardly any – and from the size of the hole in the window there should have been much more. The glass must have fallen outwards she realized, but that could only mean that the damage had been caused from inside. Instead of the wind blowing something against the glass, something – and it must have been heavy – had been hurled out.

Still puzzling over what this could mean, Thea paused and looked around her. The camera, she thought, it must have been the camera. But why? And who would do such a thing?

Adie? Had she rushed up here after quarrelling with Vernon and taken her spite out on his precious camera?

No, she might just be strong enough to lift the camera and the tripod it was attached to, but she could never have lifted them both and raised sufficient force to hurl them through the window.

Why hadn't Vernon come?

Just as she wondered where he could be, she heard a movement behind her. She turned towards the door, expecting to see her husband entering the room, but there was no one there.

And then she saw a dark figure detach itself from the shadows on the far wall. The figure advanced a little into the room – she saw it was a man – and instinctively she stepped back towards the gap in the glass. She felt the wind tug at her hair.

At that moment the moon sailed free from the clouds, lighting her as if she were in a spotlight on the stage, and the figure retreated into the shadows again.

'Have a care, missus,' she heard him whisper. 'Divven't step back any further.' And then he turned and fled through the door.

After a stunned moment Thea gathered her wits and ran after him. He was well ahead of her and she had no idea what she would do if she caught him, but he hadn't harmed her when he'd had the chance and she wanted to ask him why – why he'd done such a thing.

It was no good. He must have heard her coming down behind him but he didn't look back. When he reached the ground floor he continued down to the semi-basement. Was that the way he'd come in? Through the back door? Thea remembered the flash of lightning and seeing the garden gate swinging free in the wind.

By now Thea knew that she would never catch him. He would be out the back door, through the garden and away through the city streets long before she reached the bottom. But in any case that was not her concern any more. She could hear someone sobbing. Loud anguished sobs that alternated with cries of pain.

The frightening sounds were coming from the darkroom.

Chapter Thirty

The intruder had left the back door open in his haste to escape and a keen wind blew along the passage. Cold seeped up from the stone flags to strike at Thea's bare feet as she stood hesitating at the door. The door was ajar and a thin slice of light cut across the floor. Whoever was sobbing sounded exhausted now, despairing, and Thea was reluctant – fearful almost – to enter although she knew she must.

She had only been in the darkroom once before, when Vernon had explained briefly what he did here, but he had not encouraged her to come again, either when he was working and needed to keep the light out, or when he was simply looking at the finished work.

'Adie's domain,' he'd said, and he'd smiled at Thea in that way he had, including her in his amusement. 'She's protective about her work space. Don't want to upset the funny little thing.'

Adie herself had made it plain that Thea was not welcome in this part of the house. Thea supposed it was because the girl, living in her employer's house, set store by her privacy, so she'd respected her feelings.

Thea drew in her breath, pushed the door open and walked in. The room was in chaos. The dishes and trays where the photographic plates were processed lay on the floor; some of them were broken, so were the plates. Boxes of photographic paper had been opened and the paper tipped out; and worse, bottles of chemicals had been smashed and the contents dripped from the workbenches. A pungent smell lingered in the air.

A tall filing cabinet had been pushed over, the drawers opened; the floor surrounding it was covered with roughly torn bits of card. Sitting amidst the wreckage were two people: Vernon and Adie. It was Vernon who was crying.

Thea walked towards them hesitantly. Her husband sat with his knees up, his head clasped in his hands, his shoulders heaving spasmodically as he sobbed. Adie knelt beside him, bending forward as if she were trying to see his face through the gaps between his fingers. She was holding a towel.

Thea frowned as she noticed the fragments of brown glass scattered across Vernon's shoulders. She looked closer and saw that his fine blond hair was matted and streaked with something dark . . . blood?

Was he wounded? Was that why Adie had the towel? But if so she had made no attempt to staunch the flow; the towel was white and unstained.

'What has happened here?' Thea asked. She wanted to go nearer, talk to Vernon, comfort him, but Adie's attitude, the way she was crouched beside him, was protective, hostile. It was as if she were warning her off.

Vernon stopped sobbing at the sound of her voice but he did not remove his hands from his face. Adie looked up and stared at her angrily.

'Can't you see? He's hurt him. Smashed a bottle over his head.'

Then Thea saw the rest of the glass on the floor, the bottom half of the bottle still intact with all that was left of the liquid it had contained still inside. She leaned over to look at it and an acrid smell caught at her throat – some kind of chemical. She backed away and stared at Vernon, who was still clutching at his face with clawed hands.

'Who has done this?' Thea whispered, although she knew it must have been the same man who had thrown the camera through the studio window. 'And why?'

Adie's angry stare was replaced by something more furtive as if she could have answered both the questions, but she simply shook her head in denial and turned her attention once more to Vernon.

'Let me see,' Thea heard her whisper, and Vernon shook his head violently. But the sudden movement made him scream in pain.

Thea sank to her knees beside them just as Adie reached for Vernon's hands. She watched as the girl took hold of his fingers and gently prised them away from his face. Thea stared in horror at what they both saw.

His eyes were closed, the lids puffed up to twice their normal size, an angry red stain spread down across his forehead and beyond. In places it looked as though the skin had blistered and broken, with shreds of discoloured skin hanging from his cheeks.

After a moment of recoil Adie leaned forward as if to dab at the blisters but he sensed her movement and shouted hoarsely, 'No! Don't touch!'

'A doctor,' Adie said, 'we must get a doctor.' She turned to look at Thea.

'Of course. No . . . he must go to the infirmary. Adie, go and get a cab from the stand in the Haymarket, run.'

'You go.'

'What?'

'You go and get a cab.'

'But I'm not dressed. It will be quicker if you go.'

Thea could hardly believe that Adie was speaking to her like this, and that they were arguing over who should get the cab when Vernon was so badly in need of help.

Vernon's assistant leaned forward and placed her hands on the floor to push herself to her feet. By the time she was standing she was out of breath. 'Well, I'm not running anywhere,' she said. 'Not in my condition.'

Thea stared at her. One of her hands was resting on the curve of her belly; it was obvious what she meant. Vernon had also turned his head in her direction. He could not open his eyes but the way he held himself so still showed that Adie had all his attention. She looked down at him.

'Yes, Vernon,' she said softly. 'I am with child.'

Vernon's lips, almost as swollen as his eyelids, moved, 'Why?' he whispered. 'Why didn't you tell me before . . .?'

'Before you became a bigamist?' Adie said, and laughed. 'Would it have stopped you?'

Thea could see Vernon's eyelids moving as if he were trying to open them. His cracked lips moved again but Adie leaned down and placed her hands gently on his head. 'Don't speak,' she said. 'We'll talk later – when we're alone.' She turned to glare at Thea. 'I'm staying here with my husband. Go and get the cab.'

Thea, her heart pounding with shock, merely nodded. She left the room and paused at the bottom of the stairs to hang on to the banister for a moment until her breathing returned to normal. Then the better part of her nature took charge. Whatever she had just learned, Vernon still required urgent medical attention. She didn't go up to her room to dress, she simply went to the cloakroom on the ground floor, pulled one

437

of Vernon's overcoats over her nightgown, and slipped her feet into a pair of her house shoes.

She opened the door to find that the wind had died and the rain had eased to a slight drizzle; uncaring that her long hair streamed out behind her she began to run towards the city centre.

Luckily the streets were quiet because of the recent storm and she passed no one until she reached the Haymarket. Once there, however, diners from Alvini's mingled with the audience leaving the Palace Theatre. She was thankful that they were too full of their own concerns, turning up the collars of their coats and dodging the puddles, to notice an oddly dressed young woman. But her relief drained away when she saw the length of the queue waiting for cabs.

She was too distracted to be aware of the hansom returning to the rank until she was pulled roughly out of the way of the steaming horse. The cab pulled to a stop, the horse's hoofs skittering on the wet cobbles, and the driver got down from his seat.

'Thanks,' he said to the man behind her, who was still holding on to her arms. 'Drunk is she?'

'Likely,' her rescuer replied, and then he backed into the crowd and left her before she could turn and thank him.

'I'm sorry,' she gasped. 'I'm not drunk. It's just—'

'Miss Richardson?' The cab driver stared down at her. 'It is you, isn't it? Poor Miss Gibb's niece? It's me – Tom McGrath. What are you doing here, on your own, at this time of night? Hawway, pet, divven't cry. Here, get in, tell me where you want to go.'

As Tom McGrath, who for love of her late aunt had asked no questions, helped Vernon up the stairs to the ground floor and then out of the house, Thea remembered how he had helped her carry her belongings out of her old home in Jesmond. When had that been? December . . . less than a year ago.

So much had happened since then. Her aunt had died – cruelly murdered by the father of a girl she had been trying to help – Thea herself had been ill and near to death; she had been saved by Vernon – she had married him . . . or had she?

After they had gone, Adie cradling Vernon in her arms in the cab, Thea allowed herself to think about what she had discovered. Certainly there had been a ceremony in a church, a celebration afterwards with her friend Ellie, and Ellie's husband, Lewis Sinclair, but now it seemed that the ceremony had been a sham, had meant nothing . . . for Vernon had already been married to Adie Hall. So what did that make Thea?

Rather than go up to her room – she would not be able to sleep even if she did – she went back down the stairs to the darkroom. She had to know why someone had broken into the house tonight and wreaked such havoc; had attacked Vernon so ferociously and in such a manner that he may have blinded him.

She looked around helplessly and finally her eye settled on the scattered bits of torn card on the floor. She sank to her knees and began to gather them up. They were bits of postcard. The pretty postcards that Vernon made of children. Why would anyone want to destroy them?

She sat amongst the bits of card and thought they looked like roughly made jigsaw pieces; she began to piece bits of them together and it was not long before she stopped and stared with disbelief and then revulsion at the picture she had made.

She pushed the pieces of card away from her, wanting to destroy the image, but as she rose to her feet she saw that in one of the fallen filing cabinet drawers there were more postcards. These ones had not been damaged; she lifted some of them out, looked at them, and felt sick.

If Vernon had taken these photographs – and she knew that he must have done – it was not hard to conjecture why he had been attacked and why his darkroom and his camera had been destroyed.

Thea rose suddenly and reached into the drawer for handfuls of the postcards. She threw them into the sink. She put the plug in and then returned and got the rest. Then she looked in the other drawers, taking all the postcards she found there without looking to see what they were.

One of the large bottles of chemicals had fallen on to the floor but it had rolled up against the bench without breaking. She had no idea what it was but she lifted it up and took out the stopper. She poured the entire contents over the postcards in the sink.

She stayed long enough to see the images discolour and stain so badly that no one would ever be able to look at the photographs of those poor children and see what evil had been done to them.

'It's over . . . the photographer . . . I've done for him.'

Robert had just left the all-night soup kitchen when he heard the hoarse whisper. He stopped and peered towards the black opening of a narrow alley. Water dripped from the gutters in the overhanging roofs. Summer was over. The air smelled cold. After a few seconds a figure emerged. Luke Roper.

'You alone?' he asked, his words condensing in the air and going ahead of him.

Robert turned to indicate the empty road behind him. 'Aye.'

There was a gaslamp fixed to a bracket on a wall not far from where they stood. Instinctively Robert moved into the circle of light. There was something about the tone of Luke's voice, the heightened emotion, that worried him. Luke edged nearer, he was dressed in black, his face seemed drained of colour and his eyes glittered.

'What do you mean you've "done for him"?' Robert asked. He dreaded the answer.

Luke shook his head as if he knew what Robert feared. 'I was in his work room. They came in – him and the funny little woman – they tried to stop me – we fought – things got smashed – she was screeching fit to wake the dead. I grabbed one of the bottles – brought it down over his head.' Luke suddenly gripped Robert by the arms. 'Ah, Robert man, you should have heard him scream!'

'But he's alive?'

'Aye, he's alive, but, man, you should've seen his face!'

They stared at each other for a moment. Luke was breathing fast and each outgoing breath seemed to make him shudder.

'And I didn't care!' he started speaking again. 'I was so angry that I didn't care. I wanted to make sure that he never took any pictures like that again. I went up to the studio – heaved the camera out of the window – and I scared her – your bonny dark-haired lass – I didn't mean to—'

'Did you—'

'No, Robert man, I didn't harm her. But as for her husband . . .' Luke stared at Robert wildly before he continued. 'I got out of the house – hung about to see if they'd call the pollis – I had to know so's I'd know what to do – where to go – but they didn't. Didn't think they would. Then after a while his wife went running out—'

'Thea – where . . .?'

'Followed her – she was mad with grief – had to stop her from being run down by a hansom – pulled her out of the way

441

– waited in the crowd – heard her tell the cabby that her man was hurt bad and she wanted him to take them to the infirmary. Then I came to tell you.'

Luke began to back away and Robert made as if to follow him but the lad raised a hand to stop him. 'So you needn't do owt,' he said. 'You needn't tell the pollis.'

'Tell the police?' Robert wondered if Luke thought he was going to report him. Perhaps he did, because briefly there was a flash of menace in his eyes.

'Get a search warrant, I mean – hev him prosecuted. He won't be taking any more photographs. I telt him that if he did I'd finish him off next time.'

'I see.'

'I'd better gan now.' He backed further away. 'I divven't suppose I'll see you again.'

'No.'

Robert missed the moment when Luke vanished into the shadows. He stood for a moment wondering what to do and then he turned towards home. '*Mad with grief*' Luke had said. Thea had been mad with grief and right now she would be in the infirmary with her husband. He wondered if she knew yet why Vernon had been attacked in such a way – if he would tell her – and what that would do to her.

The night was still after the storm and the steep streets going down to the river were drenched. The drains were overflowing and water gushed down over the cobbles like a stream. But for once Robert took no pleasure in the view before him. He could only think of Thea, her distress and what she must be going through.

Luke Roper's unpremeditated act of violence might have put an end to an evil trade but it had also probably bound Thea to her husband more tightly than ever. Robert was sure that she did not love Vernon, but now that he was badly injured she

442

would probably consider it her duty to care for him just as he had cared for her.

Thea stood in the middle of the floor in the reception room on the ground floor of the house and looked at the framed photographs of beautiful children. She turned round and round, staring at them one after another.

The children did not return her stare. Thea had just realized that their eyes were blank. They weren't really looking at the book, or the doll, or the bird in the tree. They had simply turned their heads in the direction they had been told, like puppets obeying their master. And there was something else. Not one of them was smiling – not really smiling like the children on the beach the other day.

Had Vernon used some of the same children for his other photographs? She feared that he might have. And was it the father of one of them, or a brother, who had come to put an end to it tonight?

Thea felt like reaching up and tearing the photographs down from the wall and consigning them to the same fate as the postcards but she hadn't the strength. Besides, she must decide what she was going to do. She couldn't stay here, not now that she knew the truth. But where could she go?

She climbed the stairs wearily. She knew that she would not be able to face Vernon again, that she would have to leave the house before he returned, but she imagined that she had at least until the morning to pack her things and come to some decision.

The door to Vernon's bedroom was open and the light was on. Thea could hear movement – drawers being opened violently. Had the intruder returned? Surely it couldn't be Vernon?

She must have cried out loud for the movement stopped

and a voice called, 'Come in, why don't you?' Adie's voice.

Thea went in to find Adie standing by the chest of drawers. She had heaped the contents on the bed and now she had opened the wardrobe.

'I'm taking his things,' she said. 'Then I'll go down and get my own.'

'I didn't hear you return,' Thea said.

Adie looked at her contemptuously and shrugged. She began to take clothes out of the wardrobe. 'I'll take all I can pack into four suitcases, two each,' she said. 'I'll have to leave some quality stuff behind. You can sell it if you like.'

'Sell it?'

'You'll need the cash. Sell anything that's not nailed down – he wouldn't like to see you go hungry,' she sneered.

'He – Vernon – he's not coming back?'

'As soon as they let him out of the infirmary – in a few hours' time, probably – we'll be off.'

'Where are you going?'

Adie stopped her work and turned to look at Thea. 'Do you really think I'd tell you that?'

'But will you tell me why he took those – those pictures?' Thea had not planned to ask Adie that question but she found that she had to know the answer.

'Why? How do you think he could afford to buy you all those clothes? Drive you about in a motorcar? Pay the rent on this big house?'

'Rent?'

'Didn't you know? Did you think he owned it?' She was holding one of Vernon's coats and she clasped it to her body as she continued, 'Vernon always planned ahead. He thought the day might come when he would have to move on quickly, so the house is rented, just as the staff are hired from an agency and – before he brought you here – most of the food was sent in.'

'And why did he bring me here?'

'You were ill.'

'Yes, I know. He probably saved my life, but why did he—'

'Marry you?' Adie smoothed the arms of the coat as she laid it in the suitcase. She looked down at what she was doing and Thea couldn't see her face. 'Because he wanted you – desired you – and he knew that he would not get you into bed without a wedding ring on your finger.'

Thea felt the heat rising to her face. 'But he was already married to you.'

Adie looked up and her eyes flashed. 'And that surprises you, doesn't it?'

'What do you mean?'

'Don't pretend that you don't find it strange that such a handsome man should be married to a plain woman like me.'

Thea remained silent and Adie laughed. 'Oh, you're too well brought up to say so, but I never heard you protest when Vernon called me "little frog" or "that funny little thing".'

'I'm sorry.'

'Well don't be, because I'm his legal wife and you're the loser here.'

'Then if you are his wife, why did you allow him to marry me?'

For the first time Adie lost some of her composure. 'Vernon knows how to get his own way. He persuaded me that it would make no difference to us.' She raised her head and some of her assurance came back. 'And that, at least, was true. He spent more time in my bed than in yours.'

Thea felt uncomfortable as she remembered how relieved she'd been on the nights Vernon did not come to her. She'd imagined that he'd gone to his room late after working downstairs but in truth he'd been with Adie.

'Why have you always pretended to be simply a servant?'

she asked. 'Why couldn't you take your proper place as Vernon's wife?'

'Bad for business.'

'What do you mean?'

'Vernon presented himself as a society photographer. He needed a classy, good-looking wife like you. I could see the sense in that. His wealthier clients – the respectable ones – came from the so-called "upper classes". They wouldn't think much of him if his wife was a common creature like me.'

'If he loved you he wouldn't have cared what people thought,' Thea couldn't help saying.

'Love!' Adie said. 'Vernon is incapable of real love. You thought he was oh, so tender when you were ill, didn't you? But he was driven by lust, not love. He'd waited so long for you that he didn't want you to die. He married me because I know how to please him in ways you wouldn't dream of. And because I was invaluable to him in his work.'

'His work?'

'When you and that silly friend of yours had your portraits taken, didn't I dress you just right? Do your hair? Help you to pose? I'm just as much an artist as he is, Vernon told me so, and in one part of his work I'm more of a help. Can you guess what I mean?'

'I don't want to.'

'That means you've guessed already. Yes, the work that brought the real money in, the pictures of the children. Vernon needed a woman for that – a woman who could persuade the children, make friends with them, show them what to do.'

'How could you?' Thea said. 'How could any woman bring herself to harm children in that way? Why do you do it?'

Adie looked at her as if she were stupid. 'For the money.'

'But that's evil. Surely there are other ways of making money.'

'What do you suggest? Should I become a shop girl? Or a factory hand? What else is there for the likes of me?'

Thea shook her head. 'What would be wrong with that?'

'Listen to me.' Adie almost spat out her words. 'I made up my mind a long time ago that I would never be poor again.'

'Again?'

'Of course. Where do you think I came from? I came from the streets – just like the children you feel so sorry for. How do you think I know what to do? With the models, I mean?'

'I – I don't know. How could I?'

'Because I was taken off the streets of London and I became one of them myself. Oh, don't look so surprised. They didn't want me for my face, they wanted me for my poor childlike little body. But I was cleverer than most of the other children. I watched and learned, and when I'd outgrown my usefulness, I persuaded Vernon to take me on—'

'Vernon?'

'He was the photographer's assistant. He was from a good family, they'd fallen on hard times and he had debts. The bailiffs were after him. We quit London and set up for ourselves in Manchester. He paid off his debts in no time.'

'So why did you go on?'

'Because he'll never change. Soon we had to move on again. And again – always keeping one step ahead of his creditors. We ended up here.'

'But he's a good photographer – he needn't have . . . needn't have . . .'

'Turned to pornography? It's clear you have no idea of exactly how much money there is to be made.'

'At the expense of the children.'

'Listen, have you ever thought that photographs like that might be doing the children a good turn?'

'That's crazy.'

'No it isn't. The sort of men who buy them like to look, not touch. It keeps them out of the brothels.'

'But Vernon—'

'Never touches them. Like a lot of his class I don't think he sees the poor as truly human. They're there to be used; just like the bodies of paupers are cut up in medical schools and the bits thrown away like rubbish. At least these children can make some money while they're alive. They might even enjoy it.'

'Don't!' Thea could take no more. 'You're wrong – terribly wrong. But I don't want to hear what you believe – or what you did. Just take anything you want and go!'

Adie laughed. 'I don't need your permission for that, remember? But, anyway, I'm nearly done here,' she said. 'I'll take these down and collect my own things. I want to be all ready to go when Vernon gets back.'

'He's coming here?'

'Don't worry, he won't want to see you. He'll get a cab from the infirmary to the backstreet and I'll have the cases waiting in the old stable. We're taking the motorcar.'

'But—'

'Oh, yes, you've never enquired how he is, have you? Well, he hasn't been blinded and the swelling is beginning to subside. He'll manage. And, just in case you're interested, so will I.'

Thea closed her eyes but the image of Adie's taunting stare lingered. She brought her hands up and pressed hard against her eyelids until the hateful vision blurred to a dim silhouette. She felt moving currents of cold air as Adie flounced about making the final preparations for departure; and then heard the girl's laugh as she pulled the door wide and dragged the cases one by one on to the landing.

Thea remained where she was and listened to Adie's progress as she took first one case down the stairs to the next landing and returned for another. When the sounds had receded she breathed deeply, lowered her hands and opened her eyes. She flinched at what she saw; Vernon's portrait of her hanging above the mantelpiece.

She remembered the day it was taken. Vernon's intensity as he approached her; Adie moving quietly to do his bidding . . . taking the ribbon from her hair, opening the buttons of her dress and easing the neckline down over her shoulders . . .

What had Vernon said? '. . . *this pose is for me . . .*'

Black rage rose within her. She reached up and took hold of each side of the portrait. She was tall enough to grasp it firmly and pull it from the wall with such force that the picture cord was wrenched from the frame.

She must have moved quickly for she could still hear Adie lugging her cases down the stairs far below. Thea carried the portrait across the landing and without even looking she raised it high and hurled it into the stairwell. She heard it ricochet from side to side and then she heard Adie cry out in alarm before the portrait crashed over the banisters and landed on the stairs. There was a sound of breaking glass.

'You're crazy!' Adie screeched and began to laugh.

Thea sank to her knees and clutched the banister rails as Adie's high mocking laughter echoed away into the darkness.

Chapter Thirty-one

September

'Thea, is that you?'

'Ellie – I'm glad you called . . .' Thea sat at the desk in the small morning room on the first floor, pleased to hear the disembodied voice of her friend.

'Aren't telephones wonderful?' Ellie said. 'Do you know, Lewis has worked a telephone into the plot of the book he's just finished. The suspect's alibi – do you know what an alibi is?'

'Yes it's—'

'Good, well, the alibi depends on the timing of a telephone call. Isn't that clever?'

Thea smiled. 'Very clever, but you didn't call just to tell me this, did you?'

'No.' Ellie paused. 'I called to say that I'm home with Lewis—'

'I deduced that. I also deduced that he must have had a telephone installed. Elementary.'

'Very clever. We . . . well, we worked everything out and you were quite right.'

'Right?'

'About not giving in to blackmail. And I . . . I wanted to thank you.'

'Why?'

'For talking to me that day. For being honest with me.'

'Look, I'm sorry if I hurt you.'

'I deserved it. I didn't stay away because I was angry with you. I've been helping Lewis with the book and we haven't visited anyone – even dear Mama.'

'I understand.'

'Thea . . . we'll always be friends, won't we?'

'Of course.'

'I think I need you to bring out the best in me.' She paused and Thea wondered what was coming next. 'And I've been good for you too, haven't I?' she asked.

'Well . . .'

'I mean, I've been thinking, if it wasn't for me you wouldn't be happily married like I am.'

'Ellie—'

'No, listen, if I hadn't persuaded you to enter the Blondes and Brunettes contest with me, you might never have met Vernon, just as I might not have met Lewis. Isn't that so?'

Thea's hand began to shake. She gripped the receiver more tightly. Her mouth went dry.

'Thea? Are you still there?'

'Yes.'

'So you could say the contest changed both our lives, didn't it?'

'Yes.' When she spoke her tongue seemed to want to cleave to the roof of her mouth.

'So you should be grateful to me, shouldn't you?'

'Oh, Ellie, if only you knew—'

'No, you don't have to thank me. I have to go and start packing.'

451

'Packing?'

'Yes, we're going to America.'

'America?'

'For goodness' sake, Thea, don't just keep repeating what I say – although I admit the news is rather startling. You see, Lewis has been invited to some sort of detective story writers' convention – the Americans are keen about these things – and we're going almost immediately, and we'll be touring a little and then staying over there for Christmas.'

'Oh . . .'

'I know. I was hoping that the four of us would get together soon. But we will as soon as we come back in the New Year, I promise you. Thea? Are you still there?'

'I'm here.'

'I do wish you'd say something.'

'Oh, of course, goodbye – or rather *bon voyage*.'

There was a small silence and then Ellie said, 'God bless you, Thea.'

Thea heard the click which meant that Ellie had replaced her receiver. She put her own receiver down and picked up her coffee cup. The coffee had gone cold and it tasted foul; she hadn't mastered the percolator yet.

So Ellie didn't know anything of what had happened, Thea reflected. Somehow she had thought that, leaving the more dramatic elements aside, she might at least have heard that Vernon had left her. But she couldn't have done. For if she had heard anything she would have called round, wouldn't she, in spite of having to help Lewis?

For a moment, remembering the way her friend had treated her in the past, Thea felt a moment of despair. Ellie hadn't changed; she was as selfish as ever. Then: no, that's nonsense she told herself. Ellie still believed that she was happily married to Vernon and somehow she owed it all to her old friend!

And Thea realized that in one way she was glad that Ellie would never change. She would always want to be happy and, to be fair, she wanted Thea to be happy too. In the circumstances it was as well that Ellie didn't know what had happened. Thea was pleased that she and Lewis had sorted things out, and she was generous enough to be excited for them about their trip to America.

She sighed and turned her attention once more to the papers spread out on the desk. It was going to be all right, she thought. She had taken Adie's cynical advice and sold everything that Vernon had left, as well as most of her own clothes, but she wasn't going to profit from the transaction.

The money raised had gone to pay off Vernon's debts, and as they had lived well the sums were considerable. Thea had worked out that she could afford to pay the rent until the end of September and that would give her time to sort everything out and find somewhere else to live.

She'd paid off the formidable Mrs Collins straight away but kept on the two housemaids and the skivvy, asking them to clean the house out thoroughly. Then she'd sent them back to the agency too, and closed up all the rooms except the kitchen, her bedroom and bathroom and this small sitting room. These rooms she kept in order herself, making a much better job of housework than she had at her aunt's house.

She thought about that often as she swept and dusted and polished and she'd decided to forgive her own ineptitude. After all, although she hadn't realized until it was almost too late, she'd been ill, as well as being grief-stricken over her aunt's death.

She wasn't grief-stricken over Vernon's desertion of her. He had saved her life, she would always have to remember that; it was a burden she would have to carry. But now she knew his true character, the thought that such a man had desired her made her flesh crawl.

Her poor aunt had been delighted to accept Vernon's help, never guessing that he was prompted by greed and self-interest. Aunt Marjorie had been prepared to devote her life to improving the lot of the poor, and in that cause she'd lost her life. Vernon and men like him didn't even regard the poor as being human. They were there to be exploited.

In her darkest moments Thea remembered something Adie had said about the men who fed their perversions by looking at the kind of photographs Vernon took. She wondered if her father – or rather Samuel Richardson – had been such a man. Were the cruel beatings he had inflicted on her as a child an expression of something dark in his nature? Now she thought they had been.

At these moments she thanked God that she had discovered the truth – that she was not his daughter – and she began to pity her mother. Because she'd been with child, her mother had agreed – had probably been compelled – to marry a man she did not love, and that man had proved to be a stern and unforgiving husband. Perhaps worse. It was all the more harrowing that the child she'd been carrying had been Thea herself.

Each day Thea experienced an overwhelming feeling of relief that she and Vernon had not had children, and that they had not had to grow up with such a man as their father. No matter what the moral implications were, she was glad that she had never been Vernon's wife. She was free.

She returned the invoices and receipts to their folder, ready to hand over to Mr Blackwell, and picked up the letter that had arrived the day after Vernon had gone. At first she had been going to hurl it into the fire without opening it, thinking it might be from Vernon, or perhaps Adie, but she'd quickly come to her senses.

First she couldn't imagine why either one of them would write to her and, secondly, the envelope bore a French postage stamp. They couldn't possibly have reached the continent so soon, even if they had abandoned the car and taken the train to Dover.

The letter was from her mother. The tone of the letter was gossipy, as if mother and daughter were on loving terms with each other. Amy Richardson had returned to Biarritz and taken a small villa. Nancy had come to look after her and, of course, that meant Ellen went too, and they were all very comfortable.

It was amazing how the child was learning the French language, her mother told her. They could even send her along to the *pâtisserie* to choose the fancy pastries they treated themselves to each morning.

At this point Thea had been more hurt than she would ever acknowledge at the idea of her mother lavishing attention and possibly affection on another child. But her mother went on to say that she wished with all her heart Thea would come and visit them. Perhaps Vernon would allow her to spend a few weeks in France, she said, although she knew that might be asking much of a new husband.

And what of the underlying reason for her visit to Biarritz? At the end of the letter her mother told her that she had begun to make enquiries and had even hired a private investigator who was at the time of writing in Spain, in San Sebastián to be precise, but she was schooling herself not to be too hopeful of ever finding Carlos.

And, of course, even if she did, he may not want to see her. And perhaps that was for the best, she joked, for he had fallen in love with a carefree girl, not a middle-aged woman.

In spite of the attempt at gaiety Thea sensed her mother's anguish and she marvelled at a love that could have remained so strong over the years. And she thought how different her mother's life and her own would have been if that carefree girl had married the man she truly loved.

One result was that Imogen would never have been born. Her younger half-sister, Imogen, who had sent Mr Blackwell to see Thea the moment that she had heard, somehow, what had happened. He was coming back this morning, which was why Thea had all the documents ready. She hoped that after today she would never have to see him again.

When he came he surprised her with a gift: a small wicker hamper containing coffee, tea, biscuits, a fruit cake, a tin of ham and some preserves. He saw Thea staring doubtfully at the labels: they told her that the hamper had been bought at Richardson's.

'My wife bought them,' he said quickly, obviously fearing that she would reject the gift. 'I . . . we thought it would help you. I feel so guilty about what happened at your aunt's house, you know. Your being so ill . . . and all alone . . .'

Thea looked at his long lugubrious face and was moved by what she saw there. 'Thank you so much,' she said. 'And please thank Mrs Blackwell. It was very kind of her to go to so much trouble. Now, will you have some coffee? I've made a fresh pot.'

He accepted the coffee and Thea felt guilty that she hadn't taken particular care in making it. But when she sipped her own cup she realized that this attempt was the best yet.

She watched him go through the papers she had prepared for him and felt gratified when he smiled. 'It's all in order,' he said. 'You can leave this property with a good conscience. You will even have enough money to secure yourself comfortable lodgings and, combined with your allowance, keep you there until your twenty-first birthday when you come into your inheritance.'

'I'm not going to take any of Vernon's money,' Thea said.

'Whyever not?'

'I'm not entitled to it.'

'Oh, I see.' Mr Blackwell frowned. 'You mean because you are not his wife – you were not legally married to him? But, if you are telling the truth, and I'm sure you are, his legal wife gave you permission, in fact she instructed you, to sell what you could to raise enough to keep yourself?'

'She did. But—'

'Nobody is ever going to challenge your right to do what you have done. They're not going to come back, you know. I asked you to be completely honest with me about what happened that night – and don't worry, I'm your solicitor, it will never go further – and I can assure you that Vernon Gray will never show his face in Newcastle again.'

Thea winced when she remembered what Vernon's face had looked like the last time she saw it. 'It's not that,' she said. 'It's the way he made his money – the money that bought all those things . . . household goods . . . clothes . . . whatever. I could never profit from that.'

'I see, and I admire you for saying that. So what will you do with the money? Have you decided?'

'Give it to the children, of course. My aunt's friends will advise me. In fact, I've invited one of them here this morning.'

'I accept your decision. But how will you live?' He looked worried. 'Your sister will not increase your allowance, you know.'

Thea smiled. 'I didn't think she would. And I would never dream of asking her.'

Mr Blackwell looked even more unhappy. 'I'm sorry that it has to be like that and I'm even sorrier to tell you that she has asked me to – er – advise you that—'

'She doesn't want to see me.'

'She wasn't quite so blunt. She just thought that until any –

457

er – scandal that might arise has died down, for the sake of the family business, of course, it might be better if you—'

'Went into purdah like a maharajah's wife. Shut myself away – became invisible. What an inconvenient person I am!'

'Please, Miss Richardson, you were in no way to blame. I am sure that you did not know that Mr Gray was already married.'

'I didn't. But do you know, Mr Blackwell, I am reminded of something my fa— that Mr Richardson said before he asked me to leave the house. He said that "no decent man would want to marry me". If he were alive now would he be happy to have been proved right, I wonder?'

Thea saw Mr Blackwell's obvious dismay. 'I'm sorry. I shouldn't be talking to you like this. You've been so kind. And don't worry, I'll be able to manage on my allowance, so please tell Imogen that she need never see me again.'

'My dear, this is lovely.' Miss Moffat looked at the luncheon set out on the table as she undid the ribbons of her old-fashioned bonnet. 'Such a treat.'

Thea had opened the tin from the hamper, sliced the ham and added it to the hard-boiled eggs, tomatoes and lettuce that she had already prepared. She'd also cut into the fruit cake.

'I decided a cold offering was the safest,' she said. 'I'm still learning to cook, you know.'

'I was so pleased to get your letter,' Miss Moffat said as they took their places. 'Until then I thought that you had gone . . . left town with your husband.'

'My husband . . .' Thea frowned. 'Miss Moffat, how much do you know about what happened?'

'Very little. You have been so discreet. Only those of us who know you personally have heard . . . have wondered . . .' She looked unhappy.

458

'Please don't worry about sparing my feelings. It's better that I know the truth.'

Miss Moffat sighed. 'Well, my dear, the consensus is that his business had failed and that you and he fled from debts. No one blamed you, of course.'

'Ah.' Thea smiled at her across the table. 'Now why don't we have our lunch and we'll talk afterwards?'

After the meal, while they were enjoying a cup of tea, Thea made the decision to tell her aunt's old friend as much of the truth as she thought she would be able to bear, or understand. In fact, because of her work with the poor and homeless, Miss Moffat understood all of it.

'I wish I could say I was shocked, but I'm not,' she said. 'Sadly, I know these things go on. I'm only sorry to have been wrong in my judgement of Mr Gray. And poor Marjorie was too, otherwise she would never have allowed him anywhere near the children. And as for you, my dear, what a dreadful thing for you to discover – along with the fact that he was already married. Poor Thea.'

'But at least I know now what I want to do with my life.'

'And what's that?'

'First, I want to give you any money that's left over after I pay off Vernon's debts, for you to give to whatever children's charity you approve, and then I want to find somewhere to live and try to carry on with the same kind of work as my aunt did.'

'I see.' Miss Moffat smiled.

'I wish Mr Blackwell had been as pleased as you seem to be about it,' Thea said.

'Oh, my dear, this must be providence! Do let me tell you.'

Miss Moffat helped Thea carry the dishes down to the kitchen and they discussed their plans while they washed and dried the dishes together. When they had finished they sat at

459

the kitchen table and had one more cup of tea.

'I shall be glad to let that beast finally go out,' Thea said as she nodded towards the kitchen range.

'Have you been seeing to that yourself?' Miss Moffat looked suitably impressed.

'It gave me great satisfaction to master it.'

'A practical young woman. Just what's needed!' Miss Moffat said and they smiled at each other.

They made arrangements to meet again and Thea said, 'But remember, I'd be grateful if you wouldn't tell anyone else at all, any of my aunt's friends, that you've seen me and what I'm going to do.'

'I won't, dear, if that's what you want. But I'm not sure why. None of them will blame you for any of it, you know.'

'I need some time to come to terms with what has happened. I don't want people to feel sorry for me. To be honest I need time to stop feeling sorry for myself. I must be anonymous for a while before I can face people with some sort of composure. Can you understand any of that?'

'Of course I can. I'll respect your decision and I won't tell a soul.'

After her aunt's old friend had gone Thea looked out of the first-floor window at the street below. The day was bright but cold, and passers-by kept their heads down against a bothersome breeze.

So, she would soon be leaving here. She was glad of that, and the irony was that most people thought she had already gone. Including Robert Hedley, she imagined. From what Miss Moffat had told her, Robert must believe that she had gone with Vernon.

Robert . . .

Thea remembered the nights she had lain in bed and wished herself in his arms; the guilty pleasure of imagining his hands

460

on her body. Guilty because at the time she had believed herself to be Vernon's wife.

And since that dreadful night when she had discovered Vernon's secret she had tried to repress all memory of it. Where had it come from, that yearning, that unfulfilled desire? Could it have been prompted by Vernon's brutal lovemaking? She hoped not, for if it had, she would be filled with shame. And how could she go to Robert with those feelings unresolved? She knew that she needed time to allow the turmoil within her to settle.

And there was another kind of shame – Vernon's coldhearted abuse of the children, which was all the more terrible because he had been driven by greed. She felt that she must share that shame because his despicable trade had fed her, clothed her and kept her in luxury. She must find a way to redress the wrong Vernon had done before she could face Robert Hedley.

Meanwhile she must risk him thinking that she had gone with Vernon. Was she asking too much to hope that he would care?

'I'd be obliged if you'd eat yer supper, Mr Hedley. I'm sick of wasting me time cooking hot dinners that only get hoyed in the bin the next day.'

Robert looked up from the table in surprise. Lily Roper had never talked to him in such a manner before. Her face, which had filled out until she was quite bonny, was set in disapproving lines and she had her arms akimbo, her fists resting on her hips like a fishwife.

'I'm sorry, Lily, I was woolgathering.'

'Woolgathering be blowed, you were sulking like a bairn that's had its toys taken off it. And letting that good plate of stew gan cold into the bargain.'

Robert picked up his knife and fork and started to eat. Lily watched for a moment and then began to wash a few pots in the sink behind him. She didn't say any more but, by the time he'd finished, she put a steaming mug of tea on the table and smiled at him as if he were a child who'd done as he'd been told.

'That's better now. And here's a bit apple pie. I never used to be much of a pastry hand but that gas oven of yours makes things easy.'

'It looks good.' Robert smiled at her. 'But you shouldn't have stayed late like this. You work hard enough.'

'I wanted to, Mr Hedley. I wanted to make sure you ate your dinner up for once. Do you know you've lost weight? I've been worried in case you were sick.'

'No, I'm not ill, Lily. Just a little . . . distracted.'

'Aye, well, no doubt there's a woman in it. Or if there's not, there should be.'

'I beg your pardon?'

'Mr Hedley, forgive me for saying this, but you're a fine strapping man – as well as being clever. I have no idea what's making you so miserable, but I would guess that you're either pining for some lass or, if there's no lass in particular, it's probably time that there was. It's time you took yourself a wife.'

Robert stared up at Lily in astonishment. How different she was from the downtrodden bedraggled woman who had first come to work for him. It wasn't just that she was clean and decent-looking. Having a proper job of her own, earning her own bit of money, had given her a confidence she'd never had before.

She became aware of the way he was looking at her and flushed. 'Hev I been impertinent?' she asked. 'I didn't mean to be. It's just that you've been good to me and I worry about you – like family.'

'No, Lily, you haven't been impertinent. I'm touched that you care.'

'Aye, well, I'd best be going.' Lily put on her bonnet and shawl, and before she left she poured him another cup of tea. 'Good night, then, Mr Hedley.'

'Good night Lily.'

Robert took his tea over to the window and looked out across the river. There was some kind of ruckus, some kind of fight, going on on an old sailing ship moored nearby. He could hear raised voices and the thump of angry feet on the wooden deck above the rising wind. He listened with idle curiosity, wondering what had started it, and was taken completely by surprise when someone knocked at the kitchen door behind him.

He turned quickly to see Lily re-entering the room. 'Ee, Mr Hedley, I'm sorry to disturb you. It's our Luke. I got as far as the front door and there he was. He wants to see you. Is it all right? Can he come in?'

'Yes, of course.'

Robert felt uneasy. The last time he and Luke had taken leave of each other they had both assumed that they would not meet again. He frowned when Lily left the room. Wasn't she staying? What could this be about? He heard the murmur of voices and then footsteps going down the stairs. Lily must not be going to wait for her son. Luke entered the room.

If Lily Roper's appearance had changed for the better then so had her eldest son's. But in Luke's case he had almost become a different person. He was clean and smartly dressed, his hair cut neatly and dressed with brilliantine. He'd lost that feral look; he was no longer a denizen of the underworld; he looked like a respectable tradesman. And, of course, that's what he was these days. Lily had told him that Luke was working for Donkin, the master butcher.

463

Nevertheless, he looked grave. He closed the door carefully behind him and came to sit at the table. He raised a hand to gesture to Robert to take a seat opposite to him and Robert smiled. Whatever this visit was about, it had not affected Luke's self-assurance.

'What is it, Luke? Is there a problem?'

Luke nodded as if pleased that Robert had got straight to the point. 'I hope not. But that's what I wanted to ask you. If there's going to be any repercussions, I mean.'

He had even begun to talk like a gentleman, Robert noted. He knew exactly to what he was referring. 'No. Nobody knows your part in what happened that night. Vernon Gray and his assistant have fled—'

'And his wife too?'

Robert paused for only a moment before he said, 'Yes, and his wife too.'

'Where have they gone?'

'To France, I think. The police have told me that if he returns to England they will endeavour to make sure that he doesn't begin his evil trade again. He'll be easy to trace. His face—'

'I know.' For a moment Luke looked grim.

'Well, that's that, then. I think we can forget about it.' As if I ever could, Robert thought. Forget that Thea has gone . . .

'I'm sorry,' Luke said, and Robert looked into his knowing eyes. 'That lass, with the long dark hair, I know what she meant to you.'

Robert held up his hand 'Don't. I've told you all you need to know, so—'

'So bugger off! Is that what you want to say?' For a moment the old Luke grinned across the table at him.

'Something like that,' Robert said, and warmed to Luke's smile.

'I will. But I've got one more favour to ask you. I need a witness.'

'A witness? But why? What have you done?'

Luke shook his head. 'Divven't jump to conclusions, man! I've done nowt – I mean *nothing* – wrong. I don't mean that sort of witness. It's before the parson I'm called to make an appearance, not the beak. I'm going to be wed.'

'To Lucy Donkin!'

'You've heard?'

'Your mother did mention—'

'For goodness' sake, me mother don't half let her mouth run!' He was pretending to be vexed but his grin was wider than ever.

'She's proud of you. And of course I'll be your witness.'

'That's settled then. Me mam'll keep you informed of the details.' Luke rose to leave and then hesitated before he said, 'There's something else – if it's not too much cheek. If you were thinking of giving us a wedding present, I'd like a portrait of Lucy. Is it in order to ask for that?'

'Of course it is.'

'That's grand, Mr Hedley. Just wait till you see her. She's pretty as a picture!'

After Luke had gone Robert sat at the table, cradling his cold mug of tea. He had neither the will to make some more nor to leave it and go to bed. He was still sitting there when the old sailing ship slipped out on the morning tide.

December

The tide was out and a hundred yards of wave-ribbed wet sand stretched before him, glistening in the cold winter light. Robert

465

walked towards the water line and the constant sound of the waves breaking and frothing on the shingle.

Out at sea a single coble made its way south towards the bay at Cullercoats, its red sail the only flash of colour against the grey of the sky and the sea. Behind him, apart from a group of squabbling gulls, the beach was deserted. He had not been here since the day of the picnic.

Thea . . .

He could see her now, stretched out on the sand, laughing as she tunnelled into the sandcastle. When she stood up the sand had retained an imprint of her body. Then standing with him on the shoreline, the wind lifting her dark hair, moulding her summer dress to her long limbs. Then holding his hand and running from the waves . . .

Where was she now? Nobody he had spoken to seemed to know. Not able to work, not able to eat or sleep, he had even gone to see Thea's sister, Imogen, who had received him coldly and treated his garbled explanation about needing to see Thea about some charitable concern of her late aunt with contempt. She had not believed him. But he had believed her when she told him that she had no idea where her sister was. And it was plain that she did not care.

So he was forced to believe that wherever Vernon Gray had fled, Thea was there also, taking care of him because she believed she owed him her loyalty. He could not accept that she loved him.

Robert turned from the bleak view of the sea and began to walk back up the beach. The wooden café was closed for the winter, shuttered against the winds and weather; a tattered poster warned customers that no drinks would be served with their own food but hot water could be bought to fill teapots to take out.

At the top of the slope he set out northwards across the

links. He had not seen Marjorie's old friend Miss Moffat since she too had left town some months ago, and now she had invited him to a Christmas party.

Alice Moffat had surprised everyone by leaving her brother's home and becoming the matron of a new charitable institution, a home for children who had been rescued from dire circumstances. The children of prostitutes, in fact. Robert understood that the home had been suggested by her brother, whose work took him amongst such people, and that much of the money needed to set up the home had come from her brother's wife, the formidable Mrs Julia Moffat.

Dr Moffat's wife was not only rich in her own right but she had a heart after all, it seemed, although Cissie Shaw had hinted half-seriously that perhaps the money it cost her was well worth it to get poor unfashionable Alice out of the house.

Robert understood that Alice Moffat had been running the place with a small staff but there had been little or no contact with her old friends. The children she was taking care of had not only been badly neglected, some of them had been abused, she'd explained, and until the home was established she'd wanted them to be left in peace.

But it was nearly Christmas and she had arranged a party. She'd written to Robert and asked if he would like to come to help amuse the children – that is, if he was not already committed to helping out at the Charity School. In fact the Barretts had asked him but he'd made some excuse – the real reason being that he found it more and more difficult to face Grace.

He knew that she loved him and that she still hoped they might have a future together, but how could he marry any woman when he had given his heart so completely to Thea?

It was mid-afternoon but the skies were growing dark and on the lawn in front of the old stone house there was a coating of frost. Lights blazed from the windows, and as he got nearer Robert glimpsed the red and green Christmas garlands decorating the rooms. Someone was playing carols on a piano.

Robert stopped on the gravelled drive and remembered his own childhood. He was the child of a prostitute although he had never been abused. His mother had loved him and his sister, and no one could blame her more than she did herself for what had happened. Thanks to the Barretts, Robert's childhood had not been too harsh, although the orphanage where he'd been raised was probably a much grimmer place than the home he was just about to enter.

Thea was in the dining room. She had just finished setting the table for the children's tea and she stood still for a moment to admire it.

The table itself, instead of being a bare wooden trestle, was a proper dining table with a white linen tablecloth. There were proper plates and cups and saucers instead of enamel plates and mugs, and each of the twelve children had a napkin rolled up in a named wooden napkin ring.

There was a Christmas cake on the table, of course, along with a large dish of red jelly, and also plates heaped high with sandwiches, sausage rolls, jam tarts and mince pies. Mrs Farthing, the cook Alice had hired, had never worked in an institution – in fact she had never worked outside of her own home before – and she didn't intend to feed the children on anything less than the sort of food she had cooked over the years for her own now grown family of twelve.

She'd worked hard to make today special and so had the other two members of the domestic staff, who were in the kitchen with her now, no doubt snatching a quick break and a mug of tea.

The food alone looked marvellous, Thea thought, but she

had added to the occasion by putting sprigs of holly in any available space on the table and placing a Christmas cracker on each plate.

Her friend Alice Moffat knew that not one of the children in their care would ever have had what she called a 'proper' Christmas, just as they had never had a secure and loving home. She was determined that every one of the children would think of the house as *his* or *her* home, not just *a* home.

And Thea had come to think of it as home too, as she suspected Alice had. Without previous experience, all Alice and Thea had to offer was intelligence, good will and love but, even so, it had taken the children some time to respond. But it was getting easier. When they realized no one was going to beat them, or worse, abuse them, they began to respond more naturally and even believe that they deserved to be happy.

And am I happy? Thea wondered. At least she was not unhappy. At first, after her life had fallen apart yet again, she had concentrated on getting through a day at a time. But at last she was beginning to think about what tomorrow might bring. She had even written to her mother, telling her only the barest details of what had happened and saying that, yes, she would like to visit her, perhaps next summer.

Thea had come to realize that in one way she and her mother were alike. They had both married men they did not love with disastrous consequences. And, in truth, her mother's need had been more pressing than her own. They had both suffered for it, and her mother's suffering had been much worse than hers because it had gone on for so long.

Thea could not condemn her for what she was doing now. The hope of finding Carlos surely must be small, and Thea suspected that her mother knew that. But whatever the outcome she had made a new life for herself. Even if that meant severing ties with Imogen.

And what of me? I have been given a chance to change my life too. I am doing what I wanted to do. And yet . . .

Although her work with the children was rewarding, she knew there was something missing. Someone. Someone to share her hopes and dreams with as she would share his. Someone who would understand why the sight of this table that she'd helped to prepare brought her so much joy.

Thea realized that Alice's enthusiastic playing of Christmas carols had ended some time ago, and she was probably longing for the moment when Thea would announce that tea was ready. She glanced once more at the table and smiled as she imagined what the children's reaction would be. Then she left the room.

She paused by the Christmas tree in the wood-panelled entrance hall, thinking what fun they'd had putting it up the night before, and having it ready for the children to discover first thing in the morning. Then she turned and smiled apologetically as Miss Moffat came hurrying out of the drawing room.

'Sorry – have I kept you waiting too long?'

'No, dear.' Alice's cheeks were flushed and she looked happy, but also a little nervous.

'Well, anyway, tea's ready,' Thea said.

'Oh, good, but we'll have to wait a moment. They're just finishing off a game.'

As she spoke Thea heard a burst of laughter. 'It sounds like fun.'

'Yes, it is. Wait a moment, dear, don't go in yet. I have something to tell you.'

'What is it?'

'No, don't be alarmed. It's just that we have a visitor. He arrived while you were setting the table. I had played every carol I knew, so I put him to work. I hope you don't mind.'

Thea was puzzled. 'Why should I mind? You're entitled to

470

put your visitors to work, especially at a Christmas party.'

'No, my dear, not that. It's just that it's someone you know – and you might not want to see anyone yet . . . Oh dear . . .'

Thea didn't reply. She left Alice standing in the middle of the hall and walked to the door of the drawing room. Just as she entered a great shout of laughter went up.

'You've pinned it on his nose!' a childish voice exclaimed.

Of course, Thea thought, Pin the Tail on the Donkey; I watched some children playing that last Christmas – and she looked across the children's heads to see Robert standing there.

'Well, I'm not sure who came the closest but I think they should all get a prize, don't you, Mr Hedley?' she heard Alice say as she hurried into the room.

The children all shrieked, 'Yes', and surrounded Miss Moffat who, laughing as excitedly as any of them, led the way into the hall where a sack of prizes lay beside the Christmas tree.

If Thea was disturbed it was nothing to the shock she saw in Robert's face. In fact he appeared to have drained of colour – whereas I have flushed bright pink, she thought, as she felt the heat rising.

'How long have you been here?' he asked quietly.

'Since the beginning.'

He knew what she meant. 'You didn't go with Vernon?'

'No.' She walked towards him but she stopped just an arm's reach away.

'Before you say anything, Thea, I have to tell you that I know what happened – and why,' he said.

'You knew what he was doing? How he betrayed the children he was supposed to be helping?'

Robert nodded. 'I can't condone the violence but if I hadn't been forestalled I would have seen that Vernon was prosecuted, even though . . .' he hesitated.

471

'You don't have to say any more. I understand. And now must tell you something. I am not married to Vernon – I never was.'

'Not married to him? But . . .'

'He was already married. Isn't that wonderful?'

'You were deceived by a bigamist and you think that's wonderful?' He reached for her hand. 'But, yes, I agree, it's wonderful.'

Then he took the other hand and pulled her forward until she was in his arms. At first he simply held her close but she could feel his heart beating, and her own. And then as his embrace became more urgent and he held her more tightly she reached up and put her arms round his neck.

She looked up into his eyes. What she saw there made her shiver with anticipation. But just before his mouth closed on hers, dark memories made her draw back. Robert looked at her questioningly.

The way he looked at her, wanting her and yet waiting for some kind of signal from her, released all the feelings that had been suppressed by Vernon's brutality. She knew that with this man it would be different; she would be different; that she would find the ecstasy that for her could only come with love.

She leaned towards him, into the warmth of his embrace. After the weeks, the months, of cold and isolation she was coming to life again. She gave herself up to the wonderful sensations that were flooding through her body, closed her eyes and raised her face to accept his kiss.

For Love And Glory

Janet MacLeod Trotter

Growing up in Jericho Street, Tyneside, Jo Elliot has always enjoyed a special friendship with her brother, Colin, and his best friend, Mark. However, when Mark joins the merchant navy, Jo finds herself seduced by Gordon, Mark's ruggedly masculine older brother. It is a secret and short-lived affair: Mark, returning on leave, finds Jo recovering from a broken relationship with a man she now hates and whose identity she will never reveal.

Mark's tender love begins to heal her and their affection flares into a deep passion, but then something comes to light that shatters Jo's hopes for the future and ultimately destroys her wonderful relationship with Mark. As war breaks out in the Falklands both Colin and Mark are called up to fight. It's then that Jo realises that the tragic secrets of the past must not be allowed to affect the future. And that life is too precious to spend it without the man she truly loves – if it's not too late . . .

Praise for Janet MacLeod Trotter's previous novels

'A passionate and dramatic story that definitely warrants a box of tissues by the bedside' *Worcester Evening News*

'A gritty, heartrending and impassioned drama' *Newcastle Journal*

'A tough, compelling and ultimately satisfying novel . . . another classy, irresistible read' *Sunderland Echo*

0 7472 6003 6

headline

Now you can buy any of these other bestselling books from your bookshop or *direct from the publisher*.

FREE P&P AND UK DELIVERY
(Overseas and Ireland £3.50 per book)

My Sister's Child	Lyn Andrews	£5.99
Liverpool Lies	Anne Baker	£5.99
The Whispering Years	Harry Bowling	£5.99
Ragamuffin Angel	Rita Bradshaw	£5.99
The Stationmaster's Daughter	Maggie Craig	£5.99
Our Kid	Billy Hopkins	£6.99
Dream a Little Dream	Joan Jonker	£5.99
For Love and Glory	Janet MacLeod Trotter	£5.99
In for a Penny	Lynda Page	£5.99
Goodnight Amy	Victor Pemberton	£5.99
My Dark-Eyed Girl	Wendy Robertson	£5.99
For the Love of a Soldier	June Tate	£5.99
Sorrows and Smiles	Dee Williams	£5.99

TO ORDER SIMPLY CALL THIS NUMBER

01235 400 414

or e-mail <u>orders@bookpoint.co.uk</u>

Prices and availability subject to change without notice.